Blood-Borne Series

~BOOK FIVE~

Heart of Betrayal

C.R. QUINN

Printed in the United States of America

Library of Congress
ISBN-13: 978-1-7371931-0-4

Heart of Betrayal

For Charlie, the light bringer

Prologue

Brianna

"I'm going to kill her. Smoking? Smoking! And in the school bathroom for crying out loud."

"Bri," Cameron said and pumped his hands out in front of him, "we cannot fly off the handle on this. That is what she wants us to do. We need to understand why she is acting out."

"Good luck with that. She barely talks to us, and if she does, she's either arguing or being condescending."

"She is a teenager, love. I believe that is how they generally behave."

"Why aren't you as angry about this as I am?"

"Because you seem angry enough for the both of us," he replied with a crooked smile. I tightened my lips and he pulled me down next to him on the couch. "Brianna, our daughter is first in her class, and she will have taken enough accelerated classes to enter college as a sophomore. What she cannot do is participate in sports and many other extra-curricular activities because they could expose her. She has never had many friends because she cannot be truly open with them, or bring them to her home. She has missed out on so many things other girls her age get to experience."

"We don't have this problem with Jack-Jack," I replied and curled into Cameron's side.

"Jackson is a boy, which is inherently different, and he also has William," he said and wrapped his arm around my shoulder. Even after twenty years together, just smelling his autumn scent seemed to make everything else go away. "Love, she was given in-school suspension and we will ground her. I believe that is enough punishment for getting caught smoking."

"You're such a softie when it comes to her."

"I am not," he replied in an offended tone. "I am simply aware of the fact that this is normal for girls her age, especially with those that have restrictions elsewhere in their lives. I believe you rebelled in a similar way when you were Olivia's age."

I rose up from his side. "I was eighteen."

"And Olivia will be eighteen in two weeks. Do you want her going off to a party and sleeping with the first guy who flirts with her?"

I narrowed my eyes at him. "Sam was extremely manipulative and knew I was an easy target. Olivia is smarter than that. At least I hope she is."

"Love, all I am suggesting is that you not kill her because then I would have to send Devin to kill you, and frankly, I enjoy our life together."

I shook my head and flopped back down into his side. "Fine. I won't kill her, but she's mega-grounded. Seriously, she loses everything, I mean everything."

Cameron sighed and kissed me on the temple. "Yes, love."

"And you have to do it."

"Why is that?"

"Because then maybe she'll hate you the same amount she hates me. Even if it's for a day, it'll be worth it."

"Yes, love."

Chapter One

Olivia

Tomorrow I was officially an adult. Hello, eighteen. Once you hit your senior year in high school, it really hits you that the days under your parents' thumb is coming to an end. Their hold over you would lessen, and you would be set free to blossom in the world. That's all I wanted – freedom. Freedom from the constricting life of the Warriors and the world associated with them. I wanted free of vampires and battles and blind allegiance to someone else's will. It was hard being the only free-thinking person in my entire family. If only they could see beyond the black gate that surrounded the prison they called home. But I wouldn't be one of them, I was going to be free.

Sadly, even though I was almost an adult, I was still required to wear my heinous private school uniform. The green and white plaid skirt with matching sweater vest was literally the itchiest and most unflattering outfit ever created. Considering how much of a fashion snob my father was, I was surprised he hadn't considered what we would have to wear every day. Only a couple more months and I would be free of this uniform like everything else.

Wills will be here in ten minutes, my brother said in my head.

I'll be ready, I replied.

Liar. Will said if you aren't ready, he'll leave without you.

He didn't say that. Wills would never leave without me. I have to talk to Ada first. I'll meet you downstairs.

When no response came, I brushed my curls back from my face and gave them a spritz of hairspray, not that it would do much good, they'd be flopping in my face a minute from now. Most days I wished I'd gotten my mother's pin-straight hair rather than Ada's big floppy curls. On him, they looked distinctive and handsome. On me, I was either a frizzy mess or Shirley Temple. I also got his height and really long legs, which I definitely couldn't complain about, but I also got my father's fangs. Living life as a teenager was hard enough. Try going through puberty with fangs that would poke through your gums when a cute guy would merely smile at you. The first time a guy I liked held my hand, my fangs almost cut through my bottom lip. There was no end to how screwed up my life was because of what I was.

Before Jack-Jack and I were born, there was a clear line between hybrids and vampires. My brother and I straddled that line which made it difficult for either side to accept us. The fact that we were also the only ones, we had no one else to confide in or commiserate with about the struggles we faced being true hybrids. Even the name they gave us was stupid. True hybrid? Was there a false hybrid? Dumb, just dumb.

After shoving my things into my school bag, I left my room and headed to my parents' suite. The only nice thing about living in such a big place with so many others was that our parents weren't monitoring our every move. There was only one landing between us, but there were stairs and a lot of stone and concrete in between. I decided to take the back stairs, zipping down the banister and landing softly on my right foot. Sliding down the banister was prohibited since I turned nine. Something about sliding down and flipping dismounts in my dresses was no longer appropriate. Thankfully no one ever used the back stairs so I could do whatever I wanted.

My parents' suite was on the first floor in the back corner of the manor. At one time it had been my grandfather Victor's suite, but soon after he resigned as the coven leader, my parents moved in. I always wondered if my dad and Uncle Devin had to draw straws for it, but maybe not. Devy was generally more of the bare necessities kind of guy, much to Uncle Fabi's dismay. It's probably why Uncle Fabi had kept his own place outside of the manor.

Thankfully the door to my parents' suite was already open since it was important that I talk to Ada before I left for school. Generally, Ada was always available to us first thing in the morning, and most evenings around dinnertime. Any time outside of that was pretty much a crap shoot.

Although I hated giving her credit for anything, Mom did her best to create some sense of normalcy to living here and making us feel like a family. It wasn't until we were older did Jack-Jack and I start to have fears of her not coming home after a mission. That fear started to spread to our other aunts and uncles to the point where we would be in tears and clinging to people's legs. Yet another reason why I would be getting out of here as soon as I could. I would never raise a family in this place.

Even though the door was open, I knocked gently before stepping inside. "Ada?"

Mom came out from her walk-in closet in the left corner of the room. "He's outside, honey. Did you need something?" I ignored her and walked across the room to the tall glass doors that led outside. "Well, have a good day at school."

"Like you care," I muttered and opened the glass door to the veranda. She was the reason my life was miserable; I wasn't about to acknowledge her. When I stepped outside, I found Ada sitting at the small wrought iron table with his sketch book. "Morning, Ada."

He looked up from his sketch and smiled. "Good morning, Monkey."

"What are you drawing today?"

"The gardens," he replied, keeping his head down and his pencil scratching along the paper, "although I am not doing them justice."

"Gotta sec?"

"I do," he replied and placed the sketchbook on the table with his pencil, "but do you? William should be here any minute to pick you up for school."

"It'll be quick," I said and stepped up next to him, shaking the nerves out of my hands. "I know you said tonight was supposed to just be family, but I'd really like Nessa and Stephanie to come."

Ada stood from his chair and kissed my forehead. "No."

"Why?" I shouted, but he didn't flinch.

"Because you are grounded."

"It's a party celebrating my birthday. Shouldn't I get a choice of who is there?"

Ada took a step back and crossed his arms in front of his chest. "Shall I remind you that your actions at school are why we are having a family-only party in the first place? If you wanted to have a party with your friends, you should not have been smoking at school."

"But Jack-Jack gets to have a friend come."

He knitted his brows together. "Friend? I would not classify William as just a friend. William is family."

"Not blood-related family."

Ada raised his eyebrows. "Olivia, where is this coming from? We were very clear that you were grounded until tomorrow. Why are you arguing with me now?"

"Because it's not fair!"

"Lovey, it is a bit cliché, but life is not fair," he replied in that calm, steady voice that drove me crazy. "Because of your actions, your brother must also only have a family party celebrating his birthday. Is that fair?"

"It always comes back to him, always. Screw Olivia, what about poor Jack-Jack."

"That is absolutely not true, and you are lashing out because you know you are in the wrong," he said and sat back down in his chair.

"You can't stop me from bringing whoever I please."

"*Whomever*," he corrected and picked up his pencil. "And I absolutely can stop you from bringing someone. Do not make this into something, Olivia."

"I cannot wait until tomorrow when you and Mom can't boss me around anymore."

He smirked and returned to his sketching. "Olivia, I am not exactly sure why you think you will have endless freedom simply because you turn eighteen. Whether you are technically an adult tomorrow, rules for living here still apply."

Hey, dumbass, Will's here. We're leaving without you, my brother said in my head.

I'm coming.

Not fast enough. You're not going to win with Ada, dumbass.

"Shut up!" I yelled aloud.

"Excuse me?" Ada said sternly, only moving his eyes to glare at me.

"That wasn't to you, sorry. I've got to go. Thanks for not understanding anything about my life."

"One last thing, lovey," he began, keeping his eyes on his sketch, "if you continue to treat your mother as you have of late, including just a moment ago, you will swiftly see just how comfortably you live in my home, and how quickly I can take those comforts away. Is that understood?"

"Yes, Ada," I grumbled and leapt down from the veranda, sliding down the side of the hill into the gardens, and then jetted around to the front of the building. It only took four seconds, but I was just in time to see Will pulling toward the black gate in his red Honda sedan. Damnit! With a grunt, I leapt over two cars, pushed off an SUV with my right foot, then another with my left, and finally slid to a stop at the gate causing Will to slam on his brakes.

"You're insane," Jack shouted out the passenger side window.

"Better to be insane, than be you," I replied and jumped into the backseat of Will's car.

"I love our morning car rides," Wills said and looked in the rearview mirror. "Happy last day of seventeen, Liv."

Even though I'd had the worst morning, Will Ryan could always make me smile. He'd been doing it since we were babies. Maybe it was the way nothing ever got to him, or maybe it was as simple as his blue-green eyes that only ever had caring in them. Wills was just as much my best friend as he was Jack's. In the seventeen years the three of us had been alive, we could count the days we'd been apart on one hand.

"Wills, I can't believe you were going to leave without me."

Wills shrugged and pulled through the gate. "Just another strategy to keep you at salutatorian."

"Well, that could be easy enough with our Russian exam today. I didn't study at all."

"Like you need to," he replied with a smirk and rounded the corner which got us out of eyesight of the manor's cameras, and allowed Wills to put the pedal to the metal. Jack-Jack and I were always jealous that Wills got a car when he got his license. Our parents had endless amounts of money, yet they refused to buy us our own cars. Jerks.

"Hey, man," Jack-Jack began, "how come you didn't wish me a 'happy last day of seventeen?'"

"Because I don't like you as much as I like your sister," Wills laughed.

"Please," Jack scoffed, "you can't get through the day without me. I am the true love of your life, Wills, just admit it."

"Jack-Jack, there are days where I hope you'll forget who I am," Wills replied.

"You're an asshole."

"No, you're the asshole."

"Do the two of you want some time alone?" I said annoyed and rolled down my window to air out the pent-up boy smell.

"You know, Livy, we do. Jump out of the car, will ya?"

"Drop dead."

"You first. And another thing, as of tomorrow, no more calling me Jack-Jack. I'm a man now, not a toddler."

"You sure act like a toddler most of the time."

"Ok, Burke twins, turn it down," Wills said, looking at me in the rearview mirror, and then over to my brother. "So, we just call you Jack now?"

"No," my brother replied and turned in his seat. "I've actually given this some thought. I want to be called...I can see that you're trembling in anticipation...my new name is...Jax."

"Jacks? Like the really old-fashioned game with the ball and the metal spikey things?" I teased.

"No! J-A-X. Jax. The X is what makes it cool."

Wills shook his head. "I'm probably still going to call you Jack-Jack in front of as many people as possible."

I laughed and Jack-Jack glared at me. "Keep it up, *Monkey*. I swear I will call you that in public if you keep calling me Jack-Jack. I will make a banner with your picture on it and put it up at school, I swear I will."

"Do what you want. I'm not calling you Jax."

"Yeah, man, no promises from me either," Wills said and pulled into the school parking lot.

"I should have known you'd take her side. You always take her side."

"That's not true," Will and I replied in unison, and then laughed.

"I hate you both," Jack said as Will pulled into our usual parking space and was out the door before the car was even in park.

Will and I grabbed our bags and walked into the school's entrance together. Honestly walking side by side was how we spent most of our day. With the exception of homeroom, Will and I had all our classes together because we were in the accelerated academic track. Through our entire high school life, we had bounced around in the top three of our class. When we started our senior year, it was a constant battle of who was valedictorian. My in-school suspension hurt me, but I was at least back up to number two. It was a shame that Jack-Jack didn't give a shit about school because it could have been a battle between the three of us. But no matter how hard my parents pushed, Jack did the bare minimum and stayed in the middle of class rank. He had no desire to go to college which was fine, but he didn't have any plans at all. Ada's requirement was that if he didn't have a job once he graduated, he had to get into the family business. We were not allowed to live solely off our Trust funds. We needed to be contributors to society, our family, or to the world in general.

"So," I said to Will as we headed to our lockers, "are you ready for the big competition next week?"

He shrugged. "As ready as I can be," he replied humbly. Wills was a martial arts champion. He had never lost a competition, and now would be on an international stage. "Devy's been driving me hard with practices every day, but he gave me the night off tonight for the party. So, my body thanks you for the rest."

I rolled my eyes. "Thank my parents, they're the ones forcing this on us."

He put his arm around my shoulders and squeezed me into his side. "Turn if off, Liv, it won't be that bad. Being a whiney bitch doesn't look good on you."

I punched him in the ribs lightly and got out from under his arm. "You're an asshole."

"Hey, hey, I'm sorry," he said and kissed me on the cheek. "Happy last day of seventeen."

"Thanks," I replied and started walking again. "Enjoy your final few hours as valedictorian. You'll be number two by third period."

"Oh, it's on," he replied. "Let's see if you can stay out of trouble until then." I forced a laugh. "You ok?"

"Why wouldn't I be?"

"You can lie to everyone but me, Liv."

I sighed in frustration. "I hate everything and everyone, and I don't want to be here. How's that?"

"I think you're overexaggerating. Life isn't that bad, Liv. I mean, you have me. I'm a delightful person who brings nothing but sunshine into your life."

It was hard not to smile at him. "I'll see you in first period."

Turning on my heels, I headed down the hallway to my own homeroom. With each step I was reminded how much I didn't want to be here. The locker-lined walls were closing in and the smell of hormones mixed with floor cleaner was stifling. Everything was strangling the life out of me. I didn't want to be here. I had no desire to put a fake smile on my face and pretend I was interested in anything they wanted to teach me. I wanted freedom and air and the chance to finally be myself.

The warning bell rang as I approached my homeroom, but an invisible force took me by the shoulders and steered me into the stairwell across the hall. Immediately I ran out the stairwell's door and bolted across the parking lot. I didn't know where I was going, but in that moment, I had never felt so free. It was the feeling I had been searching for with my heart pulling me along more than my legs. My parents would kill me and I didn't care. I wasn't coming back here. Today I took the steps I needed to start my future. I was going to live my life how I wanted, and the hell with anyone who stood in my way.

But first thing's first, I had to get rid of this stupid uniform.

Chapter Two

Will

When Liv didn't show up for first period, I thought maybe she'd been called to the office for something, but by third period when she wasn't in Russian class, I knew something was up. Liv never missed an opportunity to show me up in that class. The only reason I took Russian was because it was considered one of the elite classes in the school. I got by, everyone else kept begging the teacher to make it a pass/fail class instead, but Liv thrived. It wasn't surprising considering she spoke three other languages fluently. It worried me that she'd missed one of her favorite classes, but even more when she missed all of her classes.

Her brother, on the other hand, didn't give a shit.

"Let her get expelled," he said as we walked out to my car.

"Have you heard anything from her?"

"No."

"Don't you think you should contact her?"

"No. You do it."

"I can't talk to her in my head like you can."

"Why is that always the default?"

I shrugged and unlocked my car. "It just is. Just try, ok? You know once Awbie and Cam find out she skipped school, they're coming to us. If we say we didn't try to contact her, you know we'll get blamed somehow. Just do it."

He growled and placed his hands on the roof of the car. When he looked down and to the left, I knew he was doing their telepathy thing, and Olivia would be looking down and to the right. Basically, they were bookends. When Jack's face started to twitch, I knew he was arguing with his sister.

"So?" I asked. "What's up?"

He looked at me with an annoyed expression. "She's fine, and she's being an asshole."

"Where is she?"

"She didn't say, but just to tell Mom and Ada she'll be at the party at some point," he replied and ducked into the car.

"Do you want to go to the manor instead of my house?" I asked as I slid behind the wheel and threw my backpack in the backseat.

"Definitely your house," he answered. "That way I can avoid my parents' questions about where my dumbass twin is."

"She's not a dumbass."

"Yes, yes, Wills to the defense, as always," he groaned.

I sighed and drove us out of the school parking lot. Having my own car was both a gift and a curse. It meant I had freedom to go where I wanted, when I wanted, but it also meant I had to drive the Burke twins everywhere. I wasn't exactly sure why they were so against driving one of the company cars. Another reason to complain about their parents, I suppose, although I didn't understand it. Brianna and Cameron, or Awbie and Cam as I had called them all my life, were my godparents and two of the best people on the planet. I never understood why the twins gave them such a hard time, but I guess that's normal for most teenagers. According to everyone, I was abnormal when it came to teen angst and drama. Frankly, between school, training, and competitions, I just didn't have the time. I believe you generally had to see your parents in order to make their lives miserable.

My parents were successful, hard-working people, especially my father being the Chief of Medicine at Facility West. It came with long hours and few holidays, but also a tremendous amount of respect. Unfortunately, because my father was so successful, there was an incredible amount of pressure on me to be at that same level. It's what pushed me to work so hard in school. The happiest day in my dad's life was when I was accepted to the Pre-Med program at UCLA. The look on his face when he read the acceptance letter was seared into my brain. At that moment, all my dreams of becoming a martial arts superstar, or god forbid a Warrior, were gone. I couldn't disappoint my family by being something as trivial as a Warrior. The only thing that got me through it was spending time with the twins.

The twins were my best friends. Jack-Jack was like a brother, but Olivia, well...well, I was in love with Olivia Burke, I always had been. Of course, that love evolved as we got older. When we were younger, I would give her whatever she wanted. I can't remember having a snack that I didn't give her half of. I was always the peacemaker between her and Jack, and would be there to comfort her when he went too far. It wasn't until we hit high school did I realize how strong my feelings were for her, and that was mainly because I realized that once we graduated, for the first time in our lives we wouldn't see each other every day. But I was afraid to confess my feelings to her because of the fear that if she rejected me, I'd lose one of my best friends. Today, that all changed. I wasn't going to be afraid anymore.

After thirty minutes of Jack-Jack jamming and playing air drums to his playlist, we finally pulled into my driveway. Considering the size of our house, I had to assume that my parents planned on having more kids. Three of the five bedrooms stayed empty most of the time, and the in-law apartment over the garage intended for when my grandparents came to visit had only been used three times that I could remember. I was thankful to have Awbie and Cam, and their extended family as my own. Without them and the twins I'd have a pretty lonely existence.

Jack-Jack stepped out of the car, but then froze.

"What's the matter?" I asked and jumped out of the car.

"Don't you smell it?" he said and looked back at me.

I sniffed the air and after a couple of seconds the smoky, charred smell hit me. "Oh no," I groaned and closed my car door, "she cooked."

"Did she burn down the kitchen?" he said and dragged his feet across the driveway.

"Jack-Jack, be serious, my mother only set it on fire that one time," I said and then we both laughed.

My mother, God help her, was the worst cook in history, yet she insisted on torturing all of us with her endless attempts. If it weren't for eating at the manor from time to time, I'd think that all food tasted like charcoal.

"Why is she even home?"

I looked back at Jack and smiled. "Because it's someone's birthday."

He groaned behind me as we approached the side door of the house that led directly into the kitchen. The smell got so bad I thought Jack might have been right and my mother had burnt down the kitchen. When I opened the door, there was a grey haze swirling around making it difficult to see. My mother stood at the kitchen island looking like a parody of a cooking show host with her hair disheveled with white flour covering her face and clothes. Pans and ingredients were all over the counters while she spread thick canned frosting over a cake that should have been yellow or white, and was instead dark brown and even black in some places. She was concentrating so much on the cake that she didn't even notice we'd come in until Jack shut the door.

"Hey, Mom."

"Oh my god," she said and dropped the frosting knife on the counter, "you're early!"

Jack leaned in behind me and muttered, "Imagine if we were late."

I swallowed my laugh down and turned the exhaust fan on over the stove. "Is everything ok?"

"Of course," she replied and patted the flour off her shirt. "That oven cooks so hot sometimes, but no worries, the cake can be saved." Mom stepped over to Jack with her arms outstretched. "Happy birthday, Jack-Jack."

Jack hugged her, rolling his eyes at me over her shoulder. "Thanks, Aunt Re, but you didn't have to make me anything."

"What kind of a 'godmother' would I be if I didn't make you a cake on your birthday," she said with her air quotes. "I've made you and your sister a cake for your 'birthday' every year since you were born. Wait," she stopped and looked around, "where's Livy?"

Jack laughed. "She cut school."

"What?" she shouted. "Does your mom know?"

He shrugged. "None of my business."

"I have to call her," she said and started out of the kitchen, but then quickly turned back around. "But first things first, you have to have some of your cake."

Jack's eyes widened. "That's ok, Aunt Re, I'm..."

"No, no, no, I insist," she said and had to put some weight behind the knife to cut a wedge of the cake. "Don't worry, the frosting will soften it, just give it a couple minutes."

The piece of burnt cake slathered in chocolate frosting made a clinking sound when it hit the ceramic plate. I could hear Jack's stomach turning.

Mom put a fork on the plate and handed it to him with a giant expectant smile. He looked between the cake and his aunt who was waiting patiently for him to take a bite.

"You know, Jax, we gotta get started on that history project," I said and waved him out of the kitchen. "You can eat in my room."

"Oh yeah," he said relieved, "that's gonna take forever. Thanks for the cake, Aunt Re. Livy doesn't know what she's missing."

My mother jumped and stepped quickly to the far corner of the kitchen where her phone sat on the counter. "That's right, I have to call your mom. She's probably packing your sister's stuff as we speak."

"We can only hope," Jack replied and followed me into the living room. "Hey, you called me Jax. It sounds cool, doesn't it?"

"No," I replied as we headed upstairs, "it was weird, but I felt bad for you. When your mom makes me a cake for my birthday, I don't have to worry about having digestive issues later."

"It's really not fair. I don't understand why this weighs so much," he laughed and held up the cake plate.

I laughed with him as we ducked into my bedroom and closed the door. Being an only child had its perks. It meant I got the biggest bedroom that had its own bathroom. I had complete privacy, which was a big deal once I hit puberty. Jack-Jack plopped down in the cushy leather chair in the corner, which was his usual spot. If Livy were here, she would be sitting cross-legged on the left side of my bed while I sat at my desk between them. Her absence was noticeable.

Jack placed the plate on his chest and began picking at the cake with his fork. "I think there's a gumball in here."

I sat down on the edge of my bed, and prepared to tell my best friend the last thing he wanted to hear. "Hey man, I uh…

"Nope, just a ball of flour," he interrupted and wiped his hands on his pants.

"Yeah, um…I just wanted to let you know that uh…"

Jack's eyes moved slowly from his cake to me. "Oh shit, you're stuttering, this isn't good."

I put my hand up. "It is, it is good. I just wanted to tell you that I've decided to finally tell…your sister…that…I…love her."

Jack froze. I don't even think he drew breath. Finally, he said, "No."

"No? What do you mean no?"

He sat up in the chair and placed the cake plate on the floor. "What I mean is that you can't do that. You can't tell my sister that."

"Why not?"

His chest welled up like it would explode any moment. "Why not? Because she's a horrible human being, that's why."

"Jack-Jack, come on…"

"No!" he shouted and stood from the chair. "If this was the Olivia from four years ago, sure, maybe I'd be ok, but now? Wills, she literally has no redeeming qualities. She's a vain, arrogant, know-it-all, snobby bitch."

"That sounds a lot like you, actually."

"Fuck you," he replied dismissively and sat back down in his chair. "I'm serious, man, don't do this. She'll mess you up and not give a shit that she did. And you know why?"

"Because she's a horrible human being?"

"Exactly," he replied with wild eyes. "Horrible, horrible human being. The absolute worst that ever lived."

I shrugged and had to smile. "She's different with me than she is with you. Maybe if I'd told her how I felt earlier she wouldn't be so…"

"Horribl-ly?"

"I'm really worried you're not going to graduate," I said and it broke the tension between us. "I can't keep it in anymore. I've got to tell her."

He picked up his cake plate from the floor and began picking at it again. "When are you going to do this really stupid confession?"

"Tonight, at some point," I replied, opened my nightstand drawer, and pulled out a small silver box.

"You do realize it's my birthday, too."

"Do you want me to tell you I love you?"

"Yes. Yes, I do. What does she have that I don't?"

"Boobs."

"Gross."

"Sorry," I laughed. "Do you know how long I've waited to do this."

"Probably since we were six years old, but tonight?"

"I'm going to give her these," I said and handed him the silver box.

He opened the lid of the box and then shot me a look. "You're shitting me, right?" he said and held up the pair of pear-shaped diamond earrings. "Dude, they're fucking real."

"I hope so," I said and took the box from him, "or else I'm out a lot of money."

"You're such a dumbass. Where did you get that kind of money?"

"My competition money."

"And your parents haven't noticed?"

"Not yet," I replied and sat down on the bed. "But I have Internationals coming up and I'll be able to put it back in and then some."

Jack nodded his head several times and took a bite of cake. As the cake crunched loudly in his mouth he began to nod again and gave me an odd look. "Two things, if I may?" he said in the uppity, formal voice he used to imitate his dad.

"Of course."

"One, I know I'm not the smart one in the room, but the way I understand math is that if I have a certain amount of money, then I take some money away, and then I add some back in, I'm going to be left with less than if I had just added the money to the original amount. Right? So, how exactly are you going to explain that to your parents?"

"Honestly, I'm hoping they won't notice."

"Ah, I see. Great plan."

"Was there a second thing?"

"Yes, the second thing," he began, "you're an idiot and my sister is going to destroy you."

"It's going to be fine," I said and pulled a notebook out of my backpack, but turned around when I heard that crunching sound again. "Are you still eating that cake?"

He nodded while his face contorted with every chew. "I'm hoping that whatever is in this thing will kill me before I have to watch this car wreck happen tonight."

"It's going to be fine. I just need your support on this."

He didn't answer, but put another bite of burnt cake into his mouth. He chewed several times before spitting out another lump of flour, or maybe there really were gumballs in the cake. "I don't support it, man, but I won't stop you either. It's your funeral."

Chapter Three

Will

The earring box was burning a hole in the pocket of my hoodie. I kept catching Jack shaking his head at me. He thought I was being stupid. I thought I was stupid not to say something to Liv. But it would be fine. Yes, it would be fine.

"Will, honey, are you ok?" my mother asked from the front seat of our car.

I jerked to attention and looked up. "Yeah, why?"

"You just seem quiet, that's all."

"Just tired," I replied and looked over at Jack who started shaking his head at me again.

"Once Internationals are over with, you should think about taking a break. You're stretching yourself too thin."

"I will," I replied, although the thought of it made me depressed.

"I think it'll be good for you. I'm happy you took tonight off too. It's been so long since we saw Sera and Eris, I'm glad they came over from the island."

"Wouldn't that be nice one day, Re? An island to ourselves," Dad said.

Mom laughed. "You couldn't stay there more than ten minutes because there wouldn't be any patients anywhere."

"That's not true," he said and looked at me in the rearview mirror. "Son, defend me here."

"Sorry, Pop. Mom's got you on this one."

"Come on, Will," Jack interrupted. "He could last more than ten minutes."

"Thank you, Jack, at least my nephew has my back."

"Of course, Uncle John. You'd last at least fifteen or twenty minutes."

The car erupted with laughter while my dad pretended to be offended. My father was the hardest working man I knew. I often assumed he'd work until the day he died. Being a doctor was everything to my dad. His parents never understood him. They were academics, and he needed to be hands-on. I hoped that I could find that same passion in medicine, and make him proud of me. I worried about that. I worried I wouldn't like being a doctor like he did. He'd always find a reason to bring me to the Facility's clinic and spend hours unloading his knowledge on me. You could hardly tell the difference between my sutures and his, and I could definitely dress wounds in an emergency. It would be fine. Just like tonight with Liv, everything would be fine.

Several minutes later we pulled into the driveway of the small ranch-style house tucked away from the city and hidden among a thick wooded area. Even though they had passed several years ago, it was still Daddy O and Maddy's house. As kids, the Burke twins and I spent nights sprawled out on the living room floor watching old movies with Daddy O while Maddy made us endless junk food. They weren't technically my great-grandparents, but I was closer to them than any of my own grandparents. Sometimes blood wasn't thicker than water.

I stepped out of the car and checked my pocket one more time. It surprised me how something so small cost me most of my savings, but it was worth it. She'd love them, I just knew she would, and that would be worth whatever punishment my parents put me through when they realized what I had done. It would be fine.

I followed my dad and Jack inside the house with Mom bringing up the rear. The family had already filled the living room and kitchen. Alex and Kyla were talking with Jared in a corner in the dining room while Devin stood with Cam at the back of the couch. Sera sat in a chair in the living room while Fabi, Devin's partner for over twenty years, examined the scarf she was wearing. My dad split the moment he saw Awbie coming toward us, and she was coming in hot.

"No, Mom, I haven't talked to her," Jack said without being prompted.

Awbie looked from her son to me. "Wills? Anything?"

"Sorry, Awbie. The last time I saw her was right before homeroom."

"I can't believe she skipped a whole day of school. What is going on in that head of hers?" Awbie said, red tears lining the edges of her eyes.

"I'd like to point out that I'm here, where I'm supposed to be, so I should get all of her presents in addition to my own," Jack said.

Knowing this would start a long debate where Jack would try and wear my aunt down, I decided to step away and say hello to the others. The first being Sera who stood from her chair as I approached.

"Hi, Sera," I said and leaned down to hug her, burying my face in her long grey hair. Each time I saw her she had more age lines cutting into her face, and seemed to shrink in size.

Sera pulled my face up with her hands on either side and looked at me intensely. "Oh my, you are a young man with a mission. N'est pas?" she said softly with her thick French accent.

My stomach flipped and I nervously patted my hair down. "Um...not really. Just getting ready for Internationals."

"Non, non, it iz more important zhan zhat," she said and then her face fell slightly.

"What?" I asked in a panic. "What's the matter?"

"Nozhing, sweet boy," she answered and patted my cheek. "Just a long day pour moi."

"I'm sorry I can't speak French with you as well as Liv."

She smiled sweetly. "Zhat is fine, my sweet boy, she will be here momentarily."

"She will?"

"Ah oui, your mission can stay on course," she replied and the blood ran from my face. Sera would always say that her psychic abilities faded the night the twins were born and Awbie was Turned, but she always knew way too much to not have something.

"Those who are eating, food is ready," Awbie said from the kitchen, her voice sounding tired and sad.

In a house so full, there were only five people that could actually eat real food, yet Awbie cooked enough for an army. I always assumed she was channeling Maddy and how she used to cook. Maddy and Daddy O's absence could certainly be felt at family gatherings. By the time you walked into the house, Daddy O was putting a drink in one hand, and Maddy was shoving a plate of food in the other.

Jack was already at the table scooping a mound of mac and cheese onto his plate. When he added a second scoop, I knew he was upset. Unlike Liv, Jack wasn't a big eater. Olivia could eat more than me and Jack put together, and then still ask for more. Jack was mostly an emotional eater.

"Hey, man," I said to him and took a plate for myself.

"She's not even here and is ruining my birthday," he said and slapped a heap of mashed potatoes onto his plate so hard that some of it splattered in my face. "Sorry."

I took a napkin from the stack sitting on the table and wiped my cheek. "The only one who can ruin your birthday is you."

"Will there ever be a day when you don't take her side?"

"I'm not taking anyone's side."

He glared at me. "I hate you."

"Sure," I replied sarcastically.

"Jack-Jack, I made Mama Jo's cornbread just for you," Awbie said as she placed a plate of cornbread wedges down on the table. Mama Jo, Awbie's grandmother, was a real Southern cook and her cornbread was made in a piping hot cast iron skillet that had about a half-inch of oil at the bottom that basically fried the batter. It was heaven.

Jack placed two pieces of cornbread on his plate before setting it down on the table. "Everyone, I'd like to make an announcement," he began, causing the room to become quiet and all eyes to turn in our direction. "As of today, Jack-Jack is dead."

"What?" Awbie asked with a scrunched-up face.

"Mom, I am an adult now, and no adult male wants to be called Jack-Jack. Actually, no one of any age wants to be called Jack-Jack."

Awbie rolled her eyes. "So what exactly are we supposed to call you?"

"I'm glad you asked. From now on, I want to be called Jax," he replied, but the room remained uncomfortably quiet. "Seriously? Isn't anyone going to say something?"

"Like with an S?" Jared asked.

"Like the old game with the metal pieces and the ball?" Alex asked next.

"No," Jack groaned. "Not the game, and with an X, not an S."

"But we called you Jack-Jack, the S makes more sense, as in more than one Jack," Jared continued to tease.

"Never mind," Jack-Jack groaned and walked to the couch with his full plate of food.

"Now, son," Cam began, "if you no longer want to be called Jack-Jack, we will all try not to do so."

"I can't promise anything," my mom answered with no apologies in her tone, but then again, she never apologized for anything. She did not possess a filter, nor did she want one. "But just for tonight, I'll try it out to see how it feels."

"Thanks, Aunt Re, I know I can always count on you."

"Ok, we'll all agree to try and remember to call you Jax," Awbie said with little affirmation from the family.

"Your enthusiasm is overwhelming. Happy birthday to me," he said dramatically and sat down next to me. "This is bullshit."

"Jackson, your language," Cam scolded from the backside of the couch.

"Ada, I'm eighteen. I should be able to say what I want."

"Tomorrow, son, you can say whatever it is you want, but tonight I would like you to pretend you were raised better than that."

"But I wasn't," Jack laughed, causing Cam to smile and shake his head. But suddenly Jack stopped laughing and his eyes darted to the left. "Fucking bitch."

"Jackson Thomas!" Cam said angrily and came around to face his son who quickly put his hands up.

"I'm sorry, Ada, sorry…uh…your daughter is down the street."

Suddenly all the vampires in the house perked their ears up, leaving us humans in the dark as to why they had a mix of anger and shock on their faces.

"Is that a motorcycle?" Awbie said and stepped toward the door just as a single headlight flashed through the living room window. "I'm gonna kill her. Who the hell does she know who drives a motorcycle?"

"Brianna," Cam began and blocked her from opening the door, "we all know why she is doing this. She wants to get a rise out of you, out of all of us. We cannot give her what she wants. We must have no reaction."

I looked over at Jack. "Is it someone we know?"

He nodded his head and sat back in the couch to simmer in his anger. "That loser who got kicked out of school last year. At least you're seeing the real Olivia before you do something stupid."

In all honesty, I knew exactly what I would see coming through that door. Olivia would be fake and pompous, throwing some random person in her family's faces to prove she wasn't going to follow their rules. But it didn't change my mind on what I was going to do. Why should it? I could see through to her heart and soul that I loved, that I had always loved. She was always the real Olivia with me.

Jack's eyes were burning a hole in the side of my face, but I refused to turn and acknowledge him. "You're still going to do something stupid, aren't you?"

"Probably."

He sighed and stuffed a huge forkful of mac and cheese into his mouth. Like I said, an emotional eater.

Chapter Four

Olivia

With a family like mine, it was hard to get off the grid and be completely un-trackable, especially with an uncle who could hack into any system possible to find his niece on any camera in the city, or even satellites for that matter. But to his detriment, Uncle Jared had also taught me how to avoid said technology, so I considered today a success in his training as each hour passed and there were no Warriors in sight.

With the exception of the last couple of hours, my day was rather boring, but I liked that. First, I went shopping to get out of my uniform. Then I sat and enjoyed a sandwich with a view of the bridge. Next, I people-watched in a park with the sun on my face, and then went down to the marina to look out onto the ocean. I let my mind go blank in order to truly relax and enjoy my life for once. As expected, once school was out, Jack-Jack's voice rang in my head asking where I was, and then calling me a selfish bitch. I knew the later I stayed out, the more my parents would pressure him to talk to me again and again until I told them where I was. But just as much as I was standing up for myself, he needed to do the same. The connection Jack and I had was a curse, and my parents constantly abused it. They had no idea what it was like to have another person, even worse, your brother, in your head at all times. I hated it, and today I refused to play. I responded only once to say I was fine, and that's all anyone needed to know.

But in my defense, my day was innocent enough until a guy on a motorcycle caught my attention. I recognized him from school, he had been a year ahead of me, but was expelled before he could graduate. I don't know what possessed me to say hi. I had never spoken to him in my life, but the little devil that had possessed me to sneak out of school took over. He had rebel written all over him with his windblown hair, leather jacket, and bad boy smirk. I smoked a cigarette when he offered it, and drank from his flask. My throat still burned from whatever kind of alcohol was in it. And then when he suggested we go for a ride, I wrapped my arms around his waist and squeezed my legs to hold on tight. The freedom I felt as the wind whipped through my hair was like nothing I'd ever experienced. This was what I wanted; this was how I wanted to feel every day.

"Turn left here," I said loudly in his ear. Daddy O's old house was just up the street and my stomach fluttered with nerves at what I was going to walk into. But I would stand up for myself and what I needed in order to be able to live a meaningful existence.

I'm coming, with a guest, I said in my head to Jack and sent a mental image of my view from the bike.

I really fucking hate you, he replied.

The feeling was mutual, but I didn't reply to him.

"It's there on the left," I said and pointed to the small house nestled in the woods. The lone little house with so many good memories, but today it was yet another symbol of my oppression.

The bike slowed and we turned into the driveway that was full of my family's vehicles. Soft lights glowed from the living room's windows with the shadows of those inside darting back and forth in front of the sheer curtain. Once the engine was cut off, I climbed down from the back of the bike and tried running my fingers through my matted hair. I probably looked like I'd been electrocuted. Butterflies were fluttering wildly around in my stomach, there was no way of knowing the kind of shit storm I was going to walk into, especially walking in with Tanner. God, even his name would infuriate them.

"This is it?" Tanner said in a judgmental tone. "Were you a scholarship kid at school?"

"Oh no," I laughed way too loudly, "this is my grandfather's old house. Our mansion is attached to my family's business, so we like to come out here to have a little more privacy at family gatherings."

He sighed and looked annoyed. "I thought we were going to a party."

"We are! We are," I replied nervously, trying to sound cooler than I was. "This isn't it, of course, I just need to stop in and say hi first."

"And piss your parents off."

"Well, yeah. It shouldn't take long, and then we can…uh…go to the real party…that I…will take you to."

I sounded like such an idiot, mainly because I didn't really know what all he wanted to do. If I had to smoke more cigarettes or drink more of what was in that flask, I wasn't sure how much I wanted to party.

"Then let's do this," Tanner said and took a swig from his flask.

I wrapped my hand around his arm and led him across the driveway to the little house that I secretly loved, but obviously couldn't admit. All conversation, all noise inside the house stopped when we stepped up to the front door. They were waiting for me, and I was ready to go into battle. With a deep breath, I threw my shoulders back and shook the nerves out of my hands. When I opened the door, everyone was already focused on us, judgment and disappointment plastered on their faces.

"Hi everyone," I said happily and pulled Tanner into the house. "Sorry we're late, we lost track of time."

Mom looked as though her head was going to explode. Ada stepped away from her side and said, "Perhaps you can introduce us to your friend."

"Oh, sorry, this is Tanner Simpkins. Tanner, this is my family. Usually they're a little more hospitable. *Perhaps* we could all relax a little."

Mom stepped forward angrily, but Ada quickly stepped in front of her. "Tanner, please forgive us, we were expecting this to be a family event, but welcome. Would you care for some food or a beverage?"

"Is there somewhere I can have a smoke?" Tanner answered.

"Absolutely not!" Mom said loudly, but Ada put his hand up to her.

When he turned his attention back to us, he gestured toward the front door. "Tanner, perhaps you could smoke your cigarette out front while we have a moment with our daughter."

"Whatever," Tanner replied as he turned and stepped back out the front door.

"He's a real winner, sis," Jack-Jack said sarcastically.

"Jackson, enough," Ada chided.

Jack-Jack threw his hands up. "What? I'm being honest, Ada. Of all the guys in this city, she finds good ole' Tanner Simpkins. I mean, look at the guy, he's got high school dropout written all over him."

"Technically he's not a dropout," Will corrected and I glared at him.

"You're right, Wills, he was expelled for dealing prescription drugs at school."

"Oh dear lord," Mom groaned from the kitchen.

"Jackson, I said enough. Olivia, you cannot simply disappear, ignore our calls, and then show up with a stranger who…"

"I should be allowed to bring someone to my own birthday party," I interrupted and pointed to Will. "You don't care when Jack brings someone."

"It's Wills," Jack shouted. "He's more a part of the family than you are."

"Fuck you, Jack."

"Olivia Sera," Mom shouted, "you will watch your mouth."

"My mouth?" I shouted back. "You have no idea the things he says to me. You always take his side."

"Maybe it's because your brother isn't bringing chain-smoking drug dealers to our house!"

"Brianna," Ada said and tried pushing her back into the kitchen.

"No, Cam, we can't just let her waltz in here like this after what she's put us through today."

"What I put you through? I'm surprised you even noticed I was gone."

"Despite what you think, we are not the horrible parents you portray us to be. We have been going out of our minds worrying about where you were today. Jared broke at least a dozen state and federal laws today looking for you."

"Maybe I was doing what I wanted on my eighteenth freakin' birthday, Mom."

My mother's eyes bugged out of her head. "Do you think your brother wanted to celebrate *his* eighteenth birthday like this? Did you for a moment think about how your actions affect those around you?"

"Of course not. Right, Jack-Jack?" I replied. "I'm just a selfish bitch, aren't I?"

"You said it," he grumbled and shoved some food in his mouth.

Tanner came back inside, the smell of cigarette smoke wafting around him.

"Fine, since no one wants me here, I'll just go so that everyone can shower love and praise on the favorite child. Tanner, let's go find a real party."

Tanner shrugged and I pushed him back out the door, slamming it behind me. As we walked across the driveway, he reached into his leather jacket and pulled out his flask again.

"Need a drink?"

I took the flask from his hand, took a big swig, and tried not to cough as the nasty alcohol burned my throat. "Sorry that was such a disaster."

He shook his head and took a drink that was twice as long as mine. "Nothing my family hasn't done to me. Ready to really party now?"

"Absolutely," I replied as we jumped back onto his motorcycle. I was ready for the wind to whip through my hair and have that feeling of freedom again.

Tanner started the motorcycle and I tightened my arms around his waist. I nestled my head into his back in order to take in the smell of his leather jacket. Unfortunately, the only thing I could smell was the cigarette smoke. It wasn't quite as romantic as the movies made it. Tanner revved the engine and I smiled at the adventure we were about to embark on. When he revved the engine again and didn't move, I lifted my head from his back and realized something was wrong. Tanner pulled back on the accelerator and squealed the back tire on the driveway, but we still didn't move. I looked behind me and gasped at the sight of my father holding the back fin of the motorcycle. With a jerk of his arm, he flung the bike backwards, and then caught the handlebars to hold us in place in front of him.

"Cut the engine," he shouted, and Tanner instantly complied.

"Hey man, what's your problem?" Tanner said, causing Ada to tilt his head in disgust.

"My first problem is you referring to me as 'man.' My second problem is that you gave alcohol to my underaged daughter. Lastly, and my biggest problem, is that you were about to take my daughter on your motorcycle while intoxicated. Now get off."

"Look, man, you can't tell me…"

"If you call me 'man' one more time, I will have you crawling on all fours and barking like a dog for the rest of your life. Now get off the bike!"

Quickly I unwrapped my arms from around Tanner's waist and jumped off. Tanner hiked his leg around and stood up from the motorcycle, but then stupidly puffed his chest out and stepped up to Ada.

"You have no idea who my father is," Tanner replied and Ada smirked.

"And you do not know mine," he said and gestured to someone behind him. "For the safety of our city, my brothers will escort you home."

"Oh they will, will they?"

To my left, Uncle Alex and Devy stepped out of the darkness. They couldn't kill him because he was human, but they could still make him uncomfortable.

"Alex," Ada began, "please load Mr. Simpkins' motorcycle into your truck."

Without a word, my incredibly large uncle took hold of one of the handlebars, raised the bike up off the ground, and then lifted it up onto his shoulder. Tanner stepped back and watched in shock as Uncle Alex walked across the driveway with the bike in the air as if he was carrying a bag of flour.

"Now, *Tanner*," Ada continued in a deep, growling tone as he looked fiercely into Tanner's eyes in order to Glamour him. "Firstly, you will never offer alcohol to anyone underage ever again."

"Ada, please…"

Ada put up his index finger in order to silence me and not take his eyes away from Tanner during the Glamour. "You will also never drive while intoxicated or under the influence. Is that understood?"

"Y-yeess," Tanner said lazily as his brain was invaded.

"Good. You will also forget you ever met my daughter today. You will not even remember her name. You will forget you ever came here, and you will not remember how you got home. And lastly, you will quit smoking. It is a disgusting and deadly habit." Ada's eyes flared as he completed the Glamour and then looked over to Devy. "Brother, please take him away before I make good on my threat to turn him into a dog."

"With pleasure," Devy responded and pulled Tanner away by the back of the neck, but didn't miss the chance to look over his shoulder and shoot me a disappointed glance.

Once Alex pulled away, there was no one to protect me from my father's hurtful glare.

"I'm sorry, Ada…"

"Do not begin by lying to me."

"I'm not!"

"Olivia, I realize your upbringing has not been traditional, and I understand the struggles you and your brother have had to go through because you are unlike others your age. Because of that, I have allowed you certain liberties. Perhaps that is where all of this has gone wrong."

"Ada…"

"I have tried to understand your rebellious nature, I have even pressured your mother to overlook it. But this…I simply do not understand. What has gotten into you? Tell me, Olivia, what is so terrible about your life that could cause you to behave this way?"

Every emotion I had been suppressing for months melded together and rose up into my chest until it finally burst through my mouth. "I can't breathe, Ada! Every day I wake up and I feel like I'm being suffocated."

"Olivia," Ada groaned, "do not be so dramatic."

"Dramatic?!" I shouted. "I live in a house with a rotating door of people, going off on missions and not always coming back. I practically have to make an appointment to see you, and Mom overcompensates for us not living a normal life. Then there's the constant need to hide who I am. 'Don't move too fast, Livy, they'll see you're different.' 'Pretend you don't hear what people are saying across the room.' 'Sorry, Livy, you can't have your friends over to the manor.' 'Don't put yourself in situations where your fangs will come out and expose what you are.' And the fact that I have fangs to begin with, Ada, is enough to make me want to scream! I'm miserable, Ada. There isn't one aspect of my life that makes me happy to wake up in the morning, oh, of course that's when I actually do sleep. I want nothing to do with violence and war and vampires…I'm…I'm sick of it! I'm sick of the manor, I'm sick of the Warriors!"

When my outburst was finished, Ada stood frozen and stoic, and it made me burst into tears. My hands covered my face and I must have cried for nearly thirty seconds before Ada even put his arm around me. When I finally caught my breath, and the hysterics passed, he said, "I cannot change what you are, lovey, and I am sorry that it causes you such pain. What can we do to make your situation better?"

I laughed and pushed away from him. "You won't do anything."

"I deserve more credit than that," he said firmly.

"Fine, let me leave."

"Leave? And go where?"

"Abroad," I replied and he raised his eyebrows questioningly. "Let me study in Europe. Italy, maybe. I love foreign languages, Ada. I want to learn more and maybe be an interrupter or something."

"And when you think about living abroad and studying languages, you no longer feel suffocated?"

"Yes," I answered honestly. "I can't wait until the summer, I need to leave now, Ada, I can't stay here."

"You do not graduate for another couple of months."

"I'll talk to my teachers and see if I can take all my finals now. I'll apply for my GED. I'll do anything, Ada, I'm very serious about this. I can't live here anymore."

He sighed and crossed his arms in front of his chest. "Olivia, leaving will not change what you are. You will still have to be careful not to expose yourself."

"But I will have space to myself, and privacy, and independence. I won't be surrounded by vampires and blood donors and people with powers. I want normalcy, and I don't want anything to do with the Warriors. Nothing."

Ada shifted his weight between his feet while he pondered his response. Just as the silence was becoming unbearable, he finally said, "Fine."

I didn't wait for him to say another word before I leapt forward and hugged him tightly. "Thank you, Ada," I cried, but instead of comforting me, he pulled my arms from his neck and stepped back.

"Olivia, my decision in no way should be looked upon as though I condone any of your behavior. I hope, I sincerely hope, that living abroad and being away from us will bring you the solace you need because I do not think that we can handle your outbursts anymore. Your behavior is tearing our family apart."

"That's a bit harsh."

"It is nothing compared to what lies ahead of you in the real world. We will pay for your studies, but you will be responsible for all other expenses now that you have access to your Trust."

"Fine, but how are you going to get this past Mom? She's not going to be happy that she can't monitor my every waking moment."

"And that is the last time you make a snide or insulting comment about your mother," he said and my face fell at how cold his expression became. "She sacrificed everything, including her life, to have you. I was there when she died, Olivia. I heard your mother's heart stop beating. I saw her lying lifeless on the table with her stomach cut open and blood everywhere. If we had not been able to Turn her, that is the last image I would have of her. I would only be able to tell you about your mother, and you would never know the tremendous love she has for you. You should thank God that you have had your mother for your entire life. I felt the incredible loss of life without her, and I sincerely hope you will never have to suffer what that feels like. She has dedicated her life to your protection and upbringing, and she deserves some goddamn respect. One more dismissive comment, or nasty look, our arrangement will terminate. You will quickly discover what life is like without the protection and comfort of our family that you are suddenly so ashamed and disgusted by."

Tears streamed down my face. Ada's disappointment in me hit so deeply that it was hard to breathe.

"Now, I need to speak to your mother and try to salvage some kind of celebration for your brother since not only did you ruin your birthday, which was what you wanted in the first place, but you also ruined his. It saddens me, Olivia, it truly saddens me to see what you have become. It obviously reflects my faults as a father."

"Ada, no…"

He held his hand up and I stopped. "I will see who can take you back to the manor. I think it best you not go back inside."

"I can get back on my own."

Without another word, he rushed past me into the house. No doubt everyone inside would be talking about how horrible and ungrateful I was. Well, let them. I didn't care. They didn't need me, they had Jack-Jack. They liked him better because he didn't stand up to them, he didn't do anything. They'd be happier without me.

Tears welled up in my eyes, but why? I'd had an exit plan for months. The woods were right there, I could just run, but suddenly a loud sob burst out of me. I covered my mouth to quiet the sound when someone opened and closed the front door to the house behind me.

I peeked over my shoulder and saw Will crossing the driveway. "Leave me alone, Wills."

"Can't," he replied.

"Why the hell not," I said angrily, wiping my cheeks before turning around and facing him. But the instant I saw him, my anger faded. Everything faded - the sense of suffocation, the feeling of being trapped, everything. He was always able to do that to me with just one look into his bright blue-green eyes.

"You're one of my best friends, Liv. I always know when you need me. So what's going on? Why are you so upset?"

"Wills," I groaned, but he put his arms around me and I instantly felt safe, as I always did. I cried into his shoulder, but I didn't know why. What was wrong with me? I looked up and found him looking at me with eyes that said only one thing, and I'd been avoiding it for years now. Quickly I stepped back and turned away from him. "I can't do this anymore, Wills. I'm leaving."

"Ok, I'll grab some keys and we'll take a drive to clear your head."

"No, Wills, I'm not talking about going for a drive. I'm really leaving, away from here, away from everyone."

"Liv, you've been saying that since Sophomore year. College is just around the corner."

With a frustrated sigh I turned around. "I'm leaving the country, Wills."

"Liv, come on," he laughed.

"I'm serious. Ada said I could study abroad."

"W-what? Abroad? What do you mean abroad? When?"

"Right away. I can't deal with this anymore."

He shook his head wildly. "No, Liv, come on, you can't just go."

"And why not?" I shouted and once again he looked at me like no one else did, and I didn't deserve it. I wanted him to just go back inside and stop this from going any further before we could never go back. When he didn't break, I turned away from him again. "Just go, please, Wills."

"Olivia, I...I can't let you go without..." he cleared his throat and stepped up behind me. "I've tried to tell you so many times, Liv."

"Will, don't," I begged, keeping my back to him.

"I love you, Olivia. I always have. I can't remember a time when I haven't," he continued and touched the outside of my left hand with his fingertips. "I've been so scared to tell you, but...I do. And I know you have feelings for me."

My bottom lip trembled, and I could feel the burning of tears in my eyes. This had to stop because in no way was I good enough for Will Ryan. "That's not true."

"Then why are you so upset? Liv, I know you better than anyone else. You open up to me more than anyone. When you're upset or having a hard time, you come to me. You are yourself when you're with me, not this person you think you need to be with other people. I see you, Liv, I see the real you, and I love her...ah you. I-I got you something..."

Slowly I turned around and found Will holding a little silver box open with two pear-shaped diamond earrings that sparkled even in the dark. Nothing he said was wrong. Will was a good person, the best person, and yes, I loved him. He was a part of me. Where there was one, there was the other. But sometimes you had to cut off a limb in order to survive. Loving him would keep me here, grounded and suffering. I couldn't let him do that. He deserved better than me, and he wouldn't do it on his own.

"Will, your whole life all you've done is try and be like us," I said nastily. "It's pathetic really. You don't love me. You love the fact that I'm the coven leader's daughter."

"Wh-hat?" he replied, frozen in place.

"Go get your own life, Will, and stop trying to be a part of ours. You don't belong, you never did. Everyone just humors you because our moms are friends."

"You don't mean that, Liv, I know you…"

"You don't know shit about me! You have this idea of who I am and that's who you're in love with, Will, and it's exhausting trying to be what you want me to be. I don't love you. I don't need you, and I don't need your stupid gift," I shouted, took the box from his hand, and threw it into the woods.

It was an impulse; I didn't mean to do it. Will's face was frozen in horror as he looked out into the woods. Even in the dark I could see he had lost all color in his face. He opened his mouth but then closed it, opened it, closed it, and then finally turned around in silence and walked back into the house.

When the door shut behind him it was as though it had cut a string that released a floodgate of grief. If this was what I wanted, why did it hurt so much? Why did my chest feel as though there was an anvil resting on top of it?

You goddamn bitch, Jackson's voice rang in my head. *You fucking evil bitch. Go overseas, fall in a hole and drop dead, you piece of shit.*

I took a step onto the grass, and then another, and another until the woods covered me like a blanket, deafening the sound of my brother's hatred. My knees felt weak and my feet stopped moving. The base of the tree next to me was split, forming what looked like a chair, inviting me to sit in silence. My head was heavy and achy, my chest burning from crying. I sat down on the ground and pressed my back into the trunk of the tree, just looking out into the darkness where only slivers of silvery light peeked through the branches as they waved in the breeze. At least it was silent now. Peaceful solitude. It was what I wanted, it was.

I could hear movement and cars being started in the direction of the house. I turned my head to look toward the sound when a spark caught my eye, the tiniest sparkle among the darkness. I leaned over in its direction, the trunk of the tree digging into my ribs as my fingertips touched something hard with edges. Finally, it fell over into my hand and I pulled myself back up. In my hand was a silver box, still open with diamonds sparkling. They were real, and they were flawless, something my true-hybrid eyes could see clearly.

"I love you too, Will," I whispered.

And for his own good I would never say it again.

Five years later...

Chapter Five

Will

"Yeah, Will, come on," Jax encouraged from the other side of the heavy bag.

Jab, jab, cross, cross, uppercut. Jab, jab, cross, cross, kick. Cut, cut, turn, back kick. It was a good back kick, even pushing Jax back a couple inches.

"Nice, man," he said and brought the heavy bag back into place. "So uh, how are you feeling today?"

"What?" I huffed and caught my breath. Jab, jab, cross, uppercut.

"Just wondering how you're feeling."

"Fine, why?" Cross, cross, cross, cross, knee.

"Come on, man," he groaned. "She's coming home today. Everybody's worried about you."

I jumped into the air, turned, and round-housed the bag causing Jax to grunt from the bag's impact into his chest.

"I'm fine," I said and pulled at the strap of my right glove with my teeth.

"Yeah, you seem it."

Once I pulled my right glove free, I replied, "I don't know what you want me to say. Your sister was bound to come home at some point, I mean, it's been five years."

"Five years of bliss," he laughed, but then his face got very serious.

"Doesn't change the fact that everyone is worried about you."

I hated that phrase, and hated the look that came with it. I'd seen it so many times from everyone at the manor, and I was sick of it. It was a reminder that at one point I hadn't been fine and almost didn't find my way back.

"Everyone just needs to chill. I'm going to go teach my classes, then go to work at the club, get a few hours sleep, and come back here for training tomorrow morning. Just like every other day. We won't even see each other, which I'm sure is what she wants too. The more attention everyone brings to this, the more awkward it will be."

Jax looked down at his watch. "Ok, well you should get going then, she's supposed to be here any minute."

My head flinched and I looked at my watch. "How did it get so late?"

"You've been hitting the bag for the last thirty minutes."

"And you didn't stop me!?"

"A semi-truck couldn't have stopped you, man."

"You could have said something," I grumbled as I ran to the wall and grabbed my bag. Unfortunately, from the training room the only way out was through the front door. I'd walked through these corridors for as long as I could remember, this was a second home to me. Yet today I couldn't get out of here fast enough. I couldn't see her, I just couldn't see Olivia. I'd had weeks to prepare for this day, but here I was panicked that I wouldn't get out in time.

"Slow down, man," Jax said behind me.

"Shut up."

"I thought you were fine," he laughed.

"I am," I lied. "I've got a class to teach."

"And you don't want to see my sister and her boyfriend."

"Shut up."

"But how can I blame you, I don't want to see my sister and her boyfriend either. Such a douchebag."

"Which one?"

Jax laughed and patted me on the shoulder as we rounded the corner. "Don't worry, man, it's not like she's going to be coming through the…"

Door. That's what he was going to say. Yet there she was, tall and statuesque. Her black hair was longer and curlier, overall looking more mature as she hugged her mother in the foyer. Her big, dark eyes caught sight of me for a second before darting away.

"Damn, she has bad timing," Jax said softly, but Awbie still heard him and we caught her attention.

Quickly Jax stepped in front of me, providing enough protection for me to slip out the door while he distracted the rest of them. The air outside was refreshing and I gulped it in as I rushed to my car. My old red Honda had seen better days, it was practically held together by duct tape. I'd had it since high school, and it was my prized possession at the time. However, when I practically emptied my savings buying Olivia those stupid diamond earrings, my father made it clear that financially I was on my own. Teaching classes at Facility West and bartending at night provided enough to squeak by, but I was having to save for my life as a Warrior. There were dues, boarding, and general living expenses for centuries to come. After all of that, I still had to drive a piece of shit.

Just as I reached out to open my car door, "Wills?"

I jumped and turned around, falling back into the side of my car and finding Awbie smiling apologetically. "Sorry, Awbie, you snuck up on me."

"I'm sorry, honey, I..." she paused, visibly uncomfortable. "I...we, mostly me, I just wanted to see if you were going to come to dinner tonight. Remember? All the family will be here, even Eris and Sera are coming in this afternoon."

I shook my head. "Sorry, Awbie, I have to work tonight at the club."

"I know," she pleaded and began wringing her hands in front of her. "But we're getting together at five, and you don't need to go to work until seven."

"You talked to Mom."

"Of course I did," she replied sheepishly.

"Awbie, I can't."

"Wills, I know having Livy come back after all this time is awkward. Believe me, we're all trying to figure out how to act."

"I have to work."

"And I need my three little angels together again." Her eyes were both pleading and yet somehow challenging. "We all need to move on from those bad times when she left, and I include myself in that. We're all adults now..."

"Jax is an adult?"

She smirked and rolled her eyes. "Perhaps not. Speaking of, I've left him alone with Livy and Niall too long. Please come tonight, Wills?"

It was hard to say no to the woman who was a second mother to me. There were times I saw her and Cam more than my own parents.

"I...I can't stay long."

She threw her arms around me and kissed me on the cheek with her cool lips. When she pulled away, I could see red tears lining her eyes. "Thank you, honey. You have no idea how happy this makes me."

"Yeah, I gotta get to the Facility."

"Oh, yes, yes, sorry. I'll see you tonight."

She gave me one last kiss on the cheek and then was a blur as she ran back into the manor. My stomach sank and I suddenly felt nauseous. Was there no end to the abuse I would put myself through?

Chapter Six

Olivia

"Only a few more minutes," the young Warrior said from the driver's seat.

"She knows, David," Trevor Roberts groaned from the front passenger seat. "She grew up in the manor, she knows she's almost home."

"Oh, right," David replied and then looked in the rearview mirror at me. "Sorry."

I smiled. "Don't be sorry. You must be new."

He nodded. "I was inducted last year. Roberts has been here much longer than I have."

"She knows," Roberts sighed loudly, then looked over his shoulder. "I apologize for young David, Livy."

I smiled. "It's fine."

Poor David looked like he wanted to crawl into the floor and die. Niall seemed to get a kick out of it, either that or he was delirious from the jet lag after over fifteen hours of flying. His smile and his reassuring hand on my knee kept the vomit from coming up from my stomach. I hadn't been home in five years. When I left, I couldn't get on the plane fast enough. I went to University and became fluent in seventeen languages, and then used that knowledge to be a translator. My most rewarding job was volunteering to help translate for refugees all over Europe and Asia. But several months ago, Ada had declared that I needed to come home, if not to stay, then to discuss and plan my future.

Thankfully I had Niall to help me through. We'd been dating for almost four months, and we'd practically been living together since our second date. He was only a year older than I was, but his cut jaw and extremely straight posture made him seem older. He prided himself on his sandy-blonde hair as well as the amount of time and product he used in it. I hoped he wouldn't mention that to anyone in my family because they would torture him about it. He was a typical looking Brit - pale, thin, and lanky. The only dark feature he had were his hybrid eyes.

When I told Niall that I needed to go home for a while, he insisted that he come with me to meet my family. I had a feeling there was more about his visit than he was letting on about, and the thought gave me butterflies. Unfortunately, he had the daunting task of meeting all my family. I'd be lucky if he lasted a day with the most judgmental people on the planet. They barely showed me any mercy, there was little hope of showing Niall any. God help us.

"Yes, David, I've known Roberts since I was a little girl," I said with a gentle tone.

"If I remember correctly," Roberts began, "you chased your brother through the ballroom during my initiation ceremony, knocked over a candelabra, and set a curtain on fire."

"It is hard to believe you were so naughty," Niall said with his cute British accent and rubbed his index finger down my cheek.

"I wasn't," I replied. "I was just responding to my brother tormenting me."

"I'm pretty sure it was half and half," Roberts laughed.

"Ah, so considering the timing, that means both of you are newer sires of Olivia's father," Niall said. "The famous Day-walkers, I believe people are calling you."

Both Warriors shifted uncomfortably in their seats. I wasn't sure why Niall was even mentioning it, he knew it was a sensitive subject.

"I don't know anyone who calls us that," Roberts responded firmly.

"Well, perhaps not to your face. Believe me, those of you who are not sun sensitive are talked about quite often."

"So, Roberts," I interrupted quickly to change the subject, "do you still keep in contact with Toshy...um, Tosh?"

He nodded as we headed up a large curve, meaning the manor was literally moments away. "She and Beckett come to visit every now and then. They've been staying out at their country house a little more lately. Will sees her a lot, though, her boys take his classes at the Facility."

"Classes? What could Will be teaching at…" I began, completely taken by surprise at why Will would be teaching anything at Facility West, but the thought completely left me when the tall black gates came into view. They were exactly the same, not even the guards who stood outside of them had changed.

"Connor's here," David groaned and I looked through the windshield to see Connor standing at the foot of the front steps. "Did he think I'd mess up picking someone up at the airport?"

"It's not just anyone, young David, it's the boss's daughter."

"And boyfriend," Niall chimed in. "That must count for something."

"Of course it does," I replied with a hand squeeze, and then looked back to the front seat. "Are you two on Connor's crew?"

Roberts nodded. "I have been for a while, but Davey-boy is new and Connor doesn't let him forget it."

My stomach leapt into my throat as we pulled in front of the manor, and Connor stepped up to the passenger door. Once the vehicle stopped, Connor opened the door and thankfully fresh air wafted in my face.

"There she is," Connor said happily and extended his hand.

I shifted my legs toward the open door, took his hand, and stepped down to the ground. Connor instantly put his arms around me, and I couldn't help but hug him back. When I rose from his shoulder, I reflexively patted his breast pocket. He smiled, reached inside his pocket, and pulled out two silver-wrapped sticks of gum.

"I can't believe you have those," I said and took the gum from his hand.

He laughed. "Some things you just don't forget, Livybean."

"Livybean? How charming," Niall said as he stepped down from the backseat, and extended his hand to Connor. "Niall Cummings."

"Oh sorry, Connor, this is my boyfriend Niall. Niall, Connor."

"Welcome," Connor replied and shook Niall's hand. "I take it young David and Roberts took good care of you?"

"Yes, they both took tremendous care."

"Not from around here, are you?"

"Doesn't he have the cutest accent?" I said proudly.

Connor nodded. "Adorable. I told your mother you were pulling up. She'll meet you inside. Roberts, David, bring their luggage inside."

I exhaled deeply, squeezed Niall's hand, and pulled him up the wide stone steps. As we stepped through the front doors I was transported back in time to my childhood, but I needed to remember that I was a grown woman now, and couldn't let my family forget that either.

"Baby girl, baby girl, baby girl!" my mother squealed before her arms pulled my body forcibly into her and squeezed me within an inch of my life. It was so hard to breathe that I turned my head on her shoulder so that my nose wasn't crushed. Just down the corridor I saw my brother walking with...Will? Dear lord was that Will? I couldn't tell at first, but the blue-green eyes gave it away, and I had to look at the floor.

I rose from my mother's shoulder and her eyes darted past me for a moment, but then came back. "How was the flight?"

"Long, but fine."

"Good, good," she said and looked to her left. "Jax, oh good, stay with your sister for a moment. I'll be right back."

Before I could say anything, my mother blurred past me. I looked over at Jack who gave me a blank, lifeless expression.

"Um...hi," I said and awkwardly tried to hug him, but he stiffened and patted my back as though I had the plague. "So the Jax thing stuck?"

Jack gave a forced smile and shrugged.

"Well, uh, this is my boyfriend...this is Niall Cummings. Niall, this is my brother Jack-Ja...um Jack, or Jax."

Niall shook Jack's hand, but Jack hardly put any effort into it. "Jack or Jax, it's lovely to meet you, I've heard so many good things."

"I doubt that," Jack laughed.

"Jack, please..."

"Sorry about that," Mom said as she stepped back through the door. Immediately she hugged Niall, which took him by surprise and he squirmed uncomfortably. "Welcome, Niall, we're so happy to have you. Sorry, I'm a hugger."

He laughed as she released him. "It is very nice to meet you, Mrs. Burke."

"Listen to that cute little accent."

"*Mom*," I groaned.

"What? It's adorable, and call me Brianna."

"Can I go now?" Jack said and rolled his eyes. Eye rolling was a family trait deep within our DNA.

"Sure, honey," Mom sighed. "We'll see you later tonight."

"Tonight?" I asked.

"Just a little cocktail party to welcome you home."

"Hooray, forced family frivolity," Jack said snidely and stepped away.

Mom sighed loudly but I didn't care because Ada and Devy were coming our way with big smiles on their faces.

"Lovey," Ada cooed as I sank into his chest, instantly feeling the love and safety that was always there. He kissed my hair and said, "Welcome home."

"Thanks, Ada," I replied and stepped out of his arms. "Ada, I'd like you to meet Niall Cummings. Niall, this is my father Cameron."

"Mr. Burke," Niall said and began vigorously shaking Ada's hand, "it is a great honor to meet the coven leader of the great Warriors."

"One of them," Devy grumbled behind me.

I smiled and stepped out of the way to expose my uncle. "And of course this is my Uncle Devin."

Niall's eyes became wide as he gave a nervous smile. "Of course I know who you are. It isn't every day you get to meet the Warrior Assassin."

"Generally, if you do, you're dead a second later," Devy said flatly. Even though Niall laughed and took it as a joke, the rest of us knew it wasn't. "Now, Monkey, may I get my hug now?"

"Devy, you have to stop calling me Monkey."

"And why is that?"

"Because I'm not five years old anymore."

He scrunched his brows together and was definitely offended. "But I have always called you Monkey. You used to climb on everyone and everything, and slide down the bannister. I call you Monkey, you call me Devy. I do not understand why…"

"Brother," my father thankfully interrupted, "if she prefers not to be called Monkey, then we must oblige. It is nothing personal."

He sighed and gave a scowl. "Fine. But I can't promise I'll always remember."

Ada turned to me. "It is the best we can hope for."

And with that I gave my uncle a proper hug. "I missed you, Devy."

He harumphed and stepped back just as David and Roberts came through the front door, each carrying arms and shoulders full of our luggage.

"This is all of it," Roberts began, "if you tell us whose is whose we'll carry everything up to your rooms."

"Rooms?" I questioned and looked at Ada.

"Yes," he replied with scrunched brows, "we have prepared separate quarters for you and Niall."

"*Ada*," I groaned through my teeth, "we don't need separate rooms."

Ada's mouth opened to respond, but my mother took his arm and said, "It's fine, honey. Right, Cam?"

Ada took a second and swallowed before he replied, "Yes, of course. Gentleman, you can take everything to Olivia's quarters."

"Yes, sir," Roberts and David answered in unison and jetted away.

"Cam, while the boys take the luggage up, why don't you and Devin give Niall a tour of the manor."

"Mom, I don't think…"

"That is a wonderful idea, Mrs. Burke."

"Please call me Brianna, Niall. With the exception of Cameron, we're all very informal here."

"Yes, Brianna, I will certainly try to remember." Niall turned to me and kissed my cheek. "Won't you join us?"

"I've seen it," I laughed.

"Yes, but you could show me all the nooks and crannies from your childhood."

"There will be plenty of time for that," I replied and kissed him back on the cheek. "I'll see you in a little bit. Don't lose him in one of the dungeons, Ada."

"No promises," he responded and smiled. "Niall, this way."

Niall skipped off like a schoolboy. To him, this place was a piece of history, a museum, but I didn't see the allure.

Mom put her arm around my shoulders. "I'm so glad you're home," she said and guided me down the corridor toward the big spiral staircase. "And now we have some time to ourselves to catch up."

"Are we in my old room?" I asked as we started up the stairs.

"No," Mom replied, "we moved Jax to a bigger suite a couple of years ago, so your father felt it was only fair to put you in the same area."

"Is Jack-Jack officially working for Ada now?"

"Yes, but only because he isn't doing anything else."

"So who's coming tonight?" I asked as we reached the second floor and Mom pulled me onto the landing.

"Just the family. Eri and Mémé are flying in this afternoon, and then all your aunts and uncles. A couple others might just stop in and say hello. Everyone is excited to see you and meet Niall."

Roberts and David exited a room at the end of the corridor and gave us a wave.

"Thanks, guys," I said and David gave a nervous wave. "It was nice to meet you, David."

"Nice to meet you too," he replied excitedly, and then tripped over his own feet.

Roberts rolled his eyes and picked him up. "Welcome home, Olivia."

"Thanks, Roberts," I replied and Roberts pulled David down the corridor like a hyper puppy.

Mom laughed softly. "He is such a sweet kid."

"He seems young."

"Everyone calls him young David. He's going to be another Jared, but he needs more field training. Roberts and Connor have been great mentors. Jax's room is there," Mom said as she pointed to a door on our left.

"So Jax stuck, huh? It's hard for me to call him that."

"He's definitely happier when we don't call him Jack-Jack," she replied and then gestured to the door on our right. "This is you."

Mom opened the door and revealed a large room with a king-sized bed at the opposite end, a bathroom on the right, and a small sitting area with a large TV.

"I think you two will be comfortable in here," Mom said and sat on the corner of the bed.

"Why did Ada make a big deal about me and Niall staying in the same room?"

"He's your father, honey, you'll always be his little girl."

"I'm not a child anymore, Mom."

"Yes, but the last time you were here, you were."

"Well, I need everyone to remember I'm not, especially in front of Niall."

"Ok, honey, calm down," she said and put her hands up. "No one will intentionally embarrass you."

"No, it's not..." I began and brushed fingers through my hair as the butterflies started to flutter in my stomach. "What did you think of Niall?"

"From the three seconds I spent with him he seemed very nice."

I stepped over to the bed and sat down next to her. "Mom, I think Niall is going to ask me to marry him."

Her eyes widened and she blinked slowly several times before finally saying, "Marry?"

I nodded. "I think he's going to ask Ada's permission while we're here."

"And that's what you want?"

I rolled my eyes. "Yes, Mom, it's what I want."

"Ok, ok, but don't you think you two are a little young?"

I stood from the bed in frustration. "No, I don't think we're too young. I'm sorry, Mom, I don't want to wait until I'm in my late thirties to get married like you did."

She cleared her throat in judgement. "Marriage isn't easy, baby girl. There are so many days I want to kill your father, but I don't, because I remember I love him. There are stresses you can't even imagine..."

"But I love Niall so much, Mom," I said and leaned up against the dresser. "It's not easy to meet men when you have fangs and the family that I do. He loves me despite that."

"Well I hope so," she said in her judgmental voice.

"Mom, stop."

She put her hands up defensively. "I'm not doing anything. I'm happy you've found someone, and that we'll get to know him better while you're here."

I didn't believe it, but I opened a suitcase and began to unpack. "Will you make sure that Jack-Jack isn't an asshole."

"Baby girl, there is only so much I can do about your brother. You two really need to talk through whatever started this rift between you."

"That would involve him actually talking to me."

"Please? For your dear old mother who literally died for you?"

I shook my head and put some clothes into the drawer. "We'll never live that down, will we?"

"Not if it makes you feel guilty and I get what I want."

I closed the drawer to the dresser and turned around to face her. "So can I ask," I began and had to take a deep breath, "was that Will who was walking with Jack-Jack when we came in?"

"It was."

"Was that why you ran outside?"

"Yes, I wanted to make sure he was coming tonight."

"Is he?"

"Yes."

"Will he be cool about meeting Niall?"

"I'm sure he will be."

I sighed and took another armful of clothes out of the suitcase. "Why was he here?"

"He works out with Jax and the trainees."

"Why? Doesn't he have a job?"

"He does. He teaches marital arts classes at the Facility and he bartends at night."

"You're kidding," I said and put my final pile of clothes into the dresser.

"Be nice."

"Wasn't he supposed to be a doctor?"

"Sometimes things don't work out."

"Yeah, but the valedictorian of my high school class is now a bartender? That's a bit of a fall, don't you think?"

She sighed uncomfortably. "Just tread lightly, please? There is a lot you don't know about the situation."

"There's a situation?" I replied, but Niall and Ada suddenly came through the door.

"The tour is over already?" Mom asked.

"Coven leader work is never done, I suppose," Niall answered.

"I am sorry, Olivia, there is an issue that your uncle and I need to attend to."

Niall turned to Ada and shook his hand. "I completely understand, Cam. My father is taken away all the time. I'm sure Olivia can show me the rest of the manor."

"We'll give you some privacy to unpack your things. Niall, I'm sure you're exhausted from the flight," Mom said and stepped over to Ada near the door.

"You're quite right, I wouldn't mind a short nap."

"Very well," Ada said and gestured to the door, "we will see you later tonight. Welcome home, lovey."

"Thanks, Ada," I replied and my parents closed the door behind them.

Niall sat down on the bed and then fell backwards with an exhausted sigh. "I may very well sleep the rest of the day, love."

"Have I told you how much I like it when you call me that?"

"Yes, love, you have," he laughed.

"Don't laugh," I pouted, "I've heard my father call my mother that my whole life. I just love it."

"And I love you."

I smiled and pulled his suitcase up onto the bed. He rolled over and unzipped the top.

"Did you enjoy your condensed tour of the manor? Was it everything you wanted it to be?"

He shrugged. "Honestly, I thought it would be bigger, but what I saw was very nice. It's homier than I thought it would be."

"You pictured something darker and ominous with armed Warriors walking the halls."

"That sounds more like it," he replied as he removed his shirt and began rummaging around in his suitcase.

"Basically, you were looking for a replica of your father's headquarters."

"Something like that," he laughed. "Speaking of my father, do you think Cam liked me? You know how important it is for him to like me."

"I think so, but I would suggest not calling him Cam."

He scrunched his brows. "Your mother called him Cam."

"Yes, and there are only three other people in the entire world that call him that," I replied and put my hands on his bare shoulders. "It's no big deal, just call him Cameron from now on."

"It would have been nice if you had told me that beforehand."

"I didn't even think about it, Niall, it's not a big deal."

"Apparently it is if there are only three people allowed to call him that. You should have told me."

I took a step back, knowing the look, knowing the tone, and seeing the vein in his forehead begin to pop out. "I'm sorry. He's not upset about it, Niall. Usually he corrects people and he didn't, so that should tell you something. Please calm down. You're just tired and nervous."

He took in a breath and the vein began to recede. "You're right, I just need some sleep." Niall wrapped his arm around my waist and pulled me into him. My hands once again rested on his thin, bare shoulders. "You know what would help me sleep?"

Gently he kissed up the side of my neck, but it was having the opposite effect that was intended. "I'm not sure I can have sex in my parent's house."

Niall's head popped up. "It's not like we're shagging in their bedroom, love."

"I know, but it's…weird." Slowly I pushed out of his arms. "I'm sorry. Just not right now."

He tightened his lips and nodded curtly. I knew he wasn't happy, but I just couldn't, not right now. The door wasn't even locked and people had a tendency of just walking in. I was too uncomfortable to even think about having sex.

"I'm going to finish unpacking and then go downstairs while you sleep."

"No," he said firmly and pulled off his jeans, "I don't want to be in here all by myself."

"But you'll be sleeping."

"As will you," he said plainly.

"You know I don't sleep, Niall."

"Then you will today," he snapped. "What part of I don't want to be here all alone don't you understand? Now finish unpacking and then come to bed." I froze, but didn't know what to say. "And don't pout."

"I'm not pouting," I grumbled, pulled my toiletry bag from my suitcase and stepped into the bathroom. I hated when he spoke to me that way. I opened the medicine cabinet and began putting my creams and other smaller items away when I heard Niall shuffle inside.

"Do you need the bathroom?" I asked as I closed the medicine cabinet and he was suddenly standing behind me. In a split second his hand was on my neck and then pushed me forward over the sink. I tensed when he lifted my skirt before I could brace myself against the mirror. Roughly he pulled down my underwear and was inside me. It was rough and uncomfortable as he banged into me, again, and again, and again. I didn't resist since it would be over in…three, four, five, and then a grunt came. He slumped on my back for a moment before releasing his grip on my neck and pulling out. I stood up from the sink and put myself back together.

Niall kissed my shoulder and looked at me in the mirror. "Now come to bed."

I forced a smile and nodded. "Be right there."

Chapter Seven

Olivia

Only sleeping an hour or two a week had never been an issue until I started living with Niall. I was now used to streaming movies on my phone, and had mastered reading in little to no light. But I found that taking long runs at night was my favorite nighttime activity. Hours would go by before I'd feel even the slightest bit of fatigue. Running helped clear my head of all the voices speaking at once in all different languages cycling through endless loops. I wanted to go for a run now and clear my head before facing my entire family in what Jack described as "forced family frivolity." He wasn't wrong.

While Niall brushed his teeth in the bathroom, I was questioning my dress choice, which was the fourth I'd put on in the last thirty minutes. My nerves were getting to me. The slim black dress hugged what little curves I had, and even though it had a high neckline, it was practically backless. I was running out of time, so it would have to do. Now, the most difficult part of getting ready - my hair.

My floppy curls were the bane of my existence. Roughly I raked my fingers through my hair and piled my long curls on top of my head. Twirling my fingers, I wrapped my hair in a tight bun, jabbed a dozen pins around the edges and examined myself in the mirror. It wasn't bad, just needed a little clean up on the sides. As I picked up the comb, two little reminders sparkled in the mirror. A year after I left home, in a moment of loneliness and weakness, I pierced my ears with a needle and shoved Will's earrings through my lobes. If I took them out, the holes would heal over, and honestly, I just couldn't bring myself to take them out. I was pathetic, and scared of Will's reaction if he saw them. Quickly I pulled the bobby pins out and shook my hair loose to let it fall past my shoulders. Messy curly-haired girl it would have to be.

Niall stepped out of the bathroom and tilted his head. "I thought you were going to wear your hair up. You know how I like to tickle your neck."

"Sorry, dear," I replied and pulled my hair in front in order to cover the earrings, "my hair didn't want to cooperate today."

He smiled and stood behind me, wrapping his arms around my waist and kissing my shoulder. "I wonder if our children will have unruly hair like their mother?"

I laughed. "The Burke genes are pretty dominate. Think you can handle that?"

"I'm counting on it," he replied and I turned my head to kiss him. It was moments like this that reminded me how much I wanted to be with him. When he pulled his lips away, he wrapped a large strand of my hair around his fingers. "However, you might want to try straightening your hair every now and again."

"A fruitless effort. Ada used to say my curls were as stubborn as I was." Niall smirked and stepped away from me. "Are you ready?"

"As ready as I ever will be," he said and pulled on his black dinner jacket. With his slim-cut pants and dark jacket he reminded me so much of Ada, well, a blonde version of Ada. "It will be fine, love."

I nodded nervously and bit my cheek to keep the tears from coming. Niall took my hand and lead me from the room. As soon as we stepped out into the hall, I heard another door shut and looked up to see Jack coming out of his room a few feet ahead. He'd let his hair grow out, which developed into the Burke signature curls. From behind, you wouldn't necessarily be able to differentiate between him and Ada.

Jack, I said pushed to him, but he didn't even flinch. *Jack, can you hear me?*

With his back still turned to us, Jack held up the middle finger of his right hand.

Niall looked over at me as we started down the hall. "Was that to us?"

"Just me, I'm sure."

"How did he even know we were out here?"

I shrugged, feigning ignorance because I hadn't told Niall about any of my gifts, especially the fact that my brother and I could talk to one another with our minds.

"She wears too much perfume," Jack said loudly before disappearing down the spiral staircase.

Niall squeezed my hand. "Pay him no mind, love. I rather enjoy your perfume."

Forcing a smile, we continued our way to the stairs and traveled down to the first floor. Warriors I knew waved or gave a nod, while others who must have been newer just slowed and stared. It made me uncomfortable, although Niall seemed to enjoy the attention. A wave of nostalgia hit me as we turned down the corridor for my father's office. The door was open and I froze. Niall took an extra step ahead before having to stop and turn around.

"Just breathe, love," he whispered in my ear before kissing my cheek. "Remember, no one loves you as much as I do."

With a nervous smile, I snaked my arm through Niall's and we stepped inside the office. The carpets had changed, but Ada's and Devy's desks were the same and still sat on the opposite wall. The tall stone fireplace on our right was ablaze in front of couches and chairs where several people were already gathered.

Aunt Kyla squealed loudly and came running toward us with her fairytale wavy orange hair floating behind her. Instantly she wrapped her arms around me and squeezed me tightly while pecking me endlessly with kisses.

"For crying out loud, Ky, let her breathe," I heard Uncle Alex say, although I couldn't see him through the curtain of orange hair covering my face.

When she finally released me, Uncle Alex was in front of us with a smile as big as he was. Thankfully Niall didn't gawk since I had warned him earlier about how big my uncle actually was.

"Niall, if you haven't guessed, this is Uncle Alex and Aunt Kyla."

"Aunt Kyla?" she said and looked at me curiously. "Well, aren't we formal. Are you taking after your father now? Hello, Niall, I am apparently Aunt Kyla, even though this little girl has called me Auntie Ky her entire life. You can too, of course, but Ky, Kyla, hey you, they're all fine too."

"It is a pleasure to finally meet you both," Niall said.

Aunt Kyla's eyes grew wide. "That accent of his is adorable."

"Yes," I replied a little embarrassed, "and he can hear you, too."

"All right, all right," Mom said as she came up behind us, "let them breathe a little, Kyla. Niall, can I get you something to drink?"

"Red wine would be lovely," he answered.

"Certainly. Livy, the same?" I nodded. "Wonderful. Kyla, why don't you help me." Mom said and forcefully took Auntie Ky away with her.

Uncle Alex looked sheepishly at Niall. "You'll have to forgive her, she's very enthusiastic when it comes to her favorite niece. It's good to have you home, Livy."

I hugged my uncle and practically disappeared in his chest. Sometimes it felt good to be home. After a handshake with Niall, Uncle Alex excused himself and stepped back toward the fireplace.

"You weren't exaggerating," Niall whispered. "I have never seen someone so..."

"He's the nicest man you'll ever meet," I interrupted.

"Livybean Sassypants Burke," a woman said behind me that I instantly recognized as my Aunt Renee.

When I turned around, I found her and Uncle John coming through the office door. Her hair was just as red as the day I left. Mom always said Aunt Re's hair was as fake as Auntie Ky's was real.

"Aunt Re," I said and wrapped my arms around her. Being human, there was always a different connection with her. She was batshit crazy, but somehow brought normalcy into my life. When I pulled back, I looked to Niall. "Aunt Re, this is Niall. Niall, meet Renee and John Ryan."

Niall took Aunt Re's hand and kissed her cheek. "It is wonderful to meet you. Now, what was that name you called Olivia?"

Aunt Re laughed. "Livybean Sassypants," she replied. "When she was little it was just Livybean, but I added Sassypants when she got older because well...that's what she was."

"I am beginning to believe I am the only one in her life that calls her Olivia. It seems everyone has their own nickname for her."

Uncle John laughed and extended his hand. "In this family, that's pretty normal. Dr. John Ryan, nice to meet you, Niall."

"Dr. Ryan, nice to meet you as well. Ryan, Ryan, why does that sound familiar? Olivia?"

"Uncle John is the medical director at the Facility here in San Francisco."

Niall nodded and smiled. "Oh yes, and you have a son, don't you?"

"Yes," Aunt Re responded. "Our son Will. He and the twins were the Three Musketeers. He should be here at some point."

"Ah, very good," Niall said happily, "I look forward to hearing about all the naughtiness Olivia got into when she was young."

"Oh, Niall, we don't want to scare you away so soon," Aunt Re laughed and I rolled my eyes.

As she stepped away, Uncle John gave me a hug. "Welcome home, Livybean."

"Aunt Re hasn't changed a bit."

"The one thing in life that you can count on is that your aunt will never, ever change."

As he stepped aside, Niall wrapped his arm around my waist. "How many adorable names do you have?"

"There is an endless supply," I groaned just as my grandmother burst through into the room.

"Petite singe!"

"Told you," I laughed as I stepped away from Niall and melted into my grandmother's chest. "Mémé."

"My little monkey, how I have missed you," Mémé said in French. Besides Ada, she was the only person I could speak French with, and we did as often as possible until someone, usually Mom or Eri would get upset. I looked over her shoulder and smiled at Eri who was already tightening his lips in frustration. "And what a handsome young man you have brought to see us."

"Mémé," I replied embarrassed.

"What? Can he understand what I'm saying?"

"No, no."

She kissed my cheek quickly three times. "Then I will say it again, he is very handsome."

I shook my head and opened up to see Niall looking confused. "Sorry, dear, this is Seraphina, my grandmother."

"Miss Seraphina, I have heard so much about you."

"All good I hope?" she replied in English.

"Your granddaughter thinks very highly of you."

"She is a good petite singe."

Niall glanced over at me.

"It means little monkey," I answered.

"You must have been climbing on everything around you," he laughed.

"It was hard to keep her feet on the ground," Eri replied and went to hug me, but Niall stepped in front of me.

"You must be Eris," Niall said in awe and took Eri's hand, although my grandfather didn't seem too happy about it. "In my wildest dreams I never thought I would meet an icon such as you."

"How lucky for you," Eri replied flatly and removed his hand from Niall's. "Do you mind if I hug my granddaughter now?"

"Eri, don't be grumpy," Mémé said as Niall backed away.

"I am not grumpy," he grumbled with his thick Italian accent. "I merely want to get to my bellissima nipote."

I hugged my grandfather quickly, but then opened up and gestured to Niall. "Eri, you are being very grumpy, and I need you to be nice to my boyfriend."

"Why?"

"Dad, be nice!" Mom shouted from across the room.

Eri growled softly under his breath and reluctantly smiled. "Nice. To meet. You."

"Thank you, Eri," I said and hugged him once again. "I'm so happy you're here."

"Anything for my favorite grandchild."

"Hey!" Jack-Jack said near the fireplace.

"Oh dear, Jackson, you are my favorite too," Eri sighed.

"We can't both be favorites, Eri," Jack said bitterly, and Eri gave me a wink. I knew I was his favorite.

Suddenly a pair of hands cut through the space between Mémé and Eri, and pushed both of them aside.

"Step aside, step aside," my grandfather Victor said in his signature raspy voice, "I hear there's a beautiful woman walking the corridors of my manor that resembles my granddaughter."

"You could have just waited your turn, Victor," Eri grumbled and directed Mémé away.

"But I'm not used to waiting for anything," Grandfather grumbled. "Olivia, how nice it is to see you."

"Grandfather, I'd like you to meet my boyfriend Niall. Niall, this is…"

"Olivia, I am very aware of who Victor is. It is an honor, sir."

Grandfather shook Niall's hand and gave him a cursory nod. "Hello, welcome to the manor."

"Thank you, sir. It truly is an honor to be here among your Warriors.

My father is a coven leader…"

"An established coven?"

Niall's face fell. "Not yet," he replied and then forced a smile. "We like to call ourselves the Warriors of Europe."

"No, I don't think so," Grandfather replied curtly.

Niall swallowed and forced another smile. "Well, between meeting you and Eris, I feel as though I am in a dream. My father has told me stories about all of you my whole life."

"How nice for you," Grandfather replied uncomfortably and then smiled at me. "We are very happy to have you home, little one."

I blushed. "I'm not little anymore, Grandfather."

"That may be, but I am your grandfather and you will always be my little one. I suppose you are too old for one of our special breakfasts."

"Well, perhaps not *too* old," I replied, making Grandfather give me a sly smile in return.

"Special breakfast?" Niall asked. "Please tell me more."

Grandfather's smile fell. "It is time specifically for my grandchildren and great-grandchildren."

"Great-grandchildren?" Niall interrupted. "I wasn't aware…"

"Yes, my grandson Beckett has two sons."

"Oh yes…but they're wolves, aren't they?"

I squeezed Niall's hand tightly. Unfortunately, Niall and his family did not have as much of an open mind about werewolves as our family did.

"Magnificent creatures, the wolves," Grandfather said in a low gravely tone. "A little odorous, perhaps, but still fascinating. I have found my joy in my grandchildren's and great-grandchildren's eyes, no matter what color they are." Grandfather cupped my cheek and I leaned down in order for him to kiss my forehead. "Welcome home, little one."

"Thank you, Grandfather."

He gave a nod and stepped away, but I could see Niall was upset. "Well, I made a hash of that, didn't I?"

I squeezed his hand again. "He's just protective, that's all."

He nodded, but not convincingly. Impressing Victor was very important to him, but I refused to let it ruin his night. Especially since the mood was going to instantly change at the sight of my youngest, and most rebellious uncle coming through the door.

"Niall this is…" I began but Uncle Jared ran into me, lifted me up, and twirled me around.

"Welcome-home-Livybean!" he cheered and finally placed me back down on the ground, keeping his arms around my waist while I caught my bearings.

"Niall, this is my Uncle Jared."

Uncle Jared extended his hand to Niall. "Jared Ranger, otherwise known as Livy's favorite uncle."

"Niall Cummings," he replied and shook Jared's hand. "Nice to meet you. You were young when you were Turned."

"Yeah, they still treat me like the baby of the family."

"Only because you act like it," Ada said as he stepped up next to us.

"Thanks, bro," Uncle Jared laughed. "I have that report you were looking for earlier."

Ada nodded and gestured to the door of the office. "Wonderful. Olivia, Niall, please excuse us for a moment."

The Warrior work was never done, no matter if your daughter was home for the first time in five years.

As Ada and Jared left the office, Niall released my hand and took a step away. "I believe your mother has forgotten our wine."

I looked over and saw the reason why. "She's talking to Aunt Re and Auntie Ky, all bets are off."

"Do you still want a glass?"

"Yes please," I replied and gave him a quick kiss.

Once he stepped away, I felt an odd sense of loneliness. Everyone else was huddled in their tight little groups. It was uncomfortable being alone in the center of the room. When I looked behind me, I caught Niall speaking to Victor with wide, excited eyes. Since my glass of wine would be awhile, I stepped forward to close the door to the office at the very moment Will filled the doorway. We both froze for a moment, neither of us knowing quite what to do. His warm blue-green eyes looked nervously over at the crowd near the fireplace, all of whom I assumed were staring at us, wondering what we would do.

"Will...uh...hi," I stuttered and awkwardly took another step forward.

Will continued to look everywhere else but at me as we struggled to figure out what to do with our arms, and ended up half hugging, half patting each other's back.

"Welcome home," he said when he stepped back and looked uncomfortably down at the floor.

"I saw you earlier today...I just didn't realize...until after you'd gone."

"Yeah, I had to get to the Facility…"

"Mom said…I heard you were uh…teaching now."

He nodded with tight lips and went to take a step away when Niall came up behind me.

"Ah, and who is this?" Niall said and handed me a glass of wine.

I took a big gulp of wine before replying, "Niall, this is Will Ryan."

"Ah, now I see," Niall said and forcibly shook Will's hand. "One of the Three Musketeers, isn't that right?"

"Yeah, something like that," Will replied. "I was more of a referee between the twins."

"That must have been a big job," Niall laughed and Will gave a tense smile.

"The only time Wills got a break from us was at school," I replied.

"And why was that?" Niall asked.

"Will and I were in honors classes, and Jack…well, he didn't care about school. Will was the valedictorian of our class."

"Only because you left," Will corrected, and then a shadow passed across his face.

"Not true, we were always neck and neck."

"And what is it you do now?" Niall asked and my stomach sank.

"I teach at the Facility and I'm a bartender," Will replied.

"Will, you were going to be a doctor. What happened?" I asked, ignoring my mother's request to tread lightly.

"Long story. Believe me, it's as disappointing for me as it is for my parents."

"Wills…"

"I can't stay long, actually. Your mother guilted me into coming, but I have to work a shift tonight. Nice to meet you, Niall."

Will quickly stepped away and walked toward my brother standing by the fireplace. I guess it could have gone worse, and from the eyes I felt staring at us, everyone else thought so too.

"Are you alright, love?" Niall asked as I gulped another large amount of my wine.

"Yeah," I answered and patted his cheek. "Sorry there's such a barrage of people to meet."

"Sorry? Whatever for? Some of the most famous vampires in history are all here in one room. What more could I ask for?"

"More alcohol," I laughed just as Ada came back through the door, but without Jared. "Ada, is everything ok?"

"Just a typical day, lovey. Unfortunately, your Uncle Jared is needed elsewhere on coven business. He says he will catch up with you later."

"It's ok, I understand."

"But there is someone in the hall asking for you," Ada said and gestured to the door.

I quirked my head and stepped through the door to find Julian, the Warrior's jailor, standing in the hall. He stood very straight and rigid, as he always did, his expression stern, as it always was. When I came to stand in front of him, I tucked my right foot behind me and curtsied. As I rose, he clicked his heels and bowed. Once he stood back up, he broke a smile and I hugged him tightly.

"Miss Olivia, welcome home."

I released him and gave him a questioning look. "Why are you out here? Why didn't you come inside?"

He shook his head. "The gathering is for family, and I didn't want to intrude."

"Julian, you're being silly. Come inside, please."

He shook his head again. "Sadly, I cannot. I must get back, but it is wonderful to have you back home. I hope that…perhaps we will be able to catch up while you are here."

"Yes, I will make a point of it," I replied and kissed his cheek.

If he could have blushed, I'm sure he would have, but his rare smile was priceless. "I look forward to it," he said and quickly disappeared down the corridor.

Julian was a very stern, very complicated man who was only liked by the men that worked for him, and me. In one of my worst moments as a child, he gave me a little doll to make me feel better. I never forgot that, and from then on, we had a connection that no one else understood.

Stepping back inside the study I found Niall surrounded by my aunts, mom, and… "Uncle Fabi!"

Fabi was very flamboyant, and not ashamed to flaunt it. He was wearing one of his signature suites, today choosing a mint green color with a pink satin scarf hanging around his neck. Dramatically he took in a deep breath while he looked me up and down. "The dress, the heels, put the hair up and add some pearls and we have Audrey Hepburn in front of us."

I gladly accepted his hug. He was another man who only came up to my chest when I wore heels. Good thing he didn't care about breasts.

"You haven't changed a bit," I said and ran my fingers over his buzzed cut hair.

"Honey," he began and draped his pink scarf dramatically across his neck, "why change perfection?"

I laughed. "When did you get here? I didn't see you come in."

He cocked his eyebrow at me. "When you befriend Victor, you learn about all the sneaky ways in and out of here. I know more about the secret passages than Devy does, just don't tell him that. I don't think Devy could handle that Victor likes me better." We laughed when we caught Devin glaring over at us. Fabi waved and blew him a kiss. "You can't help but love me."

Devin shook his head with a smirk and then continued his conversation with Uncle Alex.

"Did you meet Niall?" I asked and Fabi nodded.

"Well done," he replied. "Very English-looking. He matches his accent perfectly. How did you two meet?"

"It was very random, actually. I was just sitting at a café and Niall tripped over my foot. He fell right to the ground, and I felt so bad."

"Oh dear," Niall said as he came to stand next to me, "I heard someone fell to the ground. I fear you are talking about our first meeting."

"Yes, dear," Fabi replied, "it is incredibly cute. I'm guessing she helped mend your wounds?"

"The embarrassment had to wear off first," Niall laughed. "But then I couldn't believe who I was meeting - Olivia Burke, one of the miracle twins. I was just amazed, and it's been a dream ever since."

Fabi squinted his eyes slightly and tilted his head.

"Uncle Fabi? Are you ok?"

His eyes fluttered and he came back from wherever his thoughts had gone off to. "Yes, yes, terribly sorry, my mind wanders so easily when in the presence of a handsome young man. But as I have to say to so many, I am taken and he's the deadly jealous type. I truly hate breaking so many hearts, but at least you have Livy to comfort you," he said with a flourish and stepped away from us.

Niall pulled on my elbow and nuzzled me into his side so that he could whisper in my ear. "How is he your uncle?"

Quickly I realized he seriously didn't know. I leaned into his ear and whispered, "He's Devin's partner." Slowly Niall pulled away, his eyes blinking quickly in confusion and shock. "You knew he was…"

"I'd heard the rumors, but to have it so blatant. I'm just shocked, that's all."

I sighed and finished my glass of wine. Niall's family wasn't as accepting of gay relationships, which was probably why I avoided the subject of Devy and Fabi.

"Another wine, love?" Niall asked and took my glass.

"Yes please," I replied.

Just as Niall stepped away, my mother came to my side. "Are you hungry? Everyone's here if you want the food brought in."

"Sure. I'm sure Niall is starving too."

Mom patted my hand and then kissed my cheek several times. "You look so beautiful tonight. My baby girl is all grown up."

"I couldn't stay the little girl with floppy curls my whole life."

"Well, that was only when your brother wasn't cutting your hair," Mom laughed.

Reflexively I pulled at the ends of my curls. "Just proves he's always been a jerk to me."

Mom sighed and squeezed my hand. "One day the two of you will be the best of friends."

"You can dream, Mom."

"I don't have to dream. I know my babies, and I know the bond that you share. You can't ignore that for the rest of your lives. Now that you are back, I guarantee that things will change. Just watch," she said with a wink and then disappeared quickly through the office door.

With Mom gone, I was by myself again since Niall had cornered Eris. Niall was fascinated by my family. He was never short of questions wondering what was true and what was myth. Since they were my family, I never understood the appeal. To me they were just Grandfather and Eri, not uber famous vampires.

I exhaled nervously and stepped over to the group by the fireplace. Thankfully Mémé was on the couch so I quickly sat down next to her. My head slumped down on her shoulder and her soft, worn hand patted my cheek.

"No need to be nervous," she said in French.

"I don't know what to say to anyone," I replied in her native language.

"Then smile and nod at everyone else's conversation until you do. That is my strategy most times."

I laughed. "I missed you."

"But of course you did. I am your favorite grandmother."

"My only grandmother," I corrected.

"Then it is an easy title to win," she laughed and patted my cheek again.

It was nice to be able to speak in a different language. Eri liked to test me on my Italian, and I always passed. Grandfather liked Latin, which wasn't a specialty of mine since it was a dead language, but I could get by. It was a shame no one spoke Farsi or Mandarin. I could use the practice.

"And what are you two ladies laughing about," Niall asked as he handed me my glass of wine.

"You must know zhat ladies will never reveal zheir secrets," Mémé said sweetly as Eris handed her a glass of wine as well. "Merci, mon amore. You and Niall seemed to be having quite zhe conversation."

"Yes quite," Eri replied with one eyebrow raised and sat down next to Mémé. You didn't need to be an Empath to see Eri's annoyance.

Suddenly the smell of food wafted through the room. It was only a matter of seconds before my mother would say…

"Food for the humans," she said on cue.

For my mother, the worst part of being a vampire was not being able to eat food or drink alcohol. I could think of many things that were worse.

"Brianna, love, just a moment," Ada began and walked over to stand in front of the fireplace holding up the glass of blood he had in his hand. "I would like to make a toast. To our Olivia, we are so happy to have you home. It is hard to believe that it has been five years since your smile has brightened our corridors. All of us here are so proud of what you have accomplished, and we know there is so much more to come. To Olivia."

Others in the room echoed my name and raised their glasses. Jack-Jack remained silent and chugged back whatever brown alcohol that was in his glass. Will patted him on the back and stepped toward the door.

"Are you leaving so soon?" Mom asked as she stepped in front of him.

Will looked uncomfortably around the room before answering, "I have to work, Awbie, I told you that."

"I know, but I thought you'd at least stay for dinner," she said, but then looked over Will's shoulder at my brother who was walking up behind him. "And where are you going?"

"I have to work, Awbie," my brother said mockingly which caused my mother's eyebrow to raise. "Fine, Will has to work and I should monitor him while using his employee discount."

"Jack, please stay for a little longer."

"Sorry, Mom, I just don't want to," he replied and stepped toward the office door. "Bye, everybody."

Will gave an awkward wave in my direction. "Welcome home," he said and followed Jack out of the office.

With a quick breath, my mother plastered on a smile as if nothing was wrong and gestured toward the food trays that had been brought in. "Now that the boys are gone, there will definitely be more food for everyone, so help yourselves. Livy, Niall, guests of honor first, of course."

I rose from the couch but Niall placed his hand on my arm. "Sit, love, I will fix you a plate. Visit with your family. Seraphina, can I get you anything?"

Mémé stood from the couch and took Niall's elbow. "I never trust a man with my food," she laughed and the two of them walked over to where the food was set up.

I took advantage of the moment alone with Eri and slid over next to him. His face brightened with a wide, toothy grin. "Eri, I'm sorry if Niall is a little too eager to meet you. He's just excited, and probably a little nervous."

He patted my hand. "I usually like to tell my stories rather than have someone tell me my history, and very inaccurately I might add. But I prefer if my war stories are not shared in front of your grandmother."

"Mémé knows everything about you."

"Yes, but I don't like to remind her of the monster she married."

"Eri, you're not a monster," I replied and kissed his cheek. "I'll make sure Niall tones it down."

Gently he pulled my head down and kissed my forehead. At same time, the couch cushion on the other side of me slumped down, and when I turned around, I found Aunt Re sitting with a plate full of pulled pork, mashed potatoes, macaroni and cheese, green beans, and a piece of cornbread on top. My mouth was watering just waiting for my own plate.

"Livybean, you need to get food or else your mother will think she completely failed," Aunt Re said with half a mouthful.

"Niall is fixing me a plate," I replied. "Mom needs to chill out."

She laughed and shook her head. "Your mom chilling out is about as probable as me letting my hair go naturally gray."

"Well someday it'll have to, won't it?"

Her head flinched. "Surely you jest. I'll be ninety-six years old and going into that coffin with my fire engine hair."

I laughed just as Niall came back to the couch with two plates in hand. "Your mother has told me this is a real Southern meal. I just don't know what that means."

"Whenever she says that, it just means it's good food that's terrible for you," Aunt Re replied and stuffed her mouth with the piece of cornbread.

Sadly, my face fell when Niall handed me the plate he fixed for me, which only had small dollops of each side, a bite of pulled pork, and no cornbread.

"Goodness, Niall, did you forget to put food on Livybean's plate?" Aunt Re asked with a look of disgust.

"I didn't want anything to go to waste," Niall answered with a defensive smile. "Your Livybean eats like a bird."

"Since when?" she replied loudly, which caused Uncle John to step over and place his hand on her back. "Oops, that's the sign that I'm either too loud, embarrassing myself, or terrorizing someone."

"Or all of the above," Uncle John laughed.

I picked at my food and was able to finish my macaroni and cheese in one bite. I couldn't remember the last time I had had it. The creamy noodles mixed with dripping cheese was to die for, and the one measly bite was certainly not enough to satisfy me. Maybe I could sneak down to the kitchen later for a secret midnight snack.

"I'm sorry that Will had to leave so early," I said as I scooped up the measly amount of mashed potatoes on my plate. "Where is he working tonight?"

"He's bartending at a club downtown," Uncle John replied and took a swig of his drink. "Not something I imagined him doing, but he makes a ton of money for only a few nights' work, so I can't blame him."

"You two should go visit him at the club tonight," Aunt Re interjected.

"Renee, they just flew across the globe. Going to a club tonight is probably last on their list of things to do."

"But that sounds wonderful," Niall said and I had to stop chewing my pulled pork since his response was so shocking. "Don't you think so, Olivia?"

"Um, if you want. I didn't think you liked places like that."

"I've never been to a nightclub," he replied and then looked to Aunt Re and Uncle John. "My father is a bit strict and looks down upon such establishments, but I think it would be fun. A real American nightclub, sounds delightful. Oh this will be fun."

"Sure," I replied, although I expected a lot of dirty looks from my brother and awkwardness from Will.

"Baby girl," Mom said as she came around the couch, "you're not eating. You didn't like the food? I had all your favorites made...do you want something else."

Aunt Re leaned in and looked at me through her lashes. "I tried to tell you," she said, and then quickly leaned the other direction to face my mother. "Bri, according to Niall, Livybean eats like a bird."

"Since when?"

Chapter Eight

Olivia

"Overall, I think that went well," Niall said for the third time since we'd left the manor, but I just smiled. Niall had met my family and he didn't run for the hills. I was taking that as a win. "What is this nightclub called again?"

"Lotus," I replied just as I found a parking spot on the street. It was only a couple of blocks from where the GPS said the nightclub was so I figured the walk wouldn't be too bad in heels.

As I pulled up to the spot, Niall touched my arm. "I believe that space is too small, love."

I put my blinker on, and put the SUV in park. "Or is it," I challenged with a wink and darted out of the vehicle. After a quick look around and finding no one in sight, I pushed a small car that was parked over the line backward into its rightful place. I was back in the SUV in a flash and Niall was stunned. "What?"

"I don't think I knew you were that fast...or strong."

I shrugged. "What reason do I have to use it," I replied and smoothly parallel parked into the space. "I have you, don't I?"

"I suppose," he replied and opened his door. "Ready to have a little fun?"

"Definitely," I answered and jumped out of the SUV. Once I joined him on the sidewalk, he wrapped his arm around my waist, and we headed for the Lotus nightclub. I was still having trouble picturing Will as a bartender. So much potential thrown away. It was sad really. You could tell how disappointed Aunt Re and Uncle John were. "You do realize my brother will probably be an asshole."

Niall shrugged. "Perhaps a bit of drinking will ease him up."

If only alcohol had a lasting effect on us. Even the strongest drink would only be felt for maybe a minute or two. Our bodies just burned through it.

When we were less than a block away, you could hear the deep thudding music coming from the nightclub. That meant it would be deafening.

"This must be it," Niall said as we came to a white building with bright purple lights shining up from the ground. He removed his arm from my waist, took my hand, and kissed it. "Let's have some fun."

Butterflies fluttered in my stomach as we went through the purple-lit doorway that led us into a colorfully lit space and a sea of people bouncing up and down to the beat of the music. To our right side was a large U-shaped bar, and behind it stood Will Ryan throwing a liquor bottle behind his back and catching it with one hand in front to the cheers of the crowd.

Niall pointed toward the bar and I nodded. At that moment the crowd parted and I found my brother standing with his back up against the bar surrounded by drunk, scantily-clad women. Knowing it would piss Jack off, I purposely took Niall's hand and pulled him to my brother's harem.

"Jack!" I yelled over the music and pushed the girls aside. "Has the chlamydia cleared up?"

He glared at me, and all the girls around him fled for the dance floor.

"You're an asshole," he shouted back and turned to face the bar. "Why are you here?"

"Something to do," I replied, turning to the bar as Niall came to stand between us.

"I can see why you wanted to leave and come here," Niall shouted to Jack.

"It's mostly because I get cheap drinks," Jack replied and pointed to Will who stepped over to our end of the bar. "Barkeep, another!"

"That's still annoying," Will said as he pulled a bottle of clear alcohol from one of the higher shelves behind the bar, and then poured a decent amount into Jack's glass. "And this isn't cheap."

"Is that how you're spending your inheritance?" I asked.

Jack held up his glass. "Maybe it'll make me hate you less."

"Jax, stop," Will said and rested his hands on the bar.

"She's been home for five minutes and you're already taking her side?"

Will shook his head and looked at me, his bright blue eyes still able to shine through the colorful lights flashing wildly against him to the beat of the music. "What can I get you?" I shrugged since I really had no idea. "Something strong?"

"And sweet?" I said and caught him exchanging a smirk with Jack.

"Niall? What's your poison?"

"A beer," he replied with a smile. "A real American beer."

Jack laughed into his glass and Will gave another smirk as he pulled a light beer out of the cooler in front of him, handed it to Niall, and then walked to another station.

I turned in Niall's arms and he tried to pull me out onto the dance floor, but I resisted. I wasn't a good dancer, especially to this kind of music, and my dress didn't allow for too much movement.

"You go," I said to him and pushed him toward the crowd. He paused for a second, but then joined in. Niall wasn't a good dancer either, but he clearly didn't care.

From the corner of my eye, I watched as my brother downed his drink in one gulp. I wondered how many drinks he'd already had. When I turned back around, Will was placing a very pink drink in a martini glass down in front of me.

"Let me know what you think," he said and I took a sip.

The sweetness hit first which made me take in a little more. It wasn't until after I swallowed did the burn of the alcohol come through. For one brief moment I could feel a rush go through my body.

"It's good," I said and he gave a curt nod before walking away to handle a group of girls just down the bar from us. I turned away to face the dance floor and watch Niall flail about.

Your boyfriend looks like he's having a seizure, Jack said in my head.

Be nice, please.

Why?

I sighed and drank half of my pretty pink drink down in one gulp. *Could we just get along while I'm here?*

He laughed. *I doubt it.*

You don't have to be an asshole, you know that right?

I treat you like you treat everyone else.

I drank the rest of my drink and placed the glass down on the bar. At that moment I happened to look down the bar to see Will twirling a bottle of alcohol in his hand, catching it, and pouring it into a shaker. The girls across from him were squealing in amazement. When he completed making their drinks, I noticed that several of them snuck a napkin, a piece of paper, and even a coaster across the bar to him.

He gets fifty of those a night, Jack said.

Talk about desperate women, I replied.

Not everyone can snag a winner like Nail.

I sighed and turned to face him. *You know his name.*

I do, he replied with a challenging smile. *But I like calling him Nail.*

This was something I didn't miss. I missed having a brother I could talk to. I didn't miss hearing and seeing the disdain he had for me for reasons I didn't understand.

"Uh oh, time out Burke twins," Will shouted over the music, even sliding his arm down between us as if cutting the connection.

When I broke eye contact with Jack, I turned to find Will setting down another pink drink in front of me. "Thanks, how did you…"

"I assume you burn through alcohol like your brother does."

Jack pushed his empty glass across the bar. "How come she gets a refill first? This better not be a trend, because that's bullshit."

Will shook his head and poured another three fingers-worth of alcohol for Jack. After placing the bottle back on the shelf, he jutted his chin toward the dance floor and said, "Does he need another?"

I shook my head. "He's not a big drinker."

"How sad for him, it might help his personality," Jack said snidely and drank his drink in one gulp.

"Come on, Jax, bring it down," Will shouted and then went back to the other end of the bar.

While I slung back my drink, Niall came in from the dance floor, his forehead beaded with sweat which transferred to me when he kissed my cheek. "Come dance with me, love."

"I'm fine."

"Huh?" he said and leaned in closer.

"I said I'm fine," I said loudly in his ear. "Go have fun."

Niall squeezed my arm, and it made me flinch ever so slightly because I wasn't ready for it. Out of the corner of my eye I could see that it caught

Jack's attention, and I worried he would take it the wrong way.

"Let me just finish my drink," I said quickly and downed the rest of what was left in my glass. Niall smiled and relaxed his grip, eventually leading me out onto the dance floor. This wasn't my kind of music. Ada had ruined me with all the formal parties and teaching me all the classic ballroom styles because to him that was the only way to truly dance. I could do a waltz like nobody's business, but anything else...

Damn, Livy, and I thought your boyfriend was a bad dancer.

By the end of the night Niall had had only three beers and you would have thought he'd gone through a case. He really was a light-weight. He had danced most of the night away while I watched, and Jack hit on almost every girl that came within six inches of him. By the time they announced last call, he had two girls hanging on his every word.

Jack banged on the bar as Will came down in our direction. "Come on, man, let's get out of here."

"I just have to cash out," Will replied and kept walking.

"Where are you guys off to?" I asked.

"Somewhere you can't go," he laughed and one of the girls scrunched her brows.

"That's not very nice," she said. I swear you could hear the air rushing between her ears.

"It's ok, she's my sister. I don't have to be nice to her," Jack replied and kissed her cheek. "Why don't you ladies get your things and we'll get going."

Both girls giggled, like morons, and scurried off.

"You're gross."

He flinched. "How so?"

"Two girls, really?" Jack laughed. "What? Why are you laughing?"

"I just think it's funny that you think both girls are for me."

I scrunched my brows in confusion until I saw Will come back from around the corner and slap Jack on the shoulder. "Ready, man?"

"Yeah, the girls are coming."

Will jutted his chin out to the dance floor where Niall was stumbling toward us. "Do you need any help with him?"

"Um...I don't think so," I began, just as Niall fell into me. "But..."

Before I could finish, both boys turned and started to walk toward the back of the club, the two girls falling in line on either side of them.

"Darling," Niall slurred, "do we have to go home?"

"I doubt they'll let us live here," I laughed and he kissed me on the cheek, leaving a slimy film. "You are so sweaty."

"It's a shame it's not because we were doing something else," he said and tried waggling his eyebrows.

"I doubt they'll let us do that here either," I replied and steadied him against my side.

"We could try."

"Let's just get you to the car, ok?"

He groaned but allowed me to drag him out of the club. Now I wished I had parked closer. It wasn't Niall's weight that was the problem, it was the ever-changing distribution of that weight. When our vehicle was just ahead, I shifted him to my left hip so that I could open the door. What I didn't expect was him to suddenly decide not to use his legs.

"Try to walk!" I shouted as we began to topple over.

With sudden energy and strength, Niall grabbed my arm and pushed me into the side of the SUV, pressing his body flat against mine. "Remember who you're bloody talking to," he growled, his red face only an inch away from mine.

"I'm talking to you, dear," I replied calmly, knowing it was the alcohol talking. "I just want to get you home so you can sleep."

Niall's face relaxed slightly and he flicked my chin with his index finger. "Just remember who I am."

"I will," I replied, pushing him off of me and pouring him into the passenger seat. "Welcome home, Livy."

Chapter Nine

Will

Jax was always good about closing the deal with girls. He worked hard to be my wingman, although he always kept the prettier girl for himself, but that didn't matter to me. It wasn't like I was looking for any kind of relationship, just someone to hang out with and maybe have sex. Typical male, I guess.

But if I was being honest, seeing Olivia was messing with my head. I didn't like her being at the club last night. It made me feel self-conscious. All night long I would catch her watching me, judging me. What she should have been judging was her loser boyfriend who couldn't dance, or hold his liquor. I didn't understand it, but I guess I didn't have to.

"Hey!" Jax shouted and hit me in the shoulder with the strike pad. "Get your head in the game, pay attention!"

"I am," I replied loudly and hit the strike pad.

"No, you're not. My stupid sister has been here for twenty-four hours and she's already affecting you."

"No, she's not. I wasn't thinking about her."

"You're a terrible liar," he said and put the pads back up. "Come on, let's see if you can get through one pass."

"You're a dick," I replied and then launched my assault, whirling hits and kicks into the pads, which were more for my protection than his. Jax wasn't rock hard like the other Vamps, but he wasn't soft like humans either. He could get cut, bullets would go through him, but he'd heal pretty quickly. Truly a hybrid of vampires and humans.

Our routine ended with a roundhouse kick to his chest which knocked him back a few inches on the mat. "There were go," he cheered and took the pad off his right hand and patted my shoulder. "See what you can do when you're not thinking about my stupid sister?"

"You should stop calling her that," I replied and wiped the sweat from my face with my t-shirt.

"I'll stop when she stops being stupid…which will never happen," he laughed, but then suddenly stopped as he looked past me. "Jesus-fucking-Christ."

Stupidly I looked over my shoulder and found Olivia coming through the training room's doorway. I turned back to Jax and said, "What was it you said? Don't let her affect you?"

"Shut up and start hitting me again."

"No problem," I laughed and did just as he asked. High, high, high, low, kick, turn, kick, duck, block, block, palm to the chest.

"Whew!" he cheered again. "Seriously, man, I'm tired of doing this. Just get Turned already so we can do real Warrior stuff together."

"I just need a little more time. I'll be a Warrior soon enough."

"What did you say?" Olivia said from behind us and we both froze.

"Fuck," I said under my breath before I slowly turned around to see her face fixed in horror. "What did you hear?"

She looked between me and Jax several times before finally saying, "Did you…did you say you were going to be a Warrior?"

The blood drained from my face and my heart was beating in my throat. "Olivia…" I began but Jax jumped in front of me.

"Livy, I swear to god if you repeat that, I will pack you in a suitcase and send you back to Italy myself."

"Jax, calm down," I said and pulled him away. Olivia's expression was still a mix of shock and horror. "Olivia, please…"

"You were going to be a doctor. That's what you were going to be. Not a bartender, not a martial arts instruction, and certainly not a Warrior."

"A lot has changed since you left, Olivia, including what I want to do with my life."

She took a step back and pulled at her ponytail of curly hair. "If this is what you want, then why can't anyone know?"

I shook my head. "No, that's not…my parents don't know. Your family knows, but they're keeping it secret until I can tell Mom and Dad."

"Why are you keeping it from them?"

"Because they'll freak out," I replied too loudly, causing a few of the others training in the room to look at us. "They've made it really clear they would never support this. I'm just trying to get comfortable financially before I make the move."

She shook her head in disbelief. "I can't believe everyone is ok with lying to them."

"No one's ok with it, Liv. Your family is just doing it because I asked them. Look, you may not have any respect for me, but for my parents' sake, let me tell them when the time is right."

"Why would you think I don't have respect…"

"Livy, just keep your mouth shut, ok?" Jax pressed angrily.

"Jackson, Will," Devin said as he entered the training room with Niall next to him, "come to the center mat, please."

Jax walked to the center mat, but just as I stepped away, Liv touched my arm. When I turned back around, I was surprised to see her eyes welling up with tears.

"But why, Wills? You could be normal. Why in the world would you want this life?"

I squinted my eyes and tilted my head. "Why do you care?"

My answer seemed to shock her into silence. So when she didn't answer, I removed her hand from my arm and walked over to the mat where Jax was already standing opposite Devy and Niall.

"Nice of you to join us, William," Devin said curtly. He only called me by my full name when he was displeased.

"Sorry, sir."

"While giving Niall another tour of the manor, he mentioned he would like to show a display of his talent. I thought perhaps you and Jax could humor him."

"Devin, forgive me," Niall began in his obnoxious, pompous English accent, "I was hoping to go up against someone…shall I say, less human."

Devin's eyes narrowed and his lips tightened as he replied, "You will go up against who I say you will. Perhaps you would like to reconsider?"

Niall shook his head. "No, no, I was just looking for someone more formidable, but I suppose Will or Jax will do."

"How about that, Jax," I said sarcastically, "we'll do."

"Bring it, tea boy," Jax replied.

"Tea boy?" Niall asked. "Is that supposed to be an insult?"

Jax shrugged. "Don't you guys drink a lot of tea or something?"

"You should quit while you're ahead," I said and patted Jax on his shoulder.

"Will," Devy began, "perhaps you can help Mr. Cummings display his talent."

"Sure," I replied and stepped to the center of the mat.

"What's happening?" Olivia said as she came to stand next to her uncle.

"Nothing to worry about, love," Niall answered and I suddenly wanted to jab my fist down his throat. "Just a little bit of fun."

"Let's get started, shall we?" Devy said impatiently as he crossed his arms in front of his chest.

I nodded and took a central stance, but Niall just stood there with a stupid smirk. Was he waiting for me, was I waiting for him? I couldn't tell. I inched forward and he didn't move in response. When my impatience got the best of me, I decided to launch myself at him. With my feet off the ground and my fist poised to come down on him, suddenly a clear shimmery curtain formed in front of Niall. As I came down upon it, my body bounced off and fell backwards, landing so hard on my back that it knocked the wind out of me.

"What the fuck was that?" Jax shouted as he ran to my side.

Niall shrugged and the shimmery curtain disappeared as quickly as it had appeared. "I'm a Shield."

"A what?" Jax asked as he pulled me up to a seated position.

"A Shield. I can form shields, or forcefields you might say, to protect myself."

I looked over at Olivia. "That might have been some useful information to share."

"Do you plan on every opponent informing you of all their powers?" Devy said sternly.

Devin, my sensei, my mentor, had an amazing way of making you feel like the stupidest piece of shit that ever walked the earth. I'm sure he was embarrassed by the fact that I didn't get in one hit. Olivia gave me sympathetic eyes and looked down at the ground when Niall kissed her cheek.

"Now for Monkey and Jack-Jack," Devy announced.

"What?" the twins replied.

"I apologize," Devy replied. "Olivia and Jax, it is your turn on the mat."

"Devin," Niall began, placing his hand around Devy's arm, "with all due respect, I must object."

Devy stared down at Niall's hand and then slowly lifted his eyes to Niall who cautiously removed his hand. "And why is that?"

"I object to putting my girlfriend in harm's way," Niall replied. "She is a delicate flower…"

Jax laughed dramatically. "Delicate flower? You literally have no idea who you're talking about."

"Olivia is not a fighter," Niall responded.

"Mr. Cummings," Devy began, "I'll have you know that Livy could do a 540 kick at the age of four. I taught her that, and continued to teach her how to defend herself. In many ways she was better than her brother."

"Thanks, Devy," Jax said flatly, but Devy didn't care. "Are we doing this or not?"

"Not," Niall answered.

"Niall, it's just for fun," Olivia finally said. "I'll be fine."

"If you insist," Niall sighed and traced the back of his fingers down her cheek.

Why did that gesture seem so disgusting? Initially I thought I was being oversensitive, but even Devy's face conveyed the same feeling.

"Are we good now?" Jax asked impatiently. "I really want to hit my sister and not get in trouble for it."

"I guess we'll see if you get one in," Devy replied and directed Olivia onto the mat.

Jax exhaled deeply and shook out the tension in his arms. Just as Olivia came to stand in front of him, he immediately launched himself at her with three quicks hits. She was only able to block two of them, the third hitting her in the chest and knocking her back.

"Jax, come on," I said from the edge of the mat.

"She should have blocked it," he replied innocently.

"Devin, please put an end to this," Niall begged.

"Guys, I'm fine," Olivia said and composed herself by getting into a more solid stance.

This time Olivia ran forward with her hands flying, all of which were blocked by Jax, but I could tell he was struggling to keep up with her speed. At one point he got his arms around her shoulders, but she quickly bent down and used the momentum to toss him over onto the ground. In an instant, Jax pulled her foot out from under her causing her to fall flat on her back.

"It's like I'm watching them when they were kids," Devy said with a funny nostalgic smile.

"Devin…" Niall began, but Devy put his hand up.

"One of them has to tap out. Hopefully you have faith in Olivia's ability to at least do that."

Every word out of Niall's mouth made me hate him more. He had no idea what Olivia could do, but it was obvious she had forgotten herself.

Dammit, why did I care?

In the few seconds that I had taken my eyes off the twins, Jax had picked Olivia up over his head with a hand between her legs and the other at her chest.

"Tap out, Livy, tap out," Jax shouted as she squirmed above him.

"Devin, sir, I beg you to put a stop to this," Niall shouted.

It was then that Olivia's eyes found mine, searching for help. The answer popped in my head quickly, although she didn't deserve it. "Your thirteenth birthday party."

"What?" the twins said in unison.

"You broke the table in the library on your thirteenth birthday," I repeated.

"Oh, shit," Jax groaned.

Olivia's widened with recognition before she tightened her legs around Jax's hand, crossed her arms, and twisted down to the ground. It was amazingly graceful, and also hysterical watching Jax fumble and get flipped down to the ground. To finish him off, Olivia's long leg came down and hit him in the balls. He didn't need to physically tap out, his groans and curled up position were enough.

Olivia jumped up from the ground and ran over to me with her arms outstretched. I froze when she hugged me, although she was half jumping with excitement. When she pulled away, her smile was endless. "Oh my god, how did you remember that?"

I shrugged. "I'm packed full of useless knowledge."

She took a breath and rested her hand on my arm. "Thanks, Wills."

"Yeah," Jax grunted as he stood from the ground, "thanks, Wills."

"Sorry, man."

"I knew it wouldn't be too long before you chose her over me," he said as he came to stand next to me, although hunched over slightly.

"Winners on the mat," Devy said and gave Niall a not-so-gentle nudge.

"Do you mean for me to go against my girlfriend?" Niall replied.

"Perhaps you could display something besides your shield, Niall," Devy challenged.

"Devy, I don't think…"

"You don't think what, Monkey? You have the skill, perhaps that unbelievable confidence of yours has dissipated since you left home."

Olivia shifted uncomfortably and fidgeted with her shirt. "No, I…what happened to not calling me Monkey anymore?"

"If you get Niall to tap out, I'll never call you Monkey again. How's that?"

With a sigh, Olivia stepped back onto the mat. Niall bounced up and down a little, and punched the air with his fists. It was odd how his initial reservation of fighting against his girlfriend had turned into excitement in just a few seconds.

"Don't worry, love," he began in a condescending tone, "I'll take it easy on you."

"We don't do that here," Devy said firmly. "Whoever wins will earn it fairly, or not at all."

Niall shook out his hands and was obviously annoyed.

"At least this won't last long," Jax muttered next to me.

"In whose favor?"

Jax shrugged and I laughed to myself. Niall and Olivia began circling each other slowly on the mat. Niall flinched every now and then to get her to draw first. Finally, he gave up and began throwing punches in Olivia's direction, most of which she blocked, but got knocked in the stomach hard enough to push her back a few steps. My hand instantly formed a fist and I looked over at Devin whose head was tilted down slightly and his eyes were peeking from underneath his brow, analyzing every move.

Olivia got in a few hits, although she definitely wasn't going at the same speed she had with Jax. Perhaps she was trying to protect Niall's ego. When she ducked to avoid Niall's cross hit, she was too slow lifting up and Niall jabbed his opposite elbow into her back, causing her to drop to the ground. Quickly he jumped on top of her and wrapped his arms around her chest to try and render her immobile.

"Tap out, love," Niall said through gritted teeth.

"What is she doing?" I said softly to Jax who shook his head.

Olivia refused to tap out, but was struggling to move and her face was turning red.

"Livy, come on," Jax shouted.

She looked in our direction, her eyes pleading for help, which was mindboggling since she had all the power she needed within her. Had she seriously forgotten? Could she have possibly forgotten how strong and powerful she was?

"Use your head, Liv," I shouted at her and she scrunched her brows. I jammed my index finger repeatedly into my forehead and said again, "Use-your-head-Liv!"

Suddenly there was a flash of recognition, and she closed her eyes.

"Are you giving up, lo…" Niall said but then started grunting in pain.

Olivia's eyelids tightened, and Niall's screams became louder. He raised his head painfully, as if he was fighting against it, but then his body stared to follow. His hands pulled apart from around Olivia's chest as his body continued to rise off of Olivia's back until he was practically floating in mid-air. Olivia rose from the mat and stood in front of him, not caring about his painful wails. With a flick of her hand, Niall flew backwards toward the wall, but then quickly ricocheted forward like he was being propelled by a giant rubber band. Just as he came inches away from Olivia, she extended her right arm, close-pinned him, and followed him down to the ground. She stayed on top of him for a few seconds while cheers rang out in the training room. Devy's wide smile conveyed the pride we all felt.

Niall extended his hand and tapped the floor. With a cheer of her own, she jumped up, accepted Devy's prideful smile and nod, then ran over to me and Jax. Her excitement was contagious, and the three of us hugged and patted each other's back. In that quick second we were teenagers again, maybe younger, when we celebrated each other and shared in our triumphs. In that quick second, we were happy.

But in the next second, Jax caught himself and took a step back, shifting his shoulders back as if that moment of happiness together was itchy and uncomfortable. Olivia noticed and her face fell for a moment, but then she shook her head slightly and smiled at me.

"I can't believe you remember these things," she said, still a little breathless from the excitement.

I searched her eyes out of sheer shock and confusion. "That's your gift, Liv. How did you forget?"

Her face fell again, her eyes blinking while she searched for an answer.

But the sound of a commotion behind us caused her to break eye contact with me and turn around. We both caught the sight of Niall leaving the training room, a garbage can lying with its contents all over the floor.

Olivia lowered her head. "I need to go after him," she said and gave me a half smile. "Thank you."

My stomach churned as she walked away. Something in the back of my mind was nagging me to go with her, but it was none of my business. I was no one to her. I was the only one who knew her well enough to help her earlier, but I was no one.

"Hey," Jax said and then hit me in the back of the head, "cut it out."

"Ow! What the fu…"

"I know that look," he interrupted and pointed his index finger in my face. "Don't get sucked back in by her, you got me? She's poison."

"Calm down. I'm not getting into anything."

"You better not. I mean it, Wills, I can't watch you implode over her again."

"Stop, you're overreacting."

"Are you two going to stand there or do some work today?" Devy said sternly.

"Yes, sir," we answered and scrambled to gather our things.

"What do you want to do now?" I asked.

Jax cocked his eyebrow. "Grab a weapon," he replied. "I'm going to work you out so hard you'll be too tired to even give my stupid sister a second thought."

Chapter Ten

Olivia

Winning wasn't always easy. I was so happy that I not only won against my brother, but also Niall. What was upsetting was how badly Niall was taking it. It was an uncomfortable situation I didn't want to have to handle, but this was life, right? This was what you did when you had a partner, support them through their temper tantrum.

I was only a few feet outside of the training area when I heard my name called. When I turned around, I found Devy walking toward me.

"Devy, I can't really talk…"

"Monk…" he started but cleared his throat, "Livy, I'm very proud of your work today."

"Thanks," I replied and looked down at the floor, "but it was mostly because of Will."

"He merely reminded you of what you were capable of. It was still your talent that did the rest."

"Sure," I replied unconvinced, and gestured down the hall. "I really need to go and find Niall…"

"I just wanted to invite you to train with us any time."

"Why?"

"To fix that horrid footwork to begin with," he replied. Devy was never one to mince words.

"Devy, it's just not my thing."

"It's in your blood, Olivia, you can't ignore your gifts. It concerns me that Niall is unaware of your skills. He seems to think you are some weak little girl, and that is certainly not who you are."

I shifted uncomfortably from the stern gaze he was giving me. "Guys don't want to be with someone who can kick their ass, Devy."

He raised his brow. "You shouldn't have to minimize who you are because a man's ego can't handle your abilities."

"That's not it, Devy." He was frozen with his eyebrow raised which just made you want to confess absolutely every secret you had within you. "He wanted to impress you. He wants to impress everyone, and I just embarrassed him in front of the Warrior Assassin. I only won because I can control hybrids. I was practically cheating."

Devy tightened his lips and sighed. "Your mother won her battle with Eris using her gift, and she certainly wasn't cheating. She used her gifts, just as you used yours. You should be proud of what you're able to do, you are the only one in the world who can do that. Most men might look at that as impressive," he said and started to walk away. "Join us in training at any time."

"And fix my footwork?"

He shook his head with his back to me. "It was so bad, so, so, bad."

I laughed for a moment, but then realized I still needed to find Niall. With a sigh, I pushed myself forward down the stone corridor, and then wound my way up the spiral staircase. Butterflies started to flutter in my stomach as I approached our room. I hadn't actually used my gift since the day I met Niall. When he tripped over my foot, I inadvertently saw the bright red light glowing from his forehead. I never thought I'd use my gift against him. Why would I? It would prove that I was an even bigger freak than he thought I already was. My uncle just didn't understand what I had to deal with.

My hand rested on the door handle because I was fearful of what I was about to walk into. With a deep breath, I pressed down on the handle and stepped inside. Niall was standing near the vanity on the right side of the room, just standing there with his back to me.

"Niall? Darling, are you ok?" I asked as I took several slow steps toward him, but he didn't answer. "I know you're upset, I'm sorry." Another step forward, and another. "My competitiveness took over and..."

Niall's arm swung around and he backhanded me across the face. I should have been prepared for it, but instead I nearly fell to the ground as I held my left hand up to my cheek.

"What in the bloody hell was that?" he shouted. His eyes were raging, and his entire face was reddish purple.

"I'm sorry."

"Sorry? Sorry that you made a fool out of me in front of your family? Was it so everyone could have a laugh at old Niall?"

"No, that's not what I was doing, I swear."

He grabbed the back of my neck and squeezed it tightly. "Then what was that?"

"It was my gift," I said and pulled his hand away.

"Your gift?" he responded angrily.

"Yes. Jack-Jack controls Vamps, I can control hybrids."

His eyes flared. "Why have you kept this from me?"

"Because it didn't matter! I never had to use it, I never wanted to. It was never important enough to have to tell you."

"You made me look like a bloody fool, Olivia, a bloody fool!" he shouted, stepped into the bathroom, and slammed the door.

This wasn't what I wanted. None of this was what I wanted.

What the hell had just happened?

"And would you believe it, Cameron," Niall laughed, "my father was there hiding behind his shield the whole time."

Ada forced a smile. It was a terrible story. I'd heard Niall's story about how he used to sneak down early on Christmas morning to look at all his presents, and then go back to bed and pretend to be surprised later on. It wasn't funny, at least as funny as he thought it was.

"That is adorable," my mother said in that voice parents used when trying to feign interest in their child's never-ending story. "It must have been hard to get away anything when you were growing up."

"To say the least," Niall replied.

"I don't think we'll ever know all the things the twins got away with," Mom said and smirked at Ada, "or who all in the family helped them get away with it."

"Then there was this time I..." Niall began and I spaced out again.

Mom had decided it would be nice to have a private dinner to give her and Ada a chance to get to know Niall better. The table was set in the middle of their suite. It was actually in the same place Grandfather would set up our special breakfasts. Grandfather would dress in replicas of his Roman battle attire, while Jack-Jack and I would create our own costumes. Those were good memories, ones that I'd forgotten until now.

"That was quite a battle," Niall laughed and then looked at me for validation, so I nodded, even though I had no idea what he had said.

"Speaking of," Ada began, and looked down the table at me, "your uncle informed me you were quite the champion today."

I smiled uncomfortably and avoided looking over at Niall. "Did he tell you about my horrible footwork?"

Ada smirked. "That he did, but that is your uncle. I wish you could have heard the pride in his voice."

"Let's not make more of it than it is, Ada," I said curtly, seeing Niall start to tense up.

"So, Niall, tell us more about your family," Mom said, quickly changing the subject. She was an expert at it. But while Niall answered her, she reached over and placed her hand on top of mine.

Honey, are you ok?

Unlike Jack, she needed to touch me in order to communicate.

I'm fine, I just don't want to talk about the battles today. Niall is having a hard time with losing to me.

But you shouldn't have to hide your win, he should be proud.

He didn't know about my gift, Mom. He's upset.

Even though she was still looking at Niall, she squinted her eyes in judgement. *Why are you hiding yourself with him? If you love him the way you say you do, he should know everything...*

I ripped my hand out from under hers because I didn't want to hear it, but it caught Ada's attention across the table.

"Olivia? Is everything all right?" he asked. I nodded and looked down at my hands in my lap. "Are you sure? You have hardly eaten anything."

I looked at the plate my mother had made for me – Chicken Milanese, spring salad with lemon dressing, and crispy potatoes. I could have eaten three full plates, but had only taken a few bites. It was a test of will power.

"I'm just not that hungry, Ada."

"You hardly ate yesterday too, Livy," Mom said with a worried tone.

"Why is everyone watching what I eat?" I snapped.

Mom looked uncomfortably down at the table while Ada simply raised an eyebrow at me.

Niall squeezed my hand. "I quite appreciate a woman with a small appetite. There is nothing more disgusting than watching a beautiful lady chow down like an animal. Wouldn't you agree, Cameron?"

"I apologize, Niall, I cannot," Ada replied with a crooked smile as he took the bottle of blood from the bottle warmer on the table and poured himself a glass. "Brianna always had a healthy appetite when she was human. When she was pregnant with the twins, you never wanted to get in between her and her food."

"I do miss eating real food," Mom said and sipped from her own glass of blood.

Ada patted Mom's hand. "I always thought that Olivia had inherited her mother's love of food. She could eat more than her brother and William put together."

"But I am an adult now and I shouldn't be eating everything in sight like I used to," I snapped again. "Can we please stop analyzing my eating habits and talk about something else?"

The room fell silent.

"Very well," Ada said in a cool voice, which meant he was letting me get away with my tone, but that it needed to stop. "Have you decided what you're going to do after your visit?"

"Yes, Ada. I know you wanted to discuss my future while I was here, and I have thought about it. I'd really like to go back to working as a translator. It was so rewarding helping with refugees all over the world. But obviously I can't do as much traveling as I did before now that Niall and I are together," I began and placed my hand on his, but he gave me an odd look in return.

"Niall could travel with you," Mom prodded. "Couldn't you, Niall?"

"I'm afraid not. It's important that I stay close to my family, especially at this critical time," Niall replied and then looked at Ada. "Which is something I've been wanting to discuss with you, sir."

"Of course, Niall, but first I would like Olivia..."

"As I have mentioned, Cameron, my father's coven has been established for over fifty years now, however, they are still not formally recognized."

Ada sighed and became very business-like. "Niall, for a coven to be formally recognized they must provide a distinct service to our race."

"And we believe we do," Niall replied.

"Yes, Victor mentioned you refer to yourselves as the Warriors of Europe," Ada said and then took a long drink from his glass. "That is considered an insult to many of us who have been actual Warriors for centuries on end."

Niall swallowed hard. "I mean no disrespect, sir, truly I don't, but my father developed his coven to fulfill a need in the European countries."

"And what need is that?"

"Greater protection and enforcement of vampire law," Niall replied, and Ada raised his brows. Even Mom sat back in her seat in surprise. "Perhaps you are just unaware of the rampant disregard of the law that has been occurring across the pond, as they say. My father developed his coven out of necessity, sir."

"Necessity?" Ada questioned skeptically. "Niall, I do not wish to challenge your father's passion, but our Warriors are scattered around the globe based on necessity. Europe has always had a smaller vampire population and therefore we have never needed a large Warrior presence there."

"Or perhaps it's because my father's coven is filling in where they are needed."

Ada sighed. "Niall, what your father is doing is borderline vigilantism."

"And he would have been visited by the Warrior Assassin if that were truly the case," Niall snapped and Ada raise an eyebrow.

"Niall," I said softly and touched his hand. He was pushing Ada too hard for a first-time discussion. "Ada, perhaps it's something to look into."

Ada gave a slow nod. "Perhaps it is."

Niall gave a smile and then yawned widely. "Please excuse me, the jetlag seems to still be affecting me."

Mom stood from the table. "By all means, Niall, get some sleep."

Niall stood from his chair and held mine for me. "Thank you, Brianna, for doing this. It was a lovely dinner."

"Of course," Mom replied and walked with him toward the door.

Ada still sat in his chair, although he was looking down at the table, his eyes unfocused in thought.

"Ada?" I asked and he looked up quickly. "He didn't mean to upset you."

"I am not upset, lovey," he replied and stood from his chair.

I wrapped my arms around him and enjoyed a goodnight hug from my dad. "Heavy is the head?"

He laughed softly in my ear. "That wears the crown? Yes, lovey, my head is quite heavy these days."

I pulled out of his hug and looked him in the eye. "He means well."

"I am sure he does. We still need to discuss your future plans."

"We will."

He nodded and kissed my forehead. "Goodnight, lovey."

"Goodnight, Ada," I replied and stepped away from him. Niall was already standing in the corridor just outside the door as I approached my mother. She had a worried expression on her face, it was the same look she had most of my teenage years. "Goodnight, Mom."

She hugged me tightly. "Goodnight, baby girl. You know I love you more than anything in the world, right?"

"I do," I replied and slipped out of her arms. "I love you too, Mom."

She gave a tense smile and kissed my cheek as Niall began pulling me away.

"What was that about?" he asked quietly.

"What was what about?"

"It seemed as though your mother was upset about something."

"It's nothing," I replied, thankful to see the spiral staircase up ahead. "I think we're figuring out how to communicate with each other again."

"Communicate? You barely spoke two words to each other."

"Just...in general, I mean," I replied, not wanting him to know yet another secret of how I can communicate with my family.

The rest of the walk to our room was quiet. Initially I thought it was because he was jet-lagged, but as soon as our room door shut, he immediately started in with, "Your father completely dismissed my family's coven. He's not going to be at all open to my suggestion about connecting the covens."

I took my heels off and threw them into the suitcase on the floor. "Just go easy. This isn't something they'll readily agree to, I told you that."

He pulled his shirt over his head and threw it on the ground.

"I'm not saying it can't happen, Niall, just that it will take time to convince Ada and Devy."

"Explain that to my father," he snapped and stepped into the bathroom. "You also sound like a child when you call them those names."

I took a breath. "All I'm saying is that I know my family, and you are pushing too hard. They don't know you well enough…"

"And whose fault is that?"

"Are you suggesting it's mine?"

"You certainly haven't been supporting me," he snapped again and stepped out of the bathroom in only a pair of boxers.

"Niall…" I began, placing my hands on his bare shoulders, but he knocked them away.

"Don't," he said and then pulled down the comforter.

I sighed and shook my head, not knowing what to do. "I'm too wound up. I think I'm going to go for a run."

"Fine," he replied and slipped under the sheets. "Why don't you go downstairs and crush another man's masculinity with your secret powers while you're at it."

"Niall, I thought we talked about that…"

"Goodnight," he interrupted and snapped the light off.

Unbelievable. I was a grown woman fighting with a man-child who literally left me standing in the dark. Luckily, I could see in the dark and slipped into a pair of flats. I was too upset to change my clothes. Maybe a full-fledge run wasn't in my future. I just needed some air.

Quietly I left the room and headed downstairs. What had just happened? Was he just cranky from the jet-lag?

"Hey, you ok?"

I looked over my shoulder to see Jack.

"Yeah," I lied but didn't bother trying to smile. "I just need to take a walk and get some air."

He nodded, seeming concerned. "Well, do us all a favor. If you come across a car, step in front of it."

My nostrils flared as I fought back tears. "I'll do my best," I replied and turned away from him. "Any my parents wonder why I never come home."

Chapter Eleven

Olivia

At first, I ran at a full clip, probably a little faster than I should have in public, especially in a dress and flats, but it was mainly to get out all the pent-up frustration. After an hour or so, I finally gave up and just started walking. The slower pace helped me take in the night views, but it also allowed nasty little thoughts to flood my brain and create doubt about my relationship with Niall. He hadn't been the same person since we stepped through the manor's doors. The pressure from his father often weighed him down, but tonight was a little extreme. He never knew how to deal with his anger. It would fester inside of him until he struck out at me, but it only hurt for a moment.

"Jesus, Olivia," I groaned at myself. I couldn't believe the thought had even crossed my mind. Not striking back was basically against everything my family had ever taught me. But up until a few months ago I thought I would be alone my entire life, mainly because of my fangs. It was easier for Jack-Jack. Women liked a bad boy who could protect them and make them feel like they were in a paranormal romance novel. Men were not so responsive to an uber strong woman who could kick their ass and drain them of their blood if she wanted to.

I groaned again and stopped walking. With a sigh I looked up to see where in the world I was, and I flinched. The bright purple lights were on, but the music wasn't loud enough to shake the building like it had last night. I walked across the city, and somehow ended up at Will's club.

What were the odds?

After standing and staring at the outside of the building for almost five minutes, I sighed and slowly walked inside. The club had seriously transformed. The colorful flashing lights were now just swanky chandeliers casting soft light on the few patrons gathered on couches and booths on the outskirts of the room. The dance floor was empty, probably because the music playing was softer and not really dance music. It was mainly for atmosphere, I supposed. Only a handful of people sat at the bar, unlike the madhouse it was last night, but the bartender was a young blonde woman. Damn. But that still didn't deter me, and I walked down to the bar.

With the crowd so light, the female bartender placed a napkin down in front of me before I had even fully sat down.

"What can I get you?" she asked.

"Um…I'm sorry," I began, "but is Will Ryan working tonight?"

She scrunched her eyebrows and gave me a sympathetic look. "Honey, you seem sweet, but you're wasting your time."

"I am?"

"Will gets dozens of numbers a night, women and men, they just can't help themselves. Even if he said he'd call, he won't. He does nothing but workout and work here. He doesn't date…"

"No, no," I said and shook my head. "He's an old friend. I came here last night, and uh…I just wanted to see…"

She put her hands up and I stopped my uncomfortable rambling. "He's bringing some stock up from downstairs, he'll be back in a minute. Can I get you something while you wait?"

"Sure," I replied and when I didn't answer right away, she raised her eyebrows at me. "Oh, sorry, he made me something really good last night, it was pink."

"Really strong?" she asked and I nodded. "Knowing Will, it was probably the Livy B."

I froze. "The what?"

"Technically it's called the Livid Bitch," she answered as she reached down into the well and pulled up three different bottles.

"The…Livid Bitch?"

She nodded and began pouring various amounts of alcohol into a metal shaker. "Yeah, but the name makes it tough to have on a cocktail menu, so he shortened it to the Livy B. It's our most popular drink."

"Where did the name come from?"

"It's pretty and feminine, but will kick your ass if you're not careful," she laughed. "At least that's what he says."

"Who says?"

"Will," she replied and began shaking the metal shaker, "it's his drink, he created it."

"How nice," I replied and I could feel the blood rushing to my cheeks.

She strained the drink into a martini glass and slid the Livy B over to me. Perhaps I could throw it in Will's face, but instead I decided to drink half of it down. The bartender widened her eyes in shock and then shuffled down to the other end of the bar.

A moment later the side door to my left opened and Will stepped through with two large boxes stacked in his arms. He didn't see me and headed directly to the side of the bar that was hidden around the corner. The female bartender ducked around to the other side, and I immediately tilted my head in that direction in order to hear them. I guess there were some perks to being a true hybrid.

"Thanks, Mins," I heard Will say with a slight grunt as bottles clanged.

"Hey, uh," she began and lowered her voice, making me need to close my eyes in order to concentrate on them over the music, "there's a girl here claiming she's a friend of yours."

"Is she cute?" he laughed as more bottles clanged against each other.

"Gorgeous, actually," she replied. "Way too good for you."

"A little jealous, Mins?"

"Yes," she replied. "Just sneak a look and tell me whether I need to call security, or if I can ask her out."

He laughed. "Those are my only choices?" She didn't answer, and through my hair I could see Will peek from around the corner. "Holy fucking shit. Can we check if the gates of hell have opened?"

"Security then?"

He shook his head and hid behind the corner again. "Uh, I guess not."

"So, I can go after her?"

"She doesn't hit for your team, Mins."

"Are you sure?"

"She brought her boyfriend home to meet her parents. Yeah, pretty sure."

"So why are you freaking out?"

"What? I...no...I'm not."

She laughed and stepped back around from the corner. I was flattered that she found me attractive, and honestly, I had to admit that she wasn't bad herself. She flashed me a flirty smile the same time Will came from around the corner. He looked uncomfortable, and nervously patted down his shirt.

"Olivia, hey," he said and came to stand in front of me, keeping the bar protectively between us. "What are you doing here?"

I shrugged. "I was just walking around the city, and then I looked up and saw that I was here. And then, I met...Mins, is it?"

The female bartender flinched in surprise, but the color drained from Will's cheeks. It seems old Wills had forgotten about my hearing.

"Um, it's Mindy, actually," Will said nervously. "Mindy, this is Olivia."

Mindy waved from behind Will's shoulder, and then took a slow step away from us, the kind where you wanted to stay and watch the drama, but knew you weren't supposed to be there.

I flashed Will a fake smile and tapped my nail on the rim of my martini glass. "Mindy was telling me all about the drink you made me last night."

He pulled at his collar. "She did, huh?"

"Mmm-hmm, and she made me one tonight. It's pretty good, not as good as yours, of course, but that's because you created it, isn't that right?"

"Um...yeah," he replied and licked his lips nervously.

"And named it?" He didn't answer. "I mean, it has such a clever name – the Livid Bitch. That's it, isn't it?"

"Liv..."

"Oh no, it was shortened to the Livy B, right? It's feminine, strong, and will kick your ass when you least expect it?"

"Something like that," he mumbled.

I took a moment and locked eyes with him. "I know I'm not your favorite person in the world, but I didn't think you hated me *that* much."

"Olivia," he sighed and pulled at his collar again, "it was a joke."

"Real funny."

"You weren't supposed...it wasn't directed at you."

"I find that hard to believe," I replied and swallowed the lump in my throat. "I should sue you for copyright it's so directed at me."

"I'm sorry," he said and rested his hands on the bar, leaning over and looking me in the eye. "I'm sorry if it hurt your feelings. I don't...hate you."

"Call it something else."

He sighed and nodded. "Ok, I'll come up with something."

I swallowed another lump in my throat. What was it about his eyes that could pierce right through you? Those big, blue-green eyes were incredibly apologetic.

"Want to tell me why you're here?" he said and pushed back up from the bar.

"I told you, I was out for a walk."

"Uh huh."

They weren't even words, and yet he could get anything out of me. "I...dammit...since I got here everything has gone to shit and I realized that I don't have one person to talk to, not one friend. That's how pathetic I am. I went for a walk hoping to clear my head and then I looked up and here I was, so I came in thinking maybe you'd be here...and I...don't know. But I realize now it was mistake, so..." I slid off the stool, but Will leaned over the bar and touched my hand.

"Don't...go. Just give me a minute," he said and stepped over to the other end of the bar where Mindy was washing some glasses. This time I didn't need to stretch to hear him. "Hey, Mins, I need to call in my favor."

"I didn't know you had one to call in."

He laughed. "I distinctly remember you begging me to cover your shift when your ex came in and you wanted to make up with her for the fifth time."

She gave him an incredulous look. "That was almost a year ago, don't favors expire after awhile?"

"Please?" he begged softly. "There aren't a lot of people left, and it's almost end of shift. Please, Mins?"

Mindy gave me a glance, and then looked back up at Wills. "Fine, but if things don't work out, you'll give me her number?"

He sighed and stepped back. "Fine. We're square then?"

"Yeah, I'll close her out," she replied and placed her clean glasses on the drying rack.

Will stepped past me and held up his index finger. "Wait here. I'll be back in a few."

I nodded and slung back the rest of my drink. "I guess I need my check," I said when Mindy came to stand in front of me.

"Nah, it's on me," she replied. "I've witnessed a miracle, and the least I can do is buy you a drink."

"A miracle?"

"I need to give something to the person who caused the workhorse to take a couple hours off."

"The workhorse?"

"Your friend Will, he's a machine. It's good to see him take a little time. You must be a really special friend, Olivia," she said with a seductive smile.

"You can call me Livy," I replied. "Livy Burke."

"Livy, nice, just like…" her eyes flashed as the realization hit her.

"Yeah, I guess I am a special friend."

Mindy forced a smile and took my glass from the bar. Will came around the corner a moment later with a bag slung over his shoulder. "Olivia," he said and motioned to a side door with his head.

"Thanks for the drink," I said and gave Mindy a wave before I stepped over to Will. He held the side door open for me and I stepped through into an alley. Once Will stepped outside, he pointed to the left.

"Will, I didn't mean for you to take off work," I said as we walked down the alley to a back parking lot.

He shrugged. "Mindy owes me, and you seemed upset," he replied and then stepped around to the driver's side of his old red Honda.

"I can't believe you still have this car."

He laughed and threw his bag into the backseat. "Can't afford anything new, so I just pray and pull out the duct tape," he replied and locked the door behind him. "Come on."

"Where are we going?" I asked as we headed across the parking lot.

"You'll see."

Even with his back to me, I could imagine his sly smile. I followed silently behind him, stepping into another narrow alley that emptied out onto the city street. Will stepped to the left and immediately went up the steps of a small all-night diner. Once again, he held the door for me, and as I stepped inside, I was immediately hit with the smell of grease and old coffee. When Will stepped inside, two waitresses and a cook all waved and said hello.

"Come here often?" I said as he led me to the third booth on the right.

"What can I say, it's cheap, it's close, the food is decent, and the people are nice…well, to me at least."

We both laughed as a miserable-looking older woman placed two glasses of water and menus down on the table. "Well, if it isn't my favorite customer," she said and pulled out a small pad of paper.

"Oh, Patty, you say that to everyone," Will replied flirtatiously.

"You're right," she replied, "but I really mean it with you. So, which usual order are you going to have tonight?"

"I'm going to do breakfast."

Patty scribbled on her pad and then raised her eyebrows at me, causing her very deep wrinkles to crease. "And you?"

"Oh, um, I'll just have water," I replied and Patty pursed her lips, showing each one of her deep-set smoking lines around her mouth.

"Gotta big spender here," she said loudly, took the menus from the table, and walked away.

When I looked back at Will, he narrowed his eyes.

"What?" I asked defensively.

"I've just never known you to pass up a chance to eat."

I rolled my eyes and crossed my arms in front of my chest. "Why is everyone so obsessed with what I eat? I mean honestly, I'm a grown woman now, not the child who used to stuff her face all the time. Why can't everybody understand that?"

"Wow. Been holding that in, huh?"

I sighed. "I'm sorry. Your mom said something last night, and then Mom and Ada brought it up tonight. I just don't understand why people keep focusing in on it."

"Olivia, you could out eat me and Jax combined any day of the week. You made a big deal of the fact that you loved to eat."

"No, I didn't."

"You used to steal food from my locker at school, Liv. My parents worried I was malnourished because I would always give you my snacks the moment you would start crying that you were hungry. You can't blame your family for reacting to the sudden change to your appetite."

I sighed loudly in frustration. "You don't understand, Will, you're not a woman."

"What's that supposed to mean?"

"Despite the fact that my family thought my insatiable appetite was cute, men don't."

He scrunched his brow. "I don't think that's true. I don't think men really care, actually. Our minds are usually on something else about women that has nothing to do with what you eat."

"Gross."

"What?" he laughed. "It's true. So what is it, you're not eating because Niall doesn't want you to?" I didn't answer. "Oh shit, I was just kidding."

"It's not like I'm starving myself, for crying out loud. He just likes when a woman eats like a lady and not an entire football team."

"Ok, then say that."

"He did say that to Mom and Ada tonight. You would have thought he told them that he wanted women barefoot and pregnant. Stop laughing."

"Sorry," he replied and cleared his throat, although a smirk was still on his face. "Is that why you were practically crying at the bar?"

"I wasn't crying," I snapped.

"Liv, come on," he said in his Liv-you-can't-bullshit-me voice. Unfortunately, I knew it well.

I avoided eye contact and stared at the edge of the table which had a layer of gunk on it that grossed me out, but I nervously picked at it with my finger nail. "Fine. Niall and I had a fight, which I'm sure you don't want to hear about."

He shifted in his seat and crossed his arms in front of his chest. "Not particularly, but you said you needed someone to talk to, and here I am."

Slowly I looked back up and found his caring eyes. I sighed and finally answered, "Since we got here, Niall's been a completely different person. He's snapping at me, trying to control every little thing I do, and then if I even dare to correct him, or help him when it comes to Ada, he flies off the handle." Will's jaw was clinched and pulsing. "Please, Will, promise you won't throw this back in his face."

He shook his head stiffly. "No, I'm just listening. He seemed angry after you won today."

"Angry doesn't describe it," I replied. "He was furious because I hadn't actually...told him...about my gift."

Will's entire body flinched. "You didn't tell him? Why wouldn't you tell him? That's kind of a big part of you."

"Don't be dramatic."

"Dramatic? Are you kidding? Olivia, you and your brother were given these tremendous gifts," he began and then lowered his voice, "and quite frankly, saved humankind, and you didn't think that was important enough to share with the person you're living with?"

"That's so easy for you to say, Wills, you're not like us, you're normal."

"Thanks for the reminder," he said with a forced smile.

"Sorry, I didn't mean…"

"Here we are," Patty the waitress said as she shed plate after plate of food from both of her arms. "I made sure they gave you extra crispy bacon."

"Patty, you're the best."

"I know," she replied with a wink as she put down the last plate and then looked over to me. "Still good with the water?"

"Yes, it's simply delicious," I answered and she rolled her eyes as she stepped away. I looked down on the massive spread of food in amazement. There were eggs, and bacon, and toast, and potatoes, and pancakes with butter and syrup, and lastly a small cup of fruit for good measure. "Are you sure there's enough?"

Will nodded as he shoved a forkful of eggs and potatoes in his mouth. Once he swallowed, he said, "You have no idea how many calories I burn a day. I train at the manor all morning, teach at the Facility all afternoon, and then work at the club at night. Sometimes this is the only meal I get."

"You eat like this every night? No wonder everyone knows you here."

"Not every night," he said and took a bite of toast. "Sometimes I get dinner rather than breakfast." I shook my head in disbelief. "If I can't judge you and Niall, you can't judge me and my meal choices. Besides, I need to enjoy as much of this as possible before I can't eat real food anymore."

"Why wouldn't you eat…" I began, but then caught myself. Will wanted to be a Warrior, he would become a vampire, and I hated that. I hated every bit of that.

"Liv?" Will said, muffled by the crunch of his extra crispy bacon. "No judgement, remember?"

I nodded and looked down at the design I had now carved into the grim on the edge of the table. "Right, no judgment."

"Do we want to revisit why you didn't tell Niall about your gift?" he asked and spread butter on the pancakes.

"Not really," I replied. He laughed softly to himself and drowned his pancakes in syrup. I couldn't remember the last time I had had pancakes. "It's just…I'm a hard sell."

His hand froze and the waterfall of syrup abruptly stopped. "Say that again?"

I rolled my eyes. "What I am isn't a big deal. But it's hard to be myself around people outside of our freakish little world. I'm too fast and too strong to hide it all the time, and then of course there are the things that extend out of my mouth."

"Jax has the same characteristics as you do and he doesn't hide," he replied and began cutting lines through the pancakes, slicing them into perfect small squares.

"He's a guy, it's different."

"How so?"

I sighed and picked up the fork that was lying on a napkin next to me. In a quick move, I stabbed one of the small pancake squares and popped it in my mouth. Oh my, oh my, how I missed pancakes. Between the butter and syrup, Will knew how to dress a pancake.

"Liv, how is it different?"

I shook myself back from my pancake euphoria and replied, "Because girls love this shit. They're fascinated by all the movies and novels, and when they meet him, they think they're in one. And when he's done with them, he can Glamour them if he needs to."

"Can't you do that too?"

"Yeah, but the minute guys see my...extra-long teeth...they're terrified and I have to Glamour them immediately. So, it's been hard enough to get past that point. With the pressure of who my family is, what they do, what I am, and the things that come down in my mouth, I thought it best not to share the freakiest thing about me with Niall. Why is that wrong?" He didn't answer. "Wills?" Still he didn't answer. "What's the point of me telling you all this if you're not going to..."

"He's insecure, Liv," he interrupted. "That's the only thing I can say. He's obviously insecure and is having trouble accepting all you can do. Why should you have to hide who you are so he feels better about himself? That's stupid, Liv, and you're smarter than that."

He was right, which made me stab another section of the pancakes and put them in my mouth. The syrup had soaked into the remaining pieces and didn't leave any syrup for dipping. Without even asking, Will took the syrup container and poured more on the empty side of the plate. There were things that only Will would do.

"Liv, I didn't mean it to come out that way," he said softly.

"You never did pull punches with me, why would you start now?"

"Are you saying that I've always been an asshole to you?"

"No, that would be Jack." I laughed and dunked another stacked forkful of pancakes into the lake of syrup. "You always sent us to our corners and told us the hard truths we needed to hear."

"Sounds about right," he replied and began eating his last piece of toast. "Liv, I have literally known you my entire life. You have always been stubborn, impatient, selfish…"

"Hey!"

He laughed with a cute shrug. "Sorry, it's true, but you've also been the most confident person I've ever known. You never doubted anything you did, right or wrong, you knew what you wanted to do and you were going to do it come hell or high water. You left at eighteen and lived abroad by yourself while you learned to speak fifteen languages."

"Seventeen," I corrected.

"Jesus," he laughed. "Anyway, you did that. You left because you wanted more, and because you couldn't handle being around the family business anymore."

"It was a little bit more than that, Will," I said defensively and dropped my fork. "I couldn't handle worrying that this was the time that someone in our family didn't come home from a mission. I had legitimate reasons."

Will leaned forward. "Then why are you with someone whose family does the same thing?" His statement stung me in the chest because it was true. "And is it true what my Mom said that you left your job after you met Niall. Seriously, Liv?"

"I was traveling a lot." He raised an eyebrow at me. "I needed a break."

"What were you doing?"

I picked my fork back up and dived into the eggs that he hadn't finished. Why was he pushing me so hard?

"Olivia?"

"I was working for a humanitarian organization, helping to translate for migrants and refugees," I replied and shoved a huge forkful of eggs into my mouth.

"Did you like it?"

"Loved it," I replied between bites. "I was helping people, these terrified people who couldn't communicate with anyone. I…I really felt needed."

"Then why did you give it up," he pressed.

"Niall…"

"Right. Niall. You gave up what you loved doing, you couldn't share everything about yourself, and he's bringing you back into a world you purposely left. What are you doing, Liv?"

"Why are you yelling at me?"

He closed his eyes and took a breath. After he licked his lips, he opened his eyes and said, "I'm not yelling," he said softly. "You can't live your life trying to be something different, Liv, it'll eat you up inside little by little until you completely break. It's what happened to me."

"What?"

He sighed and looked down at the table. "As you pointed out last night, I am not a doctor."

"I was just surprised."

"Yes, you made that perfectly clear," he interrupted. "I tried, Livy, I did. I was halfway through med school when I realized I wasn't trying to become a doctor for me, I was doing it for my dad. Don't get me wrong, I love my dad, but he never liked that I trained with Devy. It didn't matter if I won a competition at the local level or internationally, I'd get the same cursory pat on the back. But when he'd bring me to the clinic, you'd think he was teaching me how to turn straw into gold. I thought becoming a doctor would make him happy, and actually it did. But it ate away at my soul until I was so miserable that it caused me to go into a severe depression. I wasn't living for myself, I wasn't doing anything that made me happy, and it was destroying me.

"Once I realized that, I went back to training with Devy, and I found my way out of that depression. Liv, I'm telling you, if you start going down a path where you're pretending to be someone you're not, it's going to catch up with you. Tonight your subconscious brought you down here because you knew I would tell you the nasty, dirty truth, and that's what I'm doing. If you love Niall, fine, but how can you say he loves you if he doesn't know who you really are?"

A silence fell between us since I couldn't think of a good rebuttal. I took the grape from the fruit cup and popped it in my mouth.

"And I thought you just wanted water?"

"Sorry."

"How were the pancakes?"

"Really good," I replied softly. "I forgot how much I liked them."

He smiled. "I was never sure what you liked better, the pancakes or the syrup."

"It's probably a tossup," I replied and popped another grape in my mouth. "If you're done yelling at me, can I ask you a question?"

"Still wasn't yelling, but sure."

"Why are you becoming a Warrior?"

"Because I've always wanted to be one," he responded easily. "Remember when we were little, I would always want to be a Warrior for Halloween, and I'd get so mad at people because I couldn't understand why they didn't know what I was." I laughed and nodded at the memories of Will's tantrums. "When I dropped out of med school and came home, I was so lost, but when I started training with Devy again, the path was clear."

"But you're lying to your parents, my godparents, my parents' best friends."

"Olivia, my parents will lose their minds when I tell them. I honestly think they'll never talk to me again."

"You're being dramatic."

He laughed sarcastically. "I'm going to lose my family, Liv. I'm lying to them because I'm just not ready for that to happen."

My nose tingled with tears. "But then you won't be human anymore," I whispered. "They'll kill you, Wills."

"Why do you care?" he asked, but before I could answer, Patty the waitress came to our table.

"Can I get you anything else?"

Will shook his head. "Just the check."

Will settled the bill while I finished the remnants of pancakes on the plate. I would need to transfer money to him later, it was only fair since I'd eaten a good portion of his meal, unintentionally of course. It was so easy being with him that I forgot all about Niall's rules. I could be myself, I guess.

"Ready?" he asked and I followed him out of the booth.

Will held the door for me as we left the diner and we easily fell in step with each other through the alley back toward his car.

"I'm sorry, Liv, I'm afraid I haven't made you feel any better," he said.

"Better? Not really," I laughed and then sighed. "Does this mean you don't hate me as much anymore?"

"What would make you think that?"

"You're calling me Liv again, for one," I answered as we crossed the parking lot. "You calling me Olivia is very strange."

He sighed uncomfortably. "Well, to be honest, I didn't know who you were. When I saw you, heard your voice, it was as though I'd never met you. You were a person named Olivia," he said and pulled me to a stop.

"But tonight? The girl in the diner, that was Liv. That was the girl I knew, the girl who loves pancakes and a lake of syrup. Not the judgmental, pompous robot I saw last night."

"So the robot is named Olivia?"

He smirked and stepped over to his car. "Yeah, I guess she is."

The evening was over, but I wasn't ready to go home. Anxiety was rising within me at the thought of having to go back to the manor and get in bed with Niall. I didn't want to leave. No, I didn't want to leave Will.

"Liv?" he asked, looking back at me with a curious eye.

Slowly I stepped toward his car and pulled nervously at one of my curls. My family wasn't big on talking about things, especially uncomfortable things. We could fight to the death to protect those we loved, but we'd rather pull our eyes out than have to have a tough conversation.

"Liv, seriously, are you ok?"

With a deep exhale, I released the curl from my fingers. "I didn't know what to say to you."

"What?"

"Last night, when I...when I was the Olivia robot, it was because I didn't know how to act or what to say to you because of how we...what happened the night I left." He froze, leaning against the side of the car with no reaction whatsoever. "Do you remember? The night of my birthday when you..."

He put his hand up. "I'm well aware what night you're talking about."

I had to look down at the ground as I continued. "That night, that entire day, actually, I was overwhelmed and I felt like I was suffocating. I needed to get out, get away from everyone, and I thought if I pissed off my parents enough, they would be glad to ship me off."

"Well, you were very successful then."

I looked up and quickly wiped the tear that had leaked from the corner of my eye. "But then you came out and I knew what you were going to say to me."

His face suddenly became hard. "How could you have known?"

"Wills, you say you know everything about me, don't you think that works the other way too? I knew...I knew that if you said..." I cleared my throat as the emotions flowed down. "I was one foot out the door and I knew you would be the only one I would stay for. You'd get me to stay and then I'd be miserable, maybe even a little resentful. I just couldn't do that to you because you deserve so much better than me.

"You're a good man, Wills," I said, wiped the tears from my cheeks, and stepped right up to him. "You're *the* best man, and I knew the only way you'd let me leave was if I said the most horrible and hateful things to you. I needed you to hate me and never look back because...because you deserve the best life with the perfect woman...but then I come back and find out you're going to be a Warrior and it makes me...it...it makes me so goddamn angry that I want to scream," I shouted as tears streamed down my face. "What are you thinking?! How can you do this to yourself? And your family..."

"Why-do-you-care," he said loudly as he stepped up only inches from me, our noses almost touching, our hot breath wafting against each other's face.

His beautiful aquamarine eyes made it impossible not to admit the truth. "I can't lose you, Wills."

He blinked nervously and his breath quickened. Before he could say anything, I placed my lips on his. They were warm and soft, although stiff as he held his breath. Cautiously I opened my eyes and found him looking at me with shocked eyes. Immediately I pulled away, but Will stayed frozen in place. We stood there staring at each other for nearly thirty seconds before his eyes fluttered and he came back to life. Nervously he took a few steps back, unable to look at me any longer.

"Will, I'm sorry, I don't know..."

"Do you need a ride home or..."

"No...I'll run," I replied quickly. Will nodded as if in a trance and stepped to the driver side of his car. I had definitely shaken him. "Will, are you ok?"

He opened the driver's side door and lifted his leg to step inside, but then quickly turned around. "So...all those things you said to me, you...you..."

"I lied, Wills. I'm so sorry I hurt you. I didn't..." I cut myself off at the sight of Will closing his eyes in aguish and clawing at his hair.

"You're sorry?" he said loudly. "Do you have any idea the damage...no, no, of course you don't, because you left! You took off and left a crater in my chest, you..." he stopped and placed his hands on the roof of the car with his head hanging down in between.

Slowly I stepped forward, being careful not to startle him. It pained me to see him like this, especially since I'd caused it. When I was finally next to him, I gently rested my hands on his right arm and shoulder, and when he didn't flinch away, I leaned my weight into him. I listened as he took in deep breaths, saying inaudible words as he exhaled loudly. After a minute or so he lifted his head and I raised mine to look at him. His nostrils flared and his eyes were glassy. There was so much pain radiating from him that it brought me to tears. I opened my mouth to apologize again, but I was met with his lips resting on mine. Butterflies stirred in my stomach as I went to breathe into the kiss, but just as quickly as it began, Will pulled away.

"I've got to go," he said and jumped into his car. A moment later the engine roared to life and Will pulled away, leaving me alone in the parking lot.

What the hell had I just done?

Chapter Twelve

Will

Even with the car door closed I could feel Liv's pull on me. My bald tires struggled to get traction as I sped out of the employee parking lot. The pull, that unrelenting pull that she had on me was debilitating. Her lips were just as soft as I'd always imagined. I was shocked and unprepared for the first kiss, but when I kissed her, it took everything I had to pull away because I wanted more. I wanted her soft lips again, the feeling of her hair between my fingers, her soft skin...

"FUUUUUCK!" I yelled and hit the steering wheel three times. "Fuck, fuck, fuck, fuck, what the fuck are you doing?!"

My heart was beating wildly against my ribs. Why did she come? I should have said I couldn't help her. I should have told her to leave. It had been so easy and natural between us, as though nothing had changed in five years. Everything was normal until she said those two words – I lied.

What was I supposed to do with that? My life went into a decline because of those things she said to me, and now she's saying she lied? My brain literally didn't know how to process that. My chest was burning from the panicked breaths and painful heartbeat. I couldn't stop thinking about the feeling of Liv's lips on mine, how unbelievably soft they were. I needed her out of my head. She was already tearing me apart, and I was letting her!

I reached over to the passenger seat for my backpack. My anxiety meds would make this go away, but my hand froze on the zipper. They were a crutch. I hadn't used them in almost a year. If I took them, my blood wouldn't be clean. Another layer of anxiety started to build. I just needed to get Olivia out of my head – her touch, her smell, everything. There was only one person who might be able to help, but she was also at the manor. Could I beat Olivia there?

My tires barely held the road as I pushed the accelerator down. Would Olivia go back to the manor right away? What would happen the next time we saw each other? Would she just act like nothing happened?

"Shut. Up," I growled to myself.

My hand hovered over my backpack again. I didn't want this to turn me into a psychological mess balled up in a corner, but if I took the meds, Victoria couldn't feed from me and knock me out. That's what I really wanted. I wanted oblivion, and Tori was the only one who could do it.

My chest tightened as the manor's black gate came into view. Quickly I pulled through and looked for any sight of Liv. Even after I got out of my car, I was constantly looking over one shoulder and then other like a paranoid mess.

"Just get through the door, and get upstairs," I muttered to myself, now choosing to look down at the floor and step my pace up in order to get to the spiral staircase.

"Hey, man," someone said in passing, and I looked up to find a familiar face.

"Hey, Jared."

"Whatcha doin'?" he asked as he changed direction to walk up the stairs with me.

"Nothing."

"Uh huh. Wondered how long it would take you."

Reluctantly I looked at him through the side of my eyes. "Don't know what you're talking about. Just crashing here tonight to make it easier for tomorrow."

"Uh huh. Well, you're in luck 'cuz Tori just got back."

Oh thank god, I thought, but then had to calm the voice that came out of me. "Cool. If I see her, I'll say hi."

"Yeah, if you see her," he laughed as he started back down the steps. "Have fun revenge fucking."

I sighed and shook my head as I continued up the stairs. Everyone knew that Victoria and I fooled around sometimes. She had a strict rule of not sleeping with Warriors, but technically I wasn't a Warrior yet, so I got a pass for the time being. The pressure on my chest started to lessen as I approached Tori's room, relief was in sight. I knocked and almost hyperventilated waiting for her to answer.

"Must be a human," she said loudly from the other side of the door.

"It's Will."

A moment later the door opened and Victoria stretched her long, slim body up the side. She was still wearing her Warrior uniform, which she filled out incredibly well.

"So, are you a donor or a conquest?" she asked.

"Both, if you'll have me," I replied with pleading eyes.

Without a word, Tori stepped away from the door and glided back into her room. Victoria, or Tori as most called her, wasn't a high-ranking Warrior, more middle of the pack, and she liked it there. It put her on missions regularly, and she got along with all the different crews, which made her an asset to Cam and Devy. If there was ever an issue with two people on a particular crew, they knew Tori would fill the gap without question, and no one ever had issues with her. In her eyes, everyone was equal as long as they pulled their weight. If they didn't, well, that was another story. Tori was also incredibly and painfully honest.

"Stressful night?" she asked as she lifted her mission pack off the bed and tossed it easily on the chair in the opposite corner.

"A little," I replied and closed the door behind me. "I just need to get someone out of my head."

Any more detail than that and she would be put off. Tori didn't do drama, at all.

"Fine," she began, pulling a few pins out of her tight bun and letting her long black hair fall down her back. When she turned around, her fingers grasped the zipper of her tight jumpsuit and started pulling it down her chest. "But I'm getting over the line before I even entertain feeding from you, is that clear?"

"Hasn't been a problem before," I replied and stepped over to her, placing my hand on top of hers and taking control of the zipper. "Let me."

She pursed her lips and raised an eyebrow at me. "You're controlling me tonight, is that it?"

"Yeah," I replied and quickly pulled the zipper down below her navel.

"A little rough tonight?"

Forcefully I pulled her jumpsuit open and down her shoulders, locking her arms at her sides. "Very."

Her eyes flashed as she opened her mouth and showed me her extending fangs. Everything immediately stirred in my pants and she was quick to notice. "Come and get me then."

As she freed her arms, I unbuckled my belt and undid my pants. Can't say I was going for much finesse tonight. Once I was able to step out my pants, I turned Tori away from me and pushed her up against the dresser. Roughly I took the uniform at her hips and pulled it down until she was completely free. As soon as I stood back up, I wrapped her hair around my hand and pulled her head back, causing her to hiss and fully expose her fangs. Immediately I entered her, slamming into her from behind hard enough to rock the dresser back and forth. I slipped my fingers between her thighs to work on her from the outside, hoping to get her to climax even faster so that she would feed from me. Between her moans and the reflection of her naked body in the mirror, I was getting close way too soon.

Abruptly I pulled out of her, turned her around and lifted her up around my waist. It was easy to carry her over to the bed. She attacked my lips and traveled down my neck, nipping at the skin. Carefully I lowered her down onto the bed, stretching back up to remove my shirt and throw it on the floor. As I stood in front of her, ready to finish what we started, I sadly realized what I was truly doing. I wasn't just having sex, I was fucking someone who looked like Olivia. She was tall, thin, dark long hair, although it wasn't curly. Jared was right. I really was revenge fucking.

"Hey, I'm losing lady wood here," Tori said laying splayed out on the bed.

Without another word, I climbed on top of her and released every ounce of anger and resentment into her. Tori's moans continued to get louder and more high-pitched as she got closer and closer to her orgasm. When she finally pulled my head to the side, I relaxed and allowed everything else to happen naturally. Her orgasm and mine came freely at the exact moment her fangs sank into my neck. As my body finished its release, the heavy veil of euphoria and fatigue came over me, the wonderful effects of being fed from. They were welcomed company.

Chapter Thirteen

Will

Practicing with my Bo staff was always therapeutic for me. It was something I could do for hours, almost hypnotized by the whirring sound as it cut through the air. I was finally clear-headed, calm, and even humming along with my Bo. I was so entranced with my practice that I didn't even know Jax was behind me until my Bo swiped him in the arm.

"Watch it!" he yelled.

"Sorry," I replied. "You should watch where you're going."

He laughed and took another Bo staff that was resting up against the wall. "So you crashed here last night?"

I kept my eyes focused on the mat as I stepped away from him. "Yeah, just wanted to get an early start to the day."

"Uh huh," he replied. "Care for a volley?"

"Why? You hate using Bo staffs," I said, unable to fully look at him and finding an invisible speck on the staff to pick at.

"Yeah, but you love it," he said and stepped closer. "You ok? You seem off."

"No, I'm fine."

Jax's Bo staff whirred past my head just as I ducked away. Instantly he came back down on me and our volley began. When I finally blocked him in the center, I was able to push him back.

"What the hell was that?" I shouted.

"Since when do you keep shit from me?"

"What? What the hell are you…" but I couldn't finish since his staff came down on me again. Another volley ensued and only ended when I clocked him in the shoulder. "Cut it out!"

"What's going on with you?"

"Calm down."

"It's Olivia, isn't it?" I didn't answer. "Damn it, man, I know something…"

I put a hand up to stop him. "She came to see me at the club last night, ok?"

"And you told her to fuck off, right?"

"No," I replied and Jax hit the bottom of my staff causing it to swing to the side and hit me in the head. "Asshole!"

"I'm the asshole? Do you remember what happened when she left? Because I do. I remember watching you dive into a blackhole of depression."

"Of course I remember," I growled. "Don't throw my past at me. You know I have clawed my way back."

"Which is why I can't understand why you'd put yourself back in that situation."

"Last night I saw the Livy we knew, not the stuck-up wannabe princess."

"Jesus…"

"What was I supposed to do?"

"Kick her out!" he replied. "I saw her last night, I knew something was wrong too, and I still told her to step in front of a semi-truck. It was that easy."

I rolled my eyes and stepped over to the wall. "If you'd taken a moment to actually talk to her, you would have found out that things aren't so great with Niall, and she's struggling even being here. Maybe you could feign a little compassion for your own freakin' twin."

Suddenly Jax whipped past and stood in front of me. "You slept with her, didn't you?"

"What?! No," I said too loudly, and Jax stared me down. "She…kissed me."

He didn't lash out, he didn't yell, it was worse. All his outward anger was sucked back inside his body in a scary simmer under the surface. After another second or two he held his index finger up warningly and his lips curled over his teeth.

"I swear to god," he began tensely, "if you sleep with her, I will break your face."

"That'll never happen," I replied. "Just be cool about it, ok?"

His glare gave me little hope, and then my stomach jumped up into my throat at the sight of Liv walking into the training room.

"She's here, isn't she?" he asked. "Don't answer that. I can tell by the stupid look on your face that she is. She's going to destroy you. Again."

Jax stepped away toward the main mat in the center of the room. He had every right to be upset, but nothing was going to come of this so he needed to chill. I twirled my Bo in my fingers and went back to my routine. I was so preoccupied with pretending I didn't see Olivia, that I didn't notice Devy standing in front of me until he grabbed my Bo in midair and yanked it out of my hands.

"Sorry, sir," I said immediately.

"Sorry for what, exactly?" he replied, his intimidating expression not changing in the slightest.

"I...uh...wasn't concentrating."

"And yet you were wielding your weapon like an unruly ape."

It was hard not to look down at the ground, but if I broke eye contact with him, that would have made him even angrier. "Yes, sir. I'm sorry."

"I know there's a distraction here, Will," he said, and my heart started to race. "But I have put too much training into you to have you fall apart now."

"I'm not falling apart," I replied defensively, causing him to take a step closer.

"Will, you never even noticed I was there until I disarmed you. If you cannot handle..."

"I can handle it."

"Then prove it," he replied and thrust the Bo staff into my chest.

"Everything ok?" Liv asked, breaking the tension between me and Devin.

"Good morning, monk...damn it...Olivia. Good morning, Olivia, I hate calling you that," Devy said in a frustrated tone, but then forced himself to lighten up. "What do we owe the honor of your presence this morning?"

"I was hoping," she began, but then looked uncomfortably over at me, "that...I could talk to Will for a minute."

"No," Devy replied sharply, causing Liv's eyes to widen. "He needs to get his head out of his ass, so perhaps later. However, I'd like to work with you today."

"Oh, Devy, thanks, but I don't think…"

"If you don't like it, then leave my training room." She didn't move. "Good. I'd actually like you to work with your brother."

"Uh, sir, I'm not sure that's a good idea."

He gave me a look that turned my blood cold. "Good thing it isn't up to you, *trainee* Ryan. How about you get back to work, and perhaps keep the Bo in your hand this time?"

Nothing like being stripped down completely by your mentor in front of the last person you wanted to witness it. Even though I knew putting the twins together would end in disaster, there was only one reply.

"Yes, sir," I said and stepped away.

I'll admit, keeping my attention on my own work was difficult since I had always been the buffer between the twins. I could sense when things were going to go south with them, and that sixth sense was sounding an alarm so loud that I could barely concentrate. Across the room on the center mat, Jax threw his arms up in the air and paced around in a circle.

"Let's just get it over with, Jack," Liv shouted.

"Don't push it, Livy."

"Both of you need to shut up and take your stances," Devy commanded, causing the others in the training room to take notice.

Reluctantly the twins complied, but hardly a second went by before Jax charged forward. Liv held her own for the first few hits, but when she tried doing a roundhouse kick, Jax caught her leg under his left arm, and then threw her down to the ground. From the sly smile, I could tell he enjoyed it.

Liv was slow to get up, but Devy was instantly in her ear with what to fix. Once she shook it off, she hit her stance again. This time she didn't wait for Jax to come after her, and came out swinging. Seeing her whip her arms and legs at her brother brought a smile to my face.

But that smile dropped quickly when Jax got in a hit to her nose. Her head flinched back and her hands flew to her face. Then they froze. They stood facing each other, only their eyes and corners of their mouths flinched. They were yelling at each other in their heads, I knew those looks anywhere, and I was pretty sure I knew what they were arguing about.

I took a step forward, but Devy waved me away. Devy may be the coven leader, but there were things he just didn't fully understand, especially with these two. After another few seconds, you could see their lips almost forming the words they were screaming in their heads.

This needed to end. Ignoring Devy, I ran onto the mat just as Jax lunged at his sister, but I was able to get my arms around his waist and pulled him back a foot or so.

"Alright, alright, both of you calm..." I began to say, but at that moment both of them raised their arms and bright white beams of light shot out of their hands throwing all three of us back...

"William? William, can you hear me?"

I knew that was my name, and I thought I recognized the voice, but it still took my brain a few seconds to tell my eyes to stretch open. When they finally did, I found Cam hovering over me with a relieved smile.

"Welcome back, Wills."

"Wills? Someone write that down," I said softly.

"I have called you Wills before," Cam replied with a smirk.

"I'm not sure about that," I replied and then grunted from the pain coming from my head, and then registered the pain in my back and shoulders. "What happened?"

"We are trying to figure that out," he answered over the sounds of the twins yelling at each other in the distance. "Do you think you can sit up?"

I nodded and rolled onto my side, waiting a moment before pushing myself up to a sitting position. Cam caught me on the other side and the blood started to pound in my head so hard that stars sparkled in front of me.

"We should get you over to see your father."

"No, I'm fine," I said and took his arms as he helped me to stand. My hand instinctively went to the back of my head, and I flinched from the tenderness. "I remember trying to pull Jax away from Liv."

"Yes, apparently the twins have found a new power," he began, but then our attention was pulled by those very twins still yelling at each other from opposite sides of the room. Niall was standing next to Liv, his hand hovering in front of her to keep her in control while Devy had to practically wrap himself around Jax as he shouted and flailed about.

"Enough! All of you in my office this instant. Jackson, help William," Cam commanded and Jax quickly stepped off the mat as the others filed out.

"Sorry, man," he said softly, not even able to make eye contact with me.

"What happened? I just remember white lights, or an explosion," I replied, finding it a little harder than usual to see straight and walk.

"I don't know what that was," he replied softly, helping me around the corner to avoid the oncoming hallway traffic.

Was Cam and Devy's office always this far away? Were the walls spinning? Maybe I had a concussion. Shit.

When we rounded the second corner, the office door was a welcomed sight, but considering the look on Cam's face as we entered, I'm sure the twins weren't feeling quite the same way. Cam stood in front of the fireplace at the far-right end of the office. It was usually a place of celebration or deep discussion, but today we were transported to our childhoods when we'd get caught doing something we shouldn't be doing, which was pretty often.

"Who wants to start?" Cam began sternly. "Who would like to tell me why I walked in on my adult children behaving like wild animals?"

"Ada, before you lay into us, can I ask why the hell he's here?" Jax asked and gestured to Niall who was standing on the other side of Liv.

"You assaulted my girlfriend," Niall began in his pompous sounding accent, "I believe I have every right to be here."

"That actually makes no sense at all," Jax replied. "I'm not talking if he's here, Ada."

"Jackson, please…"

"I don't see you asking Will to leave," Niall interrupted.

"Will is family!" Jax shouted. "And we almost killed him, so I think he's allowed to be here."

Niall pursed his lips and then released a loud, frustrated sigh. "I will stay as long as Will does."

I put my hands up. "I'm fine with leaving."

"No," Jax shouted. "Ada…"

"William, perhaps it is best we have someone take you to the Facility to see your father."

I nodded, and a bit of nausea came over me. "I'll find Jared and see if he can take me. Just uh…maybe let me know if you figure it out?

Cam nodded and eyed the twins. With a wave, I turned and left the office with Niall nipping at my heels. I knew I wasn't going to be able to search the manor for Jared, so I took advantage of the bench in the hallway and sat down.

Niall began to pace in front of me. "Have they always despised each other?"

"The twins?" I said and pulled my phone from my pocket.

He nodded. "I can see why Olivia was hesitant about coming home. Jackson is just horrible to her. Have they shown that power before?"

I scrolled through my phone, found Jared's name, and texted him to come get me. In my current state, I wasn't able to text and talk to Niall at the same time, and that seemed to frustrate him.

"Niall, could you stop pacing? I might throw up on you," I said honestly, and unfortunately he decided to sit down next to me. Could this get any worse? Was this punishment for kissing Liv last night? "To answer your question, no, they have never shown that power before, and thank god because if they had, they probably would have killed each other when we were in high school. But just so you know, they don't despise each other."

He laughed. "From what I have seen, I have to disagree."

"Their bond is so deep that it's actually hard for them to get away from each other. It's like wearing a wool sweater that's three sizes too small and constantly scratches away at you. Plus, it doesn't help that Jax is actually more emotional than Liv, and he doesn't process his feelings well."

"You seem to know them well."

"That comes from knowing them all my life."

"Considering how long she's known you, it is odd that Olivia has rarely spoken of you."

It was a nice dig. I kissed your girlfriend last night, you blimey bastard. Thankfully Jared came around the corner at that moment.

"Have I suddenly become your errand boy?" he asked.

"I think the twins gave me a concussion. Can you take me to the Facility? I shouldn't drive."

"Why did they give you a concussion?"

I shrugged. "It's a Monday."

He laughed and waved me forward. "Come on then, I don't have all day."

I stood up from the bench, but then the room started to spin. Jared instantly caught me.

"You weren't kidding," he said. "Maybe it was better when the twins were separated by an ocean."

"My thoughts exactly," Niall replied which caused Jared to glare at him.

"Always a pleasure, Niall," I said and stepped away from the bench with Jared's protective arm around my back.

As we rounded the corner into the main corridor, Jared said, "Is it just in my American DNA to hate the British guy?" I laughed lightly. "Seriously, I just want to throw some tea at him and say 'go back home, Red Coat!'"

"Yeah, that might be a little much. Although, if you do, please let me be there when you do it."

"Wow, Will Ryan coming to my side of trouble, you must really have a head injury."

"No, I just really hate that fucking Red Coat."

Chapter Fourteen

Olivia

My father was the most level-headed and collected person I knew. Even in the most pressure-filled situations, he would be the even-keeled person in the room. So when an occasion arose where he lost his temper, or even slightly raised his voice, you knew you had really messed up. Although, this was not completely my fault, and I was simply defending myself against Jack. My palms still tingled from the energy burst that exploded between us. We had never done that before or even knew it was possible. Even through his anger, I could tell that Jack was just as freaked out about it as I was.

"I know that being the children of a leader of the Warrior coven brings added pressure, and because of that I have allowed both of you some leeway when it comes to your behavior. However, I do expect, no I *require* you to show some decorum and respect when you are under my roof. It has been hard enough on your mother to watch the two of you treat each other so badly, I cannot imagine how this will affect her once she hears what happened. Thank goodness she did not see the two of you try to annihilate each other as I did. You could have killed William. Let us hope all he has is a concussion. Now, one of you will tell me what started all of this."

Jack didn't even wait a beat before he pointed at me. "She kissed Will."

"Jack!" I screeched.

Ada's eyes bore into me and I was mortified. "Olivia, is that true?"

"Yes, it's true," Jack answered. "He told me himself. She's only been here a couple of days, Ada, and she's destroying everything in her wake."

"That's a bit dramatic, isn't it?" I said. "What happened between me and Will is none of your business."

"None of my business?" he shouted. "He could barely function this morning because he was so distracted by what you did. You come home, wreak havoc, and then you'll take off tomorrow and leave the rest of us to deal with the damage you left behind. Again."

"What are you talking about? Damn it, Jack, you can't blame me for every little thing that has ever gone wrong for you."

"This has nothing to do with me, and it has everything to do with Will. Leave. Him. Alone. You literally came here with the douchebag Brit, and you still couldn't keep your filthy paws to yourself."

"It wasn't like that…"

"Enough," Ada snapped. "Putting what happened with William aside, I want to know what happened between the two of you. Where did that energy come from?"

Both Jack and I shook our heads, and rubbed our hands at the same time. I assumed his hands were still tingling as much as mine.

"How did it manifest?" We shrugged. "What were you thinking before it happened?"

Jack rolled his eyes and answered, "I wanted to push her like I do Vamps. That's what I was thinking about."

"Olivia?"

"I…I just felt like something was coming at me and I put my hands up to defend myself, and then it just…happened."

"So perhaps you have had this power all along, you simply have not tried to kill each other until today." Neither of us responded, or could even look Ada in the eye. "Very well," he sighed and rubbed his eyes. "Jackson, apologize to your sister."

"What!" he shouted.

"Apologize this instant," Ada snapped.

"But she…"

"Jackson, no matter what may have happened with Will, I will not tolerate you attacking your sister in any way. Is that clear? Without your sister we never would have found you in Aidan's camp. You owe her your life, son." Jackson shuttered and looked down at the floor. "Do not smirk,

Olivia," Ada said and narrowed his eyes at me. "While you were going to school and traveling around the world, your brother has kept his life here in order to serve and help others who would be harmed like he was.

"Both of you have sacrificed, and neither has a right to attack the other. You may not need to like each other, but you do need to love one another. There is no bond closer than what you two have, and it is truly devastating what has happened between you. Now I say again, Jackson, apologize to your sister."

Jack raised his eyes, but didn't look at me. "Sorry."

"Olivia, apologize to your brother."

"I'm sorry, Jack," I mumbled.

Ada sighed. "I suppose that is the most I can expect. From now on, you will be pleasant to one another, especially when your mother is within earshot. We will look further into this new power, but you will never use it against each other ever again. Is that clear?"

"Yes, Ada," we replied in unison.

"You are both adults now, do not make me have to treat you like children because you are behaving as such."

"Yes, Ada."

Ada turned away from us. "Jackson, you may go. I need to speak with your sister alone."

Jack nodded, gave me a scowl, and then left the office.

"Ada, let me explain…"

"Sit, Olivia," he interrupted, splaying his hands on the mantle and looking like he was every one of his three-hundred years. I squeezed into the corner of the couch, and pulled a pillow into my lap for comfort and protection. Slowly he turned around with his arms crossed in front of his chest, and then leaned back up against the mantle. "I have purposely stayed out of my children's personal lives, even when I disagree with some of the choices being made. But some things are beyond the pale."

"Ada…"

"Did you kiss William?"

I sighed and squeezed the pillow to my chest. "Yes, but it's nobody's business."

"I beg to differ," he said tersely. "Because not fifteen minutes ago Niall came to me and asked for your hand in marriage."

My heart jumped into my throat. "Wha-what did you say?"

"I gave him my blessing, of course," he said and raked his hand through his hair. "What was I supposed to say, Olivia? You brought him here to meet us, there was an assumption that you were serious about him. You even told your mother you thought he might ask. If I had known it would only take you two days to fall out of love with him..."

"I haven't fallen...that's not what happened."

Ada took a step forward and dropped his arms. "Then why, Olivia? Why would you kiss another man?"

"I don't know!" I replied loudly. "Since I got home, everything's been so messed up. I want to crawl out of my skin. Everyone keeps questioning everything about who I am now, and then when I try to be who I was, Niall gets upset and feels intimidated and takes it out on me. I'm so confused and conflicted...I just...found myself at Will's club last night. We talked a lot, and for the first time in a long time I felt...comfortable. I didn't have to be anyone to Will, I could just be Liv."

When I looked up, Ada was holding a tissue out to me. I took it from him and dabbed the corners of my eyes. Ada sat down next to me and I instantly threw the pillow aside and laid across his chest. His hand rested on the back of my head and I was instantly brought back into the safety of my father's arms like when I was a child.

"Lovey," he said softly, "you should always feel comfortable being who you are no matter who you are with. You should not be acting a certain way to please certain people, and act differently to please others. Those who truly love you, love you for who and what you are. And what do you mean Niall is taking his frustrations out on you."

"Nothing," I replied quickly. "We're just arguing. It would be hard for any man to be with someone more powerful than him and who could kick his ass."

"Your mother is ten times stronger and more talented than I am, and I celebrate that. I am prideful of the fact that your mother could kick my ass. Well, in fact she has. Several times."

I laughed a little into his chest since he rarely swore, and it always sounded odd when he did. "You're different, Ada."

"How so?"

I rose from his side and wiped my eyes. "No one is like you, Ada. You're the most understanding, most perfect, loving husband. What you and Mom have is unobtainable."

"Olivia, I can attest that I am not those things all the time. You can ask your mother," he laughed, but then looked at me with worried eyes.

"Lovey, your mother and I have gone through some very difficult times, some of which I was unsure if we would make it through. When we were at our lowest, we found our way back because deep down we loved each other. It was very emotional and hard work. That is marriage, and that is why it is a decision that should not be taken lightly. If you are already seeking the companionship of other men..."

"I was not out trolling the streets for guys, Ada. I just...ended up there. My brain was telling me I needed to talk to Will."

"And that is even worse," he replied and rubbed his face in frustration. "I would rather you had kissed a stranger on the street than William."

"How can you say that?"

"Olivia, you have not lived here for almost five years. You have no idea how sensitive of a situation this is. William is...delicate."

"Delicate? Really, Ada? You'd make a delicate person a Warrior?" He flinched and his eyes grew wide. "Yes, Ada, I know about it, I found out yesterday. I can't believe you'd actually Turn him."

"What William chooses to do with his life is his business, Olivia."

"You're lying to his parents, your best friends."

"At his request, Olivia," he replied as he stood from the couch and stepped back in front of the fireplace. "But we will not change the subject here. You came here with a young man who loves you and wants to marry you. Last night you kissed another man who has had, and may still have feelings for you. How do you think this is affecting William? He did not take it well when you rejected him. Your brother has reason to worry, we all do. You need to decide what you want to do with Niall, and I am asking you to stay away from William."

"But Will is..."

"Stay away from him, Olivia," he snapped. "I have enough problems to deal with as it is."

Ada raked his fingers through his hair again. I'd never seen him look so tired.

"Like what?"

"Nothing you need to worry about, lovey."

"No, Ada, something is bothering you."

He sighed slowly. "The coven is going through some challenges."

"Challenges? Is someone attacking us again? Please don't say we have another Aidan Pierce."

He shook his head and sat back down next to me. "No, no, nothing like that. Actually, it is the absence of someone like Aidan that is the problem."

"How can that be a problem?"

He smirked. "You need to remember that with a few exceptions, myself included, our Warriors are soldiers and fighters to their core. Since the war with Aidan, we have actually had peace. Little skirmishes here and there, of course, but nothing of substance. When soldiers have nothing to fight for or against, they get restless." He paused and pulled his hand down his face. "I would say we hit restless a few years back. Now we are getting to a point of infighting and pointing fingers at me and Devin."

"Oh my god, Ada."

He placed his hand on top of mine. "Olivia, do not fret, everything will be fine. Although avoiding a scandal that involves the coven leader's daughter could help alleviate some unneeded stress."

I sighed and pulled at the fat curl that was tickling my cheek. "I'm sorry, Ada, I don't know what to do."

The office door opened, and like a graceful bird, Mémé floated into the room. "See, Eri, I told you I would find zhem," she said happily and waved Eris inside. Unfortunately, Niall took their entry as a sign that he could join them.

"Mémé, what are you doing here?" I asked as Ada and I stood from the couch to face her.

"I know when my petite singe needs me, your Mémé always knows."

Ada smirked and leaned into my ear. "I chose long ago never to question what your grandmother knows and why."

"Well isn't this a wonderful chance meeting," Niall began and rested his hand on Eri's shoulder. "Perhaps we could all grab a bite together or something."

Eri narrowed his eyes and turned his head slowly. "I don't eat," he replied flatly causing Niall to slide his hand off of his shoulder.

Mémé stepped in between them and gave Eri a glare before turning to Niall. "What a lovely thought, Niall, but I believe my petite singe needs a bit of Mémé time. You understand, non?"

"Olivia has had a tough morning, Sera, I should be with her. *You* understand, no?"

What was he doing? How could he be so condescending to my grandmother. Use that tone with me, fine, but not my Mémé, and certainly not in front of Eri.

But before I could say anything, Mémé flipped her long, gray hair over her shoulder and gave a smile. "How supportive you are," she said sweetly. "But you have had my granddaughter all zhese months, it is time for her grand-mère to be with her. But zhat means you can have some personal time with Eris."

"It does?" Eri said with wide eyes.

"Won't zhat be fun, Eri," she said. "Go, go, have fun, vite, vite," she said as she practically pushed the two of them out of the room. When the door was shut, she turned quickly around. "I thought zhey would never leave. Come, come, we don't have much time."

"We don't?"

"Again, lovey, I tend not to question your grandmother."

I nodded and stepped around the couch. "Oui, oui, I'm coming."

"Olivia, one thing before you go," Ada said and I stopped just before the door, "could you please allow your uncle Devin to call you Monkey on occasion? Even if it is in private. I cannot listen to him complain about it any longer. You know how he is with change."

I nodded. "Ok, but just him…and you, but that's it."

"I believe we were the only two who called you that," he said with a smirk.

"But just not when we're in front of everyone. I'm still an adult."

"Of course," he replied. "And remember what we spoke about, there are some things you must figure out, and quickly."

I nodded and melted into my grandmother's chest, her arms coming around me and filling me with a sense of love and light. After a few moments she shifted me into her side and pulled me out into the corridor.

"Where should we go?" she asked.

There was only one place.

There was no better place to clear your head than Daddy O's house. Even though my parents owned the house, and he had been dead for many years, it was still Daddy O's house, and not just to me. Even Mémé and Eri, who were the only ones who stayed here regularly, would say they were staying at Ollie's. He was a man that somehow still lived among us even after his death. I could still picture him hovering near the stove to steal a taste of whatever Mom or Maddy was cooking. Memories of the last night I was here kept flashing in my head – having a fit in the living room, screaming and crying at Ada in the driveway, saying horrible things to Will.

Mémé had fully stocked the house in case of an emergency. I took Ada's advice and didn't question it.

"When your mother was pregnant, I made her so much guacamole I thought for sure the two of you would come out green like avocadoes," she said in French as she stirred the fresh bowl of guacamole one last time and then placed the bowl in front of me.

"Guacamole, really?" I replied as I scooped a large amount onto a chip, and shoved it into my mouth. "It's hard to imagine Mom eating."

Mémé laughed lightly. "Ah yes, whenever there was a crisis, guacamole had to be made, and ice cream needed to be in the freezer. It seems you are more like your mother than you would like to admit."

I rolled my eyes and dug my spoon back into the ice cream container sitting in front of me. "Let's just keep that to ourselves. And it would be nice if we could keep this whole Will thing from her as well. I don't need her judging me."

"If you say so, but I think she may understand more than you think."

"Miss-perfect-in-every-way Brianna would never do what I did."

She shrugged. "If you say so," she replied and that made me think that maybe my mom hadn't been as perfect as she always portrayed.

I scooped another large amount of guacamole onto a chip and ate it in one bite. I couldn't blame Mom for always wanting Mémé's guacamole, it was divine. "Is it possible to be one person with one guy, and another person with a different guy?"

"No," she replied and ate a big spoonful of ice cream. "Then who are you being real to?"

"Niall," I answered as I brought the ice cream spoon to my mouth, and I froze. Niall would be mortified if he saw me eating like this. Will, on the other hand, would have been smiling and giving me his portion. I dropped the spoon into the carton. "Well, maybe not. I was fine and happy until I came home. Shouldn't I be working to be a better version of myself with Niall rather than reverting back to my teenage self?"

"Do you believe you are a better person with Niall?"

"Aren't I?"

"No," she replied flatly.

"No need to hide your feelings there, Mémé."

She pushed up from the counter and put her hands on her hips. "You do not benefit from me lying to you. You never would have gone to see Will if life with Niall was so wonderful."

"A moment of weakness."

"How was the kiss?"

"Really nice," I replied and caught myself. Mémé raised an eyebrow at me which made me sigh and put my head down on the table. "Mémé, what do I do?"

"Have you spoken to Will?"

"I tried to, but Devy wouldn't let me and then Jack shot me with a photon beam."

She laughed lightly. "Talk with Will, maybe he wishes to forget about it, and the two of you can move on. If that is what you want."

I lifted my head from the table. "Of course that's what I want."

"Then why are you so sad?"

I went to object until I remembered you can't lie about your feelings to an Empath. Just then the front door opened and Eri stamped his way inside.

"Eri, my darling, what are you doing back?" Mémé said, switching back to English.

Eri stood very straight and proud, but with very tense lips. "My presence didn't seem necessary. He talked and talked and talked about me, to me! My life is my life, and I do not need some puny Englishman telling stories about me, and incorrectly. Again!" he shouted. "Olivia, I thought you were gonna to speak to him."

"I did. I'll talk to him again."

"Eri," Mémé warned. "Be kind."

He took in a deep breath. "Little one, I am sorry, but I will not be left alone with the Englishman again. Punish me how you like, my love, I stand by my decision."

With a huff, Eri walked dramatically toward the back bedroom.

I sighed and looked at my grandmother. "I'll go talk to Will."

"Zhat is a good idea, ma petite singe," she replied and patted my hand. "And perhaps you could refrain from zhe kissing."

"Fine, but I'm taking the guacamole."

Chapter Fifteen
Will

Loss of consciousness? Yep. Headache? Yep. Dizziness? Yep. Vomiting? Oh my god yeah. Hysterical mother escorting you to the medical wing as though you had a gunshot wound? Unfortunately, yes. With the exception of that last one, all symptoms of a concussion. Even though Dad agreed, he still performed all the tests required to confirm. Laying down and being still seemed to calm the nausea, although my head was still pounding.

What a mess. This was my fault. If I had just kept my mouth shut, Jax wouldn't have freaked out on Liv, and I wouldn't have been hit by the twin's newfound laser beam. I had to stop thinking about it, it was making my head hurt even more. What a mess, an absolute mess.

There was a soft knock at the door, and a moment later my dad and his nurse Jeanie stepped inside. Even at his age, my dad was fit, had all his hair with a little gray mixed in, and to most people he was the coolest guy at Facility West. He had been a badass emergency physician in Boston dealing with gunshot wounds and violence only seen in big cities, which meant he was always calm under pressure. Jeanie, his head nurse who had worked at Facility West since it was built, was short, plump, and had had short grey hair for as long as I could remember. She was my dad's right hand. Jeanie kept the clinic running and everyone in check. Despite her short stature, you didn't mess with Jeanie.

"Well, it's confirmed, you have a concussion," Dad announced.

"I'm shocked," I replied softly.

Dad smiled as he hovered over me. "It's good you knew the signs. I guess your education didn't go to waste."

It was a dig I was used to from him. "Please tell me I don't need to rest and stay still for a few days, because that's not going to work."

"I figured. So, if you're comfortable, I could give you a small dose of Healer's blood. The concussion is pretty minor, so the blood should clear things out pretty quickly."

"Yeah, let's do it," I replied.

"Jeanie, can you grab a dose and an IV kit?"

She nodded and patted my leg. "We'll have you fixed up in no time."

"Thanks, Jeanie," I said before she was out the door.

My dad looked back at me and asked, "Now, how did this happen again? I had a little trouble hearing you over your mother's screams."

I wanted to laugh, but it would hurt too much. "The twins were fighting, I tried to break them up, and then this stream of light blew out from their hands, and I went flying."

"Stream of light?"

"Ball of energy, laser beam, I don't know. It was scary powerful."

His eyes narrowed and darted from side to side, it was his thinking face. His brain was going through all the possible explanations and it always looked like he was reading an imaginary book.

"They weren't able to do that before, were they?"

I started to shake my head, but he put his hand against the side of my face to keep me still. "No, it's new. Neither of them knew they could do it."

"Thank god. Can you imagine if they were able to do that to each other when they were little?"

"There wouldn't be a building left standing in San Francisco if that were the case."

He laughed, but then went quiet and shook his head. "I always warned you not to get between them. They'll heal, you won't, son. Today more than proves my point."

I sighed. "Could we push the lectures off for one day, Pop? I have a concussion, you know."

His lips folded inside of his mouth, it was his judgmental face. My father couldn't hide his feelings very well. The door opened and the pleasant distraction named Jeanie came in with a small bag of blood and an

IV. But her presence didn't stop my dad from airing his grievances. "All I'm saying, Will, is that it's time to stop playing in their world. You're not like them and you're getting hurt. It's time to think about a real career, son."

"Dr. Ryan," Jeanie interrupted, "they need you in room two. Jacob Hester has a head gash."

"Was he flying again?"

"Unfortunately."

He nodded and squeezed my shoulder. "Jeanie will set you up, kiddo. The blood should help pretty quickly, but take it easy today. Ok?"

"Sure," I replied and he left the room. "Jacob Hester can fly?"

Jeanie shook her head and laughed. "No, but that doesn't stop him from testing himself."

"Nice."

Jeanie hung the small bag of blood on an IV hook and then swabbed the inside of my elbow with an alcohol swab. "Make a fist," she instructed and I obeyed. "You should tell your dad the truth about becoming a Warrior."

My eyes flew open and then squinted close at the feeling of the needle going into my vein. After taking a breath, and letting the pounding in my head die down, I replied, "Not sure what you mean, Jeanie."

She laughed and secured the IV to my arm with tape. "Honey, I think your parents are the only ones that don't know. Or more so, they don't want to know. I can't believe they're actually buying your cockamamie story about needing to train with the Warriors every morning in order to stay fit enough to teach here."

My eyes were wide and fixated on her in shock. How did she know? How could she, and potentially others, know? When I didn't respond right away, she raised an eyebrow, daring me to answer. My head hurt so much that I couldn't think of what to say. Finally, she opened the valve to the IV, and the Healer's blood began to flow into me.

Jeanie patted my arm. "This shouldn't take too long. I'll come check on you in a minute."

"Jeanie, wait, how did you find out?"

She smirked. "Jared has a big mouth."

"Damn it, Jared," I said under my breath. "You're not going to tell my parents, are you?"

"It's not my business," she replied. "I've worked for your father for twenty years, I know he pushes you hard, too hard sometimes. No doubt he and your mother are going to be upset when you finally tell them, but they will be crushed if they find out that everyone else knew before they did."

"I'm afraid I'll lose them."

"You may for a little while, but that's their loss. They will come around eventually," she replied firmly and patted my arm. "I'll be back in a few minutes to take the IV out."

"Is it supposed to burn?" I asked as she turned away.

"Yes?"

"Wh-why is that a question? Is it supposed to burn or not?"

She laughed to herself and opened the door. "If it gets unbearable, hit the call button. Be back in a few."

As the blood flowed through the IV, I could feel it moving from the veins, through my heart, into the arteries, and then fan out from there. The science side of me was geeking out at how quickly the blood pumped through my body. It wasn't long until the burning reached my head and within seconds, the pounding headache started to lessen. Slowly but surely, as the burning began to cease, so did the rest of my symptoms. Healer's blood truly was a magic bullet.

A few minutes later, as promised, Jeanie came back and removed the IV from my arm, gave me a superhero band-aid, and sent me on my way. Just as I was about to step out of the medical wing, my dad called from behind me.

"Hey, kiddo," he said as he caught up to me, and then put his hands on my face. "Let me check you before you go."

"I'm good, Dad. Nausea is gone."

He didn't listen and shined his pen light in my eyes. "You should take it easy. You could still feel the effects for a while."

I pulled his hands down. "I'll take it easy, no need to worry."

"You're my kid, I always worry," he replied with a caring smile. "Come back if the symptoms start to resurface."

"I will."

"And be prepared for your mother to watch your every move."

I groaned. "I hadn't thought about that. Maybe you could tell her I'm in quarantine? At least for an hour?"

He laughed. "That would never work. Your mother would risk getting any disease to be in quarantine with you. But I'll think of something."

"Thanks, Pop," I said, hugging him and receiving a pat on the back.

Now came time to cross the gauntlet. Could I get through the entire atrium without my mom seeing me, that was the question. Utilizing my Warrior training, I hid behind pillars and plants, used groups of people to camouflage me, and eventually made it across the wide atrium to the training rooms. Teaching so many classes and private lessons, I was given my own training room that had an office in the back. It was still a couple of hours before my first class, so I would definitely utilize the couch in the office to rest beforehand. Although the acute pain had ceased, I was still foggy and sluggish.

When I stepped inside my training room, I flinched at the sight of a woman standing in the middle of the room. It took me another moment to realize who it was.

"Tosh?" I asked and she turned around with a forced smile. "Did I forget a lesson with Braydon?"

She shook her head and sighed. "No, I um…we need to pull him from everything, actually."

"Why? Is everything…"

"His eyes started changing," she interrupted, her eyes turning glassy with tears. "It started a few days ago, and the full moon is next week…" she paused and wiped a tear from her cheek. "Sorry."

"No need to be sorry," I said and hugged her.

After a few seconds she stepped away and wiped her eyes clean. "It shouldn't be a shock, he's fourteen, same age as Richie when it started for him. I guess I was just hoping…but…here we are. Two pubescent werewolves in the middle of a metropolis. One was risky enough, now it's just too dangerous."

"So what does this mean for the family?"

She sighed. "Beckett wants to pack up everything and move to the country house full time, even if it's just until both boys are fully acclimated and under control. Braydon's probably more upset about having to be homeschooled than the fact that he'll be phasing soon. That and…Will, he just loves you. Both boys love you. It was so hard on Richie when we had to pull him, but Braydon will take this even harder."

"That's because he was so talented, Tosh. Are you sure you have to pull him out? Maybe I could train him at the manor, or at your house, I could train both boys."

She shook her head. "Despite their smiles, no one except the family wants a wolf in the manor. If we move to the country house, that'll be way too far for you to travel. But all that aside, it's too dangerous for you, for everyone."

"What does Victor say?"

She shrugged. "He agrees with Beckett, but said not to do anything with the house here until he gets back."

"Gets back?"

"Yeah, he said he was on vacation with Alex and Kyla, and wouldn't be back for a little while."

"Hmm, wonder what that's about."

Victor didn't just go on vacation. Something was definitely up, but it was also above my paygrade.

The door to the training room opened, and the flash of black curly hair made my breath catch in my throat.

"Oh, you have a class, I won't keep you," Tosh said and took a step back.

"Ah, no," I replied as Liv fully stepped inside the training room, oddly with a bowl and spoon in her hand. "She's definitely not a student of mine."

Tosh quirked her eyebrow and turned around. "Livy?

"Toshy," Liv said with a gasp, running to her and squeezing her tightly. When she finally released her, she asked, "What are you doing here? Is…is everything ok? You look upset."

Tosh shook her head and gestured to me. "I'm sure Will can fill you in. I'm sorry we couldn't make it to your welcome home party, there's just a lot going on."

"Well, maybe we can catch up soon?"

"I'd like that," she replied and looked back at me. Her eyes became glassy once again before she kissed me on the cheek and hugged me tightly. "Thank you."

"I'll see you soon," I replied and then released her, looking her squarely in the eyes. "I mean that. We'll figure something out."

She nodded, but I could tell she was skeptical. Once Tosh left the training room, Liv immediately looked at me with concern.

"What's going on?"

"What's with the bowl and spoon?" I asked instead of answering her.

She looked down at her hands and replied, "I had guacamole."

"Am I supposed to know what that means?"

"Mémé made me guacamole, and I decided to take it to-go."

"And you walked here?"

"Walked a little, ran a little."

"Walked a little, ran a little, with a bowl of guacamole."

"I wasn't about to let it go to waste. So why was Tosh so upset?"

"Brayden, her youngest, started the wolf transition. They may need to leave the city. But on another topic, why are you here?"

She looked down at the floor. "I wanted to see how you were doing after what happened."

"What happened yesterday or today?"

She took a second before lifting her head and responding, "Both, I guess."

"Let's talk in my office," I said and waved her forward.

"Your office? That's impressive."

I shook my head and stepped to the door at the far end of the room. "Come on, your bowl can come too."

She gave an awkward laugh. "It was just an impulse grab. I don't know what I was thinking."

"Liv, you don't need to justify yourself to me," I said and held my office door open for her.

She paused in the doorway, gave me a thankful nod, and stepped inside. Immediately she went for the couch, which was disappointing since I knew I couldn't trust myself to sit next to her. So, I decided to lean against the edge of the desk that sat across from couch. It wasn't comfortable, but it was too risky to be that close to her.

"This is nice," she said as she gave the office a cursory glance.

"You wanted to talk, Olivia, so talk," I said. "I have a class in a couple of hours and I'd like to rest a little if I can."

She placed her empty bowl with the spoon clanging around inside on the small table next to the couch. "How's your head?"

"Concussed," I replied and she flinched. "I'll be fine. Dad gave me some Healer's blood, but it's...a weird feeling."

"Then sit down," she said and gestured to the cushion next to her.

"I'm fine. Can we just get on with this really awkward conversation?"

She looked down at her hands again. "I...I just wanted to say I'm sorry for last night. What I did was wrong, and I'm sure really confusing. Obviously, everyone is mad at me about it, and I'm...I'm just really sorry."

I sighed and took in a slow breath before responding, "First thing, I wasn't planning on telling Jax anything, but he knew I was keeping something and tortured me until I told him. I didn't think he'd get *that* upset about it. Second thing, don't make it sound like you assaulted me last night. It was a kiss, Liv. I'm just curious as to why you did it."

"That seems to be the question of the century," she replied and fell back into the couch cushions. "I don't know, to be honest. I was emotional and vulnerable and…it…just seemed like the thing to do at that moment. And now Ada and Jack-Jack are screaming at me and telling me that I have to completely stay away from you."

"Is that what they said?" I asked with a twinge of anger. "No, you know what, it doesn't matter. Can we talk about the fact that you lied to me five years ago? Liv, you said some horrible things to me that night which put me in such a depression that…" I paused and put my head in my hand. The blood was pumping so hard and fast that it was making me dizzy again. "You could have just said that you didn't feel that way about me. Or that you did, but you were going abroad to study."

"I did!" she said defensively. "I did say that, and you kept pushing. So I just said the worst things I could think of so you'd hate me. I was miserable so I lashed out. Don't I get a little leeway for being a stupid kid? I felt like I had no one."

"You had me, Liv. You have always had me in your corner. You used to sneak into my room at night to talk to me about whatever fight you were having with your mother, or the latest thing Jack-Jack did to you. It was exhausting being your friend, literally because you'd keep me up all night talking, but it was worth it to me. And you decided in a single moment to tear me apart.

"How many people do you know who can say they literally have a friend they've known their entire life? We had that. You, me, and Jack-Jack, but you tore it apart in one second. Then suddenly you want to turn around in one day and go back. It's a mindfuck, Liv.

"And on top of that, you bring this guy and parade him in front of all of us pretending that you have this perfect relationship, when in reality you don't. Then you pour all your relationship problems on me like lemon juice in an open wound. And yet, I take it because I'm a stupid bastard who for some reason likes to be psychologically tortured."

I stopped and took a breath, unsure where the diarrhea of the mouth came from. Liv sat frozen on the couch, her eyes wide in shock.

"I'm sorry," she said with a quivering voice.

"So, is that it?"

She shook her head and her covered her eyes. "He's going to ask me to marry him."

I let out a sardonic laugh. "Of course he does. It's why he's here."

"If he asked me two days ago, I would have said yes right away, but now...I almost had a panic attack when Ada told me."

"Shouldn't that tell you something?" She narrowed her eyes at me. "What? If it took you two days to fall out of love with him, then you weren't really in love with him in the first place."

"I haven't fallen out of love...I'm just really confused."

"About what?"

"You!" she shouted. "I do love Niall, I did bring him here to meet my family, and I thought I found someone who could put up with all the freakish things about me."

"But he doesn't know you," I interrupted. "You assimilated to everything he wanted you to be rather than him love you for who you are."

"I see that now," she replied with emotion in her voice. "I've been thinking all this time there's no one who could accept me fully for what I was and then..." she paused and gestured toward me, "...I've had you, right there all this time. I mean...didn't you feel...something...last night?"

My fingers dug in underneath the desk's edge and it took all my strength to shake my head. "No," I lied, unable to look her in the eye.

Liv jumped up from the couch and stepped in front of me. "Then why did you kiss me?"

It took nearly ten seconds for me to reply, "Doesn't matter."

"Really?" she said angrily. "I've been crucified by everyone today because I kissed you, and no one knows that you kissed me too. I have been constantly asked why I did it, so I think it's only fair if you tell me why you did it too."

She was only a few inches away from me now, and she wasn't going to let it go. It was hard to talk over the feeling of my heart throbbing against my ribs.

"I kissed you," I began slowly and stayed, "because I've always wanted to kiss you. Like you said, it felt like the thing to do."

"Do you have feelings for me?"

"Oh my god," I groaned. This was torture. "No."

"You're saying you felt nothing," she said skeptically. "You were pretty upset when you left to have felt nothing."

"Why does it matter?" I asked, all control gone from my voice.

"Because if I'm forced to tell the truth then so are you!"

"Fine, yes! Yes, of course I have feelings for you, of course I felt something last night because I'm some sort of sadomasochist. So I went and banged another girl just so I could get you out of my head, but here you are ripping all those old wounds open again."

"Girl? What girl?"

"None of your business! But none of it matters, Liv."

"Why do you keep saying that," she sobbed and took another step closer.

"Because I'm going to be a Warrior, the one thing you had to travel across the ocean to get away from. I am going to be a Warrior, Liv, and nothing is going to change my mind on that. That's why it doesn't matter."

A silence fell between us, a very awkward and uncomfortable silence.

"Ok then, I'll go," she finally said and brushed away a curl that was sticking to her cheek. "I guess I'll see you around."

I nodded and pushed myself up from the desk. "Don't forget your bowl and spoon."

She stepped back over to the couch and took the bowl from the table. When she turned back around, she paused in front of me, gave me a kiss on the cheek, and then hugged me. Her curly hair brushed against my face, giving me a waft of her flowery shampoo mixed with her natural smell. It reminded me of our young life together, and the warm memories made me squeeze her tighter. She shifted back and looked me in the eye. Our lips met again, our eyes not letting go of each other until the moment took me and I slipped my tongue into her mouth. A soft moan came deep from within her throat as our lips kneaded together. When I finally needed to breathe, I broke away and took a slight step back.

Liv looked breathless and confused. Finally, she stepped toward the door and pushed down on the handle.

"Liv," I said and she froze, "marry him because you can't imagine your life without him. You are unbelievably special, Olivia, you shouldn't have to hide who you truly are."

She didn't respond and kept her back to me as she pushed down on the door handle once again and then left the office. After the door latched closed, I stepped over to the couch and collapsed in its cushions. I wanted to do the last fifteen minutes over again. I wanted to say different things. I wanted to tell her not to marry Niall because I loved her. I wanted to kiss her again.

I covered my face with one of the upper couch cushions and screamed into it.

"Will, honey?" my mother said as she came bursting into the office. "I just saw Livy leave, is everything ok?"

"Fine, Mom."

"Why is there a pillow on your face?

"Because I was screaming into it."

She paused. "Why were you screaming into a pillow?"

Reluctantly I pulled the pillow away from my face. "No reason."

"You should be resting, not screaming," she said and began to fuss with the other pillows and cushions around me. "I'm going to cancel your classes for today."

"Don't, I'll be fine. Stop fussing."

"I'm your mom, it's what I do. I'll turn the lights out so you can rest," she said and walked toward the door.

"Thanks, Mom."

"And stay away from Livy Burke."

"What?"

"Nothing, honey," she said and turned the lights off. "Stay away from Livy Burke."

Chapter Sixteen

Olivia

When the sun began to set, I knew it was time to go home. Honestly, I should have gone home hours ago. I was emotionally exhausted and even more conflicted. The guard at the gate gave me a wave as I approached and opened the gate enough for me to get through. I raised my bowl to him to thank him, which made him very confused. He should be honored. This empty bowl and spoon, now crusted with brown smears of guacamole, had traveled the city. Not many bowls and spoons could say that. Yeah, I was weird and tired.

The butterflies in my stomach started to flutter because I could no longer avoid Niall. When I got to the spiral staircase, I took the stairs two at a time so I wouldn't lose my nerve. I didn't know what I was going to say or do when I saw him, but it was time to be an adult.

Halfway up the staircase I heard, "Hey, baby girl."

I looked up to find my mother several steps above me. "Hi, Mom."

"You've been gone all day, is everything ok? Niall's been worried."

"Don't pretend you don't know what happened today, Mom."

She knitted her brows together. "I'm well aware of what happened with you and Jack-Jack. I thought a day with Sera, and what looks like a bowl of guacamole, might make you feel better."

"Well, it didn't," I said and shoved the bowl into her hands. "Mémé's guacamole can only handle Brianna-level problems, and not mine."

Mom pursed her lips, red tears collecting in the rims of her eyes. "No matter how hard you try to push me away, I will always be your mother, and I will always be here to help you. I just want you to be happy."

"Mom…" I started to say, but she disappeared down the stairs. I wasn't mad at her, but per usual she was there and easy for me to unleash on. I sighed and trudged up the remaining stairs to the second floor. My stomach was flipping around with nerves. I had no idea what I was going to be walking into. Which Niall would I get?

With a deep inhale, I opened the door to our room and stepped inside. At the foot of the bed was a mound of pillows and blankets. Candles were lit and spread throughout, showering the room in a romantic glow.

Niall stood next to the vanity and looked up from the bottle of wine he was opening. "There you are, love."

"What is all this?"

He took the opened bottle of wine in one hand, two glasses in the other, and waved me toward the pile of pillows. "I know these last few days have been difficult, especially today with your brother. So I wanted to do something nice for you, for us," he said and knelt down in the center of the pillow pallet. "Come sit with me, love."

After kicking off my shoes, I stepped over to the pile and settled in opposite of Niall. He poured the red wine into both glasses and handed me one. I drank down half the glass in one gulp, choosing to look at the wall instead of him. The guilt of what I had done, the feelings that I had had for a brief moment for someone else was weighing down on my chest.

"Love?" he said softly and caressed the back of my arm. "Olivia, please talk to me."

I drank the rest of the wine in my glass, wiped my lip, and turned to face him. "Something's wrong with us, Niall. Can't you feel it? Since we got here everything has been…wrong."

He took a big sip of his wine, and then placed his glass down. "Yes, I know. Olivia, I need to apologize for my behavior the last couple of days. I have not expressed to you the level of pressure my father has put on me to get your father and uncle to accept our family as a recognized coven. He has basically said not to bother coming home unless it happens."

"What? Niall…wh…that's a bit extreme, don't you think? Pressuring my family to do anything has the opposite effect, I've told you this."

"What am I supposed to do, love? You know how my father is. When it comes to him, being homeless is the least of my worry. I cannot fail at this, I have to…I fear what he will do to me if I cannot make this happen. And it is that, that crushing pressure, that has caused me to lash out at you. I am truly sorry."

My heart dropped and I refilled my glass. After another large sip of wine, the alcohol finally hit me for those few brief seconds, bringing a short wave of relaxation. Before Niall had even finished his first glass, I had downed my entire second glass in order to keep that feeling going for a few seconds more.

"Would you like me to open the other bottle?" he asked.

I shook my head. "No, I…well, maybe." He smiled and rose from the pile of pillows. As he began opening the second bottle of wine, I couldn't help but ask, "How did you do all of this?"

"Your mother," he laughed lightly and popped the cork.

"My mom?"

He nodded and stepped back over to the pile. "I wanted to do something romantic, and your mother was more than willing to help. She left only a minute before you came in the door, I'm surprised you didn't run into her."

"I did," I replied, feeling the walls of guilt coming in on me. She had helped with all of this, and I spoke to her so badly. "We used to have carpet picnics when we were young. She'd spread out blankets and pillows like this, we'd eat junk food and watch movies until we fell asleep. It was usually when Ada was out on a mission. I guess it was comforting to have us with her until he came home."

"It must have been nice to have moments like that with her."

I nodded guiltily. "I've never given her the credit she deserves," I replied and tucked a loose curl behind my ear. "I don't know what it is, when I see her, I just get so defensive and I lash out at her. But then I feel guilty afterwards. Why do I do that?"

Niall put his glass down, slid over next to me, and poured me another glass of wine. "Do you remember the day we met?"

I nodded. "The day at the café."

"Yes," he began and tucked another curl behind my ear. "I walked by that café and thought, what an enchanting creature." I blushed and sipped my wine. "You were sitting there reading with that stack of books next to you. I was so mesmerized by you that I tripped and practically landed in your lap. You were so kind to let me sit next to you. I thought that maybe if I could sneak a peek at your books, I could recognize something and start a conversation. And then to my surprise, they were all in different languages."

I laughed. "I didn't know you noticed that."

He smiled and wrapped his hand around the back of my neck, circling his thumb around my cheek. "I was so intimidated, but then when I discovered I was speaking to *the* Olivia Burke, the daughter of the Warriors, I thought for sure you would want nothing to do with me. But then that first week together we were so relaxed and free, do you remember? We barely left your flat."

Niall nuzzled into me and kissed up the side of my neck, finally finding my lips. It was gentle, soft, and familiar. He pressed his forehead against mine, his fingers gliding down my cheeks and across my chest. "You told me you were the happiest you had ever been. And then you gave yourself to me, your first time. That moment was so special for both of us, wasn't it?"

"Of course it was," I replied as tears formed in my eyes.

"We were unbreakable until we came here. I take responsibility for my part, but you've become someone I don't know, love."

My entire body flinched. "What do you mean?"

"Well, the battle yesterday for one. Then at dinner with your parents you saying you wanted to go back to translating and working with refugees, when we've clearly discussed otherwise. And lastly, today you left me all alone without a word all day. I believe I deserve a little better than that. I want to give you the world, Olivia, but I need to know you are going to be at my side."

"I-I am, but..."

"Olivia, I am understanding of the fangs. I deal with the immense pressure of who your family is – your mother, your father and uncle, your grandfathers. Is it any wonder why you haven't had any other partners? A regular man would be crushed by the weight of all that you bring into a relationship, yet I am here, love. I believe I deserve a little more respect."

My stomach sank at the notion that he was right. Even I was intimidated by my family at times. But then there was Will's voice in the back of my head, criticizing me for not standing up for myself.

I swallowed down the lump in my throat and said, "I like food."

Niall scrunched his brows together. "Say again?"

"I like food, Niall. More like I love food, actually. Even when I was little, I could eat double what the boys did. I know you don't like women who pig out in front of you, so I've been practically starving since we've been together."

Niall's eyes fluttered as he processed everything I said. Finally, "I take it that is why your family has been shocked by your lack of appetite?" I nodded. "Of course, I don't wish for you to starve, love. Eat as you wish, I suppose."

"And..."

"There's more?"

I sighed. "It's just...I'm asking you to hold off talking to Ada about your father's coven."

His face hardened slightly. "I told you, Olivia, you have no idea how much pressure I am under. This is for your family, too."

"Niall..."

"Olivia, I implore you to listen to me, you do not know how bad things really are out there. I hate to say it bluntly, but people are losing respect for the Warrior coven. When vampires no longer respect or fear the Warriors authority, then anarchy ensues. Some Warriors have even approached my father, looking to transfer to our coven.

"Even with the issues you have with your family, I know that you care about them. Although my father is pushing this, I am only doing this for you. I know this is hard for you to believe."

I looked down at the ground. "Ada told me today that some of the Warriors are unhappy, restless, I think he said."

"Then don't you see," he replied and held my face between his hands, "we are meant to be together, love. I truly believe fate brought us together in that café so that my family could help yours. There is nothing I wouldn't do for you, Olivia. Wouldn't you do the same for your family?"

My heart jumped in my throat and I couldn't stop the tears from coming. "I would do anything for them. I didn't think it was so bad."

"But now we have the opportunity to help," he said, resting his forehead against mine once again. "Are you on my side, love? Will you help me?"

My lip started to tremble. Was there no other option? Helping Niall meant saving my family. But...my kiss today with Will flashed in my head, making the butterflies flutter in my stomach and send a chill all the way down to my toes. Everything he had said to me last night echoed in my head about being with Niall even though his family is similar to mine. It was the very thing I ran away from, but my family could be in jeopardy.

Wasn't there any other way? What would Will say?

I'd been silent for too long, and Niall was looking for an answer. With the full weight of my decision resting on my shoulders and tears still running from my eyes, I answered, "Yes."

Chapter Seventeen

Will

"I love forced family get togethers, don't you?" Jax asked sarcastically before swigging back what I assumed was vodka since he would never just drink water.

"Try being forced to come when it's not your family," I replied.

"Please, you're family more than she is."

Jax and I were huddled by the fireplace near the drink cart. If I didn't have to work in a couple of hours, I'd be diving into that cart head first because I knew what was going to happen tonight. Niall was going to ask Olivia to marry him in front of her family. It was the only explanation for the last-minute gathering. The fact that I was here was yet another mindfuck on top of the others of the last few days. It was one of the first times I hated coming to the manor. But if I didn't come tonight, I would look like a coward who couldn't get over his first love. In all honesty, I was hoping the real Livy Burke would show up tonight and send that slimy Englishman home.

Jax poured another drink and slammed it back. "Are you working tonight?"

"Yes, thank god," I replied and we both laughed. "I promised Awbie an hour."

"Too bad a lot can happen in an hour."

"You have no idea," I replied softly and took a sip of water.

Jax narrowed his eyes at me. "What do you know?"

Before I could answer, Olivia and Niall stepped inside the office. She was wearing another tight black dress, this one showing off her shoulders. It was hard to take my eyes off of her, and she caught me. She held my gaze, her eyes sad and...pleading? Were they pleading?

Jax stepped in front of me, breaking my view of Olivia. "Please stop."

I put my hands up, and he gave me a warning look before stepping back over to the bar cart. In those few seconds, Olivia and Niall had moved to where Sera, Awbie, and my mother were gathered. I had to smile that Eris had wedged himself in a corner and pulled my dad in front of him. It made me laugh that even Eris wanted to hide from Niall.

"What up, Wills," Jared said as he came to stand next to me.

"You've been MIA lately, you working on something?"

He nodded. "There's a group moving this way, we're not sure what to make of them."

"What do you mean?"

"You talking about that coven?" Jax asked, coming up behind me with a very full glass of vodka.

"It's a coven?" I asked.

Jared shrugged. "They're more like migrants. They set up camp for a few days and have these big gatherings. Most of what I have are satellite photos, so I have no idea what they're actually celebrating, but they sure look like they're having a good time. It's just the fact they're doing it out in the open, and they seem to be heading this way."

"Who's heading this way?" Niall asked from behind Jared, causing our small circle to open. Olivia filtered in next to him, looking even more uncomfortable now than when she walked in the room.

"Sorry, Niall, official Warrior business," Jared said.

"Yes, but I hate to point out that Will is not a Warrior," Niall replied smugly.

"He's family," Jax said, almost with a growl. "You're not."

Niall smirked. "Well, perhaps I'll be able to change that someday."

Olivia kept her eyes focused on the ground. She was retreating, this wasn't good.

"I'm curious," Niall began, "will Victor be joining us?"

Jared shook his head. "He's traveling with Alex and Kyla."

"Oh, I wasn't aware he still handled Warrior business?"

"He's on vacation," Jared replied flatly, and it was obvious to everyone that it wasn't true.

Niall seemed to feel the tension he'd created in the circle and cleared his throat. "Very well then, I think I'll have a drink. Olivia, would you like something?"

"No, I'm fine," she replied, giving him a forced smile, although I wasn't sure he knew that.

Jared stepped away the same time as Niall, leaving me, Jax, and Olivia alone. It should have felt as though celestial powers had reunited, but instead it was awkward and tense.

Slowly Liv looked up at me. "How are you feeling?"

"Don't talk to him," Jax said tersely.

"Jax, calm down," I replied.

"I'm looking out for you."

Liv pursed her lips and sighed. "I'm not the sea witch from the deep, Jack-Jack, I just asked how he was."

"I'm fine, Liv. How are you? You seem…"

"Don't answer that," Jax interrupted and put his index finger in front of her face. "Neither of you need to be concerned with how the other is doing."

"Jax," I groaned, but before I could say anything else, Awbie stepped toward us with open arms.

"Please, please let me get a picture of my three little angels before you all start fighting," she said and held up her phone.

"Mom, come on," Jax groaned, but one look from Cam caused him to straighten up.

With Olivia on one side, and Jax on the other, I was a Burke twin sandwich. Our smiles were thin, but we stood together for a picture that looked similar to the hundreds we had as kids. The nostalgia brought on a wave of sadness. I missed the three of us being friends, and I missed Liv being so close to me.

As soon as Awbie brought her phone down, the three of us relaxed and started to step away when Niall spoke up. "Brianna, if I may, could you take one with all four of us?"

"Oh, um, of course," Awbie replied and Niall jumped in next to Olivia. The twins and I adjusted uncomfortably to stand together again. I'm pretty sure the only one smiling in the picture was Niall.

After Awbie gave the thumbs up, Jax and I tried to step away when

Niall said, "So, gentleman, what exciting things are you doing tonight?"

"I am going to work," I replied and looked at my watch. "And look at that, it's almost time for me to go."

"You're leaving?" Olivia said almost in a panic.

"Gotta get to work."

"The hardest working man in the family," Niall said and I couldn't tell if he was being condescending, or if it was just his accent. "But could you wait just a bit, I want to..." he said as he crossed in front of me and tapped his glass. "Everyone? May I have everyone's attention for a just a moment."

The room became very quiet as everyone turned to face the fireplace. From the corner of my eye, I could see Liv fidgeting nervously.

"I'm sorry to interrupt this wonderful gathering," Niall continued, "I just wanted to take a moment to thank Brianna and Cameron for your wonderful hospitality these last few days. It has been such a pleasure meeting all of Olivia's wonderful family and friends. I can see how each of you have shaped Olivia into the wonderful person she is."

Jax went to open his mouth, but I squeezed his shoulder to stop him from making what I assumed would be a snide comment.

Niall took Olivia's hand and pulled her away from my side. It was happening, and he was literally going to do it in front of me. Olivia looked over Niall's shoulder at me with her pleading eyes again. What did she expect me to do?

"Olivia, I have never loved anyone as much as I love you," he began, reaching into his pocket and kneeling down to the ground. My mother and Awbie both gasped in anticipation from across the room. "Will you make me the luckiest man in the world by becoming my wife?"

Niall held out an obnoxiously large diamond ring and looked up at Olivia expectantly, but she didn't answer. Her jaw began to chatter, but she didn't answer. Slowly her hand reached up and tucked a large section of her hair behind her ear. I nearly choked on my own spit at the sight of a pear-shaped diamond earring shining from her earlobe. Jax squeezed my shoulder as if he had recognized the earring as well.

What was she trying to do to me? How did she even...when did...maybe they weren't...no, they were the same earrings. I would never forget them.

"Olivia?" Niall asked softly and squeezed her hand.

A tear dripped down her cheek as she answered, "Yes."

The site of Niall slipping the ring on her finger and the sound of the cheers in the room didn't really affect me. I was numb. My brain couldn't process the fact that she had the earrings I had given her, but then said yes to marrying Niall. I drank the rest of my water and wished it had been vodka like Jax's. While others moved to congratulate the couple, I pushed past Jax and placed my empty glass on the bar cart.

"You ok?" he asked softly next to me.

"Yep."

"Did you see..."

"Yep," I interrupted just as my mother touched my arm.

Even though she was smiling, she was giving me her worried mother eyes. "Everything ok, honey?"

"Of course, Mom, I've got to get to work," I replied and kissed her cheek. "I'll see you tomorrow."

Jax patted me on the back, we didn't need to say anything else. I gave my dad a wave goodbye across the room and headed out the door. The air seemed cleaner out in the corridor, or maybe it was because I was finally breathing again. Once I made it around the corner, I pulled my phone out of my back pocket and called Mindy at the club.

"Please tell me you're coming in early," she said without any greeting.

"Sorry, Mins, I'm not coming in."

"We're slammed, Will."

"I'm sorry, I wouldn't do this unless it was an emergency."

"Is it that girl?"

I sighed. "Yeah, I just can't be there tonight."

"Will?" Olivia called behind me.

I didn't turn around and instead quickened my pace to the spiral staircase. "You know what, Mins, I'm going to give my notice."

"Are you serious?"

"Will, wait," Olivia called again.

"I've never been so serious in my life. I'll talk to you soon, sorry again," I said and hung up the phone.

"I know you can hear me," Olivia said and I continued up the stairs. A breeze came by me and suddenly Olivia was standing in front of me. "You're seriously going to make me chase you?"

"No, you're choosing to chase me. Shouldn't you be celebrating somewhere," I said and stepped around her, but she continued to follow me up the stairs. "I'm surprised you can even hold your hand up with that iceberg on your finger."

"Will, please…"

"Go away, Olivia."

"Then tell me why you didn't say anything."

I rounded on her. "I'm sorry, what?"

Her eyes were glassy and her lip trembled. "Why didn't you stop me?"

"Stop you?" I replied with a laugh and started back up the stairs. "No one has been able to stop Olivia Burke from doing anything. You have always done exactly what you wanted to do and never given a moment's thought to anyone else."

Olivia flew past me again and stood at the landing. "I gave you signs I needed help."

Instantly I grabbed her elbow and pulled her into the corridor. "Signs? Is that what you call them? The pitiful looks and pleading eyes? And then…" I paused and pulled her hair back on both sides to expose the diamond earrings in her ears. "The earrings that remind me of one of the worst days of my life? I literally cannot process how you even have them, but honestly, it's just yet another mindfuck from you. What did you expect to happen? You show me you have had the earrings this whole time, and I would suddenly jump in front of Niall and confess my love to you? Did you seriously think I would do that again?"

"I thought I could do it, but I've been nauseous all day…"

"You're a grown-ass woman, Olivia. If you don't want to marry someone, then say no, it's that's simple. I told you yesterday that you had to make the decision yourself, and you did. Now go and enjoy the first day of the rest of your miserable life."

I walked away from her and knocked on the third door on the right. Victoria's room.

"You don't understand…"

"No, Olivia, I don't care," I said and knocked on Tori's door again. As soon as the door opened the slightest amount, I pushed my way in and closed the door behind me. Tori glared at me and I instantly put my hands up. "I'm sorry to barge in, but I need you to put me out, please. I don't care what you do to me afterwards, but please, please just drink from me to put me out."

"Look, Will, whatever you got going on…" Tori stopped at the sound of someone banging on her door.

Oh please no.

"Will?" Olivia shouted. "Will, we're not finished!"

Tori's glare intensified. "Is that Olivia Burke?"

"Just ignore her," I said as Olivia banged on the door again.

"Will, you know I don't do drama, and I especially don't do drama that involves my boss' daughter."

"Tori, I'm begging you, I promise I won't bother you again. I *need* you to do this, please!"

She sighed and stepped over to her bed. "Fine, take your shirt off, but..." Olivia banged on the door again and shouted my name, "...this better not come back on me, do you understand?"

I nodded and pulled my shirt over my head. There was a sense of relief that came over me as I sat down on the edge of her bed. Tori came up behind me and my eyes closed in anticipation of what was to come. She pulled my head toward my right shoulder and I took in a deep breath to relax myself when I heard the door open. My eyes flew open and there was Olivia standing just inside the doorway.

"What are you doing?" she asked with a mix of shock and judgement.

"Um, sure, come on in," Tori said annoyed and stood from the bed. "Is there something I can help you with?"

Olivia completely ignored her and zeroed her eyes on me. "You dare to judge me when you're in here doing that?"

"It's none of your business what I do with my life."

"But it's your business to judge mine?"

I jumped up from the bed. "You made it my business! You heaved pound after pound of your baggage on me. I told you to stand on your own and remember who the hell you are, and you went right back to being the fucking robot, Olivia."

"I'm trying to help my family," she yelled. "Maybe you don't understand that since all you're doing is lying to yours. You sit up on your high horse looking down at me when what you're doing to them is ten times worse."

"Ok, I'm going to ask both of you leave," Tori said firmly.

"I'm sorry, Tori. Olivia is leaving, she has to get back to her sham of an engagement."

Olivia's eyes became glassy as she took a step back into the corridor. "You'll see. When my engagement saves this coven, you'll see," she said and slammed the door behind her.

"What the hell is she talking about?" Tori asked.

I shook my head. "I have no idea," I replied and picked my shirt up from the floor.

"I'll still feed from you if you want," she grumbled. With a big sigh of relief, I stepped over to the bed and sat down, seeing our reflection in the mirror of her dresser. Tori draped her arm over my shoulder as she asked, "She's who you're thinking about when you're screwing me, isn't she?"

"Not always," I replied truthfully, although she raised a skeptical brow. "I wish you could Glamour her out of my head."

"That might cause some problems with my boss," she replied, trying to make me smile. When that didn't work, she cradled my head and neck, letting it fall toward my right shoulder. "I'll make it a good, deep sleep. Ok?"

"Thank you."

"And then you'll never bring your drama into my room again."

"Never..." I began just before Tori sank her fangs into the side of my neck, "again."

Chapter Eighteen

Olivia

"You'll see. When my engagement saves this coven, you'll see," I shouted and slammed Victoria's door behind me. How dare he judge me! "Screw you, Will Ryan."

Quickly I walked down the corridor toward the spiral staircase. I needed to go back and face the decision I had made. I'd been struggling with what I'd do all day. There were doubts right up to the second Niall asked. I don't even know what I thought Will would do. But it didn't matter anymore. It was the right thing to do. So, what if our relationship wasn't like my parents' or others like Uncle Alex and Aunt Kyla. Niall and I were different, and in the end, I would be helping my family. Will didn't know shit, and who was he to judge me while he was running away and getting his neck sucked. I would show him. He would be jealous at how happy Niall and I would be.

"Livy, honey?" my mom's voice sliced through my thoughts. I stopped just before colliding with her. Looking around I couldn't believe I was already on the first floor. "Everything ok?"

"Why wouldn't it be? I told you I wanted to call Auntie Ky," I replied defensively and stepped past her.

"That's pretty tough to do without your phone," she said and I froze.

Slowly I turned around and found my mother holding my phone in her hand. I felt like I was back in high school and trying to come up with an excuse. Finally, I was able to say, "I needed a moment, ok?"

She took a step forward and lowered her voice. "Of course it's ok, honey. With everyone there, I hope you didn't feel pressured…"

"How can you even say that to me?" I snapped. "I just made a huge decision in my life and needed to get some air. There's no need to create some fake drama in your head. I know you think I'm too young, but I don't want to be like you at wait until half my life is over before getting married."

It was harsh, I know it was, and from the pinched expression on her face, I had hurt her. After several tense seconds, she exhaled loudly and then said, "What you seem to forget, Olivia Sera, is that I was with you every day of your life until your eighteenth birthday. I know the look you give when you're worried. I hear the change in the timber of your voice when you're lying. And I see when you project your feelings onto others, mostly me, when you're scared. Perhaps what frightens me is that in the last ten minutes I've seen all of those even though this should be one of the most exciting moments of your life.

"As your mother, all I want to do is help you, and you never want me to. So, I won't. Whatever this is, figure it out yourself," she said and walked past me.

"Can I have my phone?"

"Guess you'll have to figure that out on your own, too," she replied as she disappeared around the corner.

With a sigh, I slowly walked back to the study where Niall was already waiting at the door. "Everything all right, love?"

"Of course," I replied and took his hand. "I just couldn't get ahold of my aunt to tell her the good news, but it's fine."

He kissed my hand and held us in the doorway. "For a moment there, I was afraid you were going to say no."

I shook my head. "I was just surprised, that's all."

He nodded and we stepped back inside the study. Aunt Re immediately came toward us, arms open with a big smile on her face. "Ok, bring out the champagne," she said and then looked behind her to the others in the room, "sucks to be a vampire on days like this."

It was a beautiful morning. The sun was burning off the fog causing thick, white rays of light to shine through the room making the dust motes sparkle like glitter. I was having to concentrate on those sparkling bits of dust rather than the pain of Niall trying to shove his flaccid penis inside me. My head had banged against the headboard twice already, and my hips were starting to ache from being splayed and pressed down upon for so long.

"Niall, maybe we should…"

"Bugger all…stop talking," he hissed before flipping me on my stomach and pressing me uncomfortably into the mattress as he pushed inside me.

When my head hit the headboard again, I was done. "Niall…"

"Bloody hell," he said as he smacked my hips and rolled off of me. Quickly he stepped around the bed and ducked into the bathroom, slamming the door behind him.

Happy engagement to me, I thought begrudgingly. So my first morning as an engaged woman wasn't going well, but he was a little hungover from the champagne last night, perhaps that's why he was having trouble.

I looked at the clock and realized we only had ten minutes before we were supposed to meet my parents for breakfast. "Niall? We've got to get going. We're meeting my parents, remember?"

The bathroom door swung open and a naked Niall stepped back into the bedroom. "Well, you best get dressed then. We wouldn't want to be late for your dear, dear parents."

It was his tone that bothered me, that sarcastic yet stoic tone that sounded so proper with his English accent, but he was really being nasty. With the ten minutes I had to shower and dress I was thankful I could move almost as fast as the vampire members of my family. But the second I pulled a pair of jeans up my legs, Niall immediately scoffed.

"Is there a problem?" I asked as I pulled a soft t-shirt out of the dresser.

"No," he replied and snapped his watch on his wrist, "I would hope that my fiancée would present herself a little better, that's all."

"It's just my parents, Niall. I could go in my pajamas if I wanted to."

"Olivia, it's an important day," he said tersely. "It's imperative that I have your support."

"Niall, dear," I began gently, "if you're thinking about bringing up merging the covens again, I think you should wait. I know my father, the engagement is enough to swallow. Just let the dust settle a little."

Niall stood stoic for what seemed like five minutes. Finally, he relaxed his face and said, "Fine."

It was all I was going to get, and he didn't mean it. "Can we go?"

"If you're happy with looking like that, then I guess we can."

As he stepped past me, I touched his arm. "Honey, if you're upset about earlier…"

"DON'T," he growled, pressing his index finger against the tip of my nose. After a breath, he stepped toward the door and I followed in line behind him, but when we reached the spiral staircase, he reached back for my hand and pulled it into his chest. Here was the Niall that I loved. He looked back and gave me an apologetic smile. Hand in hand we went down the spiral staircase to the first floor, and eventually down the corridor toward my parent's suite.

The door was open and the room was filled with sun spilling in from the double French doors at the far end of the room. Just as we entered, Mom stepped through the French doors from the lanai.

"Ah, right on time," she said and waved us outside. "I thought we could have breakfast out here, if that's ok?"

"Splendid," Niall replied and pulled me across the room. When we reached my mother, he released my hand and kissed her on both cheeks. She gave him a pleasant smile that didn't reach her eyes, but Niall probably didn't notice.

"Good morning, Mom," I said as I kissed her left cheek and peered out over her shoulder. "No Ada?"

"He's coming," she replied and stepped away from me, obviously still mad at me for snapping at her last night. "Don't wait for Cameron, Niall, he'll be here momentarily."

Niall nodded and sat down at the table which had large platters of eggs, potatoes, and pancakes. I sat opposite of Niall and immediately stabbed my fork into four pancakes at once. Since I didn't have to hide my appetite anymore, I was going to make the most of it. First, I spread a nice layer of butter on the top of each pancake. Second, I allowed the butter to melt into the pancakes before pouring the syrup like a waterfall of sugary goodness on top and all around the plate. Lastly, I cut the tower of pancakes into quarters, allowing the syrup to seep down to the bottom layers.

"I have suddenly been transported to your childhood," Ada said as he came out onto the lanai and then kissed the top of my head. "Although, I am happy to see that you have graduated to cutting your pancakes rather than eat them whole and hanging from your fork."

"Please tell me she didn't," Niall said as he stood and shook Ada's hand.

"It made her even more adorable," Ada replied and winked at me. "I apologize for being late."

"Warrior business?" Niall asked.

"Always," Mom replied and Ada gave her an apologetic look.

While everyone else engaged in small talk, I took a deep breath in order to prepare myself for my delicious breakfast. Once I shoved a portion of my pancakes into my mouth, I realized I truly was a master at creating a perfect bite. Why had I given these up? A sudden image of Will popped in my head – sitting across from me at the diner and letting me eat his pancakes. I shook my head and faked a cough to get the image to disappear.

"Are you all right, lovey?" Ada asked and I nodded.

"A piece just went down the wrong pipe, that's all."

"Perhaps you should slow down," Niall suggested.

He didn't like that I was eating like this, but that was too bad. He would just need to get used to Olivia Burke with the endless appetite. Who's a mindless robot now, Will, with your smug face while Victoria sucks on your neck. Tori? Seriously? The thought made me shove another portion of pancakes into my mouth.

Niall gave me a disapproving look before clicking his smile in place and saying, "I spoke with my father last night, and of course he is thrilled about the engagement. He was hoping, if it isn't too presumptuous, that perhaps you would throw us an engagement party where we could bring the families together in person."

Mom smiled. "We can absolutely do that," she replied but with little energy. "We would just need to know when your father could make it out here…"

"He's already on his way," Niall interrupted. "He has some business to take care of on the East Coast, and hoped that perhaps we could do the party in a couple of days while he is already in the States."

While reaching for the container of syrup, I covertly looked over at

Ada. His face had hardened and he was looking down the table at Mom. Niall was pushing already, like I told him not to. Would he ever listen? Even though I didn't agree with what he was doing, I needed to support him, right? For better or for worse had to start somewhere.

Placing my hand on top of Ada's, I gave him my biggest eyes. "Please, Ada? It'll be great for everyone to meet each other." I turned my head to look at my mother down at the other end of the table. "Mom, I know it's short notice, but I know you can pull it off. You're always so great at planning parties."

I'll admit I was laying it on a bit thick, and from her expression, she knew it.

With a sigh she replied, "I'm sure we can put something together."

"Wonderful," Niall said with a wide smile. "My family has always dreamed of seeing the manor, this will be..."

"No," Ada interrupted, causing all of us to turn our heads.

"No what, Ada?"

"We cannot have the party here," he replied.

"Why not?"

He looked to Niall. "No offense to your family, Niall, but we do not know them."

"But that is the point, sir. If I may..."

Ada held up his hand. "The manor is not just our home, it is the Warrior headquarters. We cannot have a group of individuals wandering about who have not had even the slightest amount of vetting."

"But if you don't mind my saying, sir," Niall began, "you've had galas and ceremonies where non-Warriors are coming into the manor."

"Niall, I do not wish to be insulting to your family, but they are not a recognized coven. Every vampire that steps through our doors are either members of an established coven, or have been personally vetted. Having the event elsewhere will give Devin and I an opportunity to spend some time with your family and become comfortable enough with allowing your father and perhaps a few of those closest to him come to the manor. I know we can find another place to hold the engagement party as well as accommodations. Right, Bri?"

Mom blinked in shock several times. "Sure," she finally said in an unconvincing voice. "Should be easy."

Once again, Ada gave my mother an apologetic smile. "Thank you, love."

"Yes, thank you, Mom," I said and she gave me a slight nod in return.

"Niall, who in your family will be joining us?" Mom asked with a sigh.

"My father is my only blood family, but he has about a dozen of his sires with him. I may not consider them uncles like Olivia does for so many in your coven, but they are the closest thing I have to family."

"What about your mother?"

"My mother is not in my life," Niall replied. "I honestly can't remember the last time I spoke with her, and that's probably for the best. She is not a pleasant person, and makes sure everyone around her feels the same."

Mom's face fell. "Sadly, I can understand that."

Niall tilted his head slightly. "But you and Sera seem to get on."

She smiled and nodded. "Sera is my stepmother. My birth mother was...not very fond of me and reminded me how I had ruined her life every chance she got. I'm sorry that you and your mom don't get along. I know how difficult that can be."

"It is what it is, and thankfully I have my father. May I ask, where is your mother now?"

"She died while I was pregnant with the twins," she replied uncomfortably. I guess we were going to skip the fact that my mom had actually killer her birth mother, but I was pretty sure I wasn't supposed to know that.

"Well, now that that is settled," I said with a mouthful of pancakes as I put a heaping helping of scrambled eggs on my plate, "I was thinking..."

"Olivia, if I may interrupt and allow you to chew your food," Niall began, causing me to self-consciously close my mouth. "Cameron, I am trying to understand your hesitancy with having my family at the manor, as you stated, because we are not a recognized coven. But may I ask, how can we ever become a recognized coven when we cannot get even the slightest support to do so? This is why I believe when Olivia and I marry we should combine our covens. Why shouldn't our families..."

"Niall, honey," I interrupted and he froze, "we have so much time to have that conversation. Today is supposed to be about celebrating our engagement, figuring out the details for the party, all that fun stuff. Let's save the coven talk for another time."

Niall's stone-cold expression sent a shiver down my spine. I knew he was angry, but he wasn't going about this the right way. He just needed to trust me.

Before he could say anything, Uncle Jared came up the back stairs of the lanai. "Hey, sorry to interrupt," he began and then came to Ada's side, "you said you wanted to know when they were on the move."

Ada nodded and stood from his seat. "Yes, thank you, Jared. I apologize, everyone, but there is urgent business I need to attend to. Niall, we can pick up this conversation at another time."

Ada stepped behind my chair, kissed my head, and then kissed Mom before going inside.

Mom cleared her throat and gave an apologetic smile. "You'll have to get used to that, I'm afraid. But vampires all over the world will need to be on their best behavior the day of the wedding, because we won't have anyone leaving in the middle of the ceremony for Warrior business, I'll see to that."

"Thanks, Mom," I replied and looked over at Niall who was looking everywhere but me. "Well, maybe we can pick this up this afternoon. Niall and I can think about what we'd want for the party and get a guest list going."

"That sounds fine," she replied. "I'll start looking for a venue."

The three of us stood from our chairs and Niall left the table with only a curt thank you to my mom.

"Is he ok?" she asked.

"He's fine," I replied and took a step toward the French door, but Mom stepped in front of me.

"Maybe you should wait a little bit and let him cool off," she said with worried eyes.

"Don't be dramatic, Mom," I said and tried to push past her when she squeezed my arm.

"Let him cool off," she said warningly.

"You are unbelievable," I replied and ripped her hand from my arm. By the time I got into the corridor, Niall was already going up the spiral staircase. Ok, he was mad. He was also being a baby. So I was going to be mature and not chase after him. I took my time going up the stairs, and halfway up I heard the bedroom door slam. His tantrum was annoying and embarrassing, and certainly not how you wanted to act in front of my family.

When I finally reached the bedroom door I took a breath, patted down my hair, and then stepped inside. Niall was standing in the middle of the room. Even with his back to me I could tell that he was fuming.

"Niall, I know you're upset." He didn't flinch so I took a few steps forward. "But I told you not to talk about combining the covens today. As soon as you brought it up, I could tell Ada wasn't going to be receptive."

Niall turned around and I froze. His expression was hard to gauge. His face was relaxed, but his eyes were cold.

"I think you saw very clearly that once my father makes a decision, he doesn't change his mind. All I was doing was trying to help you..."

Niall wrapped his fingers around my chin and jaw so tightly I couldn't move. "Your *help* made me look like an ass in front of your father while you sat there like a pig at a trough."

In an instant, I allowed myself to see his red hybrid light glowing from his forehead and hit him with my mind, knocking him down to the ground. A look of shock flashed on his face before he stretched his hands out in front of him and created a translucent shield between us. His hybrid glow completely disappeared. I tried hitting him again, and he didn't even flinch. Somehow his shield was able to cut my connection.

He must have noticed that something was wrong since he jumped up from the floor and plowed his shoulder into my stomach. The breath was instantly knocked out of me and lights sparkled in front of my eyes when my head bounced off the stone floor. Niall straddled me and stretched his arms through his shield. The blow to the head was causing double vision, so I couldn't stop him from slapping me across the face and then pressing his knees down on my chest.

"You stupid cow," he shouted over me, "you will never do that to me again. DO YOU UNDERSTAND ME?"

"What the fuck is going on?" someone shouted.

Chapter Nineteen

Will

My internal alarm went off in a panic and I shot straight up. It took a few seconds for my eyes to adjust, and from the sight of the dresser in front of me, I knew I was still in Tori's room. She was nowhere to be seen, and she wasn't the kind to leave a note. She was pissed, and I would be surprised if she ever spoke to me again. Drama was a no-go for her.

With a sigh, I shrugged my t-shirt on, patted down my hair as best I could, and headed out. Olivia's room was only one floor below. Bottom line, I needed to apologize to her. It wasn't like I was going to get down on my knees and grovel at her feet, but she deserved a simple apology. My stomach started to flip as I reached the landing, so much so I had to stand up against the wall and bend over to let the blood run back into my head. I hated feeling this way, it felt weak. All I had to do was say that I was sorry for what I yelled at her, and then turn around and leave. Simple.

With a deep breath, I stood back up and headed to the last room on the right. When I got to the door, I froze at what sounded like a yelp. I put my ear closer to the door just as I heard a scream from inside. Immediately I threw the door open only to find Niall on top of Olivia. Initially I thought I'd interrupted them having sex, but then he slapped her.

"You stupid cow you will never do that to me again. DO YOU UNDERSTAND ME?"

"What the fuck is going on?" I shouted.

Niall jumped up and took several steps back. His eyes were wide and fearful, his body shaking with uncertainty of what to do. But then he decided to panic and ran to the door.

"Oh you better run," I growled, allowing him to run past me as I went to Olivia. She was coughing and had rolled over on her side. When I brushed her hair away from her face, she smacked my hand away.

"I don't need your help," she said and pushed herself up to a seated position.

"The handprint on your cheek says otherwise," I replied, although the redness was already beginning to fade.

"Where's Niall?" she asked as she stood unsteadily from the floor.

"Who the fuck cares. Olivia, why…"

"I need to find him."

"What is wrong with you? He hit you, Olivia, he was sitting on your chest and screaming at you. What would he have done if I hadn't walked in?"

She whipped around and jabbed her finger into my chest. "You don't understand anything, Will. He was upset, and it's my fault. He never means it…"

"Oh my god, this wasn't the first time, was it?"

"W-what?" she replied, catching herself.

"Has he hurt you before?" She didn't answer, and I got angrier. "Jesus, Olivia, has Niall hit you before?"

"It's none of your business!"

"None of my…how could you allow him to do that to you?"

"You don't understand…"

"I can't believe you're defending him, you of all people. After everything that happened with your mom."

"My mom? What does my mom have to do with this?"

I sighed. "Come on, Liv, you don't need to lie about it to me. I know everything that happened with your mother's first husband. Which is why I can't understand…"

"First husband…Will, what the hell are you talking about?"

I froze for a few seconds, waiting, hoping she'd relax and concede. But when she didn't, my face fell. "Oh shit, you really don't know."

"Don't know what?" she shouted. "What are you talking about?"

I took a step back. "You should talk to your mom…"

"Tell-me-what-you-know!"

"Ok, ok, just calm down," I said and pumped my hands in front of me. She took a breath and sat down on the corner of the bed. "I don't know the specifics, but she married a guy Sam…Sam Lee, or Lewis, something with an L. They married young and he uh…used to…hurt her, abuse her."

"My mom? No way."

"Apparently, he was completely controlling, and if she didn't do things exactly right, he would attack her. Mom said sometimes she wouldn't see your mom for weeks until she healed enough to cover her injuries up."

"Wh-what?" she said with tears forming in her eyes. "But…what happened to him? How long were they married? Didn't Eri or Sera know? What about Daddio, he wouldn't have stood for that."

"You should talk to your parents…"

"What the hell, Livy," Jax shouted as he came through the door with his hands holding his head. "Stop screaming, I'm here, what do you want!"

"Did you know that Mom was married to someone before Ada?"

Jax raised an eyebrow and blinked slowly. "Are you high?"

"Will says she was."

Jax looked over at me. "Are *you* high?"

"It's true, Jax," I replied. "She was already married when she met Cam, but that's not what we…"

"No," Jax interrupted, "Eris had Ada specifically assigned to Mom as her Gatherer. They fell in love at first sight, he almost left the Warriors to be with her, but then Grandfather made her a Warrior and they lived happily ever after."

"Is that seriously what you were told?"

"Yeah," Jax replied innocently.

"Apparently it's all a lie," Olivia said and stood from the bed. "Mom was married and he was abusive to her."

Jax laughed. "Are you kidding? Our mom? Our mom who's almost as feared as Eris?" When neither Liv nor I joined in, his face fell. "Oh my god, you're serious. But…there's just no way."

"It was before she even knew what she was," I said. "My mom said she would see bruises and cuts on her all the time. The first time my dad met her she had road rash up her back because the guy dragged her up the driveway."

Jax shook his head in disbelief. "It's…it's not possible."

"He picked asphalt out of her skin, Jax."

Jax and Olivia exchanged glances, and in unison said, "Tell us everything."

I sighed because I knew they wouldn't talk about anything else until I told them what my mom had told me one night in a drunken stupor.

"Fine," I began. "Like I told your sister, there was a guy named Sam. They got married young and he began abusing her pretty soon after. And one day Awbie decided to escape, this Sam guy got to her and dragged her back in the house. I guess that's when your dad came in, beat up the guy, and then got Awbie out of there. For some reason, Cam drove her to my mom's condo. That's when my dad met her and patched her up.

"After that, they went down and stayed at Ollie's in North Carolina, and at some point, the husband got down there, but your dad got to him first."

"What do you mean, got to him first?" Jax asked.

I sighed again. "Cam killed him."

"Ada killed a human?" they said in unison.

"Yes!" I replied loudly in frustration. "Victor put him on trial, and he got a stint on the board and chains. It's in the Warrior archives. It's all there."

Jax put his hand up. "In our defense, you're probably the only person who has ever read the archives. But to sum up, you're telling us that our mother was married before."

"Yeah."

"And that this asshole used to beat her?"

"Severely."

"Then our father, the current coven leader of the Warriors, killed this guy who was human, which is basically the number one rule vampires aren't supposed to break."

"Correct."

He put his hand up again. "Please hold," he said and closed his eyes.

I looked over at Olivia who looked shell-shocked. She wouldn't make eye contact with me, and we'd gotten so off track. I stepped toward Jax, but the second I opened my mouth, a cloud of black smoke filled the doorway and eventually took the shape of Awbie. This was really bad.

When she had completely formed, she looked wildly around the room. "Jax? Livy? What's the matter? What happened?"

"You've been married before," Olivia said nastily.

Awbie's expression looked as though she had been punched in the gut.

"How...how do you know that?"

"So it is true," Jax said and turned to face his mother. "How does Will know and we don't?"

Awbie looked over at me. "How did you find out?"

"Who cares!" Olivia shouted. "You've been lying to us our entire lives, Mom."

"Can we all calm down and take a step back," I said calmly, stretching my arms out to both corners. "We've gotten away from the real issue here."

"And what's that?" Jax asked.

"Shut up, Will," Olivia growled, but I didn't care.

"Awbie, I'm sorry, I thought they knew. The only reason it came up was because I walked in on Niall hitting Olivia."

"What!" Awbie shouted and then immediately started crying hysterically. "I knew it, I knew that look in his eyes."

"Livy, what the fuck!" Jax said and ran to his sister, who batted him away.

"That's not what happened," she yelled and glared at me.

"Why are you covering for him?" I yelled back.

"Bri!" someone shouted from the hallway outside. "Olivia!"

A split second later, Cam came running through the door with Devin and Jared right behind him. At this rate, the entire Warrior coven would be crowding in here within the next few minutes.

"Bri, Brianna," Cam shouted as he took her by the shoulders, "you have to stop screaming in my head, love. What's going on?"

Awbie's head fell into Cam's chest and she pointed to me.

"William?" Cam asked curiously.

"No!" Olivia shouted. "I want everyone to leave this instant."

"Shut up, Livy," Jax yelled.

"This is none of your business," she shouted back.

Cam put up one hand while the other held a sobbing Awbie against his chest. "William, would you care to shed some light as to what is going on?"

I didn't bother looking at Olivia before replying, "Last night I said some things to Olivia that I shouldn't have, so I was coming to her room to apologize. When I got close, I heard a scream and when I came in, Niall was on top of her, cursing at her and...then he...hit her." Awbie let out a wail, and Cam's head jerked in Olivia's direction.

"That's not what happened!" Olivia shouted.

"I saw him slap you across the face, Liv! And you implied this wasn't the first time."

"Oh my god," Awbie cried.

"In the heat of the moment," I continued, "and as she was defending him, I mentioned how I couldn't believe she'd put up with that considering what Awbie went through. I didn't know that was a secret, I swear."

Cam's face hardened. "Where is Niall now?"

"He ran."

Cam looked over at Devy. "Find him," he said firmly. Devy gave a curt nod and gestured for Jared to follow. "Bring him back alive, brother."

Devy growled but left with Jared right behind him. Awbie stepped out of Cam's arms and wiped the red tears from her face, although more leaked from her eyes that followed the same tracks.

"William," Cam began, "would you excuse us? I believe a family meeting is in order."

"Yes, sir," I replied.

"How did you find out?" Awbie asked with a trembling voice.

I sighed and looked down at the floor. "Mom had had a couple glasses of wine one night and a movie came on about an abused woman who escapes and then eventually kills her husband. She looked at the TV and said 'that could be your aunt's life story.' Needless to say, I had some questions. I'm sorry, Awbie."

"It's ok, honey," she interrupted and wiped her face again. "Thank you for helping our girl."

I gave a nod and then took one last look at Olivia who wouldn't even make eye contact with me. Ungrateful bitch. The signs from the Universe couldn't be more clear - Olivia Burke was not the person I used to love. She would never be the person I wanted or needed her to be. She could rot for all I cared.

Chapter Twenty

Olivia

If my parents and Jack hadn't been standing in my room, I would have clawed Will's eyes out. To say I was humiliated was an understatement, but on top of that I felt betrayed by my parents. They lied about an entire lifetime, one that everyone else in our family and the coven knew about. Nothing felt worse than realizing you were the idiot in the room.

As soon as Will closed the door behind him, Ada sighed and put his hands on his hips. "I am not sure where we should start. Olivia, perhaps you could start by telling us what happened today."

"No," I replied angrily, "not until you tell us about mom's first husband."

Jack turned to Mom who had her back to us, and placed a hand on her shoulder. "Mom, I'm not going to be a bitch like Livy, but I'd like to know what happened too."

Mom patted his hand and wiped her face as she turned around.

Ada gestured toward the bed. "Perhaps both of you could sit."

As we sat down on the bed, Ada put his arm around Mom to keep her steady. I'd never seen my mother look so fragile. Ada took the chair from the corner of the room and placed it in front of us.

Mom crumbled into the chair and it took her nearly a minute to speak. When she finally did, her voice was soft and timid. "I have rarely spoken to you about my mother because there are hardly any good things I could ever say about her. I had ruined her life by being born, and she never let me forget it. In fact, probably one of her favorite pastimes was telling me how useless I was, and how I would never amount to anything. After awhile you start believing those things. It beats you down as a person, and makes you an easy target for manipulative, abusive monsters," she said and finally lifted her head to look at us. "I met Sam Lewis when I was eighteen years old. We both had terrible upbringings and saw each other as a way out. I got pregnant, and our families pushed us to get married.

"A few months later I lost the baby, and he hit me for the first time. It only got worse from there. Gradually he began isolating me, making me dependent on him financially, and became more and more abusive. The only time I would get a semi-break from it was when I was pregnant, but I lost the baby every time." Ada squeezed her shoulder as she covered her mouth for a few moments. "Eventually we moved to Connecticut where he became very successful, and I basically became a prisoner in my own house. Sam abused and violated me in every possible way, and I felt like there was no escape for me so I just waited for the day that he would inevitably kill me."

"Mom," Jack said, "how could you just let that happen to you? You're not like that."

Mom took a breath before she replied, "Honey, when someone beats you down enough, you start to feel that it's just easier for you to take it, and I believed I had no other options. I am not the same person I was back then. I didn't even know that I was a hybrid, or that I had powers, or even the strength to defend myself. Your father helped me with that," she said as she smiled up at Ada who looked down at her with a loving expression that brought me to tears.

"Will said something about you escaping though," Jack said. "Saying you got hurt and that's how Uncle John met you."

She nodded and nervously tapped her lap with her hand. "The day I met your father, something snapped inside me and I decided that I couldn't take it anymore. I thought I'd just run or die trying. I got as far as the driveway before Sam rammed my SUV and he literally dragged me back into the house. He threw me around and I thought for sure he was going to kill me, but then your father broke down the door and saved me."

"Is that when you killed him?" Jack asked and Ada's face hardened.

"No, son. That was later."

"How? When?"

Ada sighed and clasped his hands behind his back. "I had taken your mother down to Oliver's, and we were there for several weeks before Sam found her. He made it clear he was coming to kill your mother, so another Warrior and I stopped him."

"And you killed him," I said flatly. "You killed a human."

"Yes I did, and I was punished for it. The only reason I am alive is because of the extenuating circumstances regarding his abuse of your mother, and the fact that Victor felt she would be an asset to the coven. This is not something I am proud of. I had taken an oath to protect humans from our kind. But," he paused for a moment, "Sam Lewis was a vile piece of human garbage who did not deserve the privilege of drawing breath."

"But why didn't you tell us any of this?" I asked angrily.

"Because I'm ashamed, Olivia!" Mom snapped. "I didn't want to tell my children about how I allowed a man to do this to me. How sometimes I would worry I would bleed to death because I couldn't get a wound to stop bleeding. Or that I worried I wouldn't wake up in the morning because Sam's punches had caused internal bleeding. And how I would stay awake half the night because I was afraid he would just kill me in my sleep. I didn't want to think about it anymore, so I certainly didn't want you two to know. But in all honesty, I didn't think I needed to talk about what happened to me in order to prevent it from happening to you! Olivia, we have always taught you to stand up for yourself, and frankly you have never had a problem with that. Never would I think you would..."

"You don't get to judge me," I interrupted, "and everyone is exaggerating what happened."

"Are you saying Will is lying?" Jack asked and stood from the bed.

"He doesn't know what he saw."

"If Will said he saw Niall slap you, Niall fucking slapped you," he replied, eyeing me down.

"Everyone needs to calm down," Ada said as he took Jack by the shoulders and nudged him over by the windows, but then he gave me a stern look. "Olivia, did Niall hit you?"

"It's not what you all think, it was a misunderstanding."

Mom stood from her chair. "Honey, I can assure you that it will not get better, this is where it starts. Please don't make the same mistakes I did."

"Mom, stop!" I shouted. "I'm not like you, and Niall isn't your first husband."

"Olivia, this is serious," Ada yelled with wild eyes. "I have seen your mother battered and bruised. I will not see my daughter in the same state. Only a coward lays a hand on a woman, and I will not permit that in my own home! If they find Niall…"

But Ada couldn't finish his statement since the door to the bedroom flew open and Uncle Jared stepped inside with Devy who had Niall bent over his shoulder.

"He's alive," Devy said and then threw Niall down in the floor. "For how long is up to you, Brother."

Niall grunted as he rolled over and said, "I am a hybrid, and therefore protected."

"Well, from what we just learned, that doesn't seem to really matter to the people in this room," I said and Niall gave me a worried look.

"You cannot harm me, especially for something I haven't done."

"Then why did you run, jackass," Uncle Jared said and nudged Niall with his foot.

"I wasn't running," Niall said as he stood from the floor, straightening his shirt and patting his hair down.

"We found you running down the street," Devy said flatly.

Niall patted his blonde hair down again nervously and replied, "Very well, I was running from this," he said and gestured to everyone in the room. "I knew that what happened would be misconstrued, and you all would have this reaction."

"Misconstrued?" Jack said and took a step forward. "So you're saying you didn't knock my sister to the ground and slap her across the face?"

"Jax, I know Will is your friend, but this is a misunderstanding."

"You're going to look us in the eye and tell us you didn't hit my sister, you piece of shit," Jack shouted and launched himself toward Niall, but Devy caught him in midair. "You fucking coward, you lay another hand on my sister and I will kill you, I will fucking kill you and give your body to the prisoners in the dungeon. Do you hear me?"

Ada stepped in front of Devy and squeezed Jack's chin between his fingers. "Jackson Thomas Burke, you will control yourself."

"This is what I feared," Niall said. "This is why I left."

Ada turned to face Niall, his body tense with control. "Niall, I am sure you can understand that we are all a little sensitive after finding out that you have hit my child."

Niall put his hands up. "All I am asking is for a chance to defend myself, and before I can do that I need to speak with Olivia."

"You have to be friggin' kidding me," Mom groaned. "You think I am going to let you get within reach of my daughter?"

"I can speak for myself," I shouted.

"Because you've been doing a hell of a job so far," Jack grumbled.

I glared at him. "If everyone could just let me and Niall have a few minutes to talk alone."

Mom shook her head and placed her hand over her mouth in disapproval. Ada stood stoic but looked at the wall in disgust.

"Stupid bitch," Jack muttered, not bothering to hide his feelings.

"Thanks, Jack, you're always so supportive. We'll go in the bathroom then."

"You have two minutes before we take that door off its hinges," Ada said and pointed to the bathroom door. "Are we clear?"

"Yes, sir," Niall replied. "Thank you, sir."

Niall scurried across the room and ducked inside the bathroom. Once I closed the door, Niall held up his hand and created a shield across the wall and door. "No need to look panicked, Olivia, I just want some privacy from your family."

"I'm not panicked," I lied.

"Olivia, I'm sorry that I lost control…"

"Control? Niall, you tackled me to the ground and slapped me for eating pancakes. And Will, of all people, saw it. Then come to find out that my mother was married once before and that he was abusive to her. So now, they're comparing you to him, and that's all they see. If you wanted my family's support to combine the covens, well, you just lost it. Was your loss of control worth it?"

The color left Niall's face as he sat down on the edge of the tub. "Bullocks."

"You can't hit me, Niall. You can't lose control like that anymore."

"What do you want me to do, love? There is only so much I can put up with. Between your family, my family, you keeping your gifts from me, the constant feeling as though I'm in competition with Will, I'm at my wits end. Everything was perfect before we came here, we were perfect."

"No, Niall, we weren't," I replied and he straightened up. "You pressure me for sex, you've backhanded me, talked down to me, and I never say anything because I didn't want you to… break up with me, I guess. But I'm going to speak up and tell you when something is not ok. I can't stand for anyone else in my family to tell me I'm not standing up for myself."

Niall slowly stood up from the tub and I took a small step back. "Olivia, you were a virgin when I met you, and incredibly sexually naïve. You have no idea what it's like to have your girlfriend's fangs coming at you when you're trying to be intimate with her. So maybe I haven't handled everything in the best way, but I am doing the best I can under the circumstances. I just want us to be happy. Don't you?

"Our families are tearing us apart, don't you see that? Let's go back home, and to hell with what my father wants, or how your family thinks you should behave," he said and stepped in front of me, taking my left hand and kissing the engagement ring. "I love you, Olivia. I want to start a life with you, but on our terms. Isn't that what you want?"

I didn't answer right away. All his words were registering in my head, and none of them put together an apology. Tears were welling in my eyes from too much being thrown at me at once. Was Niall worth his temper? I looked down at the sparkling engagement ring. It was what I had wanted, but I wasn't prepared for what came with it.

Niall squeezed my hand. "Olivia, you are twenty-three years old and I am your first relationship. What you are, and who your family is, is too intimidating for most men. It's not like they've been knocking your door down. I cracked under the pressure, but I am here, promising to accept all of you. How many other chances do you think you'll have?"

My stomach sank. Men had never been banging down my door. Maybe going back to our little Italian apartment where we were happy was the answer. Our families really were tearing us apart.

When Niall realized I was giving in, he seized the moment and said, "We'll need to convince your family that Will was wrong." I nodded. "We have to be a united front."

I nodded again, and after he took down the shield, he led me out of the bathroom. Everyone in the room snapped to attention as we entered the bedroom. My mother's face was completely stained red from crying. Jack stood with his back against the wall, his arms crossed tightly in front of his chest. Devy and Uncle Jared were hovering by the door, both looking like they were itching for a fight.

No one was going to be happy, but it wasn't their business.

"I know all of you are upset because of something you think happened. Will walked in on Niall and I in a…private…moment. He didn't see what he thought he did, and Niall shouldn't be judged for it."

"So you're saying Will can't tell the difference between sex and a coward abusing a woman?" Jack said nastily.

"I'm saying he made a mistake."

"You're an idiot."

"Jackson, please," Ada scolded.

"No, Ada," he said and pushed himself off the wall. "She's lying and covering for a...Niall, I believe they would call you a wanker."

"Jackson..." Ada warned.

"I'm leaving, I'm leaving," Jack said and stepped toward the door. "If you stay with him, Livy, you deserve what you get."

Once Jack left the room, I looked at Ada. "I'm serious, Ada, this is a misunderstanding and I won't stand for anyone treating Niall like he's done something wrong."

"Livy, don't do this," Mom pleaded.

"If anyone can't handle this, we'll just leave tonight, it's that simple."

Ada pulled Mom into his side and gestured for Devy and Uncle Jared to leave. "You and Niall are welcome here as long as this was, as you say, a misunderstanding," Ada began, but then narrowed his eyes and lowered his voice. "However, Niall, if you dare lay a hand on my daughter in any capacity while in my home, I will use the full force of my Warriors to remove you. Is that understood?"

"Sir, I assure you..."

Ada held up his hand. "Do not insult my intelligence more than both of you already have."

Before either of us could say anything, Ada turned around and pulled Mom out the door, slamming it angrily behind him.

Niall exhaled loudly. "Thank you, love, I know that was difficult."

I nodded and pulled out of his grip, stepping over to the dresser to fix my hair and shirt. Just then, a howling like a wounded animal sounded from the corridor outside.

"What is that noise?" Niall asked.

I swallowed the lump that had formed in my throat before answering, "It's my mother."

Chapter Twenty-one

Will

"I just don't understand why her engagement party has to be at our house?" I said huddled against the door of the kitchen that led outside, subconsciously keeping an exit strategy close.

My mom sighed and huffed as the caterers bustled around her. "Honey, I told you, your aunt didn't really give me a choice," she replied and then directed one of the waiters where to put a pallet of glasses. "Cameron didn't want Niall's family in the manor, and Livy didn't want it at the Facility. They needed a neutral location, and this was the only option on short notice. Believe me, I'm not happy about it either. Honestly, no one is 'happy'," she said with her air quotes. I did wonder if she'd ever outgrow using them. But at this point she'd probably be ninety years old stretching out her arthritic fingers to use them.

"This is bullshit, Mom. It's not real."

"I know, honey, we all know it. Everyone will be putting on fake smiles and trying to ignore the big, abusive, piece of shit elephant that's in the room that has a thick English accent. But there's nothing we can do. This is what Livy wants."

A few of the catering staff gave side glances in our direction, making my mom roll her eyes. She never apologized for things she said or how she said them. To her, she always said what no one else would. It got her in trouble, but she stood by the fact that things needed to be said.

HEART OF BETRAYAL ~ 183

"Honey, I know this is hard," she said and walked over to where I was huddled, placing her hands on my shoulders.

"But how can everyone just let her do this? She doesn't love him, and he…" I didn't finish what I was going to say, I couldn't.

She cupped my cheek. "Honey, Livy's going to do what she wants, she always has. She needs to make her own mistakes, and you need to move on." I shrugged her hand off my cheek. "Look, I love my goddaughter, I would throw myself in front of a bus for her, but she's tearing you apart and I can't stand for that either. Honey, she's not going to be who you want her to be. You need to move on with your life. I can't bear to see you keep getting hurt by her. You've been doing so well, and as soon as she came home, I saw the dark clouds form above you. Let tonight be your final send off. Let her go so you can move forward and not make me worry that you'll sink back into that dark hole."

"I'm fine, Mom," I lied. "I'm not going back there, I promise."

"I just want to see you happy," she said and kissed my cheek.

"Uh, Mom, I've been meaning to talk to you and Dad about something."

"What's that, honey?"

"It's uh…well, I have something in the works, and when this is all over, I think we should sit down and talk."

"Ok, we'll talk about it tomorrow after work. I'll make sure your dad comes home on time."

"Thanks, Mom," I said, kissing her cheek before heading out of the kitchen and into the party. The main living area was already halfway filled, and the guests of honor hadn't even arrived yet. I was dreading the moment when Olivia would come through the door with that fake smile on her face and that English asshole on her arm. But like Mom said, I needed to move on and let Olivia suffer with the consequences of her actions.

A bar had been set up in the far corner of the room, and I pushed people out of the way in order to get to it. The young guy behind the bar stood very straight and stiff, but with a pleasant smile. I wondered if I truly understood the people he'd be serving tonight.

"What's the strongest thing you have?" I asked and rested my hands on the bar.

"I'm assuming you're looking for a human beverage then," he replied.

"You have blood?"

He nodded and gestured behind him. "In warming stations, of course.

You seem surprised."

I shrugged. "I'm surprised my mother didn't freak out about that."

"Is she the red head?" I nodded. "She threatened my life if I spilled a drop of blood on her floor."

"Sounds about right. I'll take the strongest human thing you have."

"Scotch or bourbon?"

"Bourbon, three fingers, straight."

"Make that two," Jax said suddenly next to me. "So things are starting off well."

The bartender had barely finished pouring my drink before I snatched it and took a big gulp. My eyes bugged out from the burning in my throat and chest as the bourbon went down. From the side of my eye, I caught sight of Olivia making her way through the congratulatory crowd. Her hair was pulled back in a tight bun and she was wearing a white jumpsuit. It made me angrier at myself because I thought she looked so damn beautiful.

"Quit looking at her," Jax warned before drinking half his bourbon.

"Old habits die hard. Did you meet his family?"

He sucked in air through his teeth as the bourbon burned down his throat as it had mine. "Just at the airport when we picked them up, and that was enough. Niall is a gem compared to these guys." He drank down the rest of his bourbon and put the glass down on the bar. "Can I get another one, please?"

The bartender nodded and poured nearly half a glass, which made Jax smile.

"I'm going to tell my parents everything tomorrow," I said softly.

"Really? Why tomorrow?"

I shrugged. "No reason to wait anymore. Honestly, it'll feel good to get it off my chest. I'm just worried about the blowback."

Jax rested his hand on my shoulder. "But we'll be here for you, remember that."

"I know. I just want to get on with it."

"Get on with what?" my dad's voice rang behind me.

Slowly I turned around, trying to keep my face relaxed. "Hey, Pop, how's it going?"

"Fine. Your mother tells me you need to talk to us tomorrow night about something."

I went to speak, but the smallest amount of spit decided to get caught in my throat, causing me to cough uncontrollably for several seconds.

"You ok, son?"

When I finally caught my breath, I answered, "Yeah, sorry. I uh…yeah, I gave my notice at the club a couple of days ago."

His raised his eyebrows and his eyes brightened slightly. "Although I like the sound of that, I do hope you have a plan for something new."

"Yeah, that's what I want to talk to you guys about tomorrow."

"You can't just tell me now?"

"Let me get through this party first."

He nodded slowly with recognition. "I gotcha. I'm excited to hear what you've lined up."

I nodded, although I knew his excitement would not last long. Right at that moment, Cam came through the crowd with another man that was almost as tall as he was, but with a thicker build and very broad shoulders. Since I didn't recognize him, or the dozen or so others that were filing in behind him, I assumed he was Niall's father and his coven. Although, Niall must favor his mother since he didn't resemble his father in any way. Niall's entire body was the size of his father's thigh.

"John," Cam began, "I would like to introduce you to Miller Cummings, Niall's father. Miller, this is Dr. John Ryan, Chief Medical Officer of Facility West, and husband of our host."

Miller extended his hand, although he seemed either unimpressed or bored. "Pleasure is mine. Your wife is very…energetic."

Dad nodded slowly, the way you would when someone said something odd, but you didn't want to make them uncomfortable about it. "She is, but we are both honored to have you and your coven members in our home."

"Thank you," Miller replied. "Your home is definitely grander than I had expected."

"Well, we try," Dad replied diplomatically, and then opened himself up and gestured to me. "This is my son Will, and I'm assuming you've met Jax."

Miller chose not to extend his hand to me, and instead gave a slight nod. "Will, the childhood friend, yes I have heard a lot about you. And yes, I have had the pleasure of meeting my future daughter-in-law's twin brother. It is amazing to see how different twins can be."

"Thank god for small miracles," Jax replied.

"Jackson," Cam grumbled.

"Oh, Cam, it's fine," Miller laughed, and you could literally see my godfather's hackles raise at Miller using a nickname that only three people in the world were allowed to call him, me being one of them.

Cam forced a smiled and directed Miller and his crew to a different area of the party.

When my dad felt they were far enough into the crowd, he looked at me and Jax and said, "Well, I think we now know why Niall is such a dick."

Jax spit his bourbon across the room before choking and coughing for nearly fifteen seconds. Dad just smirked and turned back into the crowd. I swigged back what I had left in my glass and placed it down on the bar.

"Another, please," I said, but the bartender already had the bottle ready and was pouring.

Just as I brought the newly filled glass to my lips, Jax grabbed the same elbow and tried pulling me away. The only thing he accomplished was having me spill my drink on myself. "Dammit, man. Wha…"

"Will Ryan is drinking?" Olivia's said behind me, "now that's a sight to see."

After a deep exhale, I turned around to find Olivia standing in front of me looking more beautiful than I had ever seen her. The white jumpsuit she was wearing was cut halfway down her abdomen, exposing more of her breasts than I had ever seen. Her hair was pulled back in a tight bun exposing the diamond earrings I'd given her. It was the biggest fuck you she could give me.

I raised my glass and said, "Some occasions merit it, I suppose."

She sighed as I took a big drink and burned my throat. "Can you be nice to me for one night?"

"Me?" I said too loudly, and Jax put his hand on my shoulder. "You have treated me like shit since you came home, and now you're telling everyone I lied."

"I didn't say you lied," she began in a terse tone, "you just misinterpreted what you saw."

"If that's how you're having sex, you're doing it wrong."

Jax put his arms between us and pushed us apart. "All right, everyone back to their corners."

"She started it," I muttered.

"And I'm finishing it," he replied, and then caught himself. "Never, ever, make me sound like Ada again. Livy, just get your drink and leave us to suffer alone."

"If you're suffering so much, you should leave."

"Halleluiah, I'll go tell Mom and Ada," Jax laughed, just as Niall stepped up to our group.

"Well, this gathering looks ominous," he said, making quick eye contact with me, and then turning to Olivia. "Do you need me to save you, love?"

"She can defend herself just fine," Jax replied, but when he gave his mischievous smile, I knew he was going to be an asshole. "Then again, after the other day, maybe she can't."

"Shut. Up," Olivia growled.

"No need to get upset, love," Niall said and put his arm around Olivia's waist. "We know our truth."

"I'm sure you do, you're just not telling it," Jax laughed and placed his empty glass on the bar.

The bartender was certainly getting a show, and without a word, filled Jax's glass with bourbon.

I placed my hand on Jax's shoulder. "Come on, man, back to our corners. Remember?"

"Hold up," Niall said, and waved two men over to us. "I'd like you all to meet Mason and Duncan, my father's closest advisors."

Closest advisors? Niall's father had certainly created an incredible fake reality around himself. Both Mason and Duncan looked like uptight, judgmental assholes. Mason was a little taller than Duncan, but both had short blond hair and chiseled out cheeks. Were they former members of the Arian nation? Hitler youth?

"I know you both know Olivia," Niall continued, "but if you can't tell, this is her twin brother Jackson."

"Are you a Warrior?" Duncan asked in a tone I couldn't tell if he was curious, or was questioning the fact Jax could actually be a Warrior.

"Well, one of the Burke twins had to be," Jax replied snidely.

"Really?" Niall began. "The way your sister put it was that you had no other path in life, and your father forced you to work for him."

Jax flashed his crooked smile. "My sister hasn't lived here in five years, so what the fuck does she know."

"I'm right here," Olivia growled.

"Are you though? Or are we just misinterpreting what we're seeing."

Niall cleared his throat. "And this is Will Ryan, a childhood friend."

Reluctantly I shook the hands of the two "advisors", and they looked about as happy as I did.

"And what is it you do?" Mason asked, his cheeks sinking in even more as he spoke. "Are you a Warrior?"

Niall laughed and I wanted to punch him in the face. "No, no, no, Mason, Will is a..well, what would you call yourself? A bartender or a waiter? You also teach something, don't you?"

I bit the inside of my cheek to keep my control, but finally answered, "Yes, I teach martial arts at Facility West. And yes, I was a bartender until recently."

Olivia's face fell. "Until recently? Why just until recently?"

I met her gaze and replied, "Just moving on. Time to make a change."

"When?"

"Soon," I replied and finished my drink.

As soon as I put my glass down, the kid behind the bar filled it right back up. The alcohol was already hitting me. I'd be drunk in the next ten minutes at this rate.

Niall gave me a hit in the arm. "Well done, Will. Good things can happen even if you don't go to University."

"Like how soon?" Olivia asked, obviously stuck in her own conversation.

"A couple of days," I answered and then looked back at Niall. "And I did graduate from college, Niall. I just didn't finish medical school."

Niall tilted his head condescendingly. "Well then, let's hope your new venture is something that will make your parents proud. I'm sure it's disappointing for them not to have another doctor in the family."

Jax took a step toward Niall, but I put my hand in front of his chest. "Maybe I'm not a doctor, but at least I've worked for everything I have, rather than sponge off of my girlfriend's family connections to try and get my fake coven recognized."

Niall tensed, and the two advisors straightened their shoulders.

"At least he's not lying to his family about becoming a Warrior," Olivia said, and it knocked the breath out of me.

"Is that right, Will?" Niall said loudly. "You're becoming a Warrior?"

"Shut your fucking mouth," Jax growled.

"What was that?" a soft voice said as two hands came between Mason and Duncan and spread them apart, revealing my mother. "What did you say?"

I couldn't breathe. My heart was pounding so hard it was making my head hurt and my knees weak. Olivia looked at me from under her lids, challenging me to say something first, but I simply shook my head, pleading with my eyes for her to keep quiet.

"Will?" Mom asked with a trembling lip. When I didn't answer, "Well someone say something!"

"Will is becoming a Warrior, Aunt Re," Olivia blurted out. "Everyone knows and has been keeping it from you and Uncle John."

"Wh-what? What? I...John? John! JOHN!" she shouted, causing the whole party to fall silent except for the sounds of my mother's hysteria.

My father waded through the crowd and took my mother by her shoulders. "Re, what's..."

"Will...becoming...Warrior," she said between gasps of air.

Dad jerked his head in my direction as everything in front of me began to spin. My ears started to ring and I couldn't find any words. Jax stepped in front of me, trying in vain to calm down my parents. My father became beet red, his face twitching and eyes bulging until he finally blew.

"Everyone out!" he shouted.

"Uncle John, wait..." Olivia began, but Dad put his hand in front of her.

"I'm serious, everybody out of my house. Now!"

People around us began to awkwardly retreat. The ringing in my ears was deafening, and the world was spinning out of control. Jax's face came into focus in front of me, his lips moving in slow motion, but I wasn't able to hear him at first.

He shook me roughly and knocked the breath back into me. "Will? Can you hear me?"

I nodded, but still couldn't find words. When I looked up, I saw that Cam and Awbie were now standing with my parents.

"You lied to me!" my mother screamed in Awbie's face. "You're supposed to be my best friend, my sister, and you lied to me!"

"Renee, please listen..."

"You want to kill my son, you bitch!" Mom screamed and slapped Awbie across the face. Awbie was more shocked than anything. I was sure that the hit hurt Mom more than my aunt, but red tears still formed in Awbie's eyes. Mom ran across the room, loud wails echoing off the walls as she pushed people out of the way with Awbie following after her.

"I swear to god, Cameron, if you're not off my property in five minutes, I will call the police."

"John," Cam said calmly, "I know we can discuss this, just please calm down and hear Will out."

"Get out!" Dad shouted. "I will expose everything, I swear I will if you don't get out of my house this instant. Don't test me, Cameron, I will shout everything I know at the top of my lungs and enough people will hear before you can take me down. Now get out, just get out."

Cam put his hands up and began to back away slowly. "John, we will do what you ask, but please remember, you and Renee are our dear friends. We will talk about this."

With a final look at me and a slight nod, Cam turned and guided the remaining people out the front door.

"Jackson, that means you too."

Jax shook his head. "Sorry, Uncle John, someone needs to be here for Wills."

"I am his father," Dad shouted. "I have done nothing but be there for him."

"No offense, and I mean no offense, but if you were really there for him you wouldn't have just kicked dozens of people out of your house because you wanted to scream at your son in private. If you were really there for him, he wouldn't have had to keep this secret. I'm just saying."

The redness in my father's face began to recede, although the intensity of his look didn't fade. "Fine then," he said and then looked at me. "How long, exactly, have you been lying to us?"

"A year," I replied in a voice so soft and meek that I didn't recognize it as my own.

"A ye…you've only been home a year. And you felt like you couldn't tell us because…"

"Because I knew you would react like this! I've been waiting for the right time, and…and it just never seems to happen."

"And this is what you wanted to discuss with me and your mother after tonight?" I nodded. "So you were planning on joining the trainees?"

"I've already been accepted as a full Warrior, Dad. I've been training with the trainees for the last year just to prepare for when I'm ready to…"

"To be Turned? That's what you want? You want to be Turned and be…one of them?"

"Yes, it's what…"

"This is going to kill your mother," he said angrily and turned his back to me.

"Uncle John," Jax began, "Wills has a gift. He's ten times better than me, and I'm, to use your words, one of them. You saw him change when he came home last year. You saw him come out of being a zombie, and that happened because he started training with us. Isn't that what all parents want, for their children to find their calling? Well Wills has, this is it. It may not be what you want for him, but he's meant to do this."

Finally, Dad turned around. The redness in his face was completely gone, but there was a lack of emotion altogether. "Fine, if this is his calling, he can do it without us."

"What? What does that mean?" I asked as my stomach dropped into the floor.

"It means you don't have to wait," he replied. "Go ahead and get Turned now because your mother and I will not be there to watch it."

"Dad, wait…"

"I want you out of here by tomorrow night. Do not call, do not message, do not drop by. You want to be a vampire, fine. As of right now my son is dead. I hope you're happy with your decision. Now I have to go and tend to your mother," he said and walked across the living room just as Awbie ran through with dark red streaks running down her face.

Suddenly Jax's hand crushed my upper arm, pulling me back up to standing. Everything was spinning as my world crumbled around me. I could feel the tears coming up and I had to get out of here before they overflowed. I pushed Jax's hand off my arm, ran through the kitchen, and out the side door. The night air hit my face and I quickly began gasping for breath. I grabbed at one of the pillars on the covered walkway that led to the garage, I wasn't sure if I was going to faint or throw up.

Jax patted me on the back and wrapped his arm around me for support. "Are you happy now," he shouted over me and I looked up to see Olivia standing at the far end of the driveway with Niall and his family. "You ruin everything, Olivia, you fucking bitch. Just go back to the other end of the world and wreak havoc over there and leave us alone."

Cam was in front of us in a flash and put his hand in Jax's chest. "I know you are angry, son, but you will control yourself."

"How can you defend what she just did! Uncle John just kicked Wills out. He literally said Will is dead to them."

"William, is that true?" he asked and I was about to lose the battle of not crying in front of everyone.

"Yes…" I began, but my voice cracked. "I can't be out here, I can't…"

Cam nodded as he placed his right hand on my cheek and pressed my opposite cheek against his. "He will come around, Wills," he whispered in my ear, making me almost breakdown. "Come to the manor, you have a place to go."

I nodded as I pulled away, keeping my head low as I ran to my garage apartment's door. I was up the stairs in less than five seconds and in the solace of my bedroom. Thankfully my anxiety pills were sitting right on top of my nightstand. My hands shook as I tried opening the bottle once, twice, and then on the third attempt the bottle's cap went flying, causing the pills to scatter in all directions.

"Fucking, fuck," I shouted, throwing the bottle across the room and falling to the floor with my back against the wall.

"Will?" Jax said, filling the bedroom doorway. "What happened?"

"I was trying to take my anxiety meds," I replied, placing my elbows on my knees and letting my head fall into my hands.

Jax stepped inside and knelt down next to me. "You know the problem with relying on your meds is, right?" I shook my head. "You can't take them once you're Turned. You can't run to the pills to help you through something like this. You've got to figure out how to do it without them, man."

Feeling the tears coming again, I pinched my thumb and index finger between my eyes. "You're right," I replied. After several deep breaths I said, "Why…why would she do that?"

"Because she's a miserable human being whose aim is to make everyone else as miserable as she is."

"Had that one locked and loaded, didn't ya," I said and rolled my head back up against the wall, making a loud thud. "My worst nightmare just came true. I mean, I was worried I would lose them, but…what am I going to do?"

"You heard Ada, just come to the manor. Pack your shit and let's go."

I shook my head. "I can't do this now, plus she'll be there. Jesus, I'll be there and she'll just be walking around like she didn't just drop a bomb on my life."

"Then show her," he replied adamantly. "Show her she can't do shit like this. Don't give her the response she's looking for."

"What if I don't ever see Mom again," I said and the tears finally came. "This was not how I wanted to tell them."

"They'll come around, Wills," he replied and hit my leg lightly with his fist. "Your mom can't go a day without speaking to you, she'll come around, man. Your dad too."

"Did you see his face?" I said and then completely broke down. Jax didn't answer and just let me have my moment. After a couple of minutes, I wiped my face with the back of my hand. "Sorry, man."

"It's all right, Wills. We're Warriors. We're not afraid of anything, including a little crying. Well, Devy might be afraid of crying." I smiled, but didn't have the energy to give a full laugh. "So, you're going to stay here tonight?"

I nodded. "I'll pack tomorrow. I'll never be able to sleep tonight."

Jax stood up from the floor. "Who needs sleep? Got any vodka?"

"Yeah, in the cabinet next to the sink," I replied and he instantly left the room. "But that's not going to solve anything."

"You're right," he replied as he came back in the bedroom with the big bottle of cheap vodka. "But it'll make you forget for a few hours, and if you get blackout drunk, you'll forget the whole night."

Jax opened the bottle and handed it to me. After a big exhale, I chugged three big gulps of what tasted like gasoline.

"You should never be a counselor," I replied with a cough as the vodka burned down my throat.

"Bullshit. I'd have the happiest clientele in the world."

"You'd have alcoholics."

"And I'd treat them for that too. It's a brilliant business plan."

I smiled. "Thanks, man."

"You're my brother, it's what I'm here for. Now drink up."

Chapter Twenty-two

Olivia

Mom and Ada thought perhaps Niall and I would be more comfortable at the residence they had rented for Miller and his coven members. Which meant Niall went back to their rental house, and I went for a run. Last night had been a shit show, but my head was a little clearer after a near five-hour run. The only thing I couldn't get out of my head was the look on Will's face when I outed him. Saying my parents were furious was an understatement. Hell, I was surprised they allowed us to pack our own bags for the night and they weren't waiting for us at the gate. That's why it was so surprising when at hour four of my run I received a call from Ada suggesting Niall and his closest family come to the manor for an intimate sit down. Miller jumped at the chance, although I wasn't sure that Ada would have considered the family accountant a "close" family member.

Simon was a short, mousy, nervous little man who had no combat skills, but was a brilliant accountant, and had made Miller an incredible amount of money to sustain the coven. I believe it was the only reason Miller had Turned him, and I had a feeling he knew he didn't belong, but he stayed because he didn't have anywhere else to go. But on important occasions like today, Simon was a common fixture since Miller felt that every meeting had a financial aspect to it.

With last night being such a disaster, I really wanted today to be the beginning of an…adequate life with Niall. There was still an ache in the pit of my stomach that wouldn't stop burning. It seemed to be linked to that tiny voice in the back of my head telling me that every step I was making was a mistake. No matter how many times I told that little voice why I was doing this, she wouldn't shut up. She was a constant droning that churned my stomach.

"Olivia?" Niall asked next to me and startled me slightly. "You're awfully quiet this morning."

I forced a smile and squeezed his hand. "Yes, just a little nervous, I guess."

"Perhaps today won't be as dramatic as last night," Miller said from the front passenger seat.

"One can only hope," I replied just as we rounded a corner bringing the manor's tall black gates into view.

"Whether it is or not, it has been a dream of mine to just step into the famous Warrior manor, and the two of you have made it possible," Miller said and then gasped softly like a child as we drove through the gate.

Simon leaned into me and nudged my side. "Seeing the manor has been a dream of mine as well. How lucky you were to have grown up here."

"Well, I can't say I ever thought of myself as lucky."

"Oh but you are," he replied with a kind, innocent smile, "your family is so lovely. I'm sure we will be able to come to agreeable terms today."

"Terms? Wha…"

"Simon," Miller interrupted, and Simon squeezed his portfolio nervously into his chest.

I knew there was no use in getting anything more out of Simon, but what the heck did he mean by terms? But I suppose I would find out soon enough. Ada and Devy stood stoically at the front door as we pulled around. I was used to seeing Devy have little to no expression, but seeing it on Ada was unnerving.

"Miller, welcome to the Warrior manor," Ada said with a pleasant smile as we all filed out of the SUV and stepped up next to Miller. Niall looked nothing like his father. Where Niall was lanky and fair-haired, Miller was thick with wide shoulders, and dark brown hair.

Miller looked down the length of the manor and back again. "Yes, thank you, it is a pleasure to be here," he said and then gave a disappointed sigh. "I thought it would be bigger."

"We don't need to prove we have the bigger penis," Devy said and turned to walk inside. "We know we do."

Miller gave a side glance to Niall who squeezed my hand tightly. I wasn't sure what he expected me to do. His dad was being a dick, and Devy gave it right back.

Ada gestured to the front doors. "Please, if everyone will follow me, Brianna is waiting for us."

As soon as everyone had stepped into the manor, Niall pulled me back slightly. "Why is Devin here? I thought it was just family."

"Your father brought his accountant. I don't think you can judge. Besides, Devy is family, Niall. What's the matter?"

Niall grimaced and lowered his voice. "You know how my father is with...people like Devin."

"People like Devin?"

"His partner isn't going to be here, is he?"

"Uncle Fabi? Not that I know of, but it shouldn't matter. What do you want me to say, Niall? Everyone is going to have to deal with each other," I replied, ripping my hand out of his and walking inside.

Everyone just needed to grow the fuck up and pretend to like each other for one fucking day! How hard was that?

When the door to my parents' suite came into view, I took a breath and reached back. Niall took my hand and I was reminded why I was doing this.

"I'm sorry, love," he whispered in my ear and then kissed my temple. "I'm nervous."

"Me too. Just keep thinking, we'll get through this and soon enough we'll get to go home and be us again."

He squeezed my hand. "You look lovely, by the way."

Self-consciously I smoothed down my dress. It was a simple fit and flare black dress, but also conversative the way Niall preferred. "Glad I thought to pack it last night."

"Me too. This is how my bride should represent herself."

I forced a smile and Niall pulled me into my parents' suite. Mom was standing just inside the door. She looked weary. There was very little energy in her face, and the skin around her eyes was stained red.

"I had some muffins and danish brought in for you," she said and gestured toward a table near the French doors. "If you want something hot, there's the buffet in the dining room."

"No, no, this is fine, Brianna. Thank you," Niall replied and stepped over to the table.

"Mom," I whispered, "are you ok?"

Her eyes widened and she flinched back slightly. "No, Olivia, I'm not. My best friend of thirty years called me a bitch and a whore after your little outburst last night. I'm a bit confused and upset, but I'm here and doing my best to keep it together. So grab a danish and we can move this along."

I was left speechless as Mom stepped away toward the sitting area in the center of the room where two white couches faced each other. Mom joined Ada on the couch to the right, while Devy stood behind them. Mason, Duncan, Simon, and Miller sat on the opposite couch to the left. Lines had definitely been drawn between the families. Niall seemed to notice too, and pulled me to where my family was sitting.

"Well isn't this nice," Miller began. "Just think, this is only the beginning of these lovely little gatherings."

"Yes, just think about it," Devy grumbled, causing Ada to clear his throat quietly.

"Hopefully today will be a little less dramatic than last night," Miller said with a smirk. "Perhaps we could think about having another engagement party across the pond. No ex's there to cause a commotion."

"What? Will's not an…"

"Another stab at the party is a wonderful idea, Father," Niall interrupted.

Mom and Ada gave cursory smiles.

"Well, shall we get on to why we're here," Miller said gesturing to me and Niall. "Our lovely children uniting our families. With a wedding of this size, we need to start planning right away."

"A wedding of this sizz…"

"This will be the event of the century, my dear. Cam," he said and Ada tensed at the familiarity, "with the concerns you have with strangers coming into the manor, perhaps it's best the children be married at our headquarters instead. We can accommodate just as many people without the restrictions you feel are necessary here."

"I believe the location of the wedding should be up to the children. If they want to have it here, we can make the appropriate accommodations," Ada replied.

I turned to Niall. "I think it would be really nice to have it here. We have so much more family…"

"Yes, but having the wedding at our headquarters in London would be much easier. We were just talking about that last night, remember?"

His eyes were pressuring me to agree with him, more so agree with his father who had just decided to take over the plans of our wedding.

When I opened my mouth to answer, Miller continued with, "And on those lines, I think we should discuss…well, perhaps the ladies could step out during this discussion."

"And why would that be?" Mom said in a challenging tone.

Miller gave her a placating smile and then looked to Ada. "I don't mean to offend anyone, but I am of an older generation, as are you, Cam, and there are certain…expectations when a marriage occurs."

"Miller, anything you need to say to me can be said in front of my wife and daughter. In fact, I am sure they both insist on it."

Miller shifted uncomfortably in his seat before answering, "Very well. I believe we should discuss a dowry."

"A WHAT?!" Mom shouted and Ada draped his arm in front of her.

"Like I said, perhaps the women should step out."

"If anything, the women should stay before you men discuss our worth," Mom said angrily. "Are we talking money or just live stock?"

"Miller," Ada began, his voice strained with control, "as you said, you and I come from different times when dowries were commonplace, however, in today's world I do not see how it would be relevant."

Miller snapped his fingers in front of Simon who quickly pulled a piece of paper out from within his portfolio. "As my accountant has thoughtfully prepared, this is a breakdown of what it will cost us to host and care for Olivia. The dowry is just a gift to help cover those initial costs."

Ada took the paper from Miller's hand and looked it over quickly. "Who decided that Olivia and Niall would be solely living with you?"

"Your daughter," Miller replied and gestured to me.

"I don't think I…expressly said we would live…Niall?"

"Olivia," Miller began before Niall could even open his mouth, "you play such an important role in bringing our families together. By having you in our headquarters, you become the conduit between our coven and the Warriors."

My mouth hung open as both Mom and Ada bore holes into the side of my face. This was the first time any of this had even been brought up, and Niall wasn't saying anything. Not a goddamn word.

"Olivia, didn't you tell Niall you wanted to live outside of the manor?

Living at the manor was stifling, I believe your words were."

I gave Niall a side glance, but he was frozen. Where was the support we promised? He was hanging me out to dry and his father was taking everything out of context.

"That's not…we were planning on going back to our apartment…"

"But that is just throwing money away. Having you as our conduit at our headquarters…"

Ada cleared his throat and shifted both feet firmly down on the ground. "Miller, I am uncomfortable with you referring to my daughter as a conduit. What exactly are you thinking will be the relationship between our two families?"

Miller shot a look over to Niall, and then gave Ada an uncomfortable smile. "I apologize, Cam, I was under the impression my son had laid the groundwork."

"He tried," Devy mumbled.

Miller narrowed his eyes at Devy, and then turned his attention back to Ada. "Cam, let me be…"

"*Cameron*," Ada finally corrected and you could feel the tension growing in the room.

Miller straightened his posture. "Cameron, let me be frank, the Warriors are losing their standing within our race. People think you are going soft."

"Going soft against what?" Devy snapped. "We maintain the laws and we punish those who break them. Because we aren't in all-out war, people think we're going soft?"

Miller put his hands up in front of him. "I am just repeating what I hear."

"Gossip," Devy said as he began to pace behind the couch.

"Even from your very own Warriors?"

Ada and Mom flinched while Devy grabbed the back of the couch and shouted, "Who? Tell me which traitors to put on my kill list."

"Brother, calm down," Ada said. "Miller, in times of peace there is often unease among soldiers."

"Cameron, you're losing your hold, and you know as much as I do, once people no longer fear you, you will lose all control over them."

"And that is where your coven comes in?"

"Frankly, yes," Miller shrugged. "We call ourselves the Warriors of Europe because you have concentrated most of your resources to the

United States. Things were getting out of control, and we stepped in out of necessity, but I'm sure Victor can tell you that. I believe you have him snooping around over there, don't you?"

"I assure you Victor does not snoop."

"This is bullshit," Devy shouted.

"Perhaps this is a conversation best between me and Cameron."

Devy leapt forward, but Ada jumped up and caught him by the shoulders.

"Brother, perhaps he's right," Ada said calmly.

Devy pushed Ada's hands off his shoulders and left the room, slamming the door loudly behind him.

"His kind can be so emotional," Miller laughed.

"*Excuse me*," Mom said angrily.

"Miller, I would refrain from any critical or disparaging remarks about any of my brother's characteristics. He may forgive them, but my wife certainly will not." Miller straightened his posture again, and wiped the snide smile from his face. "Now, if we could get back to the part where you are relying on my daughter being the bridge between our covens."

"Very well. I think it is pretty clear that right now our covens are a bit like oil and water. Olivia will be the bridge that brings us together, and ensure we are speaking the same language. We are all fighting for the same goals..."

Acid was rising in my throat as Miller continued. I thought I could do this. I thought Niall and I were sticking up for what we wanted. My breathing started to quicken and perhaps mimicked Devy when he was angry since Mom put her hand on top of mine and squeezed.

Mom...I don't know what's happening.

They are planning your future, baby girl. Is this really what you want?

No, I...I think I made a mistake.

Thank god you see it, she replied, but sighed aloud.

I need to get out of here, but..

She patted my hand and then crossed her arms in front of her chest, breaking our connection.

"Olivia?" Ada said, bringing me to attention. "This mainly affects you. What do you think of all of this?"

I looked between him and Mom, struggling to find an answer when the door suddenly burst open and Uncle Jared came inside.

"Jared?"

"Sorry, bro," he began and then gestured to me, "we need Olivia."

Miller stood from the couch and turned to face the door. "Excuse me, we are in the middle of some highly important business. Perhaps this could wait."

Uncle Jared gave a smirk and a slight laugh. "Uh, well, since I don't work for you, I'll let my brother decide whether this can wait or not."

Ada stood from the couch and looked around Miller. "What is the problem, little brother, and why is Olivia needed?"

"There's a new hybrid at Facility West who is having an episode and no one knows what language she's speaking. I'm hoping it's one that Livy speaks."

"Yes," I replied loudly and stood up quickly, looking down at my mom who gave a nod. "Um, yes of course I'll do what I can."

I didn't give anyone enough time to object before I stepped away from the couch and followed Uncle Jared out into the corridor.

"Olivia, wait," Niall said, suddenly grabbing my arm. "You can't leave, not right now. We agreed we would support each other..."

"And when exactly is that going to start?" I answered, noticing Uncle Jared stepping closer and eyeing Niall's grip on my arm. Slowly I removed his hand and continued, "You broke your promise to me, again. I'm going to help this woman, and you can't stop me. So why don't you go back inside so you and your dad can plan my future, since it doesn't appear you need me to do it."

With a flick of my hair, I turned away from him and started down the corridor again. Uncle Jared fell in line with me and together we headed out the front doors.

"So, what kind of episode is this woman having? Any idea what part of the world she might even be from? That'll help me narrow things down."

"Uh, I have no idea," he replied with a shrug.

"Wh-what do you..."

"There's no hybrid, Livy." I scrunched my brows in confusion. "I was in the command center when your mother's voice came in my head saying I needed to get you out of that room."

Tears started to form in the corners of my eyes, and I bit my lip to stop them from streaming down my face. After everything I'd done, she didn't wait a second to help me.

"If there's no hybrid, then what am I supposed to do?"

"Run," he replied firmly. "I'm serious, Livybean. Run as far as you need to."

"I've run halfway up the coast and it doesn't make any difference. I come home just as confused as when I left."

"Then you're thinking too much." My head fell onto my youngest uncle's shoulder, and his arms squeezed me tightly. "Clear your head, and your feet will take you where you need to go. Out of the state, out of the country, whatever, just find something that makes you happy, Livybean, because it certainly isn't here or with him. And if I can see it, it's pretty damn obvious."

I half-laughed, half-cried into his shirt. Uncle Jared was never one to talk about feelings or relationships, so I took his statement even more to heart.

"I'm sorry," I said, lifting up from his shoulder and wiping my eyes.

He shrugged. "I've seen worse, mostly from your mom," he laughed. "Now go if you're gonna go, otherwise…"

I didn't wait for him to finish, and launched myself at the door, then across the parking area and through the gate. Now I wondered where my feet would take me.

Chapter Twenty-three

Will

The morning came quickly, and with it came bright sunlight flooding into my bedroom. The sun didn't care that I had a hangover the size of Texas, but neither did my dad who had boxes delivered to my door at eight in the morning. It was a gesture that cut deep, and it was meant to. My dad was a wonderful, caring physician who would do anything for his patients, but was a fierce disciplinarian when it came to his son. He was probably kicking himself for not having more children that would have made him proud. Now, he had no son, I was dead to him. I did wonder if Mom felt the same way, but since she hadn't reached out or come by, I figured she was standing with Dad.

Thankfully there wasn't that much to pack, mostly clothes, a few books, some pictures, and personal items. I could probably move everything to the manor in one trip. It was funny how I'd wanted this for so long, and now that it was here, I wasn't excited. Olivia had taken that away from me.

I shook the thought of her out of my head and concentrated on packing up my bedroom. Just as I stretched a long piece of tape across the bottom of a new box, there was a knock at the door.

"Coming," I said loudly, putting the empty box on the floor and heading down the stairs to the door of my apartment. Perhaps Dad had hired armed guards to escort me off his property. With a deep breath I turned the door handle and braced for whomever was on the other side. But when I opened the door, nothing could have prepared me for Olivia standing in front of me.

"Oh hell no," I shouted as I slammed the door closed and quickly locked the deadbolt.

"Will, please," she begged and banged on the door.

"Go away, Olivia," I shouted and ran back up the stairs.

Just as I made it up to the main floor there was a banging at the window in the living room. I turned around to find Olivia hanging from the eave by one arm, and her legs splayed on either side as far as her dress allowed.

"Please, Will, let me in."

I ran to the window and slid it open. "Jesus Christ, Olivia, we have neighbors," I said as she swung herself inside. Once her feet were on the floor, I closed the window and gestured to the stairs. "Ok, I let you in. Now leave."

She touched my arm, but I slapped it away. "Will…"

"I mean it, Olivia, get the fuck out," I yelled, suddenly realizing that I was standing in front of her in only a pair of sweatpants. I felt incredibly exposed, so I turned and headed to my bedroom in the back of the apartment.

"Wh-what's with all the boxes?" she asked.

"As if you didn't know," I replied as I picked up a white t-shirt from the floor and shrugged it on.

"No…I don't. Will, what's going on?"

When I turned around, she was standing in the doorway. "I've been disowned, Olivia," I answered and her face fell. "Dad kicked me out last night after you outed me, and now I have to be out by tonight, hence the boxes. Are we good now? Or did you want to take another pound of flesh from me?"

"Will, I'm sorry."

"No you're not."

"Yes I am!"

"Then why did you do it," I shouted and stepped in front of her. "I begged you to keep quiet about this, but you didn't listen. I told you, Olivia, I told you what would happen, and yet you decided to shout it to the world. I get that maybe we aren't friends anymore, but what did I ever do to you to deserve that?"

She shook her head and wiped a tear away from her left eye. "Nothing, you didn't..."

"Then why!"

"I don't want you to be a Warrior," she cried.

I took a step back and held the wall. "So you thought outing me would change my mind?"

She shrugged. "I don't know. You were throwing digs at me, and then you hinted that you were going to get Turned soon, and I...it just came out. I didn't know your mom was right there, I swear."

"What I do with my life is none of your business."

"You can't be a Warrior, Will!"

"Why not!"

"Because I love you too much," she cried as she stepped over to me and placed her hands on my arms. "I don't want you to die, you can't..."

"You are so full of shit," I interrupted and pulled my arms free.

"Will, please, I'm serious. I can't lose you, please don't do this, I'm begging you."

With an exhausted sigh, I sat down on the edge of the bed with my head in my hands.

"Why are you here? You did your damage last night for your own selfish reasons, but why are you here now?"

She didn't answer, but I heard her tentative steps before she knelt down in front of me. Through my fingers I could see her wet face and red pitiful eyes looking up at me. When I finally lowered my hands from my face, she began to cry again and leaned into my leg.

"We brought Miller and a few of his men to the manor this morning to...bring the families together and talk about the wedding. It was horrible, Miller was horrible...he was talking about me like I was a piece of property he was negotiating to buy. Mom and Ada are grinding their teeth and going along with it because they think it's what I want, and all I could see was my future with Miller controlling everything I do, and I can't do it. I thought I could suffer through it, but I can't. I was able to get out of there, and I just started running." She looked up at me. "Before I knew it, I was here. I didn't even mean to do it, my brain just brought me here."

"What do you mean you were going to suffer through it?"

Olivia wiped her face and fell back into the wall behind her. She sighed loudly and roughly adjusted her dress down her legs. "The coven is in trouble."

"Um…what? Since when?"

"Niall told me people have lost faith in the Warriors since Ada and Devy took over. And then this morning, Miller blurts out that some Warriors have actually come to him looking to come over to his coven."

I shook my head. "No way that's true."

"Then why did Ada tell me that some Warriors are unhappy and getting restless because there's not a battle every other day like there used to be."

"When did he say that?"

She paused before finally answering, "The day Jax and I almost blew each other up, the day after we kissed."

I licked my lips and rubbed my chin, trying to process everything she'd just said. "So let me see if I'm following. Niall and Miller feed you some bullshit that the coven is in trouble, so you decide to get married to what…fix it somehow?" She nodded. "Not because you love him." She shook her head and new tears leaked from her eyes. "It's hard to believe that you were almost the valedictorian of our class because that is the stupidest thing I've ever heard," I said as I stood and walked around to the front of my bed.

"I'm trying to help my family."

"How exactly were you going to do that? How could you even entertain that idea?"

She pushed up from the floor and wiped her cheeks. "Because saving my family is more important than me being happy, and I thought I could tolerate it until Miller started planning the wedding and talking about dowries…"

"And that's what you chose over me," I interrupted and she looked down at the floor.

"It was to help my family, Will," she began, and then finally looked up at me. "Not because I don't care about you, because I do, even though you constantly throw my faults in my face, which is why I keep lashing out."

"Las-lashing out?" I shouted and leapt in front of her. "You blew up my life, Olivia! You decided that since you didn't agree with my life choice, you were going to destroy me instead."

"I'm sorry," she replied weakly, wiping her face once again while her big dark eyes were slowly piercing through my anger. If I looked at her a second longer, I would give in, so I turned and stepped away. "I'll talk to Aunt Re and Uncle John."

"I don't want your help! Just leave, for god's sake, leave."

She sniffled behind me and her fingers grazed the side of my hand making me turn around slowly. Her other hand pulled my face gently toward her as she kissed the side of my cheek. "You really are the best of us. I'm sorry. I really am sorry, Wills."

Olivia took a step toward the door and for unknown reasons, I reached out and took her hand. She froze, keeping her back to me.

"Why can't I hate you," I said, disgusted with myself. "After everything you've done to me, why..."

Olivia whipped around and slammed her lips against mine. My hands instantly fell to the curve of her lower back and pressed her into me. She grabbed the bottom edge of my t-shirt and lifted it roughly over my head. Just the feeling of her fingers on my bare chest made me hard. Her hands traveled down to the waistband of my pants, but I stopped her and held her hands in my mine.

"Olivia, wait...we can't."

"I want this, Will," she said. "I've never been this sure about anything in my life."

After a brief pang of guilt in the pit of my stomach, I turned her around, brushed her curly hair over to one side, and kissed the side of her neck. When she moaned, my fingers went to the zipper of her dress and slowly pulled it down her back.

I couldn't believe this was happening. I was seeing her bra, the lace of her underwear, this was really fucking happening. My teenage self was giving my adult self a high five.

Olivia slid her dress off her shoulders and let it fall to the floor. I buried my face into her neck, pulling the lace strap of her bra down her shoulder. Olivia gasped and then sighed as my hand slid into the cup of her bra and squeezed her breast. Wanting more, I pinched the back clasp of the bra and ripped it away from her body, allowing me to squeeze both breasts with my hands. Her breasts were everything I had imagined they would be, and oh did I used to think about them.

As her moans grew louder, she reached back and put her fingers through my hair, scratching my scalp slightly. My body was ready for her so I moved my right hand from her breast, slowly sliding it down her abdomen and slipping my fingers underneath the band of her lacey underwear, pausing to give her a chance to stop me, but she didn't. Holy shit, this was really, really happening. Not wasting another second, I plunged my hand down and explored her with my fingers.

"Oh my god," she said breathlessly and it was over for me.

Quickly I turned her around and pulled her legs up around my hips. It was amazing how light and free she was. Her lips found mine again as she pressed her breasts against my chest. I took a step toward the bed when a horrible thought crossed my mind, causing me to pull away from her.

"Shit, I don't think I have condoms."

She shook her head while catching her breath. "I'm on birth control."

"Well thank god for that."

"You have no idea."

She leaned in to kiss me again, but I pulled away again. "Are you sure?"

In response, she slid her hand between her legs and then down my pants, grabbing my penis and pulling it upright.

It was done, I was done, there was no turning back now. I wasn't going to last long because I'd wanted this for so many years, and here she was stroking me. With thoughts of baseball stats in my head, I laid her down on the bed and slid her lace panties down her legs. She was so beautiful laying there completely naked and stretched out waiting for me. There wasn't a flaw to be found. I pulled down my sweatpants as she pushed herself into the middle of the bed, but then I froze when she turned onto her stomach. I mean, yeah ok, I'd do it, but the first time?

Not wanting to make her feel uncomfortable, I crawled onto the bed alongside her, but she turned her head away from me.

"Liv?"

"Just do it," she replied with her head still turned. Not quite knowing what was happening, I reached over and touched her hair, but she flinched. "My…fangs are out."

"Oh I hope so," I replied and she turned her head.

"You don't mind?" she said with tense lips, seemingly trying to hide her fangs. But why?

I threaded my fingers through her hair, causing her to relax her mouth enough to reveal her elongated incisors. Gently I rested my lips on hers, keeping her gaze as I rolled her on her back. Finally breaking eye contact, I moved down her neck and eagerly began attacking her breasts. Between her fingers scratching my scalp and the moans she was making, I needed to move pretty quickly or else I'd be finishing on her stomach.

With little flair, I hovered over her and entered her so fast that she gasped loudly. Afraid that I had hurt her, I started to pull out, but she dug her fingers into my hips and pulled me back into her. With each pulse Olivia would arch her back and neck, exposing her fangs which I'd fantasized about for so long. Everything felt right, inside and outside, everything was a perfect fit. As her body began to convulse around me, her face twisted into fits of pleasure. Her loud, high-pitched moans were causing me to lose all control.

"If you're going to bite me, it has to be now," I said breathlessly, unable to stop from pounding myself harder and deeper into her.

She didn't respond, and merely looked listlessly around until she was able to grab the headboard of the bed and anchor herself as she orgasmed all around me. Grabbing her legs, I pulled them around me and thrusted quickly until I finished, letting out a cry of release so loud and deep I even scared myself.

Quickly I collapsed on top of her, hearing her quick breaths against my ear. Neither of us moved for nearly a minute, living in that beautiful post-coital bliss. Reluctantly, and exhaustedly, I slid off of her and rolled onto my side. I was still catching my breath when I realized her breaths had turned into a soft cry.

I opened my eyes to see her covering her face with her hands, and her shoulders shaking. "Liv?" I said softly. My stomach sank at the thought that she was regretting what we'd done so quickly.

"Is that what it's supposed to be like?"

"I don't understand…"

Her eyes shot open as she pulled her hands away from her face. "I've never felt that," she continued to cry. "What was that? It's never been like that, never," she sobbed and I pulled her into me and allowed her to cry into my chest.

When her cries continued on for a few minutes, I reached down and pulled the blanket that was folded down at the foot of the bed over top of us. As she cried, I petted her hair softly, kissed her temple, and just held her until she finally lifted her head from my chest.

"I'm sorry."

"No, I'm sorry. Did I push you to…"

"No, no," she interrupted. "It's not that. I'm…I'm just the stupidest person on the planet."

"Well, you don't know everyone on the planet."

She smirked and shifted to lie on her back. "The naivest person, then."

"How's that?"

She sighed and then replied, "I thought I hated sex."

"I'm not sure anyone hates sex."

"Well, I thought I did because it was painful and boring, and I couldn't understand why everyone made such a big deal about it. Christ, I've barely faced him when we're having sex," she said, and began to cry again.

"Wait, what do you mean...what has he done to you?"

She began to cry again and pulled the edge of the blanket over her shoulder. "He convinced me the only way we could have sex was...behind me, so he didn't have to look at my fangs. The couple times we faced each other he could never get hard enough, and it was all my fault, because of my fangs. I thought...see, I really am the stupidest person in the world because I went along with it. I mean, it's not like I had any other experience."

I flinched back. "Wait a minute, you're saying you've only been with Niall? Ever."

"Thanks for the judgement, Will. When did you lose your virginity?"

"In high school."

"High school? When? With whom?"

"Erica Jansek, two days after you left."

She made a face. "Erica Jansek? I always hated her."

"Yeah, that's why I had sex with her. She hated you too."

"I guess I deserve that. I'm such an idiot."

Gently I snaked my arm around her waist and rolled her back over onto her side to face me. "You're not an idiot, he took advantage of you. And...I think your fangs are beautiful." She smiled and a few tears leaked from the corners of her eyes, and I couldn't help but catch them with my index finger. "Speaking of fangs, you seemed confused when I suggested you bite me. I'm guessing you've never done that." She shook her head. "Do you know how to?"

"Yeah, just not during...you know."

I smiled. "Did you like what we did?"

"I think the neighborhood knows I liked it."

We laughed and I pressed my forehead against hers. "Wanna do it again?"

She pulled her head away and had a questionable look on her face. Her eyes burned into mine as I gently kissed her lips, pulling her leg around my hips. It only took one squeeze of her left breast to make me hard again. She gasped as I slipped inside her again, and I thoroughly enjoyed watching her eyes close with pleasure. As I continued to push myself into her, I pressed my hand into the curve of her lower back. Her head whipped back, exposing those beautiful fangs of hers as she wailed and breathed heavily.

"You'll need to do it soon," I warned her.

"I don't want to hurt you."

"You won't," I replied, sliding my hand to her leg and pulling it up higher, feeling the absolute top of her. "Count to four, no more than five. I'll pass out, lick me closed. Got it?"

She nodded but I kissed her so I didn't have to see the terrified look on her face. Between her tongue plunging in and out of my mouth, and her breasts rubbing against my chest, I was ready to explode. My body was tensing and concentrating deep down in my pelvis.

"Do it now, Liv," I said, but she hesitated. I'd never wanted something so badly in my life. "Now, Liv, do it."

With a loud breath, she reared her head back and then sank her fangs into my neck. My body flinched and convulsed as I released inside her at the same time the euphoria from her bite flowed through me. My body was humming, and the uncontrollable sleep was coming over me.

"Three, four," I whispered and petted her hair. I felt her fangs pull out of my neck and then her tongue licked my wounds closed. As darkness filled in around me, I rolled onto my back and felt Olivia sprawl out on my chest and abdomen. It was perfect. Even if this led to nothing, which I assumed would be the case, this was the perfect ending.

Chapter Twenty-four

Olivia

The manor was dark and absent of all its warmth and color, just cold and empty. I was standing in the foyer that brought the two wings of the manor together. Will was running down the corridor toward me waving his arms in front of him.

"Run!" he shouted.

I turned around in time to see the front door slammed shut and lock with a loud snap.

Hands grabbed my arms and turned me back around as Will stumbled to his knees, his eyes begging me for something I couldn't understand. He squeezed my arms tightly, trying to say something when a long blade shot out from the middle of his stomach. I tried to scream, but no sound came out of my mouth. I tried again, struggling to keep Will upright, and still nothing. Will coughed loudly and bright red blood spewed out of his mouth.

He coughed again...

My eyes shot open at the same moment the real Will coughed and cleared his throat. It took me nearly ten seconds to realize where I was, and then panic set in that I had fallen asleep, which was so foreign. My body was humming throughout mixed with the adrenaline of that horrific dream. It had been awhile since I had had a dream, especially one like that, mainly because I hardly ever slept. Unconsciously it was probably by design. My dreams terrified me as a child, mostly because the violent ones seemed to come true. Mom had had the same gift when she was human. For a while it was thought that both Jack-Jack and I had inherited the gift, however, it was later determined that it was mostly me sharing my dreams with him. It was yet another gift I wish I didn't have. But why now? Jesus, was this happening again? The dream didn't even make any sense, although they rarely did until you were in the thick of it.

Will cleared his throat again, his chest rumbling underneath my ear. Reflexively my fingers circled around where the blade had come out of his stomach, causing a sleepy smile to stretch across his face. It was just a dream. My head was swimming with fear, but it could be just a dream.

Carefully I rolled over, trying not to wake Will, searching for a clock. On the nightstand sat a small digital clock and I nearly jumped out of the bed when I saw the time.

"Oh my god, it's one o'clock," I said loudly, causing Will to flinch awake. I pulled the blanket up tightly around my chest. "I can't sleep more than an hour any day of the year, but today of all days I'm fucking Sleeping Beauty? Oh my god, I'm so dead."

"Hey, calm down," Will said sleepily, his eyes still trying to focus. "No one knows you're here, right?"

"No, I didn't tell anyone because I didn't know myself."

"Ok," he continued calmly and pulled me back over onto his chest, "so let's just take a moment and let my heart get to a normal rhythm since you just scared the shit out of me."

"Sorry, I just…I've never slept like that, I don't know why…"

"Maybe you needed it," he replied and began petting my hair.

My fingers began to lazily trace circles on his chest until they brushed up against a gold cross necklace nestled between his collarbones. I took the cross and spun it between my fingers, enjoying how it sparkled when it caught the sunlight.

"I can't believe you still wear this." He shrugged, stretching up and putting his left hand behind his head. "I remember when you got this."

"You do not," he laughed.

"I do too," I replied and placed the cross back into the crook of his collarbone. "Your dad's parents gave it to you before your first national competition, which you won, and you wore it after that as a good luck charm."

He squinted his eyes in shock. "I can't believe you remember that."

"After you won that tournament, whenever you were nervous, you would reach into your shirt and rub it between your fingers. You used to do it before every exam we had in Russian class."

He smiled. "Well, it worked better on tournaments than it did on those tests."

"Why do you still wear it?"

"I don't know, just one of those things that's hard to take off after wearing it for so long." He started petting my hair again and after several quiet seconds he asked, "Are you ok?"

"Mmm-hmm. Although I think it's worse that I'm not riddled with guilt." I looked up and found his beautiful blue-green eyes looking back at me. Those eyes were so comforting in their familiarity. My old friend was holding me and making me feel so unbelievably safe, so comfortable and loved. I had never felt this with Niall. I never knew I needed to feel this way.

"Crying again?" he said, trying to laugh but sounding more worried as he wiped a tear from the corner of my eye.

"I'm sorry," I cried and buried my face into his chest again. "Things could have been so different if I hadn't...been such an awful bitch and left."

Will leaned back and pulled my chin back up to look at him. "You don't know that. What if you had stayed and we were horrible together? There's no telling what would have happened. Niall aside, were you happy over there?"

I nodded. "Especially when I was helping people, those poor, poor people who couldn't understand anyone or get anyone to understand them. I finally felt useful."

"See, if you had stayed, you wouldn't have been able to help all those people. We both had to go through our own journeys to get here."

"You're right, but..." I started to say, but then just crumbled back into his chest.

We laid quietly for a few minutes, the only sound being his heart thudding under my ear. I swallowed back the tears at the thought that one day that sound wouldn't exist.

"Can...can I ask you something?"

"Sure," I replied softly.

He waited a beat before finally asking, "How do you have those earrings? I mean, I…I saw you throw the jewelry box in the woods."

It was my turn to wait a beat and take a deep breath. "It was a fluke, really. That night of the birthday party, after I talked with Ada, I ran into the woods. I was just going to run home, but I didn't get very far, and ended up crying in the trunk of this tree. And there they were, just sitting a few feet away."

"But…you kept them."

I sighed. "I did."

"And you've been wearing them ever since?"

"Pretty much."

"Why?"

"Because…you gave them to me. It was like I was carrying a piece of you around with me."

He sighed and shook his head. "But you left to get away from me, why would you…"

"Not you," I replied, and turned my head to look up at him. "I wasn't running from you. It was everyone else. But wearing your earrings, seeing them, it was like you were always with me, my compass, just like you always were."

"But you kept them in even after you met Niall. Didn't he ever ask why you always wore them."

I swallowed and put my head back down on his chest. "He did."

"And?"

"I told him they were a family heirloom."

He laughed. "And he bought that?"

"Do you want them back?"

"God, no. The damage is done, you might as well keep them."

Another silence fell between us, his heart once again thudding in my ear. "Now, can I ask you something?"

"Sure."

"Why are people so worried about you?"

He brushed my hair back, making me look up at him as he asked, "What do you mean?"

"Well, Mom said I needed to be gentle with you. Jack-Jack is overprotective of you. And Ada flat out told me to stay away from you because you were fragile."

"Fragile? Please tell me he didn't say fragile."

"Umm…no, delicate was the word."

"Lord, that's worse."

"Why is everyone acting as though you're going to fall apart at any moment?"

Will pursed his lips and look nervously up at the ceiling. "Because I..." he paused and rubbed his face roughly, pulling his hand slowly down to his chin. "Liv, if I tell you this, I swear...I swear to god...if you use this against me the next time you're angry at me and want to punish me..."

I took his face between my hands to get him to stop, bringing his eyes in line with mine. His beautiful blue eyes were filling with tears at the rims. What could this possibly be about?

"I won't."

"Liv, I'm serious, you can't..."

"*Wills*," I interrupted, bringing my face closer to his. "I swear, but you're scaring me."

Will pulled my hands away from his face, closed his eyes painfully and sighed. Finally, he opened his eyes and said, "It goes back to the night you left. I'm not saying any of this to make you feel bad, I swear, but when you rejected me on your birthday, I fell into a really deep depression. Everything I thought was true in my life blew up in my face. I didn't know what my life was without you in it, without loving you and thinking we had this special relationship."

"Will, I'm sorry."

He shook his head. "Don't be, just...I put so much pressure on needing to be with you that when it came crashing down, I had no idea who I was or what I wanted.

"We went to the International tournament a couple of weeks later, and I made a complete fool of myself. I didn't even get past the first round. I was so humiliated, and I completely embarrassed Devy. When we got home, we started getting things ready for college, and my parents looked at my savings account for some reason and saw that it was almost empty. Of course they flipped and I was forced to tell them that I spent the money on a pair of earrings...for some girl."

"Ohmigod," I groaned, feeling nauseous.

"My dad was so mad that he said they weren't going to pay for college anymore."

"What?" I said shocked, propping myself up on my elbow.

He replied with a smirk. "John Ryan, nicest guy you'll ever meet, hardest man in the world on his son."

"Still, I can't believe…"

"I knew they would freak, and I owned up to it. I got a job and thought the only way I could get my dad to be proud of me was to become a doctor, so I kept my nose in the books. That's all I did – worked and went to class. I wouldn't even come home during the summer or intercession and would just do more classes so that I could finish earlier, show my dad how serious I was.

"I graduated in three years, double major in Pre-med and Biology, minor in Chemistry, and I immediately applied to med schools. What I didn't realize was that I was sinking deeper and deeper into my depression, ignoring everything but the drive that I needed to be a doctor and make my dad proud for once."

Will paused, placing his hands over his face and rubbing his eyes. His entire body was tense, and I stayed completely still in order not to spook him.

"So, I was finishing up my first year of med school, and I was living in this apartment with a couple of other guys. My depression turned into something much worse, and I stopped going to class, going anywhere, actually, and literally barricaded myself in my room. After about a week, one of my roommates somehow got ahold of my dad and told him he needed to come and get me, otherwise they were going to call the police."

Will paused again and took a deep breath before continuing. "My dad, your dad, and Jax all came down to my apartment that same day. Your dad had to take the door off its hinges in order to get in, and then literally had to drag me out. Dad checked me into the hospital and they drugged me up so bad I don't remember anything."

I squeezed my hand against my mouth to keep my audible sobs inside. It was silent for several minutes while we held each other. If only I had known what was happening to him, my dear friend.

"How long were you at the hospital?" I finally asked.

"Nine months, and I was worse than when I went in," he answered. "At least that's what they tell me. Since I wasn't getting better, Mom made Dad bring me home until they could find a different treatment center for me. After a couple of days of being home we were at the manor for something, some gathering, maybe someone's birthday. At some point I just wandered off and ended up in the training room. I don't even remember how I got there. My first memory is of Devy standing in front of me, it's foggy, but I remember seeing him staring me down.

"I don't know how long we were standing there when he started going through our drills, the drills we'd do every day during training. It was really slow and hardly any contact, but I remember my body just knowing what to do and...it woke me up. Next thing I remember, my mom is sobbing and screaming behind us, and then everyone was there hugging me and I went right back into zombie mode. That's what Jax called it, my zombie mode.

"That's when they started Warrior daycare," he laughed lightly. "Every day on their way to work, my parents would drop me off at the manor, and I always found my way to the training room. And every day Devy would be there waiting for me. I mean, the man is the co-leader of the coven and the Warrior Assassin, and yet he would be there and he worked with me every day. Each time we'd do a little more, go a little faster until one day we had a flat-out battle, and something broke in me.

"When we were done, I looked at him and said 'I want to be a Warrior.' Those were the first words I'd said in almost a year. He just looked at me and said, 'it's about time you said what you really wanted.' That's when I started training to become a Warrior." He slid out from under me and looked at me intensely. "That's why I believe becoming a Warrior saved my life, Liv. I'm not being dramatic, it's the truth. I spent years trying to make others happy, and it nearly killed me. I am meant to do this, Liv, and I'm sorry that makes you so upset, but I can't...I can't be that zombie ever again."

I couldn't think of any words to say, not one, so I just buried my face into his chest again. His arms draped over me and with a deep exhale I melted into him.

"I'm sorry, Wills."

Gently he pulled my chin up and I cried at the sight of his beautiful face and caring eyes. I stretched up and pressed my lips against his. His hand slid up to my breast as he slipped his tongue into my mouth. His touch was like nothing I'd ever felt before. I hooked my leg around his hips and pressed my body against his in order to feel more of him. Things were beginning to stir between us again. Just the desire to want to make love to him was overwhelming. Without thinking, I pushed his shoulders down, rolling him on his back, and climbed to sit on top of him. His hands went up to my breasts and squeezed them tightly.

And that's when my stomach growled like a lion. I froze and looked down to find Will laughing at me.

"Hungry?" he asked. I started to shake my head, and he raised an eyebrow. "Truthfully, are you hungry?"

"Starving," I replied with a sigh. "I've hardly eaten in months."

"You only have yourself to blame for that," he replied and I jerked back. "Don't look at me that way. You could have easily said 'I'm hungry, I'm fucking eating this.'"

I swallowed hard. "You're right."

He smirked. "How hard was that for you to say?"

"Very hard," I grumbled. "But we can keep going if you want."

Gently he shifted me off of him and gave me the slightest kiss. "I don't have much, but I think I may have stuff to make a grilled cheese. How would that be?"

"A grilled cheese sounds really good."

Will kissed me again and then rolled to the edge of the bed. When he stood up, I looked away at the sight of his bare backside. It was still weird. It was Wills, my friend since childhood. I shouldn't be looking at his very firm and well-developed ass.

I only heard him shuffle around the room and finally make his way into the kitchen, with pants I hoped. Once I heard the clanging of dishes and cabinets, it was finally time to think about what I had done. One, I'd just cheated on my fiancé. Two, it was the best sex I'd ever had. Three, for the first time I hadn't needed to hide my fangs. Four, my family would be furious with me for putting them through all this drama with Niall and his family. Five, I had slept. I had to wonder why that was nagging at me so much. What was my body telling me?

My stomach growled again and I realized it was telling me exactly what it needed. With a sigh, I rolled over and placed my feet on the floor. None of my clothes were in sight. I looked up to find Will's closet in front of me, the left side revealing a few shirts still hanging inside. I stretched my arm out and pulled a blue striped button-down shirt off its hanger. It was surprisingly soft and smelled of detergent. Quickly I shrugged into it and let the blanket fall from around me. Finally, I padded into the kitchen that was directly opposite from the bedroom. He looked so cute standing in front of the stove in just his sweatpants, buttering the sides of two pieces of bread. When he saw me, he flinched and then went awkwardly back to buttering the bread.

"You ok?" I asked.

He nodded, but concentrated on putting the bread into the pan on the stove. "Yup, fine."

But he wasn't fine, I knew that tone. I stepped further into the kitchen and hopped up on the counter next to the stove. "No really, what's wrong."

He smirked as he placed a cheese slice on each piece of bread. "It's nothing, I've...I've just literally fantasized about you walking around in one of my shirts."

Self-consciously I pulled at the collar. "Sorry."

"No, no, it's uh...fine, more than fine," he laughed lightly, flipping one piece of cheese bread on top of the other. "Bigger question is, are you ok?"

It took a moment to answer. "I'm not sure," I replied truthfully. "I think I feel guilty at the fact that I don't feel guilty."

He pressed down on the sandwich, making it release a delicious smell of browning butter. "Well, you are your mother's daughter, you have to feel guilty for something."

"I wasn't even raised in the South like she was, and yet her relentless Southern guilt complex was still passed to me. It's a genetic disease, I swear." I paused and watched him flip the sandwich to the other side and pressed it down. Suddenly a memory popped in my head of Daddy O teaching us how to make a grilled cheese sandwich and reminding us that you always pressed down on it. Burgers, never, but grilled cheeses you mashed.

The sound of Daddy O's voice was echoing in my head just as Wills said, "As Daddy O always said, leave your burgers alone, but grilled cheeses you gotta mash." My breath caught in my throat, my eyes suddenly watering at his familiarity. I looked away in order to catch a tear from falling. When I turned back around, Wills caught my eye and gave me a sympathetic smile. "Even after all this time I still miss him, too. He was a really good man."

I nodded and swallowed the lump in my throat. "The best. It's funny...no, not funny, it's awful that since I left, I haven't really thought about him, but now that I'm home, I see and hear him everywhere like he's right over my shoulder. I can't even imagine what he would have said about Niall."

Will shook his head, scooped the hot grilled cheese out of the skillet, and placed it on a paper plate. "You know good and well that he would have stayed silent, but would be giving you those big-eyed expressions you could hear from across the room."

I smiled and lifted my leg in order to let him into the drawer where he drew out a knife and cut the grilled cheese in half.

When he handed me a half of the sandwich, I scrunched my eyebrows. "Only half?"

He smirked. "Olivia Burke, never will I ever give you all my food again. I spent too much time as an underweight child because of you."

"Yet another thing to add to the Livy-Burke-is-a-horrible-person list," I replied and bit into my sandwich. My god it was good. Crunchy, buttery outside, ooey-gooey cheesy center. "This is really good," I said with a full mouth. "Thank you."

"You're welcome," he replied, taking a bite himself and pressing up against the counter opposite me. "Not to put a damper on things, but uh…what are you going to do now?"

I inhaled as a big ball of nervous energy rose from my stomach and into my throat. "I don't know," I answered truthfully. "I…I know now Niall isn't who I thought he was. But I brought him here, I brought his family here and forced everyone to pretend to like them. Now I have to go back to my parents and tell them 'Oh hey, sorry I've put you through hell, but I've made a mistake with Niall and decided to have sex with Will.'"

Will coughed as he choked on his sandwich. "Please, let's just leave that last part out."

I started to laugh, but it turned into uncontrollable sobbing. "What have I done," I cried, falling forward until Will caught me and wrapped his arms around to my back. Suddenly my reality came crashing down on me. "What will Niall do to me, and…Miller, he's worse than Niall."

Will squeezed me tightly. "They won't touch you, Liv, you're protected."

"What if they're right?" I continued and lifted my head in order to look him in the eye. "What if the coven really is in trouble, and the only way to save them is to merge with Miller? If I break this off, what if it destroys everything and it's all my fault because I'm just being my normal selfish self. I can't lose anyone…I can't…" I couldn't control the tears any longer and Will pulled me back into his chest.

"The Warriors have been around for over five hundred years. There is nothing going on that is so bad it would destroy them. It's just a ploy, Liv," he replied calmly. I nodded and brought my arms around his neck, realizing I was still holding the remaining piece of my sandwich and popped it in my mouth. "Did you just take a bite of your sandwich?"

"Umm hmm," I replied, slightly embarrassed.

He laughed and pulled me away, wiping a tear that was resting on my cheek. "This is the Olivia I know."

His presence was so calming. But suddenly a wave of guilt came over me as I looked into his eyes. "I don't want to hurt you any more than I already have. I'm not sure what to do here."

"What do you *want* to do?"

With a sigh I answered, "I *want* to go back into that bedroom and keep doing what we were doing, that's what I want to do."

"Uh huh, and uh...after that," he said, gliding his fingers up the outsides of my thighs, making me open my legs and pull his body between them.

"That's the problem, I can't think past that," I replied as he lowered his head and started kissing up the side of my neck. "I'll need some time to break things to Niall."

"Umm hmmm," he replied as his fingers undid the buttons of the shirt. Every part of my body was vibrating and tingling and other adjectives I couldn't pinpoint. I squeezed my legs around him, pulled down the waistband of his sweatpants, and just as he slid me toward him, his phone rang.

His eyes flew open and looked past my left shoulder, both our bodies frozen for a moment until he broke and reached for the phone.

"Are you kidding," I said, utterly befuddled.

He grabbed the phone with his right hand while pulling up his pants with his left. Quickly he took a step away and turned his back to me as he put the phone up to his ear. "Hey, Jer."

If I wanted to, I could focus my hearing on listening to why my uncle was calling, but honestly, I felt too embarrassed and exposed at the moment so I pulled the shirt closed around me.

"Now?" Will asked. "Yeah, it's fine, I just need a place to stash my stuff. Cool, I'll get there as soon as I can." Will took the phone down from his ear and waited a moment before turning around. When he did, he simply shrugged and said, "I've gotta go. There's a mission, and they're putting the trainees on it." I looked up at the ceiling to keep the tears from falling down my cheeks again. "I'm uh...not really sure how to leave this."

"Go on your mission, and I'll worry to death about it while trying to figure out my entire life."

He sighed. "I have to move my stuff into the manor, but it's probably best we stay away from each other until you figure things out...whatever your decision is. Unless you…need me, of course." I nodded and nervously combed my hair behind my ears. "Well, I need to pack up and shower so uh…you can see yourself out, or stay…it's up to you."

I nodded as he took a step out of the kitchen, but then turned back around and I leapt off the countertop. He caught me in midair just as I wrapped my legs around him. Using the velocity from my jump, he swung us around and pressed me up against the wall. Within seconds my shirt was open, my breasts pressing into his chest as he slipped himself inside me. Everything felt swollen and raw, but amazing as my insides started to flutter once again. Kissing him felt like a goodbye, and I didn't stop the tears as they streamed down my cheeks because they mirrored the ones coming down his.

Chapter Twenty-five

Will

Taking a shower was the only way I could escape Olivia's pull. When I finally came out of the bathroom, I was thankful to find that she had left. My world had been knocked sideways and back again in less than twelve hours, and I was still reeling. The only thing bringing me back down to Earth was the mission. After throwing the rest of my clothes in bags, I packed up my piece of crap car and pulled away from my home. It was full speed ahead to my new life.

My room at the manor was the typical layout for a new Warrior – small, one twin bed, a chair, and a chest of drawers. There wasn't much time, so I set out a few things and got changed. My trainee uniform was riding up my ass as I made my way through the manor's corridors toward the training room. I had my pack and a silver-coated Bo that I had never used. This mission would be my final step into becoming a Warrior. My dream was so close that it made my chest tight with nerves.

The training room was buzzing with the other trainees warming up and practicing with their weapons, nervous smiles on their faces. We all knew what this mission meant. Jax was hitting and kicking the heavy bag at the far end of the room, although I wasn't exactly sure why. He always used his gift of vampire control, and rarely had to do any actual fighting. He was also the only one dressed in a real Warrior uniform compared to the rest of us in our trainee jumpsuits. When he caught my eye, he waved me over.

"Hey, man," I said and dumped my pack on the ground, "know anything about this mission?"

"Hey, *man*," he said slowly and deliberately in a tone that put me on the defensive. "Did ya have a good morning? A pleasant afternoon?"

It seemed as though I was walking into a trap. "Um, yeah, I guess," I replied cautiously.

He took a couple of steps forward, and I felt the need to brace myself. "Good, good, that's good," he continued, lowering his voice as he placed his left hand on my shoulder. He leaned his head in and spoke softly. "Do you remember what I told you would happen if I ever found out you slept with my sister?"

"What..." was all I got out before his fist cracked me right in the jaw, knocking me to the ground.

"Everything's fine, it's fine," Jax announced to the room of trainees who were looking at us in shock. "He had something on his face, that's all. Go about your business."

The trainees slowly went back to what they were doing, and I rubbed my jaw.

"Have you lost your mind?"

Roughly he lifted me back up to standing. "I know what you did."

"I didn't..."

"Don't do it, Wills, don't lie to me over her. I know what you did because my fucking sister didn't put her fucking shield fucking up so I fucking got a head full of your fucking fuck-face all scrunched up while you're fucking my fuckwad sister! Twice I had to see that face, twice! Do you have any idea how fucked up I am right now?"

"Only twice?" I teased. "Guess I should have upped my game that last time." Jax reared his fist back again and I put my hands up. "Come on, man!"

Eventually he put his arm down and leaned into me, his chest heaving with anger. "What the fuck are you doing? She destroyed your life last night, and then you go and...idiot. I can't keep cleaning up after her when it comes to you. It's bullshit, Will, and you know it. She's just giving you a little ray of hope so she can tear you down again. It's her game, she likes it."

I pumped my hands at him, begging him to calm down. "Look, this morning there was some meeting they had with the families and she freaked out. She came over, we fought, and...you know, it just happened.

He's been lying to her, Jax, about basically everything, I can't...I can't even tell you what Niall's been doing to her."

His lips tightened in anger for a moment, but then he shook his head. "It's not your problem, Will. It's hers and his, and they have made that perfectly clear. I need your head in the game today. This is your chance to make things official, and I can just see she's crawling around in your head trying to dismantle everything you've worked for."

I shook my head. "No, no, man, that's not...it's over. It was just today, and nothing more. I'm here, all here."

"Fucking stupid," he muttered under his breath as he turned away from me.

"Who is?"

"You both are," he shouted and hit the heavy bag hard, causing it to swing wildly back and forth. "Now come on, before Jer and Devy get here."

"Do you know what the mission is about?"

"I do," he replied and stopped the heavy bag from swinging, holding it firmly in front of him with both hands.

"And you're not going to tell me anything, are you?"

"Not a goddamn thing," he answered. "Should have thought about that before you banged my sister."

"Keep your voice down," I said and started with light punches into the bag.

"Stop banging my sister and I'll keep my voice down. Oh, and seriously, man, you gotta work on your sex face. It's not pretty."

"Fuck you."

"Fuck my sister is more like it."

I shook my head and continued to warm up with Jax at the bag. After only a few minutes his hands went slack, causing the bag to sway when I kicked it. He was looking over my shoulder, his eyes squinting in confusion. "What's up?"

"What's he doing here?"

"Who?" I said and turned around to find Niall sauntering into the training room at Devy's side in a trainee uniform. My head jerked back to Jax who started laughing.

"Now this just got interesting," he said, putting his arms around my shoulders.

"Everybody gather up," Devy commanded, and we all headed toward the center of the room. "We have decided we're ready to begin selecting our final members to become Warriors. This mission is your last chance to show us what you're made of. The mission is relatively simple, just some Solitaries making some trouble in our area. Jared will give you the details."

Jared stepped through the crowd and stood next to Devy. "We have a group of twenty or so Solitaries that have been making their way from New Mexico. We started tracking them after there were reports of feeding and other activities out in the open. They have decided to set up shop here, complete idiots..."

"Jer..." Devy warned.

"Sorry, yeah, they're here and have set up camp outside of the National Forest. Your job is to capture and bring as many of them back to us. In, out, done."

"Thank you, Jer," Devy began, "even though they seem harmless enough, you need to be prepared for resistance. There will be a few Warriors going with you, and we will put you in pairs."

Jax nudged me, I assumed because he thought we'd get paired together.

"Uh, sir," Jax said and pointed to Niall, "can we talk about the new recruit?"

Devy sighed and his face went blank. "Yes, I'm sure you've noticed Niall Cummings," he said with a bit of annoyance. "Niall is engaged to Olivia Burke, and has asked to join the mission."

"Please tell me this is a joke," I muttered under my breath, and Devy gave me a look.

"Unfortunately, that means we have an odd number, so we'll have a group of three..."

"Unless there's room for one more," Olivia's voice rang from the far end of the training room. She was dressed in a female Warrior's uniform with Cam right behind her.

"What the fuck is she doing?" Jax asked me, and I shrugged.

The group parted and created space for Liv. Niall came up next to her with a smug smile on his face. "Are you having a bit of a laugh?"

She ignored him and looked up at Devy. "You have one more if you'll take me."

Devy looked past her at Cam. "You're ok with this, Brother?"

"As long as you are," Cam replied. "She is more than capable."

"I should say so," Devy replied with a bit of annoyance since we all knew that he had trained her. "Very well," he said and began putting individuals together starting from the other side of the room first, and then finally looking at us. "And as for the four of you. Jax with Olivia, and Niall, you'll be with Will."

"What?!" the four of us said loudly in unison.

Devy raised an eyebrow. "Are you questioning my decision?"

"Yes!" Jax replied, and Cam cleared his throat in warning.

"Jax, you and Olivia work better as a pair and you demonstrated a power we haven't seen until recently. That could be helpful."

"But we only used it against each other," Jax snapped back. "Will and I have trained together for a year."

Devy raised his eyebrow again and crossed his arms in front of his chest. "Yes, and despite Will's skill, he is still a human and Niall is a Shield. Niall can provide Will an added layer of protection."

"In theory," Jax mumbled.

If he heard it, Devy ignored it. "The convoy will leave in ten minutes. We will have a few Warriors with you in case things get out of hand. Cameron and I will be watching, just do your best and use your training. Good luck."

The crowd broke up quickly in different directions, and Jax glared at me.

"Why are you looking at me like that? I didn't do this."

"Tell me, love," Niall began and pulled at the collar of Liv's uniform, "how did you get the fancier uniform?"

"She was in a war when she was four years old," Jax replied instead. "You get the fancy uniform if you survive."

"That's not..." Liv started and then paused in frustration. "I took Mom's because it would fit."

"And you're allowed to wear it because you are a Warrior by birth, and you were in a war at four. Don't minimize what you've done just because he's here," Jax said and pointed at Niall.

"That's not what I'm doing. I'm just..."

Jax stepped between Niall and Liv and headed toward the door.

"Tell me more about this war," Niall began as he turned and followed Jax out of the training room.

Liv looked at me uncomfortably and then turned away. I fell in line after her as she headed toward the door.

"What are you doing?" I whispered.

"Going on the mission like everyone else."

"You'd rather pull your eyes out than go on a mission. What are you really doing?"

She shrugged as we turned the corner. "Maybe I'm changing my mind."

"Liv…"

She stopped and lowered her voice. "I need to make sure you're ok. Is that what you want to hear? When I heard that Niall was going, I had this sinking feeling…"

"I don't need you to take care of me," I interrupted and continued toward the foyer.

"Fine, I won't. Get hurt all you want," she said, coming back in line with me.

It was awkward walking with her knowing what we had done only hours before. "By the way, Jack knows."

"You told him!"

I laughed, still feeling the pulsing in my jaw. "Ah, no, you did."

Her head flinched. "How…"

"Your shields were down," I replied as we stepped through the front doors. "It got me a punch in the mouth."

She didn't reply, but the mortified expression on her face more than said what she couldn't.

The convoy was made up of various cars and SUVs, as to not attract too much attention. Jared waved us over to his Jeep where Jax and Niall were already waiting.

As we approached, Niall gave us a peculiar look. "Well, don't you two look friendly."

"Momentary truce," I replied and Jax laughed to himself.

Niall shifted his weight and puffed out his chest. "Will, let's just put everything on the table, shall we? You don't like me, and I don't like you."

"And I don't like you," Jax said, and we all turned our heads. "What? I thought we were taking a poll."

Niall licked his lips and sighed before continuing, "As I was trying to say, we don't like each other, and yet we have been paired together. I hope we can put our differences aside since both of us have a lot to gain by being successful on this mission."

"I can put my personal feelings aside if you can."

"Very good then," he replied and then looked at Jax. "And I trust you will protect my fiancée?"

Jax raised his eyebrows. "First of all, you're an asshole for even asking. Second, she literally kicked all our asses last week. She may play weak and innocent with you, but I know what she's capable of. Hopefully she's beginning to remember that too."

Jax gave Olivia a look, and she held his gaze. If they were screaming at each other in their heads, they were hiding it well. With a collective sigh, the four of us filed into the Jeep, and I pushed Jax out of the way in order to sit in the front passenger seat rather than have to sit with Niall and Olivia in the back. This mission was going to be painful enough, I didn't need to flay myself too.

The sun had already started to set as we pulled through the manor's black gates. But even in the low light of the Jeep, out of the corner of my eye I could see Niall pull Liv's hand over onto his lap. My fingernails dug into the palm of my hand. That slimy piece of shit was allowed to touch her. I had held that hand today, I had felt that hand on my back and chest and face. A sudden image of Liv lying under me flashed in my head, her lips curling into a smile before stretching up and kissing me. A shiver ran through my body, and I looked out the window to shake the image out of my head.

"You ok?" Jared asked.

"Never better," I replied.

I needed to get my head in the game and concentrate on the mission, not the bullshit that was happening in the backseat.

"So, Jared, how is your hybrid doing?" Niall asked.

"What hybrid?" Jared answered quickly.

"Your hybrid that took my Olivia away all day."

"Oh, yeah, that one," he replied, and the air in the Jeep became thick. "Livy, how did that turn out?"

"Good, um…eventually," Liv began. "She was scared, and didn't speak any English. She just needed a friend, someone to help her understand what was happening, let her know that she was safe."

"Well, I'm sure that was very satisfying for you, love."

"You could say that again," Jax muttered and my stomach sank.

"Well, you missed a, how can I put it, lively conversation with our families. Your mother is not shy of voicing her opinions."

"That's the understatement of the year," Jared laughed.

"Your father seemed more willing to negotiate," Niall said and I dug my nails into the arm rest.

"Negotiate?" Jax asked loudly. "She's not cattle."

"Cut it out," Jared shouted. "Everyone shut up and concentrate on the mission. Got it?"

"Yes," we all muttered at different times.

"Damn you all, I shouldn't have to be the adult in the car."

The rest of the ride was silent as we followed the other cars to the far outskirts of the city. Eventually the convoy pulled onto a hidden dirt road that would take us deep within the state park. You could tell vampires were driving since no one had their headlights on and it was very dark with the sun down and little city light spillage. My heart started pounding in my chest. Tonight I would prove I deserved to be a Warrior. Unfortunately, the familiar feeling of anxiety was starting to sink in.

My breaths became shallow as Jared pulled the Jeep over and cut the engine. Quickly I opened the door and stepped out. Jax was right in front of me, and placed a hand on my shoulder.

"Hey, man," he said quietly, but kept intense eye contact, "no need to get anxious."

"How did…"

"A deaf person could hear your heart racing," he interrupted. "The only one worse is Niall. I think he might piss himself." I laughed. "Now listen, be careful, he's not going to do you any favors, and he probably has no skills except helping get you killed. So just breathe, and do what you do. You're more talented than all of us."

"Right now, I wish I could control Vamps like you."

"Don't doubt yourself, man. You can do this."

"Yeah, I can," I replied.

"That's right. And then later, I'll kick your ass for what you did to my sister," he said, patting my cheek and then walking away.

"What if it was mutual?"

"You're still an asshole," he replied.

I followed him to where everyone else had already gathered in a circle. My stomach started to churn with nerves. I needed to keep Jax's voice in my head telling me to breathe and have confidence in myself. And then there was Devy's voice telling me not to think about winning the battle, but winning one fight at a time. All I had to do was use the skill I had and had practiced every day. All the other nerves and negative thoughts needed to shut up.

Jared took position in the center of the circle. "All right, everyone, listen up," he started in a whisper, "no motivational speeches here. The clearing is about a hundred yards through those trees, you'll see the path that leads to it. Get in, capture who you can, but this is more of a scare mission. We need them out of here. They have the balls to bend and break our laws only miles from our headquarters, so let's show them what happens when they do. Get with your partner and let's kick some ass."

Jared hit his chest with his right fist, and everyone except Niall repeated the action. The circle broke up and everyone started down the trail with their partner. Niall walked alongside me, and I would normally describe him as a very pale Englishman, but the blood had drained from his face leaving him looking like a blonde, skinny ghost floating beside me.

After only a few minutes, the clearing Jared had told us about was visible through the trees. Everyone stopped, nodding to each other that they were ready until it reached us in the back of the group. There was a count of three and then we all broke out in a run. In seconds the trees around us retreated and the clearing came into view. There was a low fire burning in the center of the clearing with about a dozen people sitting upright and perfectly still around it. No one moved as we approached, for a moment I thought maybe they were mannequins when someone suddenly shouted, "They're human."

When Niall and I came around, the couple nearest to us were indeed human. Their eyes were large and fixed with a distant gaze while their necks had streaks of dried blood. They had obviously been Glamoured and posed, but why?

To my right I noticed Jax and Olivia examining one of the humans near them just as a dark cloud of black smoke moved toward them.

"Jax!" I shouted just before a vampire formed in front of him, hit him upside the head with a log, and caused him to fall instantly on the ground.

"Jack!" Olivia screamed, falling to the ground next to her brother and rolling him over.

Without another word, I leapt over to where they were and plunged my Bo into the vampire's side. The log dropped from his hand as I pulled my Bo out of him and then plunged it into his heart. He froze for a moment and then crumbled to the ground.

"Niall, shield," I shouted, looking over my shoulder and seeing that Niall was standing frozen in fear.

I pulled my Bo from the Vamp's chest and ran over to Niall, grabbing the shoulder of his uniform. "Dammit, man, put up a goddamn shield or else we're all dead," I shouted at him. He held his shaking hands up in front of him, and a clear film stretched out around us. Quickly I knelt down to the ground next to Liv.

"Will," she said nervously as she held Jax's head between her hands. "He won't wake up."

"He will, we just have to give him time to heal," I replied and looked around to find our entire group of trainees struggling to defend themselves against the Vamps that somehow knew we were coming. "He'll wake up, Liv, we'll cover you until then, ok?"

She nodded nervously as I picked my Bo up from the ground just in time to see a giant vampire, almost the size of Alex, barreling toward us. I looked at Niall who was trembling. "Niall," I said scrambling behind him seeing the shiny film start to retreat. "Niall, keep your shield up." He started to whimper and the shiny film retreated further. "Niall!" I shouted just as the shield retreated completely except for around him.

The giant Vamp picked up speed and leapt forward, bouncing off of Niall's shield, and flying right at me. I planted my feet, held my Bo out in front of me, but I was nothing against his velocity and we both went flying down to the ground. The Vamp landed hard on top of me, and I felt my ribs crack. Through the pain, I reached for the silver-plated knife tucked into my pocket, but the Vamp stopped my arm just as I was about to plunge it into his neck. With one squeeze, he easily broke the radial bone in my forearm. He gave me a devilish smile and showed his fangs to me before plunging them into the side of my neck.

This was not how I wanted to die. I couldn't move, I couldn't breathe, and my arm felt dead. I had come so close, but now I could feel the blood being sucked out of me. Suddenly the Vamp removed his fangs from my neck and arched his head back with a loud, painful scream. A second later, he went flying backwards and Jax emerged in his place, blood still dripping down his face.

He grabbed my chin and yanked my head to the side. "This means nothing, man," he said before licking my neck, effectively closing the gaping hole the Vamp had left.

When I turned my head back, Jax was looking down at me with concern and anger. "Where the fuck is Niall!" he shouted and looked around. When he looked back down at me, he said, "Are you hurt anywhere else?"

"Arm. Can't. Breathe," I whispered painfully.

He knitted his brows. "I'm guessing that's two things and not that your arm can't breathe." My eyes grew wide as I squeezed his hand tightly, trying to convey some sort of urgency. Now that the Vamp was off of me, I realized that not only had my ribs broken, they had punctured my lung. If I didn't re-inflate it, I'd suffocate and die. "Ok, so this is serious," he said and I nodded.

"Will!" Liv shouted and was suddenly leaning over me, her tears dropping onto my face. "What's wrong."

"He can't breathe, and something with his arm," Jax said. "Help me get him up...oh shit, Livy!"

Five vampires were running at us. Jax grabbed Livy's hand, and a bright white bolt of light shot out of their extended hands, hitting the vampires and shooting them back at least fifty feet.

The twins looked at each other in shock for a moment before turning back around and threading their arms under my back, easily lifting me and carrying me out of the clearing.

"It's ok, buddy, we're gonna get you to the Facility in no time."

Problem was, I wasn't going to make it to Facility West with a collapsed lung, and no one else knew that. The starry night sky disappeared and the trees from the state forest blanketed over us. It wouldn't be too far to the Jeep, but I needed to stop them from taking me anywhere.

"What the fuck happened?" Jared shouted from somewhere.

"They were ready for us," Jax shouted back, jostling me and causing a sharp pain in my left side. "He needs help."

"Get him in the Jeep," Jared said and opened the door.

My right arm was dead, so I flailed my left hand about until I could find something to grab, which happened to be the collar of Liv's uniform. "Sss-top," I hissed.

She looked down at me. "Stop? Why?"

"Livy, come on," Jax shouted.

"He wants us to stop, Jack, there has to be a reason."

Jax looked down at me. "We need to stop?" I nodded. "Put him down."

Carefully the two of them lowered me to the ground, and Jared was hovering over me. "He's cradling his arm," he said to the twins, and looked to me. "Is it your arm?"

With my left hand I pulled at the zipper of my uniform, unzipping an inch or two before Liv removed my hand and pulled the zipper down.

"Is it your chest," she said as she pulled my uniform open. I shook my head and touched my left side. "Your ribs?"

"Pen," I squeaked out.

"A pen?" Jared said. "We're in the middle of nowhere and you need a pen?"

"Uncle Jared please!" Liv shouted and then looked down at me. "Your ribs punctured your lung, didn't they?"

I nodded, reached up to her vest and pulled the small knife out of the front pocket.

"What are you doing, man," Jax said as he tried taking my hand, but I waved him off.

"I can't believe I found a friggin' pen in my car," Jared said and knelt down beside me. "Are we about to do some battlefield medical shit?"

"Are you seriously going to do this yourself?" Jax shouted as Livy pulled my undershirt up.

"Well, are you going to do it?" she yelled at him. "He wouldn't be trying if he didn't know how to do it. Now take the pen apart, he just needs the hollow part. That's all I know about this."

Painfully I rubbed my thumb down my side and calmed my mind as best I could. Gritting my teeth, I cut a line across and then plunged the knife inside between my ribs. The pain was excruciating and my hand went slack.

"Give me the pen," Liv commanded and then looked at me. "I just put the pen in the hole, right?"

I nodded and she slid the pen inside. After a second or two, my body suddenly filled with air. Every breath was painful, but at least my chest was rising.

"You're a badass, man," Jax said and patted my face. "Can we go now?"

"Yeah," I replied painfully. "Pen's gotta stay in."

He nodded in understanding before he and Jared lifted me into the backseat of the Jeep. Liv scrunched down in the floor in front of me, holding my head with one hand and the pen with the other. With both her hands occupied, she didn't bother wiping the tears that were streaming down her face.

"I knew this would happen, I just knew something was going to happen," she kept muttering to herself, although it was hard to hear her over Jax shouting into his phone. The ride was bumpy and seemed hours long. Every time I would start to close my eyes, Liv would shake my head and wake me back up. The final time she did it I caught a glimpse of the guard station at Facility West. As the road curved uphill, I sighed with relief knowing that I was minutes away from getting help.

A few moments later, the Jeep screeched to a halt and the backdoor opened.

"Dear god," my father said above me with a mix of worry and anger on his face. "Livy, get out so we can get him on the gurney."

She gave me one last look and then did as he asked. Jared and Jax took hold of my shoulders and pulled me painfully out of the Jeep.

"Holy hell, is that a pen," Dad growled.

"Pneumo…thorax," I said weakly as they lifted the gurney up the stairs toward the front entrance.

"But who…"

"He did, doc," Jared interrupted and pointed down to me. "Like a fucking badass!"

Dad gave Jared a murderous glare, so much so that Jared backed away completely as they wheeled me inside.

"Will! Ohmygod," Mom screamed from somewhere.

"Keep her back," Dad ordered as we continued into the atrium.

"You can't keep me from our son, John," she yelled, and then was suddenly running alongside the gurney. "Ohmygod, look at him!"

"Re, you're not helping," Dad said angrily.

Looking up at the glass ceiling of the atrium, we were past the peak, meaning we'd be turning into the medical wing at any second. So many people were yelling and screaming in such an open area that it was deafening. But somehow through all the chaos, I heard the familiar voice of my aunt cut through.

"Re, let John do his job," she said, and I could see her hands come around my mother's shoulders.

"Get away from me," Mom shouted, and whipped around, causing me to lose sight of her. "You did this, you all did this to my son!"

I couldn't hear anything after that since the gurney took a hard left into the medical wing.

"Jeanie, we're going into room one," Dad said and we took another hard left.

The gurney came to a stop, and Jeanie's caring face hovered over me. "We're gonna patch you right up, honey, I just need to start an IV," she said and went toward my right arm, but I shook my head.

"Right is broken," I coughed painfully, and she pursed her lips sympathetically.

Quickly she came around to the other side and started an IV in my left arm while another nurse began cutting my uniform away on the right.

"Do you want the Healer blood now, doctor?" the other nurse said over her shoulder.

"No," my dad replied. "If his arm is broken, we'll have to set it first, or else it could heal incorrectly. Get the portable X-ray."

The nurse nodded and left the room at the same time Devy and Cam barged their way in.

"Oh no, no, no, out, all of you," Dad shouted and pointed to the door.

"John, we just want to know what happened and see if William is ok," Cam said diplomatically with his hands up in front of him.

"Ok? You want to see if he's ok? Look at him! Renee is right, this is all because of you. My boy is lying here broken with a goddamn pen sticking out of his chest because of you."

"And he's alive because he knew what to do. He remembered what you taught him, John…"

"Don't," Dad interrupted, "don't you dare patronize me."

"Can I get some pain meds, please," I asked up at Jeanie.

"Dr. Ryan, can we give Will…"

"Everyone needs to shut up and let me work," he yelled. "And all of you need to get out of here. I will call security if I have to."

"We will wait outside," Cam said calmly and gave me a nod.

Devy squeezed my foot, but said nothing. He was either concerned or embarrassed that I'd failed so miserably. The two of them left the room together, and Dad finally gave Jeanie an order to push a small dose of morphine. Shortly after, the portable X-ray was brought in and it was confirmed that my arm was broken, but not as bad as it certainly felt. Jax held the door open to allow the tech to push the X-ray machine out of the room, and then stepped inside. He looked like a horror show with the dried blood on his face.

"Jax, I've made it clear that no one can be in here," Dad said as he placed his hands on either side of my arm.

"Yeah, I know, Uncle John, but I'm not leaving," he replied and pressed himself into the far corner of the room.

"I will call security."

"Then do it," Jax challenged and my dad froze. "I'm not here to get in your way, I'm here to protect Will's interests."

Snap!

"Protect him?" Dad said, not even acknowledging my screams as he snapped my bone back in place. "From whom?"

"From you, Uncle John."

"How dare you!"

"Yell all you want, Uncle John, we all know you shouldn't be working on Will. You're too emotionally involved, and I want to ensure that Will has an advocate."

"Do you honestly think I would hurt my own son?"

"Technically you said last night he was no longer your son, so I have no idea what you'll do."

My father stood stone-faced, although I knew there were a million thoughts racing through his head. After what felt like an hour, although probably only about thirty seconds, he looked down at me. "This is the life you want," he said, and yanked the pen from my ribs. I gasped painfully, and for a moment I wondered if he was going to let me get close to death to make a point. It seemed that Jax had the same thought and took a step forward, but paused when Jeanie handed my dad a syringe filled with a red liquid. Quickly he stuck the syringe into the wound and pressed the plunger. "Broken arms, and collapsed lungs, you can't see it, but I can see the bruises forming all over your body. That's what you want, this is the life you want to have."

I could barely keep eye contact with him, but I found the strength to reply, "It is."

He shook his head. "From now on, the Warriors can deal with their own injured. I'm not treating their wounded who they are so callously sending into battle." Jeanie soaked a piece of gauze in Healer's blood and then handed it to Dad, who then pressed it into the open wound while Jeanie placed a new larger piece of gauze on top and taped it to my body.

"You'll have to do the Healer's blood in small doses for the arm. I'll send you with some pain meds, but you want to be Turned anyway, why not just have them come in and do it now."

"Dad, please..." I started, but he stepped away from me and snapped his latex gloves into the trash.

"You could have been anything, Will, you could have been a doctor."

"If I'd stayed in med school, I'd be dead by now," I snapped, making

Dad flinch. "This is what I want, Dad, and I'm not going to feel guilty about it anymore."

Dad tightened his lips and closed his eyes, trying to hold back whatever was ready to explode from within him. After a few seconds he opened his eyes and stepped toward the door. "Next time, go to someone else. I won't fix you up just so you can go back out and almost get yourself killed again."

Without another word he opened the door and slammed it behind him. I started to count the number of tiles in the ceiling so that I wouldn't release the agony that was brewing inside of me. Jeanie squeezed my hand, but I couldn't look at her. Gently she took my arm and placed it in a brace.

"He loves you, Will, he just doesn't know how to deal with all of this. Neither does your mother, they're grieving, honey. They just need some time. They'll come around. You'll see."

I swallowed the lump in my throat and looked away. "Can I get the pain meds and the blood, please?"

She patted my hand. "Of course," she replied and then looked at Jax. "Do you want me to clean that head wound, dear?"

Jax shook his head. "Nah, that's how I'll get some sympathy from a beautiful woman tonight."

Jeanie shook her head and stepped out of the room.

Jax came to my side and helped me sit up. "Goddamn that hurts."

"Well, if it makes you feel any better, you look probably about as good as you feel."

"I'm going to kill Niall, he caused all of this."

"I know. He's here, by the way," Jax said I flinched, and then painfully regretted it. "He and Livy are going at it. Everyone is watching, don't worry."

"I do worry, Jax, you know what he'll do…"

"Let's worry about you at the moment, ok? I have to get you through the gauntlet out there."

The door opened, letting in the noise from outside, although I couldn't tell who was shouting. Jeanie handed Jax a small bottle of pills, a few small vials of blood.

"Now, honey, you have to remember you're human and you'll take longer to heal, especially your arm, even with the Healer's blood," Jeanie began as she removed the IV from my arm. "Rest and take the blood in small doses. After a few hours you may not even need a pain pill."

I nodded and pressed my head against hers. "Thank you, Jeanie. I'm glad you were here tonight."

"Take care of yourself, honey. Everyone will come around. I've been around all of this long enough to know that."

I gave her a weak smile in reply while both she and Jax helped me off the table. Jax opened the door to reveal everyone shouting at one another.

"I would never have done this to you," Mom screamed at Awbie. "I meant it when I said I never wanted to see you again, you heartless bitch."

"I have trained and protected that boy since he was five years old," Devy yelled at my dad.

"Protected him! Look at what you did to him. You put him there, you put all those trainees in harm's way. They all could have died," Dad shouted in reply, causing Cam to place a hand on Devy's shoulder.

"Stop it! All of you," I shouted over them, and then groaned from the pain in my ribs. Everyone turned to face us. "Mom, Awbie is your best friend, you don't go a day without talking to her. She has always been a second mother to me, and you know it. She doesn't deserve this from you.

"And Dad, the only people to blame for this are me," – I looked over and pointed at Niall – "and that English bastard over there."

"Now wait a bloody minute," Niall began, but Livy pulled on his arm.

"Mom, Dad, I know you're not happy about this, but this is my choice. I'm not living my life to please you or anyone else anymore."

There was absolute silence as I stepped through them. Jax took all my weight and led me through the medical wing doors and the across the atrium.

"I think you handled that well," he said. "Good, short speech, right to the point, and you got a shot in at Niall." I nodded and the emotions that were absent only a moment ago, were rising to the surface. If I said anything, my voice would crack, or worse. "It's ok, man, you don't..." he paused and I looked over at him to find him looking down to the left. "Oh for crying out loud."

"What? What's the matter?"

He sighed and rolled his eyes. "Livy says to tell you that she'll come find you once she can get away from Niall."

"No," I snapped. "No, no, no. Tell her she has to stay away, if he finds out..."

"Dude! Calm down," he replied and pulled us to a stop. "I think she'll be fine. She doesn't seem to be drinking the Niall Kool-Aid anymore. Have a little faith in her." I knitted my brows in confusion. "I gave her a compliment, big deal. What she's doing is still idiotic, and I certainly don't want to be some secret messenger between the two of you. Let's just get that straight. This was a one-time thing. Got it?"

"Got it, but there's not going to be a need for a messenger. As I told you..."

"Yeah, I know what you told me, but you're not hearing my sister in your head, and seeing your stupid wanting face."

"My face isn't wanting."

"You don't have to look at it, how would you know?" he laughed as the glass doors slid open. "You know what I just realized?"

"No."

"We didn't drive here," he laughed and I tried to stop myself from laughing. "So let's play whose-car-are-we-going-to-steal."

"It better not be mine," Jared said from behind us and then shot down the steps to his Jeep to open the back door. "I'll give you a ride to the manor. It's the least I can do for getting you wrapped up in this."

"It's not your fault, Jer," I replied and the two of them helped me up into the backseat.

"Not totally," he said and looked over at Jax. "Once we get him all set up in his room, you are going to help me figure out how the hell they knew we were coming."

"And how they knew exactly who to take out," Jax replied, rubbing his head reflexively. "Could we have a mole?"

"Wouldn't be the first time, certainly won't be the last. Now come on, let's get Humpty Dumpty home," Jared said and pulled away from the Facility. "Now can we talk about how you jabbed a pen inside you?"

"I'd really rather not have to relive it."

"Fine," Jared groaned, "but who is going to replace my pen?

Chapter Twenty-six

Olivia

Even though I had suggested to Niall that it was probably best he stay at his father's rental house tonight, he was insistent that we go back to the manor. Unfortunately, Roberts had somehow drawn the short straw and had to drive us back from the Facility. It was the quietest, and most uncomfortable ride of my life. Roberts kept playing with the radio, turning it up, and then turning it down, changing the station, then turning the volume back up again. The trainee in the front seat, who I didn't know the name of, kept tapping the window to the beat of the music, and then made up his own riff during the commercials. Niall and I looked like bookends, facing away from each other and looking out opposite windows. At some point he went to take my hand and I flinched away, so he forcefully snatched it, causing me to look at him. His lips were thin, his eyes narrow and giving me a warning. I relaxed, letting him win the moment even though my skin was crawling at his touch. When I went to look back out my window, I caught Roberts' gaze in the rearview mirror.

"Everything ok back there?" he asked.

"She's just jumpy," Niall answered. "It's been a tense night for all of us. Right, love?"

"Yes, more so for some," I grumbled and he squeezed my hand tightly in response.

Roberts nodded and looked intensely in the mirror. "Almost there."

"Do you think there will be a debrief right away?" the trainee asked, finally taking a short break from his finger drumming.

"My guess is they'll do it in the morning," Roberts replied. "They'll gather all their facts and then interrogate everyone one by one."

"Interrogate?" Niall said. "Whatever for?"

Roberts looked in the rearview mirror again, and even the trainee turned around in shock. Thankfully the gates for the manor came into view, and within two minutes this horrible ride was over. As soon as the car was parked, I jumped out of the car and walked quickly toward the front doors, but Roberts stepped in front of me.

"Livy, I hope you know this is very uncomfortable for me to ask," he began, but before he could continue, Young David came running out the front door.

"Roberts!" he shouted. "I just heard. Olivia," he said as he hugged me tightly, but then caught himself and let me go abruptly. "Sorry, when I heard…"

"David, zip it for a second. Livy," Roberts said looking back at me and lowering his voice, "do you feel safe?"

"Safe? Oh no," David whined with wide eyes.

Trying to downplay the situation, I straightened my shoulders and replied, "I don't know what you mean."

"Olivia," he said with challenging eyes.

"Trevor," I challenged back.

Roberts tightened his lips and sank into another level of uncomfortableness. "I saw what happened in the backseat, Niall grabbing your hand like that."

"Oh no," David whined again.

"David!" Roberts snapped, and sighed in frustration. "I just need to know if you feel safe going in with him."

But just as I was about to answer, Niall's hand slid up the back of my arm. "That's an odd thing to say, Roberts, is it? Why wouldn't my fiancée feel safe with me?"

Roberts pulled his shoulders back and his chest forward. "It's been my experience when insecure men have a bad day, they tend to take it out on the person closest to them."

Niall lurched forward and I put a hand on his chest while Young David held Roberts by the shoulders.

"Thank you, Trevor, everything will be fine. I think we're all frustrated with what happened tonight."

"Olivia, are you sure we can't escort you?" young David asked and then glared at Niall.

I shook my head. "Thank you both for your concern. Everything is fine."

Niall squeezed me into his side and pulled me toward the front door. I could feel Roberts and Young David staring at us until we disappeared inside. Niall was silent the entire walk to our bedroom. From experience, I knew he would release on me the moment the door to our bedroom closed. But tonight, I wasn't going to take it. I was ready for it, and I was ready to…walk away? My stomach dropped at the amount of courage I needed to muster.

Niall opened the door to our room, and I immediately broke away from him, getting to the bed before he could even take a step inside. He stood in the doorway with his hands clenched into fists. After a moment he took a deep breath, stepped inside the bedroom, and slammed the door shut.

"I don't know what has gotten into you. Yelling at me in front of your family like that. How dare you…"

"No," I interrupted, "that's not how this is going to go."

"I beg your pardon?"

I planted my feet and inhaled slowly in order to calm my fast-beating heart. "What you did tonight, Niall, was unforgivable."

"What I did? I used my shield to defend myself."

"Yes, you've said that over and over, but you don't even see that you used your shield for yourself and no one else, especially the person who was your partner. And it was Will, for god's sake, he's the most beloved member of this coven."

"So that's what this is what this is about. It's always about Will Ryan."

"It's because you were a coward!"

Niall leapt forward and I found his bright red light shining from his head. With a deep breath, I pushed him so hard that he flew back into the wall and slumped to the ground.

After a few seconds, Niall sat up and stretched a shield out in front of him. I wouldn't be able to push him again. He stumbled up to a standing position and looked at me from underneath his lids. Evil was looking back at me. I flew to the bathroom just as he started running towards me. Immediately I closed the door and locked it as Niall started banging his fist against it.

"Open the bloody door!" he shouted and tried turning the knob.

Tears stung my eyes as panic started to sink in. I sank down into the floor and hugged my knees to my chest. How was I going to get out of this? He had his shield up, I didn't have my phone, who could I...

Suddenly I thought to close my eyes and take a breath in order to relax enough to get into the slightest form of sleep.

Eris? I thought out into the darkness. *Eri, are you there?*

The door banged behind me, and I flinched. With another breath, I closed my eyes again and relaxed back into the darkness.

Eri, I need you, please.

Suddenly the darkness whipped around me in a flurry of colors until a flowery meadow formed around me. Eri was standing a few feet away, his hair hanging loose down to his shoulders and wearing a white linen outfit. It was a look I hadn't really seen before.

"Olivia?" he said and stepped toward me. "I believe the last time you called me like this you were not more than seven. You always asked for a meadow of butterflies, do you remember?"

I nodded, remembering it fondly. "I do, but Eri, I need your help."

His smiled fell. "Where are you right now?"

"At the manor," I cried. "I'm locked in the bathroom in my room. Niall is...I just need you to put him to sleep for a little while. Can you find him?"

Eri's face settled into a fierce, emotionless expression. "I can do more than that. Your mother has told me..."

"Eri, please, I just need you to put him to sleep so I can get out of the room."

Eri stepped in front of me and placed his hands on my shoulders. "I never knew the trouble your mother was in when she was married the first time. If I had, that man wouldn't have been allowed to draw breath for as long as he did. I will do as you ask, but I beg you, do not allow the same abuse as your mother did for so many years. You deserve more, little one."

"I know, Eri, I just need you to do this for me this one time. Please?"

He sighed. "Very well. And call or come see your grandmother. She worries about you endlessly."

"I will," I replied, wiping the tears from my cheeks. "Thank you, Eri."

He nodded and the meadow whirled away back into darkness.

I opened my eyes and the bathroom came back into focus.

"Olivia, I swear to god…"

"Niall, just go to bed," I shouted into the door, and worried how long it would take Eri to find him. It wasn't like he was asleep, and Eri wasn't even in the same house. It would take a lot of effort for Eri to find Niall out of the blue.

Suddenly the banging stopped. I held my breath until I heard a loud thud on the other side of the door. After counting to ten, I stood up from the floor and carefully opened the door. I peeked out and found Niall lying face down on the floor. Relieved, I flung the door open and stepped into the bedroom. Niall didn't move, even when I nudged him with my foot. Knowing I couldn't leave him there, I pulled him up by the shoulders and threw him into the bed. I stood and watched him for nearly a minute before rolling him over and pulling the comforter around him. I wasn't sure how long Eris would be able to keep him under, so I quickly left the room and ran out into the hallway only to find Jack-Jack about to step into his room.

"Jack," I whispered and he froze with his hand on the doorknob. "How's Will?"

"Why are you out of breath?"

"It's nothing." He narrowed his eyes at me since he knew I was lying. "How's Will?"

"He's fine. He's got drugs and Healer's blood, so he doesn't need you to bother him."

"I just want to see him."

He shook his head and put a hand through his hair. "I can't let you hurt him, Livy, I'm begging you to leave him alone."

"I have to see him, Jack-Jack, please."

He glared at me for a moment and then replied, "Up a floor, forth door on the left."

"Thanks, Jack-Jack," I said and kissed him quickly on the cheek.

"It's Jax!" he said loudly behind me as I ran down the corridor and up the spiral staircase.

The hallway on Will's floor was empty, but I wasn't going to linger. Quietly I knocked on Will's door, but there was no answer. I turned the doorknob and the door opened. It was pitch black inside, but I could see Will's form lying on the bed.

"Will?" I whispered and slipped inside. I stepped over to the bed and knelt down to the floor. Even through the darkness I could see the pain etched in his face. "Will, can you hear me?" I whispered again, gently touching his arm with my fingers.

"Mmm-hmm," he mumbled and shifted, which caused him to groan in pain.

"Will, what can I do?"

"Hmmm? Liv?" he said sleepily, his hand falling open in front of me. My head instantly fell forward and my cheek sank into the palm of his hand. "You can't be here."

"I needed to know you were ok," I replied with tears burning in my eyes.

Will's thumb grazed my cheek, but then he lifted his hand away altogether. "You have to go," he said, and then flinched in pain again.

"What can I do? Will my blood help?" I asked and stood up from the floor.

"No, I've had Healer's blood," he replied and shifted painfully. "You need to go." Instead, I crawled up in the bed next to him. "Liv, no. You can't be here. If Niall..."

"No one knows I'm here."

"But if he finds you, I couldn't...if he hurts you...please, Liv."

Being careful not to touch his injuries, I stretched out along his side. His arm fell onto my shoulder and then slid to my waist. "I'll just stay for a few minutes. I just need...Wills..." I cried into his chest, "Just let me stay a few minutes."

"Ok, ok," he said, trying to calm me down. "Just a few minutes. You can't sleep here."

"I never sleep, Will."

"You did this afternoon, remember?"

"Literally a freak episode," I replied. A deep silence fell between us, the fingers of his left hand grazing my arm gently. "I'm going to leave him, but...I don't know what I'm going to do after."

"Ok."

"But I need you to get better so we can keep figuring things out. Ok?"

"Mmm-hmmm. But you can't stay here," he said sleepily.

"I won't."

"I'm serious, Liv," he said and squeezed my arm.

I reached up and brushed my fingers on his chin. He lowered his head slightly and I stretched up enough to give him a gentle kiss.

He kissed me back and then turned his head away. "How did you get away from Niall?"

I laughed. "Eri put him to sleep."

He started to laugh, but then groaned from the pain.

I kissed his cheek and rested my head back on his chest. "It was awful seeing you like that."

"I'll be ok, but you need to go, Liv."

"I will," I replied and snuggled into his side. "I'll leave once you fall asleep."

"That won't take long."

"Then I won't be here that long."

"Fine. Goodnight, Liv."

"Goodnight, Wills." I waited a few seconds before placing my hand over the bandage on his side where he had jabbed a knife into his lungs. My worst nightmare had come true right before my eyes. This was why I had left. How could I stay and see Will destroy himself? I couldn't. I couldn't stay here and watch and worry.

"Wills?"

He sighed. "Yes, Liv."

"I do love you."

He sighed again. "Not as much as I love you."

I shook my head and nuzzled into his shoulder, listening to his shallow breathing with a hint of a rasp. In and out, in and out. I concentrated on the sound of it, and sank into the warmth of his skin against my cheek.

"Run!" Will shouted before being knocked down to his knees.

Miller came around him dragging a sword loudly across the stone floor. "Tell me what I want to know," he yelled.

Will looked at me and shook his head. "Don't tell him a fucking thing!"

Before I could reply, Miller plunged the sword into Will's stomach. I turned to run and the space around me exploded in bright light.

My eyes flew open and I had to blink from the brightness of the morning sun on my face. It was almost as bright as the explosion in my dream. When my eyes finally focused, I found Will sleeping in front of me. First thought, I had fallen asleep again? Second thought, Will looked so peaceful and healed. That's when someone cleared their throat. Slowly I turned my head and found my father standing at the foot of the bed. His arms were crossed with a stern expression on his face, and then he raised a single eyebrow.

I nudged Will, but he didn't respond. "Will," I said and nudged him a little harder. He stretched his eyes open and turned his head. It took him a few seconds to wake up and realize he was looking at me, but once he did, he smiled and went to kiss me.

"Will, Ada's here," I said through clinched teeth.

He squinted his eyes and then turned his head slowly. His eyes grew wide at seeing Ada at the foot of the bed, then quickly turned his head to me, and then back to Ada. "Holy shit," he said in a panic and sat up in the bed. "Sir, I...I told her to leave."

"Will!"

He whipped his head back to me. "I told you to go, I kept telling you to go," he said and then whipped his head back to Ada. "I swear I don't know why she's here, sir."

Ada held up his hand. "William, do you feel well enough for me to have a word with my daughter?"

Will shifted and nodded nervously. "Yeah, I think I'm pretty much healed. My arm still feels a little sore, but I can probably take it out of the brace." There was an awkward silence and Ada looked intently at Will. "Oh, you mean you want her alone...here, and I'll uh...go," he said and climbed clumsily off the bed. When he stood, both Ada and I reached cautiously out to him, in case he wasn't as well as he thought, but he easily pulled the brace from his arm and wiggled his fingers. "Yeah, feels ok. I'll uh...leave you two to it," he said and left the room.

Ada turned back to me with a look of such disappointment and shame that it made me want to cry. "I do not know..." he started, but then Will opened the door behind him.

"Um, sorry, I can't find..." he stuttered as he patted his pockets and then inspected the top of the chest of drawers to his right, "have you seen my phone? I thought I put it here, but..." He turned around to see Ada and I staring at him. "You know, it's fine...it'll turn up," he said and stepped out of the room again.

"As I was saying, I…"

"Sorry," Will said as he stepped back in. "I just need a shirt. Sorry, I'm gone this time, I promise."

Will grabbed a shirt off the floor along with a pair of sneakers, and ducked out the door again.

Ada turned back around to face me, but took in a deep breath and slowly exhaled. He looked back at the door for another few seconds, obviously waiting to see if Will would barge back in again. But when he didn't, Ada said, "It is obvious that I have failed you as a father."

"What?!"

"I admit that in my guilt over what happened to you and your brother as children, and having been raised in such a non-traditional household, I allowed the two of you certain freedoms that maybe I should not have. Where I should have been sterner, I overindulged in hopes that it would make you happy. I see now that I was blind and ignorant."

"Ada, please…"

He held his hand up and I shut my mouth. "On your eighteenth birthday, you cried to me that you had to leave us, it was the only way you could be happy. Against your mother's advice, I allowed you to go, all the while, believing you were bettering yourself and creating a life that would prove I was right in my decision to allow you to leave.

"Instead, you have brought havoc into our home. You have ridiculed and exposed a young man you have known since birth. You have forced your mother and I to accept Niall even after his heinous acts. Forced to welcome his family, and then sit by while that vile excuse for a man dared to ask for a dowry, and then insulted our coven. And yet, we suffered through it because at the root of it all, you said you loved him.

"But worst of all, you got William involved in this. When you admitted to kissing him, I specifically told you to stay away from him and figure out your feelings for Niall. When you accepted Niall's proposal, I assumed you had, but here we are. I realize that perhaps I spoiled you, and did not make you as accountable for your actions as I should have when you were younger, but I know for a fact that I never taught you to behave like this. I take the sanctity of marriage very seriously, and the moment you put Niall's ring on your finger, you made a promise to him. I would expect you to respect that promise a little more than this."

"I get it, Ada, you're disappointed in me."

"No, I hit disappointment several days ago. Now I am furious."

My breath caught in my throat. Never had Ada been this angry at me. My stomach started to convulse, causing these horrible sounding gasps of breath.

Ada stood frozen at the end of the bed, completely unmoved by my hysterics. "You need to explain yourself, Olivia. I need to know why you have done all of this."

"I don't know," I cried and bent over my knees.

"Look at me!" he shouted and I bolted upright. "Why did you accept Niall's proposal if you had no intention of being faithful to him."

"I did it for you!"

His head flinched. "For me? Olivia, you are not making any sense?"

I stood from the bed and faced him. "To be clear, before I came home, I thought I loved Niall. I wanted to marry him, and have a life I thought I was happy in. Little did I know I was living in a bubble with someone who was completely manipulating me. It wasn't until we were here did that bubble burst, and I saw things more clearly. But what has never changed was what I was willing to do to help my family."

"Olivia, what have you done?"

I wiped my face and sat back down on the bed. "I was trying to help, Ada. You heard what Miller said about people losing faith in the Warriors. And you told me flat out that some of the Warriors were unhappy."

"That hardly rises to the level..."

"And we know some of them have been speaking with Miller directly. I didn't believe it at first, not until I came home. Niall convinced me you needed help. I came to terms with what I needed to do, and I truly thought I could do it, but I buckled like a...a...I don't know what, something weak and stupid."

Ada took a step around to the side of the bed, his face creased with concern. "What exactly did you think you needed to do?"

It was hard to look at him as I said, "Marry Niall so that we could bring the covens together and fix everything."

There was a long silence before Ada sighed and sat down next to me. "Well, Monkey, it seems I have failed at fatherhood once again."

"Stop saying that," I cried and fell into his shoulder.

"Olivia, I come from a time when women were treated as property, traded and used to gain power and privilege. Why, even my first wife was part of a financial transaction." I lifted my head and could see the guilt in his eyes. "I loved Chloe very much, but her father would only sell me his business if I married his daughter. It was a very different time, and never in a million years would I want you to think that you had to sacrifice your life and happiness for the coven."

"But if it helps the family…"

"I assure you, Olivia, it would not."

"You said things were bad…"

Ada held his hand up. "Olivia, I never should have mentioned there were issues. They are not your concern, that is for me and your uncle to handle. And Miller's coven certainly is not the answer. All I see here is Niall and his family seizing an opportunity to be connected with us in hopes of gaining power, and they are manipulating you to get it."

I broke down in tears again, and Ada pulled me into his side, resting his head on top of mine. The final piece that had been holding me to Niall was broken, and I had to come to terms with how blind I had been.

"Lovey," Ada said over my sobs, "I would rather the coven go down in flames than you marry someone you do not love." Gently he placed his finger under my chin and titled my head to look at him. "I know growing up in this family has been hard. The only thing I have ever wanted for you is to be happy."

I nodded. "I can't marry him, Ada."

"Thank god," he replied with a loud sigh of relief, and we laughed together.

"I'm sorry, Ada. I created such a mess."

He smiled his crooked smile and rested his forehead against mine. "And we shall get through it as we do everything else."

"Will you tell Mom?"

He nodded. "She will be elated."

"I've been really awful to her."

"You have."

"I'll fix it."

"Yes, lovey, I expect you to." I went to stand from the bed, but he caught my arm. "We still need to discuss the situation with William."

Reluctantly I sat back down. "Ada, it's complicated."

"Olivia, there is so much you do not know."

"I know about the breakdown and the hospital, and then coming home and being catatonic. He told me everything."

Ada batted his eyes in surprise. "Oh, I see. Was this before or after you outed him about becoming a Warrior?"

"After," I replied and wrapped my arms tightly around my waist. "I don't know what this is with Will. On one hand…" I took a deep breath, "I love him, Ada. But on the other hand, last night…seeing him injured like that was the most agonizing thing I've ever been through. He wants to be a Warrior, and I don't know if I can get over that. But then…then when I try to push him away it just makes me need to be closer to him."

Ada nodded. "Lovey, I know I said I wanted you to be happy, but I truly believe William is still much too fragile."

"I think you need to give him a little more credit…"

"I saw what happened to him when you left, Olivia, you did not. I pulled him out of a barricade of his own making, covered in his own filth, and speaking incoherently. I saw him locked in a padded room, and then watched him walk around like a zombie for months. You have no idea the pain our family went through seeing him like that. Right now, everything for both of you is so heightened and in flux. I urge you not to pursue anything right now with William. At least not until you are absolutely sure of what you want. I worry how he would react if you were to break his heart again."

"I'm not trying to hurt anybody, Ada. I'm just trying to figure things out."

He raised his eyebrows skeptically. "As your grandfather Victor would say, you need to get your house in order, and that starts with Niall. Do we understand each other?" I nodded. "Do you want me with you?"

I shook my head. "No. I made this mess. I need to clean it up myself."

He sighed nervously and stood from the bed. "I could have Jared or your brother stand by."

"I can do it, Ada."

"Very well." He bent down and kissed my forehead. "I love you, Monkey. Get your house in order."

"Does Grandfather really say that?"

He smirked. "Oh yes. He has said it to me several times."

"I can't imagine you not having everything in perfect little boxes."

"No one is perfect, lovey. I have lost my way several times in the three centuries I have been alive, and your grandfather has been there to knock me back onto a better path."

"Maybe we can talk about that sometime. So that I don't feel like such a screwup."

"Perhaps we will. I suppose I can tell your grandfather that they can come home. No need to keep sniffing around for information on Miller."

"So that's why Grandfather, Alex, and Kyla were there all along?"

"Of course they were," he replied with a crooked smile and stepped away from the bed. Just as he was about to open the door, he turned back around. "I almost forgot. Miller is here with Niall and looking for you. They might be under the impression you are out for a run."

"Why would they think that?"

He shrugged. "Because that is what I told them."

"You didn't have to cover for me, Ada."

"That is what father's do," he replied. "They are also under the impression that Niall was somehow visited by a certain Dreamwalker last night."

I looked away. "Really? Well, you know how Eri can be."

He smirked. "If you need help, you know where to find me."

"Yes, Ada," I said and he turned to leave. "Wait, how did you know I was in here?"

"There was only one place you would be, lovey."

He gave me one last kiss on the forehead and then left the room. My head fell onto my knees. I wanted to cry, scream, maybe cry again. Get your house in order. That phrase was echoing in my head. It was very much a Grandfather kind of statement – cold and to the point.

Fine, I would get my house in order, like a fucking boss. I bolted up from the bed and left the room. My heart was beating so loudly that it was creating a beat to walk to, a strong walk for a strong woman. That was me. I wasn't going to be that weak little girl anymore who would dumb herself down for a man so he would love her. I wasn't going to be that girl that just took a man's abuse because it didn't hurt that bad and she thought she probably deserved it. No, not me, not me ever again. All of this had taught me I was better and stronger than I thought.

My strong woman-about-to-kick-ass walking brought me right to my bedroom door. My hand went for the doorknob right when I heard Miller yelling from inside.

"Bloody hell, Niall, where is she?"

"I don't know," Niall shouted back, and then there was the sound of a slap. Like father, like son.

"Well, you better bloody find her..." Miller continued, sounding as though he was coming closer to the door.

In a panic, I ran diagonally across the hall to the first door I saw, ducked inside, and closed the door behind me.

"Hey!" someone yelled and a light came on.

I turned around and flattened myself up against the door, but instantly relaxed when I saw my brother, shirtless and sitting up in his bed with a young woman securing the sheet around her chest.

"Get out," Jack shouted just as I heard the shouts from my room spill out into the corridor.

Keep your voice down, I pushed into Jack's head.

"Why?" he said aloud.

I put my index finger up to my mouth and put my other hand out, pleading silently with him to keep quiet as the sound of heavy boots hurried down the corridor. He narrowed his eyes, and tilted his head slightly, hearing the boots as well I assumed since as soon as they couldn't be heard anymore, he said, "Get out."

"Please, Jack-Jack, I just need another minute."

"No," he replied and gestured to the woman next to him, "I'm obviously in the middle of something."

"I'm sorry," I said, still keeping my voice low. Awkwardly I waved to the blonde in the bed. "Hi, I'm his sister. Sorry to interrupt."

She smiled. "I've heard you two look alike, but wow, you really are twins."

Wow, she's a real rocket scientist, Jack, I said in his head and he glared at me.

"What are you doing, Livy?" he said aloud.

I bit my lip and exhaled. "Hiding from Niall and his family."

He titled his head and smirked. "And why's that?"

"Because I ended up falling asleep in Will's bed, and then Ada found us together this morning and lost his shit on me, and then said I needed to figure things out and fast. So I was going to go confront Niall, but then I heard Miller in there and I got really scared so I went into the first door I saw."

The room was silent for almost ten seconds before Jack burst into laughter. "Tell me about the look on Ada's face when he found you."

"This isn't funny, Jack."

"But it is," he laughed. "You're the smart one, and yet at every turn you make the worst decision. It's so mind boggling that you should be studied."

"Jack, please stop…" I started to say and completely broke down, sinking into the floor and placing my head onto my knees.

"Always with the tears," he groaned.

"Jax, that's not nice, she's upset."

"So?"

"She's your sister."

"I know who she is, Madison. You don't know the shit she's caused since she's been home."

"She's still crying, Jax."

"And I'm still naked, Madison, what do you expect me to do?"

"It's fine," I said and pushed myself back up to standing, although my knees were shaking. "I just had a moment, and now I'll go back in there."

"Jesus, you're terrified," he said, actually sounding concerned. "What's wrong?"

I wiped my face and replied, "I have to break it off with Niall, and that scares me to death."

"Good," he said and then caught himself. "The breaking it off with Niall part, not the scared part. You absolutely need to do this, Livy."

"I know!" I said too loudly, absolutely out of fear.

"Do you…do you want me to come with you?"

Tears welled in my eyes, and I could see them in his. For the first time in years, I felt the connection with my twin humming between us.

I shook my head. "No. I need to do this."

"Yes, you really do." I looked back up at him and his gaze was intense and serious. "And you need to stop sleeping with Will."

I rolled my eyes. "I get it, Jack-Jack."

"Jack-Jack, that's so cute," Madison said. "Can I call you that?"

"No," Jack said sternly. "Go do what you need to do, Olivia. But if you need me…"

"I know how to call you," I said with a smile and he gave me a nod.

"You can do this, Livy."

"Thanks, Jack-Jack."

"Nice to meet you," Madison said with a little wave.

"So nice to meet you too. In the few minutes we've spent together I can honestly say, the two of you are meant for each other. What a beautiful couple."

Jack narrowed his eyes. *And you wonder why I hate you.*

I released a soft laugh, and then exhaled a mountain of anxiety over what I needed to do. With great trepidation, I turned back around and opened the door. The corridor started to spin as soon as I stepped into it and walked toward my room. The bedroom door was already open, and from the opening I could see Niall pacing back and forth. With a sigh, I pushed opened the door and stepped inside. Niall jerked his head up, and then his expression melted into a nasty snarl.

"Where have you been?" he growled.

"First off, you need to calm down."

"Calm down?" he said and stepped forward. "The last thing I remember is you being in the bathroom, and then I wake up in bed alone. What did you do to me?"

I put my hands up, and counted to five before I responded, "I was cowering in the bathroom because I was afraid of what you were going to do to me. So I did what I had to do. But right now, you need to calm down so that we can talk."

"Fine. Olivia, your behavior these last two days has been abhorrent," he began, but then took a breath and clasped his hands behind his back. "But I understand that you are under the influence of your family. I remember you saying just days ago about how we needed to get out of here and go back to our flat where we were happy. And now, I cannot agree more. We need to go home and be away from these outside influences. I admit, I have lost my temper, but I can assure you that will not happen again. Now let's go home, love, where we can go back to being us."

For the first time in our relationship, his words bounced off of me. He was no longer the Pied Piper. A lump formed in my throat, and I struggled to swallow it down as I said, "Niall, it's over. I'm sorry. It's just not working out. We're forcing this to happen, and that's not fair to either of us."

Niall turned his back to me. "It's someone else, isn't it?"

"No," I replied quickly and he laughed.

"I'm not blind, Olivia."

"Niall, I..." I started, but suddenly he turned around and splayed his hands causing a shield to shimmer in front of me. I tried to run, but the shield engulfed me and pushed me up against the wall. Niall stepped toward me, slowly, his hands tense and shaking.

"You think you have a choice in this," he growled and jutted his right hand forward. The bubble around me closed in and I started to panic. It was as though plastic wrap was being shrunk around me. "You little bitch, you think this is just about whether you love me or not?" He placed his hands around my neck and started to squeeze. I couldn't move. I couldn't breathe.

Jack, I pushed weakly.

Niall pressed his face against mine as his shield melted against me, squeezing out what little air was left. "I will kill you before I let you go," he growled. "I haven't done all of this just for you to…"

Suddenly Niall flew backwards and the shield evaporated, causing me to fall to the floor. Hands took me by the arms and pulled me over toward the bed while I coughed and gasped for air. I looked up to find Jack staring back at me. With a mix of coughing and crying, I hugged him tightly around the neck, and he squeezed me back as never before.

After a few seconds, realization hit me and I flinched out of Jack's arms. Niall was groaning on the floor, rolling over and struggling to sit up. At the same time, Ada, Devy, Miller, and several of his men all came rushing through the door.

"What is going on here?" Miller shouted and jerked Niall up on his knees. "What have you done to my son!"

"Not near enough," Jack answered and stood protectively in front of me. Only now did I notice that he was shirtless, barefoot, and wearing a pair of pajama pants. Oddly I thought about Madison lying in bed alone, wondering what was happening and why Jack had bolted out of bed.

Miller and Jack started shouting over each other when Ada stepped between them in the middle of the room with his hands up.

"Let us all calm down," he said and caught my eye. "Olivia, are you alright?"

I shook my head. "No. Niall put his shield around me and I couldn't breathe. If Jack hadn't come in, I think he would have killed me."

"Lies, all lies," Miller shouted. "What reason would Niall have to do such a thing?"

I stepped around Jack, but squeezed his hand for support. "Because I broke off the engagement."

Miller snarled and let go of Niall, causing him to fall in a heap on the floor. Just then, at the absolute worst moment ever, Will ran into the room and slid to a stop. Miller's eyes flashed wildly. "No doubt because of that young man," he said angrily and pointed to Will.

Will looked panicked and started to open his mouth when Devy took his arm and led him safely to the other end of the room.

"Don't you dare throw accusations you have no proof of," Devy said, and it took all my energy not to react, or make eye contact with Ada or Jack who knew very well it was true.

"Don't patronize me," Miller said and stepped over to his men. "No one here supported the relationship between Olivia and my son. Since they came through the door, members of this family have done all they can to dismantle it. You brought that boy to force a wedge between them."

"Miller," Ada began, "I assure you we did nothing of the sort. But even if we did, it still does not excuse your son's attack on my daughter, albeit not the first time either. He is lucky he is human, because that is the only reason why he will get out of this house alive after what he has done to my child. Now, I suggest you take Niall and your men, and leave quietly while you can."

Miller picked Niall up from the floor again, who still seemed dizzy from the blow to the head. "Cameron, I would think long and hard about excusing me. Without our coven's support, you risk losing your control over our race."

"We would rather the Warriors implode before we have any affiliation with you," Devy said, and Miller smirked.

"Perhaps you will get your wish," he replied and gestured for his men to leave when Uncle Jared came running into the room.

"Oh good, you're all here," he said, ignoring the tension in the room, "we have a problem, bro."

"Jared, this is not a good…"

"They're back," he interrupted. "That coven, they're back and they're right in the open in the middle of the day. Same place as last time. We need to get to them before they can…"

"Jared!" Devy shouted and Jared flinched, suddenly reading the room.

"Oh, umm…I interrupted something, didn't I?"

Ada shook his head in frustration. "We were just saying goodbye to Miller and his family."

Miller growled. "We need to pack Niall's things."

"We will *send* his things," Ada replied.

Miller didn't move.

"That's American for get the hell out of our house," Jack said, causing Ada to give him a warning look.

"Brother, would you do the honors of escorting them out of the manor," Ada said, and Devy smiled.

"It would be my pleasure," Devy responded and gestured to the door.

Miller put his hand up when Devy took a step forward. "We don't need the nancy to show us out."

Jack and Jared tensed and flinched forward, but Devy merely smiled. "Well then, let me change out of my nancy clothes and into my assassin's uniform since nothing would give me greater pleasure than ripping each of your heads off and describing it in detail in my journal so that I can read about it each night and re-live the wondrous moment when I rid this world of scum like you. The choice is yours, of course."

Miller flung his hands in the air and left the room. Miller's men held Niall by his arms and followed after.

"I guess my nancy clothes are ok then," Devy smirked and then followed after them.

The rest of us stared at each other awkwardly until Jared finally broke the silence. "So uh…we need to form a team, bro, like now."

Ada nodded and then looked over at Wills. "Feel like taking another bite at the apple?"

"Absolutely," he responded and my stomach sank.

"Jared, form a team and we will meet in the next fifteen minutes. I want those Solitaries out of my city today."

"Got it," Jared replied and then jutted his chin at Will. "Come on, man, you've obviously interrupted something."

Will gave me a quick apologetic glance, and then followed Jared out the door. Ada opened his arms and I fled into their safety.

"Are you all right, lovey," he said softly and then kissed my hair.

"If Jack hadn't heard me, I don't know what…"

"Heard you?" Jack asked, causing me to turn out of Ada's arms.

"I pushed you a message before the shield…"

Jack shook his head. "I didn't hear you, Livy."

"Then how…"

"I felt you were in trouble. It was like when we were younger and could feel that stuff. But you're sure you sent a message?" I nodded nervously. "Then maybe our pushes can't get through their shields."

"Something we no longer need to worry about," Ada said and squeezed my arm. "Olivia, are you sure you are all right?"

"Yes, Ada," I replied, and wiped my eye before the tear could fall. "It's ok, I know you need to go."

He sighed. "I will make sure your mother comes up. Ok?" I nodded, and he kissed my forehead. "What you did took a lot of courage. And

Jackson, thank you for helping your sister. I am very proud of you both. I will see you in a few minutes, son."

Jack gave a nod and Ada Projected away in a black mist.

"Well go," Jack urged.

"What?"

"Go find Will before he has to leave."

"Thank you for saving me," I said and hugged him again.

"Let's just not make it a habit, ok? Now go before you miss him."

I pulled away and headed to the door. "Say hi to Madison for me," I said and he groaned. "Maybe we can all go out together sometime."

"Keep your voice down," he said behind me as I dashed up the back stairs and ran to Will's room.

I knocked only once before just opening the door and going in. Will flinched and turned around, the bottom half of his jumpsuit hanging down around his hips showing the red scars from last night's injuries. He rushed forward and crushed his lips against mine. His chest and back were red hot under my hands. The passion in his kiss and the feeling of his skin was unbelievably intoxicating. It felt right and easy. Will pulled his lips away and hugged me tightly into his chest.

"Are you ok?" he said breathlessly into my hair. I nodded, but couldn't answer through the tears. "I was heading to Jax's room when I heard the shouting, and then I saw you...what did he do?"

Gently I pushed against his chest and took a step back. "It doesn't matter."

"Of course it matters, Liv. He did something to you..."

"It doesn't matter because it's over," I interrupted, my voice shaking almost as much as my hands. "It's all over. They're leaving and...and I know what I..." I paused and took a breath, "I love you. I want to be with you, Will. Everything that's happened the last two days has proved that."

"Duh," he answered matter-of-factly.

"Seriously? That's all you're going to say?"

He smiled, took my face between his hands, and kissed me gently on the lips. He continued to walk me backwards until my back was pressed up against the chest of drawers. His hands traveled down to my hips and pulled me into him. My hands circled his bare chest and then down his abdomen until they met the fold of his jumpsuit. A shiver went through my body as the image of Will being stabbed by Miller flashed in my head, making me jerk away from his kiss.

"Don't go," I whimpered.

His eyes searched my face. "What…"

"Don't go on the mission," I said and his hands fell from my hips. "I have a really bad feeling about this."

"Olivia, don't do this," he replied, taking a step back and shrugging into a white t-shirt.

"I'm serious, Will. I had a dream yesterday and this morning, something is going to go wrong."

He pulled his jumpsuit over his shoulders and zipped it up to his neck. "Liv, I have been very clear about what my plans are. I'm not about to change them now."

My bottom lip started to tremble and tears filled my eyes. "I haven't had dreams like this in years. There's something wrong, I'm telling you. I love you, Will, I can't lose you."

He sighed and hovered near my face, our noses brushing against each other. "If you loved me, you wouldn't even ask me to stay." I opened my mouth to respond when his gaze shifted over my shoulder and his brows scrunched together. "Where did that…" he began, but then stopped and reached for his cell phone sitting on top of the chest of drawers. "I swear that wasn't there before. I couldn't find it anywhere, I…" He cleared his throat and looked back at me. "I'm sorry, Liv, this whole day has been…" he sighed. "There's a lot we need to talk about. I know you're scared, so am I, but I need to have my head on straight for this mission. And I feel terrible leaving you like this, but I have to go. This is what I'm meant to do." He reached up and slid his fingers gently down my cheek. "I'm also meant to love you, I always have been. There is so much we have to talk about, Liv. Please, let's just keep talking, ok? We'll figure this out."

I nodded and wiped my face. "Ok, we'll keep talking. But please be careful, I'm telling you something is going to go wrong, I feel it."

He kissed my cheek, my lips, and then pressed his forehead against mine. His eyes were tightly closed as he reached into his shirt and took out his gold cross. When he opened his eyes, he kissed the cross, and pressed it against my lips.

"Now I'll have good luck. I'll see you when I get back."

After one last kiss, he put his cell phone in his pocket, and left the room.

I waited until the door was closed before sinking into the floor and crying for nearly ten minutes. I couldn't get my dream out of my head.

Maybe it was just bullshit and my overactive brain was thinking the worst. When I finally had myself under control, I pushed up from the floor, and stepped toward the door. I caught my reflection in the mirror and flinched at how red and puffy my eyes were. I was also still in my mother's uniform, and my hair was a ball of frizz. I was a mess, a goddamn mess. With a deep breath, I opened the door and ran to my room with my head down to hide my puffy face. The door to my room was open, and when I stepped inside, I found my mother sitting on the bed. She immediately stood when she saw me and opened her arms. Just like I had with Ada, I ran into the security of my mother's arms. I had never felt so childish, but the need to feel safe and loved was overwhelming. She hugged me tightly and rubbed my back, kissing my hair and gently swaying from side to side. After a few minutes she slowly pulled us down to sit on the bed, but continued to hold me into her side.

Eventually I pushed out of her embrace. "Mama, I'm so sorry."

"For what, baby girl?" she replied and wiped my cheeks.

"Everything," I cried. "I've done nothing right since I got here."

"That's not true," she replied sweetly and brushed my hair out of my face. "You finally kicked Niall and his awful family to the curb."

I tried to smile but burst into tears instead. "I was so stupid, Mama, so stupid and blind."

"Yes, honey, you were," she said and my breath caught in my throat. After a second of silence, we burst into laughter.

"Did Ada tell you about…"

"Finding you in bed with Will? Yes, I believe he mentioned something."

My head fell into my hands. "I love him, Mom. That sounds so crazy. I can't stop crying and panicking at the thought of him going on this mission. There's a pit in my stomach that makes me want to vomit. I can't…it's…" I looked up and found her comforting, motherly eyes looking back at me. "How do you do it? How do you just watch Ada go on a mission?"

She petted my hair and then patted my hand. "I remember the first time I had to deal with your father going on a mission. I was a mess, and your Aunt Kyla fed me all this junk food to make me feel better. She told me that it doesn't get easier, but that we had to trust in the skills and training our loved ones had. It was all we could do. Well, that and eat junk food, or go shopping like she did. And when I got really scared or stressed, I would take a long shower or a hot bath."

"A hot bath? That made you feel better?"

"Well, there's only so much hot water can do, but it can relax you enough to think about something else. It always cleared my head, but the worry doesn't go away, baby girl. You worry because you love him."

I nodded and brushed my messy curls away from my face. It was hard looking her in the face after the hell I had put her through. "I've screwed up so many things."

"Unfortunately, you seem to have inherited my tendency to make bad decisions in the name of helping."

"I'm going to talk to Aunt Re and Uncle John. I'll fix that too, I promise."

Mom shook her head and squeezed my hand again. "Honey, we need to figure this out ourselves."

"But I..."

"You betrayed Will's confidence, and picked a very bad time to do it, but your father and I chose to lie to our best friends. That's on us, and we have to fix it, not you." Red tears lined her eyelids. "Thankfully I have a lot of time to wait it out. But then again, with Renee being as stubborn as she is, she'll probably out live us all somehow."

I laughed, and tears fell from both our faces.

"I...about the other day, when you told us about...about..."

"When I told you about Sam?"

I nodded. "I was mad because what happened to you was so bad that I didn't want to admit it could happen to me."

"I can understand that. No one wants to admit they let it happen, honey. I dealt with it for so many years because I thought I had no other options, more so I never thought I was worth fighting for." I couldn't help the tears from falling and rested my head on her shoulder. "Baby girl, I never want you to think that you're not worth it. You deserve the moon and the stars, and nothing in between. Do you hear me?"

"Yes, I hear you, Mama."

"Good. But...when it comes to Will, just make sure you are absolutely positive you want to be with him."

"Yes, Mom, I am doing my best to figure all this out. The last thing I want to do is hurt Will."

"I know, honey," she replied and rubbed my shoulder.

"Um...can...can I ask you something?"

"Of course."

"When you used to have your dreams, how could you figure out what was going to come true and what was your brain messing with you?"

She tucked a curl behind my ear and tried to hide the worry on her face. "You're having dreams?" I nodded. "Like when you were little?"

"I don't know, maybe. It's pretty much the same dream, but I can't..."

Just then, a young woman came through the door, and she looked oddly familiar.

"Cecily?" I asked. Cecily's mother used to work in the kitchen, and often played with me and Jack-Jack when we were kids.

She gave a weak smile and an awkward hand wave. "Hi, Livy, it's been a long time."

"It has," I replied. "Are you...living here now?"

She nodded with a hint of embarrassment. "I've been a donor for a little while now. I knew you had come home, but I wasn't sure if you'd even remember me."

"Of course I remember. It's really good to see you."

"You too. Well, anyway, um...Brianna, Cameron sent me to find you. Apparently, there are a bunch of unexpected Warriors here, so they need help with accommodations."

Mom stood from the bed. "How many is a bunch?"

"Fifteen, so far."

Mom flinched, and although she tried to hide it, there was a bit of worry that flashed across her face. "Thank you, Ceci, I'll come down."

Cecily nodded. "It was good to see you, Livy."

"You too," I replied, and she quickly left the room.

Mom looked down at me. "I have to go, baby girl. Why don't you come with me? It'll help keep your mind off of Will, and you can tell me about your dream."

I shook my head. "No, it's probably nothing. I need...I just need silence in order to think. There's so much to think about."

"Just don't drive yourself crazy," she said and kissed me on the cheek. "That's definitely something else that's in my half of your DNA."

I stood from the bed and hugged her tightly. Once again, it felt as though she was giving me healing energy for my soul. "I love you, Mama."

She squeezed me tightly and kissed my cheek once again. "I love you too, baby girl. Never forget that. And maybe throw my uniform in the wash."

I nodded in her arms, and after one more squeeze, she Projected away. Suddenly, I was alone. Chaos had surrounded me for weeks, and now it was scarily silent. So, what now?

A bath. I would take a bath like my mom had suggested. My brain was so overloaded I wasn't sure if it would do any good, or if I'd drown myself. But I was willing to find out.

Ten minutes later, I had peeled my uniform off, piled my hair high on top of my head, and was shoulders deep in extremely hot water with some lavender oil floating on top. And Mom was right, the hot water didn't take the worry away, but it relaxed me enough to think of other things. I thought about waking up next to Will, twice, and how comforting that felt. I thought about his smile, and the muscular indentations at the bottom of his abdomen. But most of all, the feeling of warmth and security in his arms. All of these things were more important and eclipsing the fear I felt about him being a Warrior.

Was it that simple? Love over fear. I shook my head and settled further into the bath, letting the crest of my head rest on the edge of the tub. My eyes closed and I could feel my body continue to relax in layers. But then, I heard my bedroom door close.

"Hello?" I asked, but no reply. I shifted up in the tub, causing the water to slosh back and forth. "Hello? Is someone there?"

Chapter Twenty-seven

Will

It was hard not to smile. Even though the tension was very high in the SUV, I kept thinking about looking into Livy's eyes and seeing love there. Could it actually happen? Could being with Olivia truly be a reality?

Jax hit me in the chest. "Ok, ok, tell me again, tell me about the look on Ada's face when he found you in bed with Livy."

Jared was busy looking at his tablet in the front passenger seat while Connor drove along the curving roads toward the National Forest, and both of them looked back quickly to see my answer.

"We weren't *in bed*," I replied, and thankfully Jared and Connor turned back around. "I was hopped up on drugs and she fell asleep next to me. Don't make it sound like more than it was." Jax rolled his eyes. "Fine, your father was very mad, I nearly pissed myself when I saw him at the end of my bed, and I said everything was her fault."

He laughed. "Now that's what I want to hear."

"Ok, your turn. Tell me what you saw when you went into Olivia's room, since no one seems to want to talk about that."

He sighed and looked uncomfortably out the window. "Think shrink wrap. Olivia was up against the wall and Niall's shield was surrounding her like shrink wrap. He's lucky I only knocked him out."

A chill went up my spine at the thought of the air being squeezed out of Olivia's lungs. "Thank god she could push you a message."

He gave me a nervous side glance and shook his head. "No. I didn't hear her in my head."

"Then how…"

"I just felt it, man," he replied, brushing his hands nervously through his hair. "Just that weird twin thing where sometimes you can feel when the other is in trouble or in pain. I can't remember the last time it happened with us, but…I just felt this overwhelming panic and I knew something was wrong. She said she pushed me a message, but I didn't hear it. And…and that just means we can't get through Niall's shield."

"But we don't need to worry about that anymore, right?"

"Yeah," he replied unconvincingly. "It's just…I don't know. Just waiting for the other shoe to drop, I guess."

"Things are going to change," I said and sat back in my seat. "I can feel it. Big things are coming."

"Yeah, yeah," Jared interceded while looking intently at his screen that had a satellite feed from the park. "We're almost there, get your heads in the game."

"Are they still wreaking havoc, Uncle Jer?" Jax asked.

"Oh yes," he replied with the screen only inches from his face. "No way are they going to get the jump on us this time. We are going to slap those motherfuckers in the…" Suddenly his face flinched and looked sharply from left to right to left again. "What the…what the fff…where did they go!"

Jax and I looked at each other quickly and then leaned over to get a better look at the screen, but from the little I could see, there was nothing there but an empty field.

"Jer, what do you want to…" Connor began.

"Go faster, we need to get there now!" Jared yelled.

Connor didn't answer or argue, and just simply pressed the pedal down and lurched us forward. I looked behind us and the caravan was keeping pace.

"Did they just Project away?" I asked.

"I don't know," Jared grumbled.

"Could it be your feed? Maybe…"

"I don't know!" he shouted and threw his hands up. "Connor, don't bother going to our rendezvous point, just drive right up to it. No point in being covert now."

Connor nodded uncomfortably while Jared texted the others about the change in plans. The atmosphere in the SUV changed drastically. Even Jax seemed nervous, which was rare. Going blind into any situation was bound to make even the fiercest Warrior uneasy.

Only a few minutes passed before Connor pulled our SUV to the side of the road up against an embankment. If I was right, the Solitaries should be just on the other side.

Jax pulled on my arm as I went to open my door. "Stay close to me, ok?"

"I'm not glass you know."

His eyes shot open. "Seriously? You had to stick a pen into your body to breathe the last time we were here. So that I don't ever have to see that again, could you just stay close to me?"

I put my hands up and nodded, and he seemed relieved. The others in the caravan exited their vehicles and Jared gestured for everyone to come in closer.

"Ok, everyone listen up," he began, "the satellite is no longer showing our targets. They were there one second and gone the next. I don't know what happened, I don't know what to expect to find on the other side of that embankment. The last thing I want to do is go in blind, but I want to shut these guys down, and I sure as hell want to know why they just suddenly disappeared. If you want to back out, tell me now."

"We're with you, Jer," Connor said for the group and everyone nodded in agreement.

Jared sighed angrily. "Stay together, keep your eyes open, and for god's sake let's find these fuckers."

It wasn't the best pep talk I'd had, but they couldn't all be overwhelmingly inspirational. With a deep breath, I pushed my nerves down into the depths of my stomach and trudged up the embankment with everyone else. Once we got to the top, there was nothing to see. It was the same clearing from last night, but empty and showing no signs that anyone had been there for months, let alone a few minutes ago.

We spread ourselves out in a line and slowly inched our way toward the center of the clearing. Each step was filled with trepidation, as if I was walking on a tight rope, or waiting to hear the click of a landmine. Reflexively I held my Bo staff in front of my chest, holding it with both hands as the tension seemed to grow with each step. Other Warriors pulled their weapons in front of them as well, ready for something to strike us at any moment. Jax didn't have to do anything since he was his own weapon, but from the squinting and tension showing in his face, I could tell he was scanning the area harder than usual. We all knew this felt wrong.

Suddenly one of the Warriors to my left yelled for us all to stop. He was only a step or two ahead of the rest of us, his hands held out in front of him gliding tentatively up and down. At first, and for only a brief second, I thought he looked like a goofy little mime pretending there was a wall in front of him, and then that's when it hit me. Just as I reached my hand out, the area in front of us shimmered and then revealed a ghastly scene. Dozens were running in all directions only to be stopped by the shimmering forcefield. Blood shot from their necks and chests as others dressed in all black attacked and killed them. It was mayhem, absolute mayhem.

"Son of a bitch," Jax said as a tall figure walked casually from the middle of the killing field toward us. It was Miller, a sly, cruel smile on his face. This was his shield, and these were his men, but how this was possible was beyond me.

By the time Miller reached the edge of the shield, the killings were over, the sounds of torture and death dissipating as the blood of the victims streaked down the sides of the shield like a red glaze. With a flick of his hand, the shield shimmered away and there was a horrible sloshing sound as the blood splashed down to the ground.

"So nice of you to join us," Miller said in his cocky and condescending English accent.

"You have no authority to do this here," Jared shouted. "You had no right to kill these people!"

"No right?" Miller replied as several of his men flanked him, two of them being his seconds I met at the engagement party, Mason and Duncan. "Well, it didn't seem as though the Warriors were going to handle the situation, so my men and I took it upon ourselves to enact the very laws the Warriors are supposed to be upholding."

"That's right, the Warriors, not some off-brand foreign import."

Miller narrowed his eyes. "We have their leader. And he is more than willing to talk. Now if I were the coven leader of the Warriors, I'd want to know why my mission failed so horribly last night. Are you going to annihilate us and destroy what valuable information we've obtained, or will you allow us to come to the manor freely with our prisoner?"

Jared's face flinched and contorted as he weighed the different options. Finally, he replied, "Fine. You will bring the prisoner and follow us to the manor. If you veer even the slightest inch, we will destroy you. Is that understood?"

Miller held his hands out and open. "We are only here to serve," he said in a tone so condescending that it sent a shiver up my spine.

Jared shouted orders and everyone dispersed to their vehicles. Some were ordered to lead, others to follow behind Miller's people. Jax and I were completely silent in the back of our SUV while Connor sped back to the manor and Jared shouted into his phone.

"I don't know how they got here!" he yelled. "At least twenty of them, I don't know when more of them came into town." Another point we were all curious about. There were certainly not this many of Miller's men at the engagement party. And why? The why seemed the most ominous. "Well, I'm just trying to prepare you for what's coming at you. What do you mean...at the manor? Now? Yeah, yeah, we'll be there soon."

Jared hung up and threw his phone in the floor.

"What did Cameron say was happening at the manor?" Connor asked without taking his eyes off the road.

Jared shook his head. "Not much. Just that something was going down, and to get there ASAP. This is bad, this all feels really bad, like we're heading into a trap."

I leaned over slightly to Jax. "Have you heard anything from Liv?"

"No, why?" he replied.

"Jer, Miller was in the room when you came to tell Cameron and Devin that the Solitaries had come back, wasn't he?"

Jared looked over his shoulder. "Yeah, that's right, he was."

"And Niall was on the mission last night, so he knew the location."

"What are you saying, Will," Jared said flustered.

"I don't know...just that...an hour after we kick Niall and his family out of the manor, they hijack our mission. It could have been for revenge. But I didn't see Niall there. So I'm worried about where he is."

Jax laughed. "He was probably hiding under a rock and pissing his pants."

"Just...check on Olivia, please?" I said, feeling pain in the pit of my stomach.

Jax rolled his eyes, took a breath, and then looked down to the left, his usual side when speaking with Liv telepathically. After a couple of seconds, he blinked and shook his head.

"What did she say?"

"Nothing, she didn't answer," he replied, but there was an uncertainty in his voice. "That's not new, Wills, don't get all…"

"I'm calling her," I interrupted and put the phone up to my ear. Immediately her voicemail answered and I hung up. My knee started bouncing nervously while my brain worked at a million miles a minute. This wasn't a coincidence, there was something wrong.

When Connor took the corner onto the manor's street, all of us gasped.

"What the fuck…" Jared said at the sight of vehicles parked alongside both sides of the street up to and past the manor's gate. A few individuals were crossing the street in front of us and I vaguely recognized them as Warriors. "What is Skyler doing here?"

"Isn't he supposed to be up in Vancouver?" Connor asked as he slowed the SUV and cautiously approached the gate.

"More like exiled to Vancouver," Jared said tensely as we pulled through the gate only to find the parking area in front of the manor just as packed with vehicles and people scattered about. "This would be the situation at the manor Cameron was talking about."

"You're right, Jared, this is bad. Did every Warrior come in from the field?" Connor said and skidded to a stop near the front of the manor, blocking several cars that were parked along the side of the driveway.

I looked over at Jax who had suddenly lost color in his face. It was a sight I'd never seen on Jax – fear.

"Anything from Liv?"

He shook his head and jumped out of the SUV. I did the same, and followed him and the others through the manor's front doors. Awbie was standing just inside frantically directing people to go to the Council Hall.

"Mom!" Jax shouted over the crowd and Awbie immediately looked relieved.

"Oh my god, I'm so glad you're both ok," she said and squeezed us both tightly around the necks.

"Awbie, what's going on," I asked as she pulled us over to the wall.

"We have no idea," she replied nervously. "People have just been rolling in without explanation, and then we heard about the mission…"

"Mom, where's Livy?" Jax interrupted.

Awbie flinched and suddenly looked guilty. "Her room, I suppose, that's where I left her. Why, what's…"

"We're just going to go find her," Jax said and pushed past.

Awbie gave me a worried look.

"We'll get her and bring her to the Council Hall," I said and ran to catch up to Jax.

By the time I had reached the spiral staircase, Jax was nowhere to be seen, which meant he was running at his full speed, and was more worried about Olivia than he previously let on. The hallway seemed infinitely long, and I hated to admit that I was a little out of breath by the time I ran inside the bedroom. Jax stepped out of the bathroom with a worry creased into his face.

"Well?"

He shook his head. "The bathtub is full, there's water all over the floor, but she's nowhere in sight."

I stepped over to the bed looking for any clues as to where Liv might be. "Try her again."

"I have! Don't you think I have?" he yelled, and then angrily put his fingers through his hair. "Dammit, Olivia, answer me!"

But there was no response, no sound of any kind. She had obviously come back here and taken a bath. But why leave the water in the tub? Where would she have gone?

Jax began to concentrate on the far wall nearest to the bathroom, just oddly staring at it intently.

"You got something?" I asked and stepped up behind him.

He shook his head. "No, just a weird feeling."

"A twin feeling?"

"Maybe. I just…"

"All Warriors report to the Council Hall," a voice echoed throughout the room and corridor outside. "All Warriors must come to the Council Hall immediately."

"We have a P.A. system?" I asked, and Jax shrugged.

"We should go then, maybe Livy's there already," he said unconvincingly and I followed him to the door, but gave one last scan around the room. Jax was right, there was a weird feeling. Something was drawing my attention, but my eyes saw nothing. "Wills, come on," Jax shouted from the middle of the hallway.

Reluctantly I shook the feeling off and caught up with Jax. Together we made our way back down the spiral staircase and followed the river of Warriors toward the Council Hall.

"So this is what lemmings feel like," Jax teased nervously. Around us was a mix of those that were curious and confused, and others that seemed calm and prepared. Once we finally made it through the tall double wood doors, the noise in the Council Hall was almost deafening from the number of people. Everyone was filing up onto the concrete risers on the right side of the Council Hall while the opposite side, or commonly known as the visitor's side, remained empty.

Jax squeezed my shoulder and pointed up to the fourth level riser. I nodded and followed him up, taking the seat on the very end that had a five-foot drop to the center aisle below. There was no railing to keep a human like me from falling off, so I pushed Jax to the right slightly to give me another inch from the edge. While others filled in around us, the door leading to the prison cells below opened. Julian, the Warrior warden you might call him, led a man in silver chains into the Council Hall followed by Miller and a few of his men. Awbie sat on the second row next to Jared and Connor, Tori was a few people down from them. There were only a handful of other Warriors I even recognized.

Jax leaned into me and whispered, "Livy isn't here."

My heart thudded roughly against my chest. I looked around the room and had to agree that she wasn't here. So where the hell was she?

But the opportunity to leave and look for her went away when Julian stepped up to the stone platform where two elaborate chairs sat. The meeting was coming to order. He flicked his fingers up, and we all stood. Devin and Cameron came through the tall double doors of the Council Hall and walked down the center aisle to their thrones. Devy's shoulders were stiff, jaw clenched, heaving breath. He was the angry bull I'd only seen a few times in my life. Cam, on the other hand, was better at hiding his feelings, and only looked like he was on a mild simmer. It was almost the same look he'd have with the twins when they were in trouble. But perhaps all of us were in a little bit of trouble for somehow allowing Miller's coven to get the jump on us.

Once Devin and Cameron sat, Julian cleared his throat and announced, "I now call this emergency meeting of the Warrior coven to order." He looked down at Cam who gave a slight nod, and he continued, "You may present the prisoner and announce yourselves."

Miller walked to the center aisle with his men leading the prisoner behind him. Once they all stood at the front, Miller gave a shallow bow. "I hear it is customary to bow before we begin."

"Only if you're on trial," Devy replied tersely.

Miller stood up straight and gave a smirk. "I am Miller Cummings, and

I lead a group of men who have dedicated their lives to protecting humankind and the legacy of the great Vampire race."

"Illegally," Devy interrupted, causing Miller to shift his weight and a few grumbles to echo from the crowd. "You do this illegally as an unrecognized coven."

"We are where we are needed," Miller replied.

"We have never needed an entire coven in Europe."

"Perhaps it is because of our presence," Miller said, but Devy didn't flinch.

Cam leaned on the left arm of his chair. "Julian, please proceed."

Julian nodded and stood very straight and stiff with his hands folded in front of him. "State your purpose here and why you have brought us this prisoner."

"Certainly," Miller said in a light, casual tone and began to pace. "Initially, I was asked to the manor to celebrate the engagement of my son to the Warrior's first daughter Olivia Burke. But while I was here, my son was asked to participate in a mission that involved capturing vampires that were vagrantly breaking our laws. Unfortunately, the mission did not go well. Not a single vampire was captured, and there were even some injuries to the humans on the Warrior's side. Therefore, when I heard that the same group of vampires were out again, this time in the very light of day, I could not with good conscience see more humans be injured or even killed. So I gathered my men who had come with me to celebrate the engagement, and confronted the group ourselves."

"Confronted?" Julian said. "You killed the entire group less one, that is a bit more than confronting."

"We did not go there to eliminate them, but it was quickly realized that they weren't going to go down easily. We used the force we thought was necessary to neutralize the issue."

"And as Devin pointed out earlier, you did this illegally. You do not have the authority..."

"The Warriors had already failed once," Miller interrupted. "Were we to assume you would succeed a second time around? But does it truly matter? We eliminated a group of unruly, disrespectful vampires blatantly violating our laws. Do we really care how it was done?"

"Yes, we do," Cam said calmly. "We do not outright kill..."

"Perhaps that is the problem," Miller interrupted. "My men eliminated the Solitaries and kept a vital witness. Rather than debate our tactics, perhaps we should hear his testimony about why the Warriors' mission failed."

Heads turned and murmurs rumbled through the crowd like waves lapping back and forth between the wall and the aisle.

"Present the prisoner," Julian instructed, and two of Miller's men brought the man to stand in front of Cam and Devy. It was surprising that Miller's men were holding the prisoner, rather than our own. It was probably yet another one of Miller's power moves. Julian turned his attention to the prisoner. "State your name."

The man's hands shook as he nervously brushed the hair from his forehead, the silver cuffs clanging around his wrists. "Frederick. Frederick Mendel."

"Coven affiliation?"

"Solitary," he replied and looked nervously around the room.

"The group you were with," Julian continued, "you did not consider yourselves a coven?"

Frederick shook his head. "No, that's kind of the point."

Julian smirked. "Enlighten us on the point, then."

"We are…were Solitaries, all of us. We're not like you, you know? Vampires like us don't have masters who bring us home to live in mansions or castles like this. We're the children of Vamps who drank too much and didn't want to be charged with killing a human. We're the children of a lonely vampire who wanted a companion, only to be abandoned. We were left to fend for ourselves, many of us learning how to be vampires all on our own. None us were ever taught the old ways."

"The old ways?" Devy asked.

"Yes, the old ways of the Vampire. Living life as we once did, as a true and unmatched predator. Living our infinite lives out in the open without fear, showing humans that they have never been at the top of the food chain. Being free and not limited to either being in restrictive covens or wandering the world alone. Feeding on the life force of those beneath us, and giving them the opportunity to live an infinite life."

There was an awkward silence before Devy finally said, "If that's what you think the old ways were, you and your now deceased like-minded friends were thoroughly deceived."

Frederick began to shake with nerves, and looked down at the floor.

"Are you the leader of this new thinking, reliving the old ways?" Julian asked.

Frederick's head shot up. "Me? No. I came across a group in New Mexico, and we picked up more on our way to California."

"And chose to set up camp in the city where the Warriors are headquartered to expose yourselves?"

"Can't say we knew you were here at first. It's not like anyone taught us anything about you."

Cam's face softened. Frederick's master had failed him. Cam would be sympathetic, Devy wouldn't have the patience. They'd meet somewhere in the middle, which is why they worked so well together as coven leaders.

But the mood quickly changed when Miller stepped in front of Frederick and turned his back to Cam and Devy, causing an audible rumble through the crowd.

"Now let's get to the night of the Warrior attack," he said. "From what I have been told, your group was prepared for them. Is that true?"

Frederick paused for a moment before answering, "Um…yes."

"Excuse me, Miller," Julian said, "it is my position to ask the questions."

"You knew they were coming," Miller continued, "and you were in a position to attack the Warriors, or should I say the Warriors in training. You were waiting for them, isn't that correct?"

"Yes," Frederick replied nervously, "yes, we were ready for when they came."

"How?" Miller said, and took several steps to his left coming almost in line with Julian. "How did you know they were coming?"

"We were tipped off."

"By whom?"

Frederick didn't answer right away and the man holding him on the left raised his fist causing Frederick to hold his shackled hands in the air. "By a Warrior, a Warrior on the inside!"

The Counsel Hall erupted, some Warriors even standing as they shouted that Frederick had to be lying. Even Devy's chest had started to heave.

Julian called the meeting back to order, and the shouts went down to murmurs. "Frederick, you say a Warrior tipped you off, how exactly did they notify you?"

"I got a text message."

Julian nodded skeptically. "You got a text from someone you don't know telling you that a Warrior attack was emanate? Albeit until recently you said you had never even heard of the Warriors, yet you just up and prepare for battle?"

"It was true, wasn't it?" Frederick replied, making Julian purse his lips with skepticism.

"How would a Warrior even know how to contact you?"

"He said he had come to a previous rally, and made connections…"

"And what about today's activities," Miller interrupted, stepping squarely in front of Julian. "Were you notified again today that they were coming after your group?"

"Yes," Frederick replied, but unable to keep eye contact with those in front of him. "We were told they were coming again, but we thought we had more time to prepare. That's when we were attacked by…"

"My men," Miller said proudly. "Yes, and thankfully we were able to neutralize the situation quickly." Frederick grimaced and slumped to one side, only to be pulled back upright. "Were the messages from today sent from the same number as before?" Frederick nodded. "And do you have the phone that received those messages with you?"

Frederick nodded again. Miller stepped forward and rummaged through Frederick's pockets, finally pulling out a cell phone.

"Miller, if you would hand that to Julian…" Cam began.

"Shall we see if the traitor is in the room?" Miller interrupted and put the phone up to his ear.

After a few seconds a cell phone rang, soft and familiar in the way that everyone tended to have the same factory setting ringtone. Everyone began looking around at each other, and I turned my head to Jax whose eyes were wide in shock.

"What?" I asked just before a hand wrapped around my arm and pulled me down to the stone floor so hard that I bounced. My body was still recovering from the shock of the impact that it took me a few seconds to realize that Miller's men were rifling through my pockets, and pulled out my phone. It was still ringing as they held it up in the air. It was ringing. But…how?

"Don't you touch him!" Awbie screamed from somewhere.

Duncan grabbed me by the shoulders and jerked me to a standing position, my feet barely touching the ground. Miller's men formed a large circular perimeter facing outward and held their hands up in front of them. Awbie was on the first landing and banging her hands against an invisible shield. Jax leapt down next to his mother, his hands balled in fists as his eyes narrowed and his face tightened. He was trying to push his power through their shield, and it was obvious he wasn't getting through. Cam and Devy stood and shouted over each other, shouting at Miller to stop, shouting at the crowd to calm down.

"Miller, you have no right to handle a human that way, let him go," Cam said as he held his arm out to stop Devy from jumping off the platform.

"Let him go? You would let a traitor go? Is that because of his connection to your family?" Miller hissed, causing grumbles from the crowd.

"I'm not a traitor," I yelled, grabbing at Duncan's hands.

"Put him down, Duncan," Miller instructed and Duncan threw me into the floor, knocking the breath out of me.

Miller pulled me up to my knees and waved my phone in front of my face. "Explain the texts, Mr. Ryan."

"There's nothing on there," I replied.

Miller turned to the crowd like a masterful showman. "Shall we see for ourselves?" Miller didn't wait for an answer and pulled up my messages. But the smirk left my face when he began reading aloud. "It says, 'Warriors incoming, be ready.'" I flinched and he turned to me. "That was sent yesterday, right before the first mission failed."

My head shook violently from side to side. "No, that's impossible!"

Miller shrugged and pointed to the phone. "It's all right here, Mr. Ryan."

"I was on the mission. I almost died! Why would I have…"

"'Warriors coming your way in an hour.' That text is from earlier today."

My mind was racing, I hadn't sent any texts. Who the hell would I have sent texts to? Then it hit me.

"Wait, I didn't even have my phone this morning," I said and looked at Cam. "Remember? You came to my room this morning and I couldn't find my phone. And…and then later today when I went back to my room to get ready for the mission it was suddenly there. Someone must have taken my phone."

Miller tilted his head condescendingly. "And we're supposed to just take your word?"

"Yes!" I shouted. "There is nothing I have wanted more in my life than to be a Warrior. Why would I try and sabotage that?"

"Because you're angry, isn't that true?"

"Angry?" I laughed and went to stand, but Duncan forced me back onto my knees. "What would I have to be angry about?"

Miller smirked. "Isn't it true that you are in love with Olivia Burke?"

I paused for a moment before answering, "I've known Olivia since birth, of course I care about her."

"No, no," Miller laughed. "You have been *in love* with her, deeply, for some time. Isn't it true that you were insanely jealous when she came home and became engaged to my son?"

"I wasn't jealous," I replied carefully.

"But you weren't happy about it, were you?"

"No one was happy that she was engaged to Niall. Especially when we found out that he was…"

"And you were angry, weren't you? Angry that she was going to marry Niall and not you."

"No, I was angry that your son…"

"Angry that her family, people you consider your family, were allowing her to marry someone other than you, and so you took action. You took action to destroy those who wouldn't allow you to be with the woman you thought you deserved."

"No!" I yelled, and had to take a breath to calm myself down in order to choose my words carefully. "Never in a million years would I betray the Warriors. They are my family, and no amount of fake evidence you show is going to change that. Besides, you can't really make an argument about me being angry about Olivia being engaged to your son when that's a moot point now, isn't it it?"

"Is it? Are you sure about that?" Miller replied with a sly smile and looked around the room. "It seems that there is an important member of the Burke family missing." The crowd started to rumble, and I looked at Cam who had a sudden look of terror on his face. "I have it on good authority that Olivia is still in fact engaged to my son Niall, and that her absence here is due to the pressure she felt from the family to break the said engagement."

"That's a fucking lie!" Jax shouted and brought his fists down on the shield, causing it to shimmer where his hand hit. "She broke it off because your son tried to kill her!"

"My son? The puny little hybrid against the powerful Olivia Burke? I don't see how that could happen. Another lie," he said to the crowd.

"Another lie perpetuated by the mighty Burke family. And for what? You see, my friends, what they won't tell you is that their daughter is afraid of them, afraid if she doesn't follow their every command, she'll be ostracized. But not this time. This time she has taken a stand and defied her family, and for what? The purest emotion we have in this world – love."

"You're full of shit," Jax shouted.

"And that, my friends, is why she fears her family. That is why she isn't here."

"Where is Olivia? What have you done with her," I shouted, this time getting to a standing position, only to be knocked down flat on my face, and then picked back up to sit on my knees. I could feel blood running from my nose down over my lips.

"Miller, that is enough!" Cam shouted. "I will not allow this charade to go on any longer."

Miller turned to Cam and Devy, and gestured to my phone in his hand. "In my very hand I have proof that Will Ryan has betrayed you. Members of your coven could have been killed…"

"Yeah, me! I was almost killed…" I shouted and then got punched in the face. I hit the ground and literally saw stars floating in front of my face.

"Isn't it odd that even when presented with proof of a betrayal, your leaders defend the traitor," Miller continued. "And why? Because he is part of their family. What does that mean for the rest of you?"

"Miller stop this," Devy warned.

"Stop what? I am merely pointing out the truth as I see it. If you are not part of the close-knit family, you are left in the cold. Isn't that right?" he said, playing to the crowd and receiving a scary, approving response. It was suddenly apparent that the Warriors coming in from the field wasn't a coincidence.

"My friends, what are we doing here? The Warriors were once the most feared, most revered coven that existed. And here we are, debating whether a traitor should be punished or not. What has become of the Warrior coven!" Miller pointed directly at Cam and Devy. "Them, they happened. *They* had favorites. Are you one of them? Have you seen the dark side of not being favored by them?" The crowd froze, but in a captivated way rather than in shock. "There are children, the Burke children, who have crossed the divide between vampire and hybrid, and yet they keep it to themselves. And let us not forget the biggest insult of all," he said and pointed directly at Awbie. "Your leaders gained the knowledge of how to make vampires who can withstand the sun! Yet again, they keep it to themselves. We true vampires have had the torture of hiding in the shadows, the caves, the humiliating coffins in order to hide from the sun, and yet they have solved it and hid it from all of us. Why should they hide it from us unless they mean to keep us under their boot?"

The affirmations from the crowd caused worried glances between several of us.

"And look among you," Miller continued loudly, "look at those newer members of your coven, how come they do not have to suffer the effects of the sun like the rest of us. Why do they not share their knowledge…"

"Miller, that is enough…" Cam shouted.

"Is it?" Miller interrupted, turning around swiftly to face Cam. "Is it now? How is it that in all the millennia of our existence there are only two children who are truly both human and vampire, and they both belong to you?" The crowd's reaction grew as Miller turned back to the crowd and opened his arms wide. "Why shouldn't all our children have the ability to truly be of both worlds?" He pointed to Jax. "They can live among the humans, yet they have the power and strength of the vampire. Why wouldn't we want all our children to have such power and strength? Why do they keep it to themselves?"

"That is enough!" Devy shouted and thrust his fists into the shield so hard that a wave shimmered through it, causing Miller's men to adjust their stances and flex to hold it up.

Miller didn't flinch under the protection of the shield, and merely turned in Devy's direction. "Ah yes," he said snidely, "the mighty Warrior Assassin. Of all the Warriors that Victor created, he chose you, the homosexual, to have the coveted role of Assassin. Then you became a coven leader, a homosexual coven leader."

"Shut your fucking mouth," I shouted and leapt forward, only to be stopped and thrust into the stone floor and held there.

"Obviously you have your supporters," Miller said condescendingly.

"He's ten times the leader you will ever be," I muttered while the side of my face was pressed firmly into the floor.

"Is that so?" Miller laughed, and someone pulled me up by my collar onto my knees. "Shall we take a poll? The Warriors, the reviled Warrior coven, led by liars and homosexuals, is that what you all truly signed up for? Leadership that lies and protects those closest to them, and only leaves the scraps for the rest of you, is that what you want?"

Many of the Warriors in the crowd stood and shouted. It was a mutiny. The walls around us were falling down. There was a sudden feeling in my stomach that I was no longer safe, no matter how human I was.

Miller stood in the middle of the Council Hall and turned to face Cam and Devy defiantly. "My friends, I suggest a vote of no confidence of the leadership of the Warrior coven."

There were audible gasps from the crowd.

"You cannot ask for a vote," Devy growled.

"But I can," Skylar said, standing from the middle of the Warriors. It was planned, with sudden realization everything today was planned. "I ask for a vote of no confidence in the leadership of the Warrior coven."

"I second," another Warrior said within the stands.

I couldn't believe my eyes as one, five, ten, half, and then close to three quarters of the crowd finally stood in support. It wasn't until Julian stepped off the platform and stood with those that supported the vote, I realized I was going to die. Cam, Devy, the family and I were going to die. There wasn't enough oxygen to take a full breath.

Miller shrugged. "I believe the votes have it. The majority of your coven doesn't believe in your leadership. Victor isn't here to challenge anyone. So I believe you must...well, forfeit."

Cam was stunned while Devy heaved like a wild bull. "And I suppose you will take it upon yourself to lead them."

"What else can I do but continue the legacy of this once great coven."

"You will need an army to pull me or my brother down," Devy growled.

"Very well," Miller smirked and gestured to the opposite side of the Counsel Hall which suddenly began to shimmer, revealing at least a hundred men standing along the concrete risers. Could Miller's men have been here the whole time? Walking amongst us...hiding in our rooms? It would explain how my cell phone was gone one moment and there the next, and how messages I'd never sent were mysteriously there. How long had they been here? Days? Months? Dear god, help us.

The Warrior coven was falling right before our eyes. Even Devy conceded. His chest was no longer heaving, and he knelt down to the ground, placing his hands behind his back. He looked over to the Warriors standing against him.

"I see you," he said calmly. "I see each of you that stood to destroy our coven, our family. I see you...and I will kill you. Have no doubt, each of you will die for your betrayal against us and against our father."

Miller laughed, as did his men and many of the Warriors, but not all. There were definitely some that suddenly regretted their choice.

"Any last words from you, Mr. Burke?"

"Let my family go. You have me…"

"But I don't want just you. Your family is the crux of this. Your wife, your children…"

"And you will let William go," Cam demanded.

"The traitor?" Miller shouted and opened his arms once again to his audience. "My friends, even in the midst of defeat, your leader only thinks about those closest to him."

"He is human!"

"And he betrayed your coven," Miller shouted. "Things will be different now. There will be no more trials, no more leniency. You break our laws, you face the consequences. We will no longer be the soft, ineffective coven you two have created. There will be order. There will be punishment! We will once again strike fear into those who would challenge us, and that starts today."

Miller gave a nod, and the man standing behind Frederick stretched a garrote between his hands, and sliced Frederick's head off clean, letting it roll along the stone floor as his body fell to the ground with a loud thump.

"Take the family," Miller ordered, and several Warriors took position behind Awbie and Jax who were huddled together.

"Leave them alone," Cam shouted, taking a leap forward into several of Miller's men.

I caught Jax's eye, and without words I knew he was apologizing for what was about to happen and I absolved him. There was nothing he could do to save me.

In a split second, Jax placed his hand on Awbie's shoulder and a wave of energy exploded from within them. The Warriors behind them took most of the brunt, flying backwards or toppling over the concrete steps. Miller's men were pushed back and their shields faltered long enough for Awbie to Project away while Jax leapt over the crumbling bodies and disappeared out the door.

Only a few seconds of stunned silence passed before Miller began shouting out commands again. Miller's men surrounded Cam and Devy, taking them underneath their arms and dragging them toward the dungeon doors. Miller stepped in front of me, grabbed my hair, and forcibly tilted my head up to look at him. The blood from my nose rushed down the back of my throat. I had a feeling this wasn't the only blood I was going to spill today.

"What have you done with Olivia," I said, and then spat the blood that had accumulated on my lips onto Miller's face.

He flinched and then gave a devilish smile. "Oh we have so many things in store for her. But first thing's first," he said before his fist came down between my eyes.

Chapter Twenty-eight

Olivia

"Hello?" I asked loudly, to no reply. I shifted up in the tub, causing the water to slosh back and forth. "Hello? Is someone there?"

There was still no answer, but there was the nagging feeling that I wasn't alone. Angry and frustrated, I jumped out of the tub and grabbed the clean white robe that was hanging over the edge of the sink, leaving a trail of water behind me. Quickly I shrugged my arms into the robe and tied the sash around me tightly. Water was dripping from the ends of my hair down my neck, causing a shiver to run through my body.

"Is someone out there?" I said, adjusting the top of the robe to hide my chest, but again there was no answer. With a frustrated sigh, I stepped to the bathroom door and flung it open. "I'm not deaf, I heard you come in," I shouted, but the room was empty. It was eerily silent, and yet the voice in my head was screaming at me that there was something wrong. My eyes and my brain were fighting against each other. With a deep and nervous breath, I took a step into the bedroom. Nothing. I took another step, edging toward the bed. Nothing. I closed my eyes and shook my head. "Idiot," I said aloud to myself, but then the bathroom door slammed behind me.

My eyes flew open and I jumped at the sight of Niall behind me. When I tried to back away from him, I was met with a wall. I turned around to find three of Miller's men standing in the middle of my bedroom with a clear, shimmering shield between us.

I turned back to Niall. "How did you get in here," I shouted.

"How did we get in here?" he said condescendingly. "We never really left, love."

"Wha-what do you mean," I began, but then the invisible shield began pushing me toward the wall. Quickly I turned back and pounded my fists into the shield, but inch by inch it continued to push me back until I was only a few inches away from the wall.

Niall stepped in front of me and glided his finger down the shield. "What does it feel like to be an animal in a cage?"

"Why don't you come on this side and I'll show you," I replied.

He smirked. "My god, you really are intolerable."

"My family will come looking for me, and they will annihilate you and your cronies."

"Not likely," Niall laughed, as did the others behind him. "You see, after today, your family will no longer be in charge."

"You're full of shit."

Niall began to pace in front of me, chewing at his thumbnail with a sheepish grin that told me he knew something that I didn't. "It's like this, Olivia, when my father wants something, he will do whatever it takes to get it. Today, he wants the Warrior coven."

I laughed. "The Warriors would never follow your father."

"But they already are, love. For months my father and his men have been working on those Warriors who have been, let's say, unhappy with the current management. They're coming here, all of them. Right downstairs they are already starting to fill the corridors. They have come to help us tear your family down. The others will have no choice but to follow."

"They will fight to the death before they let you take over."

"Are you certain of that?"

"You have half a dozen men, you can't take all the..."

"Well, you have me there," he said mockingly, and then gave a proud smile. "Oh, but wait a minute, we have over ninety, actually."

"But...how."

"How do we do anything? We hide behind our shields. Dozens have been coming through your front door every day undetected – waiting, watching."

"You mean..."

"Oh yes, love. They've seen everything, including when you decided to sneak into Will Ryan's bed." My jaw dropped. "They were really there to plant the evidence against Will to prove he was the mole the Warriors have been looking for. Just think of their surprise when they saw you climbing into bed with him. That only sealed his fate, I'm afraid. I never thought of you as the whorish type, you were always so stiff with me."

"Maybe that's because you couldn't satisfy a woman even if you were a life-sized vibrator." Miller's men chuckled under their breath. "Maybe if you'd face me when we're having sex every once in a while…"

"I couldn't bear to look at your bloody ugly face."

I smiled. If he wanted to play dirty, I'd play dirty.

"Is that the reason though? Not that I like to brag, but I'm gorgeous. I'm thinking you're gay and you can't tell your dad. I mean, you know how he is about homosexuals. So just admit that I was your beard, and that you basically sexually assaulted me in order to hide your secret from your dad."

Suddenly the shield that had been separating us pushed me up against the wall and melted around me, squeezing the air from my lungs. My body was in a panic but was frozen against the wall unable to scratch or claw my way out.

"You stupid whore," Niall screamed. "I have control over you, don't you see that? Don't you ever, ever say that again, do you understand? I will do what I want to you!"

My eyes were becoming unfocused, but I could see someone pull Niall away from me. A moment later the shield pulled away and I fell to the floor coughing and gasping for air.

"We have two coming this way," someone announced in the room, and suddenly arms were around my waist, lurching me upright and back against the wall. I shook my head and forced my eyes to focus. One of Miller's men stood on the other side of my shield and then cast another shield around the two of us. Niall and the two other men were huddled in the far corner on the opposite side of the room before they disappeared. What was happening? Was this how they'd been hiding in the manor all this time? They could see out, but were invisible to the outside. Damn it, I knew they could do this. Niall would tell stories about how his father would do this to him. I never put it together how they could use that against us.

The bedroom door suddenly flew open and my brother ran inside, stopping in the middle of the room and looking around. He paused and looked to the left. He was trying to talk to me through our connection, but it wasn't cutting through the shield.

"Jack!" I screamed and banged on the shield, but he didn't react. "Jack, I'm here, I'm here!"

But again, he didn't hear or see me. Frustrated, he stepped toward the bathroom, opened the door, and stepped inside. At that moment Will came into the room. Dear lord, no.

"Will," I shouted through tears. "Will, please see me, I'm here!"

"Well?" Will said as Jack stepped out of the bathroom.

"The bathtub is full, there's water all over the floor, but she's nowhere in sight," Jack replied.

"I'm right here," I cried. "Please, please see me."

"Try her again," Will commanded.

"I have! Don't you think I have? Dammit, Olivia, answer me!"

"I am, asshole! I'm right here," I screamed and sank to my knees, sobbing into the shield. But then, for a split second, Jack turned his head in my direction. I stood back up quickly and pounded my fists against the shield.

"You got something?" Will asked and stepped up behind him.

"No, just a weird feeling."

"A twin feeling?"

"Maybe. I just…"

"All Warriors report to the Council Hall," a voice sounded throughout the room. "All Warriors must come to the Council Hall immediately."

"We have a P.A. system?" Will asked.

"We should go then, maybe Livy's there already," Jack said and Will followed him to the door.

"I'm not there," I cried and sank back into the floor as Jack stepped out of the room. Will lingered for a moment and looked right at me, but then turned and closed the door.

Eventually the outer shields melted away, allowing Niall and the other men to roam about the room, whereas the bubble around me stayed intact. I was an animal in a cage, an exhibit at the zoo.

Niall stood in front of me, looking down on my pitiful position. "I told you," he said proudly. "It all ends today."

My hands wouldn't stop shaking. It had been about an hour since Jack and Wills had come in the room and left me inside the constrictive prison Miller's men had constructed around me. It wasn't just the feeling of not knowing what was going on outside my bedroom door, but also feeling unbelievably exposed sitting on the floor in nothing but a white bathrobe. It was a position no woman wanted to be in while in a room full of men.

Occasionally Niall would stand in front of me to gloat, and show me his disgust. The feeling was mutual, and it would stoke the fear I had for my family, but especially Will. It could be worse for Will now that they knew he was so important to me. And he was. My stomach churned every time I thought of him. What danger had I put him in?

Suddenly the bedroom door flew open, and Miller strolled in with Duncan, Mason, and Simon behind him. Miller exhaled a dramatic breath and announced, "It is done."

Everyone in the room cheered and congratulated Miller, shaking his hand and proudly patting each other on the back. Tears burned my eyes as my bottom lip trembled in fear. What did it mean? Where was my family? Where was Will?

Miller, sensing my distress, stepped in front of me, tilting his head in condescending curiosity. "Little bird crying in her gilded cage," he said in a soft, sickly-sweet voice.

"Where is my family?"

He raised his eyebrows and sighed. "It is truly a sad, sad day for you. The Warriors have given their vote of no confidence in your father and uncle's leadership, and have therefore forfeited the coven to me."

"That's…impossible. There's no way that…"

"Oh, but it is possible, little bird," he said. "Your family is now in custody, along with your lover."

"Will?" I asked, tears instantly burning my eyes and nose as I stood from the floor. "But he's human, you can't…"

"He's also a traitor."

"A trait…" I paused and looked over at Niall. "You said…you said they planted evidence. Is that…"

In the blink of an eye, Miller rounded on Niall and slapped him across the face so hard he fell to the floor. "Did it ever cross your mind that perhaps we didn't want that information known? Your stupidity amazes me, Niall."

Niall held his hand up to his cheek that was red and already starting to swell. "What difference does it make? They can't prove anything."

Miller turned his back to his son and shook his head in disgust. "As I said, your lover was shown to be a traitor in front of the entire coven, they saw the evidence, and we responded. He will die like the rest of your family, that is how these things work."

"Then why keep me? You kept me for a reason, otherwise I'd be in the dungeons with everyone else."

"Well done, you," Miller said with a wink. "In situations like these, you always need leverage. Right now, your mother, father, brother, uncles, and so forth are going through excruciating torture until their ultimate execution. But you can put a stop to all of that, and allow them to die mercifully. All I want is to know two little things, that's all. Two little bits of information, and your family's pain ends now."

"And then what happens to me?"

Miller opened his arms wide and smiled. "Nothing, my dear. You will go on living your life as Niall's bride, as planned. Your marriage to my son will bring our covens together as we had hoped."

Besides wanting to vomit at the thought of being forced to marry Niall, I couldn't stop imagining my family being stretched across boards, screaming in agony having god knows what done to them. But even worse, my stomach churned at the thought of what they could be doing to Will. Was he bleeding or crying out, begging for the pain to stop? My breath quickened to the point I thought I would hyperventilate. Different voices were screaming in my head on what to do.

Without looking Miller in the eye, I said, "What are the two things you want to know?"

"You are a smart little bird. The first, and should be the easiest, I want to know how the new Warriors are no longer sun sensitive."

"And the second?"

Miller stepped forward and grazed his fingers along the shield in the shape of my outline. "I want to know how they made you and your brother. How does one make a true hybrid?"

I sighed and looked at the floor. My dream from this morning flashed in head – Will on his knees and Miller circling him with a sword. Before Miller stabbed him through the stomach, Will looked directly at me and said "Don't tell them a fucking thing." Was this what he was referring to? He wasn't here, Miller didn't have a sword, but he was looking for information that I shouldn't, no, that I couldn't tell him.

"Well, little bird?"

"I don't know," I replied softly.

"I beg your pardon?"

Keeping my eyes on the floor, and bracing for the shield to suddenly start sucking the oxygen out of my body again, I replied, "I'm the last person you should ever have kept. They never told me how they were siring the newer Warriors, and I never asked. I never wanted to know anything about the coven. And as for me and Jack, we were born this way."

Silence fell upon the room, and Miller lowered his head to be inches away from me. "Stupid girl," he growled. "You will tell me what I want to know. Your loved ones will be tortured, they will be shown no mercy, and you will be responsible for that. I will get what I want, and I don't care what I have to do to you to get it."

I raised my eyes to his. "I don't know anything, Miller. If I did, don't you think I would have told Niall by now?"

"Take her to her parents' quarters," he ordered and the shield narrowed around me, forcing me forward as Miller's men circled around me with Niall falling in behind us. When they stepped forward as a unit, I planted my feet into the carpet, but then fell face first into the floor as the shield pushed me forward.

Duncan bent down and narrowed his eyes. "You will walk with us or you will be dragged. Is that understood?"

I glared up at him but didn't answer. When they stepped forward again, I quickly stood up and walked at their pace out of the bedroom and into the corridor. It was empty, but you could hear chaos echoing up from the lower floors. I tried to keep my emotions at bay, but tears kept leaking steadily down my face. They were tears of sorrow and fear of what was going to happen to me and my family. My brain was racing, trying to think of what I could do. Could I break out of this shield? Were there secret passages that I could sneak into? Who was even an ally at this point? It was overwhelming, and the tears kept coming.

Once we had descended down the spiral staircase, the reason for the noise was obvious. Miller's men steered us toward my parents' quarters, but the corridor was tight with a mixture of men from Miller's coven pushing other Warriors forcibly down the hallway. That's when I realized that no one was looking at me. I was in a bathrobe; I would think that might draw at least some attention. The shield must be disguising me in the same way Miller's men had been hiding in the corners of the manor.

As we approached the dining hall, I saw young David kicking and yelling and fighting against two of Miller's men who were dragging him down the corridor. "You are all traitors! Traitors!" he yelled.

Behind him, two Warriors held Trevor Roberts by the elbows, stoic as ever as they led him along the corridor. It was at that point I beat my fists into the shield. They were both newer Warriors, impervious to sunlight, and obviously resisting the new leadership. They would be tortured for information, just like my family. I'd known Trevor since I was a child, and David was just a baby.

"Roberts!" I shouted and pounded on the shield. "Let them go," I cried, losing my footing and falling into the floor. "I'm sorry," I cried and pressed my weight against the shield, allowing them to drag me along the floor.

Was I making the right decision? My family and the new Warriors were being tortured. Were our family secrets worth their pain? I knew what Miller wanted to know, I knew everything including the mistake my father had made, and how one moment of weakness had brought us so much misery. Were those secrets worth the pain everyone was having to endure? What would be my breaking point? How long could I play dumb to what Miller wanted to know?

"Get up," Duncan growled, trying not to look at me in order to keep up their illusion.

Anger was bubbling up to the surface. Generations of Warriors and ancient vampires were part of my DNA. I could no longer ignore it. I could no longer deny it. I secured my robe around me and replied. "You can all go fuck yourselves."

Duncan's lips curled into a snarl. "I hope you like pain, little bird."

Chapter Twenty-nine

Will

Being knocked out was not quite what I thought it would be. It was literally darkness. No sense of time passing, just the moment when you lost consciousness, and then the next moment when you woke up. I'm sure others who have lost consciousness may have had a gradual process to waking up. I, however, went from seeing Miller's fist coming at my face, to someone else's fist waking me up.

In a word, I would say the pain was – unimaginable. I'd been hit, I'd broken bones, but never every bone in my face, and what felt like every rib. My eyes were already swelling shut. Mason was definitely taking great pleasure beating me to a pulp. The pain was so intense that the only thing keeping me upright was the rope around my wrists tying me to the back of a chair, otherwise I'd be in the floor. It was hard to breathe, not that he was giving me a chance to really catch a full breath anyway.

Miller's men kept bringing in the newer Warriors a few at a time, grilling them on the same questions they had asked in the Council Hall. Being good Warriors, no one answered, and their heads were cut off. Young David was on his knees, scared and fearful, but dutiful right up to the point when they brought a sword down on his neck. Roberts was kneeling next to me. He had always been stoic and proud, but encouraging. He'd trained young David personally, and yet he was stone-faced as the blood from David's neck seeped into his pants leg.

"How did you become insensitive to the sun?" one of Miller's men asked before punching Roberts so hard in the stomach that he keeled over.

Slowly Roberts rolled back up to his knees and exhaled a deep breath. "Trevor Roberts. Sire number seventy-two of the Warrior coven. Coven leaders Cameron Burke and Devin the Warrior Assassin. Sires of the mighty Victor. Sire of the ancient Alastor…"

Roberts' tormentor grabbed him by the back of the head and slammed his head into the floor, leaving a dent in the stone before pulling him forcibly back up to his knees. "How did you become insensitive to the sun?" he demanded in a tone that was frustrated and exhausted.

"Trevor Roberts. Sire number seventy-two of the Warrior coven. Coven leaders Cameron Burke and Devin the Warrior Assassin. Sires of the mighty…"

"Last chance."

Roberts paused and looked over at me. "It would have been a pleasure serving with you, Will."

My stomach dropped at the reality of what was going to happen to both of us. "See you on the flip side."

Roberts smirked and continued, "Sires of the mighty Victor. Sire of the ancient…"

But he didn't finish. Mason swung his sword around and cut Roberts' head clean from his shoulders. His body slumped to the ground while his head rolled a few feet away. My breath caught in my throat at the thought that I would be next.

Mason stepped in front of me, dragging his blood-soaked sword along the floor, and leaned down to be eye level with me. "No one is coming out of this alive. You can stop your suffering. Just tell us what we want to know."

"Where's…Olivia," I said through the pain in my ribs.

Mason slapped me across the face in response. The door behind me opened, and Miller's men straightened to attention.

"How are things progressing?" Miller asked as he came around me.

Mason seemed nervous as he replied, "We didn't get anything, sir."

There was a pause that seemed to make everyone nervous. After several agonizing seconds, Miller leaned down and looked me in the eyes as though he was examining his prey.

"You have been a thorn in my side, Mr. Ryan."

"Where's…Olivia."

"After everything she has done to you, you continue to pine for her. Well, if you must know, she is going to marry Niall, I am going to take over this coven, and you are going to die. These are the absolutes I can provide to you, Mr. Ryan. Does it make you feel any better?"

"It does, knowing that you'll never get the information you want," I said, incidentally spitting blood and saliva in his face. "You'll never be able to control Olivia."

Miller snarled at me and wiped his face slowly. Tilting his head curiously, he reached for my cross necklace and ripped it from my neck. "Your lord and savior aren't going to save you now, Mr. Ryan," he said and put the necklace in his pocket.

The door opened behind us and Julian came to stand next to Miller. "They are ready," he said, giving a quick glance down at me. "Continuing to hurt Will Ryan could be a problem for you."

Miller smirked and patted Julian on the shoulder. "Let me worry about that." Miller turned toward me. "Now how's about we have a little fun."

In an instant, my bindings were removed and I was dragged out of the room. Breathing was difficult from the pain in my ribs, made worse by the two guards holding me up by my arms. I could put on a brave face and talk of duty and being proud to die for my coven, but my stomach was churning at the thought that my death could be moments away.

My brain started to think about all the things I hadn't done, all the people I didn't get to say goodbye to, or the apologies I wanted to make. It was hard to keep all of that inside while they dragged me painfully along the dark corridor toward the main torture room. I wondered if Roberts had been as afraid as I was. He was so stoic and brave, and I felt weak. How much would this hurt? I was so focused on the pain. I was in so much pain already, how much more would I have to be in before it stopped and I took my last breath.

Miller's men dragged me into the main torture chamber, and my breath caught at the sight of Cam and Devy stretched across two wide wood boards hanging twenty feet in the air with thick silver chains melting into their skin.

Miller's men threw me on the ground, and my face bounced off the stone floor. I rolled onto my back to catch my breath, looking up to see Cam and Devy shouting and screaming at Miller.

"He is human!" Cam shouted.

"He is a traitor, Cameron," Miller replied. "But it's not the fact that he's human that has you so upset. It's because Will is important to you. So important that you have lost your coven over him. That's the truth, Cameron. And that's why your coven has turned against you."

"Our coven has turned against us because you have appealed to the weaker minded members," Cam said, jostling his board in the air. "Those Warriors who are only happy when they are killing and torturing others. Am I right, Julian? Is that why you turned? We were unable to fulfill your need to torture and punish enough vampires?"

Julian stepped forward and looked up. "The day of your coronation was the saddest and most disappointing day in Warrior history. Perhaps now we can restore the respect and pride of our coven under Miller's leadership."

"Your entire Warrior life has been based on Father's approval. What do you think he is going to say when he finds out what you have done?"

"Hopefully he will congratulate me on seeing the error of his ways," Julian replied with a smile.

"Well, now that we have gotten some family drama out of the way," Miller began, giving a nod over his shoulder which caused two of his men to raise me up to my knees.

I was disappointed at myself when I couldn't stop the tear from dripping down my face. What hope did I have when the two strongest, fearless, and most important men in my life were hanging helpless above me.

"Will, be strong," Devy began, his eyes boring into mine. "Everything is going to be ok."

"Why lie to the boy?" Miller asked.

"I truly look forward to killing you," Devy replied.

"You can't even get yourself off that board," Miller laughed. "It's all rather anti-climactic, isn't it? If I'd known it was so easy to take over the Warrior coven, I would have done it years ago. I was certainly excited about the possibility of a big battle, but we can't always get what we want. That said, there are still a few loose ends to take care of, last chances and all that."

The men on either side of me tightened their grip and lifted me high enough to where my knees hung a few inches from the floor. The sharp, blinding pain from my ribs made me scream and cough up a bit of blood. That wasn't a good sign.

Miller took a few steps forward, looked up at Cam and Devy, gestured to me and said, "It looks like your favorite son is running out of time. Do you want him spending that time in this much pain?"

"Fuck you," I said weakly.

Mason glided swiftly in front of me and punched his fist hard into my stomach. A stream of blood came up and out of my mouth.

Devy and Cam began shouting, not that I could decipher what they were saying, especially when Miller started yelling over them. "How are you making the new sires?"

"Take your torturous desires out on us, not him," Cam yelled.

"I don't want him," Miller replied. "He is merely a nuisance. I want to know how your new Warriors are not sensitive to the sun. Now tell me, or his pain continues."

"Let it continue then," I said and let my head fall back. "Don't tell him a goddamn thing."

I could see the conflict in Cam's face, but I couldn't be the reason they let go of their secrets. Miller gave a nod and I braced myself as best I could for whatever would come, but Mason's fist came down so hard on my leg that my knee separated from my thigh.

"How did you make your children true hybrids?" Miller continued over my screams.

"Don't tell him a fucking thing," I yelled.

"William…" Cam cried.

"Don't tell him…don't tell him," I kept repeating as things started to get fuzzy. "Just…tell my parents…I love them."

"Will, look at me," Devy commanded and I weakly looked up. "Get your mind right."

To some it might have sounded insensitive considering my current situation. But Devy would often say that to me during competitions. It meant to focus the mind for what was coming, and not on what was happening in the moment.

"Enough then!" Miller yelled and gestured toward me.

Before I could blink, Mason was in front of me again and thrust his sword into my stomach. I kept searching for breath. The room around me went silent. Mason jerked his sword out of me, allowing me to look up at Devy and Cam one last time.

"I'm sorry," I said and fell onto my side.

Cam start screaming, but Devy let out a howl and flexed every muscle in his arms and chest. There was a cracking noise, and with one final wail, the left corner of Devy's board broke off and fell to the ground. He tried grasping at the thick silver chain hanging from the ceiling like a wild animal, burning his hand and causing the board to swing.

"You said these were indestructible," Miller yelled at Julian, who was quick on the defense.

"Against most, yes," Julian replied. "But you put the Warrior Assassin on it and kill his student, then maybe there's a weakness."

"Fix it," Miller commanded and gestured for his men to leave. "Or else you'll be the next one who loses his head."

"Of course, sir," Julian said, bowing his head.

The room went quiet as Miller and all his men left the torture chamber, slamming the door loudly behind them. As the blood leaked from my body, my brain started to fire odd images. I wasn't sure what was real or the final synapses showing random memories. One was of Jax and Olivia wrestling on the ground fighting over the last popsicle. Another was of Julian kneeling over me telling me to hang on. And then Olivia smiling at me, touching my cheek.

Julian was looking down at me again, and I had to think that this was real since I'd rarely had any interactions with him. "I'm sorry, I know this will hurt," he said and then lifted me up into his arms.

He was right, it was extremely painful, but I hardly had the energy to react to it. My leg dangled and shot sharp pains throughout my body as Julian carried me across the room and laid me on a table. He stepped away and came back a moment later with a thick piece of cloth and pressed it into my stomach. The feeling made me want to vomit.

"Hold that there if you can. Stomach wounds can be slow bleeders, so hopefully we have some time. Keep the pressure on."

I wasn't sure what was going on. Julian had betrayed us, stood against Cam and Devy in the meeting, had put them on boards and chains, but now he was helping me. I didn't understand and I was too weak to try. He stepped away from me and knocked on the door three times. A moment later Connor Projected into the room.

"Pull that first lever," Julian instructed as he put on a thick pair of welder's gloves. Connor nodded and pulled down on the first lever. Pulleys squeaked and suddenly Devy sailed down to the floor.

I reminded myself I needed to keep pressure on my stomach, but I started to shake. Shock was setting in. Breathe, I kept saying to myself, keep breathing.

"Pull the second lever, Connor," Julian said across the room, and a moment later, Cam's board started lowering to the floor.

Suddenly Devy was hovering over me, and then pressed his forehead against mine. "Get your mind right, child, get your mind right. We have more to do."

He lifted his head and his eyes were lined with red tears.

"It hurts," I said and he squeezed my hand. "I'm not...brave enough."

His face tensed and the red tears dripped from his eyes. "You are the bravest human I know. Lesser men would have given up to stop the pain. Now, get your mind right, we have things to do. That is an order."

I didn't understand what he was talking about, but I nodded anyway. The room was getting fuzzy and cold. Devy squeezed my hand one more time and then stepped away, going over to stand near Connor and Julian at my feet. But before my hand could hit the table, Cam was at my side and wrapped his hand around mine.

His cheeks were streaked with red tears as he petted my head. "I am so sorry, Wills. We will get out of this."

"Not sure about the we part," I replied. "Please...tell my parents..."

"We cannot think like that," he interrupted, but then I coughed up more blood. Cam looked back at Devy. "Brother?"

"He doesn't have much time," Devy replied.

As everyone had always said, Devy new death intimately, and he always knew when someone was close to it. I just never imagined he would be talking about me.

Cam turned back to me, his face strained trying to keep his composure. "William, your injuries are severe enough that..."

"I'm dying, Cam, I know."

"Brother, if we're going to do this, we have to do it now," Devy said.

Cam petted my head. "It is most likely you will not survive your injuries. The only way we can get you out of here is if we Turn you. We can do that, William, or we...we can quicken your passing."

I'd wanted to be Turned for a year, and now the choice was in my hand. It was rushed and forced and I was scared.

Devy stepped up on the opposite side and looked down at me intently. "Dying now is still honorable, Will. But if you want to be Turned, we need to do it right now before they come back. It's not how any of us wanted to do it..."

"Ok," I replied weakly. "Do it."

"Are you sure," Cam said and squeezed my hand tightly. "We cannot go back. You have to be sure…"

"Yes…do it."

Devy nodded and looked down toward the end of the table. "Connor, keep a look out. Julian, you stay here."

Connor nodded and left the chamber. Cam pulled Julian to the side of the table. "You are sure the cameras are not recording?"

"Positive," Julian replied. "Liam is seeing to it that the recordings are on loops. I assure you they cannot see us."

Cam looked across me to Devy, who gave him a nod. "Julian, you are about to become part of a small group who knows how vampires can become sun insensitive, an even smaller group after today," Devy began and Julian looked between the two of them nervously. "We stumbled across it when Brianna was Turned, and since then we have tested and administered it on our new Warriors. It is surprisingly simple."

Cam looked down at me. "Last chance to turn back, Wills. Do you consent to the Turning?"

I nodded, unable to find the strength to speak.

"We have to drain most of your blood first, and you will want to fight against it, but try to relax. Then you will drink from each of us, understood?"

I nodded and started to shake with nerves. Cam and Devy each took an arm and held my wrist at their mouths.

"Careful, Brother," Devy said. "There can't be that much blood left."

Cam nodded and closed his eyes, red tears streaking down his face as he sank his fangs into my wrist. Devy did the same on the other side, and Cam was right on wanting to fight back. It must be an autonomic response, the fight or flight instinct to being close to death. Julian put his weight on my hips to keep me still, which only made me scream out because of the pain it caused in my leg. It was only a few seconds later that my body just gave up and I went limp. I was cold, and weak, and wanted to sleep.

Devy smacked my cheek to bring me to attention. "Come on now, Will, you need to drink."

My eyes were heavy, too heavy. Devy smacked my cheek again, and my eyes flew open. Immediately he put his wrist up to my mouth. I'd already forgotten what I was supposed to do. Devy didn't waste a moment and squeezed blood from his wrist into my mouth, so much so that I was forced to swallow.

"Good boy," Devy said and stepped aside.

Cam was next, piercing his wrist with his fangs and then bringing it up to my mouth. I tried to drink, but I was too weak. Cam nodded and squeezed his blood into my mouth as well, and I swallowed it down.

Julian stepped up next to me, looking to Cam for instruction. "I am Turning him as well?"

Cam nodded. "The blood of three is the secret, for reasons we do not know."

"I've never Turned anyone," Julian replied nervously.

"He can't be too picky," Devy said, coming to stand near my head. "Bite your wrist and squeeze it into his mouth. We don't have much time."

Julian looked down at me. "I'm sure I'm not the third person you would have chosen, but it is an honor all the same."

A second later, Julian bit his wrist and squeezed his blood into my mouth. When he pulled away, I could see the red tears welling in his eyes.

"Wills," Cam said as he took my hand and held it up against my chest. His eyes were apologetic and the red tears finally crested over his lids. "Your heart will start to beat faster," he said softly, and a moment later that's exactly what happened. My heart started beating hard and painfully fast. "You will start to feel a cold, burning sensation. That is the vampire blood working its way through your body." It felt like there was Ben-gay in my veins, and it made me jerk and convulse. Cam petted my hair, red tears streaking his face. "Your heart will start beating even faster, and you will try to breathe, but…"

I gasped for breath. And gasped for breath. My heart felt like it was going to explode. Faster. Faster. Painfully fast. And then it stopped. It was silent. I laid frozen for several seconds before taking in a giant gulp of air.

I looked at Cam whose hand was clasped over his mouth. "Is it…done?" He nodded, causing more red tears to drip over his hand. I stopped taking in breaths, realizing I was doing it out of reflex. There was no pulse, no heartbeat, although there was still pain. "Everything still hurts."

"It will take a little while for your injuries to heal," Devy said, suddenly at my side. He looked over at Julian. "Bring Connor back in."

Julian nodded and disappeared. Devy placed his hand on my chest. "You're a Warrior now, child."

"We have to get…out of here…first," I said painfully, wondering when the magic vampire healing powers would kick in.

The door opened and closed again, and a moment later Connor was standing at my feet. "Wow, you Turned him?"

Cam finally released my hand and wiped his face. "Yes, and now we need to get him out of here. Are the tunnels clear?"

Connor nodded. "So far yes. That's how I've been going back and forth. Either no one has told Miller about them yet, or they can't find them. Either way it gives you time to get out. I was able to get some of Jared's old equipment. If he can get onto the old analog network, we can communicate with each other."

"Well done, Connor. Do we know how many allies we have in the manor?"

"A handful," he replied. "It's hard to know who to trust, but roughly six or seven."

Devy grimaced at the number. "How are we going to fight against this?"

"We will find a way, Brother," Cam replied confidently. "Do we have any idea where Olivia is?"

Connor shook his head. "There's a rumor they moved her to your quarters, but nothing firm. No one has seen her since before the Council Hall meeting."

"We can't leave...without her," I said, feeling a new round of burning in my stomach and face.

"You have no say in this," Devy said and looked down at me. "Looks like you're starting to heal. That's good. We'll have to be careful with this leg, though. We don't have time to locate Olivia, we need to leave now."

Cam stepped away and pulled Connor aside. Devy put his arms under me and raised me up to a sitting position. I grunted at the pain in my leg and stomach, although blood was no longer seeping out of the wound.

"Do you have tape?" Devy asked Julian who nodded and jutted his head to the corner.

Julian took Devy's place and held me upright while Devy went in search of tape, which for some reason seemed scary to me.

"I am sorry I couldn't help you earlier, Will," Julian said sincerely.

"I thought you'd turned against us."

Julian smirked. "That was the idea. Anyone who truly knows me, knows that I would never betray Father. Even though my brothers and I don't always see eye to eye, they are a part of Victor, and therefore I could never betray them or the coven. Thankfully my brothers knew that, so they knew I had a plan to get them out. I'm just sorry that I couldn't help everyone."

"Thank you for helping me."

"Not soon enough," he replied. "But at least I could help in some way."

"Here we go," Devy said, extending a long strand of duct tape. "Hold him, Julian."

"What are we…" I began, but Devy quickly placed my knee in line with my thigh and wrapped the duct tape around it. I was still screaming as he lifted me into his arms and turned to Cam.

"It's time, brother."

Cam nodded and patted Connor on the shoulder. "I'm counting on you, Connor."

"Yes, sir," he replied.

"Julian, be careful, you know they will suspect you."

Julian smiled and puffed his chest out. "I'm sure they will, but hopefully Connor can help me stage enough doubt."

"What am I doing?" Connor asked, looking confused.

Julian directed him toward where the broken boards and silver chains were hanging limp to the floor. He handed Connor the set of gloves he'd used before and pointed to one of the silver chains. "Tie that chain around my wrist, and then you'll need to press up on the lever over there to get me off the floor."

Connor's eyes grew large. "I don't think I can do that."

"You can, and you will," Devy commanded. "That is an order."

Connor nodded nervously, and put on Julian's gloves.

"It's important you stay quiet," Devy said to me firmly.

"I'll try my best," I replied, and he narrowed his eyes, which was never good.

"Don't try, just do it," he commanded.

"Yes, sir."

"You got your mind right."

"Yes, sir, I remembered."

"You're a good boy."

"Was I really that close to dying?"

He pressed his lips tightly together as he nodded. "I'm glad you made the choice you did. I've lost enough people today. I wasn't ready to lose you."

Cam opened the door as Connor stepped over to the levers that controlled the silver chains. As we made our way out of the torture chamber, I looked back just in time to see Julian assenting into the air by one arm tied with a silver chain. I couldn't believe I doubted him for one second. He was probably more honorable than all the Warriors put together.

Devy held me tightly against his chest as we took a hard left, but only a few steps and we were at a stone wall. Cam lifted a small section of the wall to reveal a keypad and entered a code quickly. A second later, the stone wall opened to expose a secret set of stairs. Devy and I went through first, the area around us darkening to pitch black by the time we got to the bottom of the staircase. Cam was right behind us, and once again we took a hard left and then ran down a long tunnel. I'd been through a few of the hidden tunnels, mostly as a kid playing with Jax and Olivia, but we had never gone down this one. Honestly, it looked as though no one had in decades. It was musty and damp, with moss growing along the walls and vines cutting into the ceiling and hanging down. It suddenly hit me that I could even see these things in the dark.

It was only a minute or two before a sliver of light penetrated the darkness ahead. As we got closer, I realized it was a vertical grate at the end of the tunnel. Cam got to the grate first and lifted a heavy lever that was holding it shut. As he pushed the grate open, the sun hit and cast shadows of the overgrowth in front and around the grate, which made it almost invisible from the outside.

The sun hit my skin as Devy stepped through the grate, and my natural reaction was to flinch. The light burned my eyes for a brief moment, but then my body relaxed when no further pain came. I opened my eyes to see the woods of the west side of the manor expanding in front of us. Jax and I used to call it the jungle since it was kept wild, but today it was hopefully our sanctuary. Cam stepped behind us to close the disguised grate door, and just as it locked into place, a loud alarm wailed.

Devy's jaw tightened and he squeezed me uncomfortably tight into his chest. Cam launched forward and we were right at his heels. The woods rushed past and nicked my face as we headed down a steep hill. Suddenly Cam whipped his head to the left, sensing something in the distance, and then pointed to a large dead tree on the right. Devy leapt from the ground and landed softly on the other side of the tree, laying me gently down on the forest floor.

"Check down near the brush," someone said in the distance.

My head jerked up, realizing there were people after us already. Devy squeezed the back of my neck and held his index finger up to his lips. I nodded as Cam quietly pulled a large fallen branch with leaves over the top of us. Then we froze. No breath sounds, no heartbeats. It was taking a bit of getting used to, but it was certainly beneficial in these circumstances.

But that's when the burning in my leg began. Was it going to start healing now? NOW? Not an hour from now when we'd be away from other vampires that were hunting us down. A stick broke not too far from us, and I put my hand over my mouth to keep from making any noise, but I could feel something building in my leg. Devy looked down at my leg, and then back up at me with wide, terrified eyes. Quickly he pressed my face firmly into his chest, trying to muffle me, but it wasn't helping. The pressure and burning was building, tightening everything up through my stomach until my leg shifted with a loud snap, and I let out an uncontrollable whelp into Devy's chest.

Suddenly the branch above us was pulled away, and the three us looked up at the same time to find a Warrior named Maxim staring down at us. No one moved, no one made a sound.

"Hey, Warrior," someone else shouted in the distance, "did you find something?"

Maxim relaxed his face, put his fist over his heart for only a moment, and then dropped the branch back over us. "No," he shouted back. "Just some squirrels."

Cam grabbed a rock and threw it, causing it to crack several feet away.

"There's someone on the northeast side," Maxim yelled and was gone. The other person in the woods streaked past us, his feet barely crunching along the forest floor. We waited only another few seconds before Devy pulled me back up into his arms and ran out from under our perch. As the trees whipped past, I realized it was the first time I was happy to be leaving the manor.

"We made it," I sighed into Devy's chest.

"Not yet, and goddamn your leg."

"Yes, sir," I laughed softly.

"We're going to be ok."

"Yes, sir."

Chapter Thirty

Olivia

"Will you ever stop crying?" Niall groaned from a corner on the other side of the room. Duncan and the other guards had dumped me on my parents' bed and placed a shield around it with a wide perimeter. At least they were allowing me to move around, although I found it hard to leave the bed. The fear and realization that my life had been a lie was overwhelming. Everything happening now was my fault. I had forced Niall on my family, and now I didn't know if they were even alive.

I wiped my nose on the cuff of my robe and pushed myself up to a seated position, pulling a pillow up into my chest. "I'm sorry, Niall, how am I supposed to react when my life is crumbling around me? Please tell me, I'd love to know. That is if you can tell the truth. You don't seem able to do that very well."

He rolled his eyes and softly began banging the back of his head against the wall. "Duncan, how much longer must I stay here?"

Duncan sighed and shook his head. He didn't seem too keen on having babysitting duty either. "Your father said to keep you with her. Until he says otherwise, you're stuck here. Now both of you shut it."

Duncan turned his back and began having a quiet conversation with one of the other guards. Niall got up from the floor and began to pace in front of the doors that led out onto the lanai. The sun was just touching the tips of the trees, deflecting yellow rays through the door's glass panes and hitting Niall in such a way it looked like he had a halo glowing above his head. Only a few weeks ago I would have made a comment about how he was truly an angel sent down to love me. And now…

"Was it always a lie?" I asked and he looked over at me.

"What?"

"Even in the beginning, at the café …did you ever have feelings for me?"

"No," he replied flatly. "My father's men surveilled you for two weeks to discover your patterns and preferences. After that, every step, every choice you made was because I put it in your head to do it. You think you're a prisoner now? I've been forced to pretend that I like your hair and the smell of your perfume. It took everything not to recoil when kissing you, and the only reason I did was because I knew the wrath of my father if I didn't make you fall in love with me."

I wiped my nose again. "You're a victim in this too, you know."

"I've been a victim since the day I was born," he replied and stepped up to the edge of the shield. "Olivia, my father isn't going to stop until he gets what he wants. He will force us to marry."

"And how exactly will he do that?"

"Do not underestimate what my father will do. We will have no choice. Please I'm…" he lowered his head for a moment and took a breath, "I am begging you, just tell him what he wants to know. Having to marry each other is probably the least painful thing he will do to us."

"I've told him what I know, Niall. You know how I've purposely stayed away from my family. I never wanted to know anything, so I never asked and they never shared. Keeping me prisoner isn't going to magically give him an answer."

He licked his lips and snarled. "It does amaze me how stupid you are."

"I'm stupid?" I said, standing from the bed and stepping toward him. "I think it's funny you believe that your family has won. The Warriors have been in existence for almost six hundred years. Do you seriously think the battle is over? My family will come after you again, and again, and again if necessary. They will be relentless at taking back our coven. They will search every cave and every rock your family tries to hide under until each of you has paid for what you've done to us. You have stepped in a hornet's nest, Niall, and you're either too stupid or too blind to see it."

Just then, as if it were a message from God, the manor's alarm began to wail. Niall's eyes widened as his confidence dropped. A few of the guards raced out of the room with Duncan, leaving the door wide open and letting the sounds of chaos spill in from the corridor.

"I warned you," I said and sat back down on the bed. "My family is relentless."

It had been hours since the alarm had echoed throughout the manor, but no one would say why it had gone off. There wasn't a second that passed that I didn't pray someone from my family had escaped or would be bursting through the doors. Honestly, the hope that alarm brought was the only thing keeping me sane at this moment. Niall still sat in the corner opposite the bed, bruting and grumbling every time a new shift of guards would come in and not tell him anything. The bubble around me would shimmer every time a new set of guards took over, and the amount of breathing room they would allow me varied. The two guards who were currently on duty had actually given me the most area to pace in front of the bed which gave me something to do, although I was still only wearing a stupid terrycloth bathrobe. Every now and then I'd catch one of the guards leering at me which made me pull the robe tighter around my chest.

"Will you stop pacing?" Niall groaned.

"Will you stop being an asshole?" He didn't answer. "Yeah, I didn't think so."

The door to my parents' quarters opened and Simon, mousey little accountant Simon, came into the room looking as frantic as the White Rabbit. He seemed surprised at the presence of the guards causing him to look spastically back and forth between me and Niall.

Niall jumped up from the floor. He knew as well as I did that if anyone would spill the beans about anything, it would be Simon. As the saying went, he crumpled like a cheap suit. "Simon, please tell us what's happening out there."

Simon adjusted his shirt nervously and avoided eye contact. "No, I mean yes, yes of course, everything is...well. In some ways, yes, but then there's...well, a bit of a snag."

I stepped up to the edge of my bubble, resting my fingers lightly on the shield. "What kind of snag?" The guards turned their heads slowly, giving

Simon a look of death. "Simon!" I shouted, catching his attention. "What kind of snag?"

"Well, you know…I…I was just going to…I mean I wasn't going to do anything of course, I just…"

"Simon, why did the alarm go off? Where's my father?" Niall asked, grabbing Simon's elbow roughly.

"Uh, uh…um…you don't…know? No one said…"

"Simon, tell us why the alarm went off!" I shouted, pounding on the shield.

"Oi, bean counter," the guard standing to my left called, "remember your place."

Simon's jaw flapped feverishly as he struggled to find words. "Yes, yes, yes, I know…I mean I don't know anything of course. I was just going to uh…check…on you, Miss Olivia."

"Simon, please tell me about my family, I need to know what's happened to my family."

His eyes were apologetic, I could see he was terrified.

"Simon wouldn't know if his own head was being cut off," Miller said from the doorframe. "Isn't that right, Simon?"

Simon's jaw began to flap again. "Quite right."

Miller stepped forward into the room with Duncan and Mason on either side of him with faces of stone. "You know, little bird, it isn't nice to try and pry information out of the weakest member of our coven. He doesn't know anything because we don't tell him anything. We can't have him telling our plans to anyone who flashes a pretty smile." Miller stepped up behind Simon and leaned in right by his ear. "It's time for you to leave now, Simon."

Simon jumped and turned around to face Miller. "Yessir, but uh…we need to discuss the…you know…the finances of…"

"Out, Simon! Or I will remove your head myself," Miller shouted.

My stomach sank as Simon ran from the room, but I didn't let it show on my face since I needed to exude as much confidence as possible. "So, based on the alarm I take it you're finding it's a little harder to overtake the Warrior coven than you thought."

The left side of Miller's mouth curled into a wicked sneer. "Hardly. Your family, as I suspected they might, found a way to escape." My stomach jumped and I tried to control my breathing. "Your mother and brother did succeed, although both of them sustained some terrible wounds, especially your brother. Some injuries you just can't heal from. Who knows how far they actually got."

"No. You're lying. I can feel my brother..."

"Your father and uncle, on the other hand..." He paused, and my breath caught in my throat. "In some ways it's a shame, killing such revered vampires, but we were going to kill them anyway so..."

"NO!" I screamed and pounded on the shield while the tears streaked down my face. "You're lying! No, you need them...you wouldn't...no."

Miller sighed and stepped right up to the shield. "They sacrificed themselves so your mother and brother could get away. An honorable way to die, I suppose, if you're into that sort of thing. But then there's the senseless death of your lover."

My crying stopped instantly, my stomach cramping from clinching it tightly to keep the vomit down. "No, no way. You wouldn't kill a human."

Miller rolled his eyes. "Why is everyone so caught up on that? Your lover was a traitor, and was executed along with the others."

My head wouldn't stop shaking. "No, no I'd know, I'd feel it...somehow. No..." But the world stopped when Miller reached into his pants pocket and pulled a thin, broken gold chain with a cross hanging from it. My knees buckled and I fell into the floor, crying hysterically into the thick carpet. Miller must have stepped through the shield since I could see his boot right in front of me. Roughly he pulled at my right hand, jerked me upright, and placed the chain into my palm. There was blood on the necklace, causing thin streaks to stain my palm and fingers.

Will was dead.

The words made my stomach jump and cramp, causing me to dry heave. I was forced to put both hands down on the floor to steady myself.

"Enough of that," Miller growled and kicked my left arm out from under me, making me faceplant into the carpet. Slowly I pushed myself up, curling my feet underneath me and looking up at Miller completely defeated. "Are you ready to tell me what I want to know?"

My breathing was staggered and my voice quivered as I answered, "I don't. Know. Anything."

Miller slapped me across the face, and I hit the floor. He certainly hit harder than Niall ever did. My cheek was already starting to swell underneath my hand. Once again, I slowly pushed myself back onto my heels, fear settling in that he would just torture me until I broke. Ada and Devy were dead. Would it matter if I told? Will was dead. Could I just die along with them? Or was I souring their memory just thinking these things.

Miller sighed loudly and shouted an order behind him. I tensed and prepared for another hit when two of Miller's men walked someone into the room. From my position on the floor, I had trouble seeing who it was until Miller stepped aside.

"Julian," I cried and leapt forward, only to have Miller catch me in the chest and throw me to the ground.

"Don't you touch her, you cowardly slime," Julian yelled, struggling against the two men who held him by the arms with silver chains.

"Slime?" Miller laughed. "You are full of surprises, Julian, just like the one where you pretended to side with us."

Julian laughed loudly, shoulders shaking uncontrollably, even leaning into his captor's faces causing them to turn away. "Brilliant, wasn't it?" he continued through his laugher. "You thought I would betray my father and brothers for your joke of a coven? I have more respect for the dirt on my boots than I do for you."

"Get him on his knees," Miller ordered, and both guards kicked Julian in the back of his legs, causing him to fall roughly down on his knees. "He is your friend, isn't he?"

I looked up at Miller and then to Julian, tears falling from my eyes at my first memory of Julian – curtseying to him in the corridor and calling him my friend. From that day on, Julian and I always had an odd connection that no one else quite understood. To me, Julian was a prideful, lonely man with the toughest job in the coven. I was his friend because few others were.

"Yes…" I sobbed, "he is my friend."

"You can spare his life, Olivia," Miller said, taking a step back and gesturing to Julian. "You have the power to spare your friend's life."

"My life doesn't need to be spared, Livy, don't listen…"

"Tell me what I want to know, Olivia. You have the power to save him."

"Don't tell them anything, Olivia," Julian said a little louder over Miller's continued berating.

"Everyone else is gone, do you want to lose him too?"

"I have lived a good long life, and I will die an honorable Warrior."

"Tell me what your parents did to make you a true hybrid!"

"Never give in to them, Livy."

"Tell me or he dies!"

"Your friendship has meant everything to me," Julian said with a red tear leaking from his right eye.

"I'm sorry, Julian," I cried. "My dear friend."

Julian smiled and closed his eyes, seeming somehow relieved. He tilted his down, exposing the back of his neck and then glanced up at Miller from under his eyelids. "You will not win."

Miller's jaw tensed as he grinded his teeth and then gave a quick nod. Mason came up from behind, a long sword at his side that he quickly raised up over his head.

"Don't give in, Livy!" Julian shouted just before Mason's sword came down and sliced through his neck as if it were made of butter. Julian's head rolled off to the side while his body fell to the ground with thick, dark blood dripping from his neck into the carpet.

My stomach started to heave again, so I ran to the other side of the bed to the small trashcan. Bile rose in my throat while snot and tears drained out of me. Miller had taken everyone from me in order to get me to tell him why I was a true hybrid, but all it did was solidify that no one else should have to suffer like me and my brother. None of this was worth it.

"I am running out of patience," Miller growled behind me.

"Too fucking bad," I choked out, wiping my face with my sleeve that was now pretty damp from all the other times I had wiped my face.

Suddenly someone grabbed the back of my head, pulling me upright by my hair. I struggled to my feet as I was dragged backwards a few feet across the carpet. Miller stepped around to the front of me and traced his index finger down my cheek. The gesture and the look on Miller's face made my skin crawl.

"I will say again, little bird," he said in a low voice, "I am running out of patience. Your family is gone. Your friends are gone. There's no one left, Olivia. It all comes down to you."

My bottom lip trembled as I answered, "Then you'll just have to kill me too because I don't know anything. I don't know how many times I can say it – my brother and I were just born this way. I know that's not what you want to hear, but that's it, that's the truth. So please, just kill me now," I said, squeezing Will's necklace in my hand so tight it pierced the skin of my palm.

Miller put his nose right up to mine, his eyes terrifying me with the evil that was behind them. "There is more than one way to skin a cat." He stepped back and motioned to the others in the room. "Get her on the bed."

"NO!" I screamed as my head was wrenched back by my hair. The two nameless guards each grabbed an arm while Mason and Duncan dodged my flailing legs. I pulled at my arms and kicked my legs wildly as they struggled to drag me to the bed. Finally my foot connected with Mason's face, hitting him square in the nose, but Duncan quickly grabbed my right leg in the air and pushed all of us backwards toward the bed. I fought against Duncan with everything I had, pulling and pushing my leg back and forth trying to get him off balance.

Mason eventually stood from the floor, and with a growl, he plunged his shoulder into my abdomen, knocking the breath out of me, and causing all of us to topple awkwardly on the bed.

"Hold her down," Mason shouted to the two guards at my arms. "She's just a woman, for fuck's sake."

Just as Mason rose from the bed, I kicked my left leg and got him right in the balls. Immediately he fell to the floor, wailing and grabbing his manhood. Miller laughed behind him while the others locked their grips and pushed me firmly into the mattress. Mason stood from the floor and lunged at me, but Miller grabbed him by the collar and pulled him back.

"She is not yours to punish, Mason," Miller said. "Now mind the shield and grab her leg."

Mason grabbed my left leg before I could react, and painfully dug his fingers into my ankle. I didn't understand what Miller had meant about the shield until he gestured for Niall to come closer. As Niall stepped forward, the shield shimmered and receded toward the bed. Once Niall was near the foot of the bed, Miller took him by the back of the neck, making Niall stiffen and struggle against him.

Miller looked down at me. "Now, little bird, if your only answer is that you were born this way, then you will simply have to bear me a grandchild. Preferably a son, of course."

"No, no please," I cried, trying to fight against the four men at each of my limbs. Their grips were so tight I couldn't move even the slightest amount. I wasn't going to get out of this so I looked at Niall and begged, "Niall, please don't do this. Don't do this! You never loved me, but you know I don't deserve this. Please."

Niall struggled against his father, breathing hard but unable to get free. "Father, I...not like this."

Miller tightened his grip on Niall and shook him violently. "If I thought you could do it on your own, we wouldn't be here, you stupid boy.

Now get your cock out," Miller demanded and pushed Niall right up to the edge of the bed.

"Niall, please!" I screamed as Duncan pulled the lower part of my robe open, revealing myself to everyone in the room.

Niall squinted his eyes painfully as Miller forced him down over me. He avoided looking at me and struggled against his father's grip. His fingers hovered and shook above the button of his pants. My sobs were deafening, my jaw chattering loudly at the prospect of what was going to happen to me. I closed my eyes and turned my head, tensing every muscle in my body to prepare for the pain and humiliation.

"I...no, I won't do it," Niall shouted.

My eyes flew open at the sight of Miller flinging Niall back to the opposite side of the room.

"Useless!" Miller spat. "Just like your mother, absolutely useless! What use are you if I have to do everything myself."

"LET GO OF ME!"

Miller turned back in my direction and unzipped his pants.

"NO!" I roared, finding sudden energy and jerking all four men in all directions. Miller climbed up between my legs, pulled the robe away from the rest of my body, and licked my cheek before entering me with pain I'd never felt before.

HELP ME!

Chapter Thirty-one

Will

We ran for almost an hour, darting in all different directions until Cam and Devy thought we were finally safe enough to rest. I'd fallen asleep several times while in Devy's arms, each time waking up with a jolt and Devy whispering "all is well" in my ear. Devy put me down on the ground, allowing the base of a wide oak to hold me in a sitting position.

"Where are we?" I asked softly, my eyes still heavy with exhaustion.

Cam knelt beside me and gently squeezed my shoulder. "We are a few miles from Oliver's house," he said, looking me up and down with concern. "How is the leg?"

I pulled the duct tape from around my leg and pressed around it without too much pain.

"I think I can walk on it now. I'm just so tired."

He forced a smile and patted my cheek. "That is normal. Your body has gone through a great deal."

My hand went to my stomach and slipped into the hole from Mason's sword. The wound itself had closed, but the skin was still sensitive. Damn. I'd been impaled today.

"Is everyone at Ollie's?"

He nodded. "Brianna pushed me a message before she Projected. Whether or not everyone made it…I do not know."

"It's a good thing we never told anyone where Oliver's house was,"

Devy muttered a few feet away. "I am looking forward to killing those who betrayed us. I will take great pleasure in killing them, each of them, how dare they…"

"Brother," Cam interrupted, "let us focus on getting to Oliver's first."

Devy nodded reluctantly and came to stand in front of me. "You think you can walk on your own?"

"I think so," I replied and took his outstretched arm. In a split second I was standing upright with the two of them staring at me intently. There was no pain or dizziness, just fatigue. "I'm ok, I think."

Both of them nodded, and slowly we began making our way to Ollie's old house. The woods around us were quiet and expansive. Bit by bit it was starting to sink in that I was no longer human. Birds were louder, trees were more colorful, and even the ground felt different underneath my feet. After about an hour of trudging through the woods, the area around us began to look familiar as distant childhood memories of playing with Liv and Jax flashed into my mind. My jaw tensed at the thought of Olivia.

"Cam?"

"Yes, William?"

"Do you think she's ok?"

He kept his eyes forward. "As long as she remains an asset to them, I hope so."

"But when she's no longer an asset…" I said before a sharp pain pierced my head and was somehow thrown back at least fifty feet.

Who are you! Jax's voice shouted painfully in my head.

I stretched my eyes open from the pain, unsure of what was going on while everyone ahead of me began to shout.

"Jackson, no! It is us…"

Devy was suddenly in front of me, grabbing my face and pulling it up to him. "Wills…"

"What was that?"

Devy smirked. "If it's what I think it is, you're feeling what Jack-Jack and Brianna are able to do to us. Can you stand?"

My head pulsed as I nodded and stood from the forest floor. Devy snaked his arm around my shoulders and pulled me forward. I could hear the conversation before I saw everyone involved.

"Sorry, Ada," Jax said apologetically. "I saw your light and Devy's, but I didn't know who the other one was so I…"

Jax stopped as Devy pulled me in line with Cam. Jax froze and stared at me with wide eyes while Jared ran up behind him with a long-range rifle in his hands.

As usual, Jared broke the ice. "Holy shit," he said and shifted his rifle around to his back. "Damn, Wills…you…have a hole in your shirt."

I looked down self-consciously and placed my hands in front of my stomach. "It's been a bad day," I replied.

"Here," Jax began and pulled his jacket off. "You're gonna want to cover that over."

He handed me the jacket but I didn't take it. "Why?"

Jax looked at Devy and spoke to him rather than answer me directly. "It's a good thing Fabi was working at the Facility today. Lana rounded him up along with Aunt Re and Uncle John, and they came here."

"My parents are here?"

Jax looked at me and nodded. "Hence why you need the jacket. You're bloody and look like shit."

"Jackson," Cam warned. "Try and be a little more sensitive."

Reluctantly I took the jacket from Jax as Devy sighed with relief. "So Fabi is safe?"

Jared nodded. "With all of Miller's homophobic rhetoric, we were worried he'd go after him. Everyone's here and they are fine." Jared paused. "Well, Renee and John have been total assholes the whole time, complaining we're keeping them hostage. Sera and Fabi are trying to mediate the best they can, but…"

Everyone in our small circle sighed loudly and nodded in understanding. I shrugged into Jax's jacket and pulled up the edge of my shirt to wipe my face. Jax and Jared turned toward the house, and the rest of us followed them up to the edge of the driveway of Ollie's little ranch-style house. My stomach sank at the thought of seeing my parents and no longer being human. It wasn't going to be pretty, and everyone knew it.

Just as we stepped onto the driveway, the front door opened and Awbie flew out, jetting across the driveway and slamming into Cam. Normally I would have seen this as a flash, but now I saw every step she took, every movement of her arms as she wrapped them around Cam's shoulders and kissed him. I looked away, but caught Jax staring at me. I averted my gaze and looked down at the ground uncomfortably.

Awbie gasped loudly, making me bring my attention back to her. Red tears were already staining her cheeks as her hands cupped her mouth and nose. "Ohmygod," she sobbed and then hugged me tightly. I could feel her tears leaking down the side of my neck. When she rose from my shoulder, she held my face with her hands and looked me over. "I'm sure there was a good reason for Turning you." I nodded. "Your parents are here."

"Jax mentioned that."

Awbie sighed and took a step back. "They're already upset even being here, so...we *all* need to be prepared for their reaction." She looked at Cam. "Do we know anything about Livy?"

He shook his head sadly. "No, love. Only that Connor believes she may have been taken to our quarters, but nothing else." Cam looked over at Jared. "Little brother, Connor did say he was able to grab your old communication equipment. If you're able to finagle something..."

"Yeah, that's awesome. I'll get on it," Jared replied and ran back into the house.

"How are we contacting people? I am worried our cell phones might have been tampered with just as Will's was," Cam asked.

She gave a tired smile. "We were afraid of contacting anyone directly, so Sera made a call to Jonah. There aren't a lot of people that would even remember our connection with him. He's been our contact for everything, including getting to Victor. They'll be here tonight. Dad is chomping at the bit for a good fight and he's contacted some of his...I don't know what you'd call them but fangs-for-hire. But we've stayed away from connecting with any of the Warriors that *weren't* there today since we didn't know whom to trust."

"Very smart, love," Cam said and squeezed her hand. "Shall we get out of the open?"

And face the music, I thought to myself. The others started toward the house ahead of me, but I found it hard to move my feet. Jax stepped over to me and squeezed my shoulder. "Do I really look like shit?"

He shrugged. "Did they beat the shit out of you and stab you in the stomach or something?"

"Clean through with a sword."

He paused, looked at the ground, then up to the sky to fight back tears. Finally, "Then, uh...yeah, you look like that and now you're...really, really pale." He looked at the ground again. "It's the eyes, man. They're...it's just different. Really different. But hey, now I can control you with my mind and make you do whatever I want. Cool, right?"

I rubbed my head as he pulled me toward the house. "That really hurts, by the way."

"So I've heard," he laughed. "You should wipe your face again and zip up that jacket."

"Have you heard or felt anything from your sister?" I asked as I wiped my face with my shirt, and zipped the jacket up to my neck.

"No. She's definitely behind one of their shields."

When we finally stepped inside the house, Sera was the first to see us. She smiled and took a step toward me, but then stopped herself and gave me a sympathetic look. Slowly she stepped toward me again, hugged me, and kissed me gently on the cheek. When she backed away, she cupped my cheek as she whispered, "You are what you are supposed to be."

My eyes burned for a moment, but I quickly pressed my fingers into the corners to stop any tears from coming out. Sera patted my hand and stepped away. A moment later someone slapped my shoulder roughly, making me turn to see Eris giving me the once over, nod approvingly, and step away. Jax tried to hide his laugh from the corner.

Fabi was next, pulling himself away from Devy and looking me up and down. "It suits you. Your parents have been a nightmare."

"I'm sorry. It's not going to get any better."

"Don't I know it."

"I'm glad you were able to get out."

He shrugged. "I can claw the eyes out of homophobic dickheads like nobody's business, but I'm glad to be here too. Oh dear, incoming…"

"Will!" Mom shouted as she and my dad ran down the hallway, causing everyone in the center of the living room to part like the Red Sea to let her through, but halfway to me she slid to a halt and fell back into my father. Immediately she started screaming and pointing at me. My father struggled to keep her upright, not understanding what was happening until he made eye contact with me, and froze. Jax's words rang in my ear - "the eyes, man."

"What have you done to my son!" Dad yelled.

I held my hands up. "Dad, no, you have to listen…"

"You killed my son!" Mom screamed and lunged at Cam. Dad grabbed her around the waist and pulled her upright. She clawed at his arms and he let her go. Awbie immediately went to her, but Mom pushed her away. "You killed my son, you bastards! You killed my son," she cried and ran back down the hallway toward the bedrooms. Awbie and Fabi ran after her, but my father stayed in the middle of the living room seething with anger.

"Dad, let me explain."

He put his hand up in my direction and looked at Cam. "You just couldn't keep your hands off of him. It's what you've always wanted, isn't it?"

"John," Cam said calmly, "there were extenuating circumstances…"

"Bullshit!" he yelled. "Jesus, Cameron, he's my son, my human son!"

"Would you have rather I let him die?"

"Yes! I would rather have a dead son than a monster. It wasn't enough what you did to your own children, you had to Turn mine?"

Devy stepped in between Cam and my father, all three of them yelling at each other, and even Jax and Eris stepped in to try and stop the chaos. I just looked on in disbelief, exhausted disbelief. My throat was burning and my fingers felt tight and stiff. What was happening to me? It felt like the flu had come on in literally five seconds.

From across the room, Sera caught my attention and waved me down the hall. I stepped around the circle of shouting men and followed Sera into the first bedroom on the right. When I stepped inside the bedroom, Sera removed the thin cardigan she had on and placed it on the bed. I froze. She smiled and wiggled her index finger at me to come further inside the room. Reluctantly I did as she asked, looking around me for any explanation for what was happening.

"Does your throat ache, young one?" she asked in her thick French accent.

"How did you know?"

She smiled. "You were Turned, but have you fed since zhen?"

"Uh…no?" I said, still unsure of what was happening, which made her laugh softly.

"You need to feed, Wills, and you need to rest. Forget what iz happening out zhere," she said and began rolling up the sleeve of her blouse.

"Oh…uh, I don't know," I stuttered and took a step back right into Eris who was in the doorway.

He looked up at me curiously, and then across the room to his wife. "Ser-a-phina? May I ask…"

"Zhe young one needs to feed, mon amie."

"Ah," he replied lightly and pushed me off of him toward the bed. "But all by yourself, that is awfully risky with a newborn."

"I knew you would find me," she said and pulled me around to the other side of the bed. Eris placed his hand on my shoulder and pushed me down on the mattress. "Now, Eri will talk you through each step."

"And I will ensure you do not hurt my bella Sera," he said in a low, almost threatening tone.

"Maybe this isn't a good idea."

"Nonsense," he laughed and shifted to sit behind me with Sera in front of me. "Ser-a-phina's blood tastes lovely."

"Oh god," I groaned, but Eris pulled my chin up with his index finger in order to look up at Sera.

"Now we must be serious," he started and I swallowed the lump in my throat. "First thing, you must extend your fangs."

"I...I don't know..."

"Concentrate on Sera's neck." I did. "Do you see the vein pulsing?" I nodded. "Now follow it down, you'll start to see it flow all around beneath her skin."

It was an uncomfortable task to do since it was like I was checking out my grandmother, but I did follow the vein down and just as Eris had said, I could see the blood running, almost glowing beneath her skin. The more I concentrated on it, the more I lost the sight of Sera and only saw the pathways of veins and arteries. They were calling to me. My throat burned, and a yearning started to build inside that was like a massive hunger without stomach pangs. Reflexively I opened my mouth and felt my fangs extend down.

"Good boy," Eris said and patted me on the back, but then kept his grip firmly on the back of my neck. "Now, Sera will present her wrist to you, and you will take it in both hands." I took Sera's wrist in my hands as she held it up close to my lips. "Do you see the vein?" I nodded. "Good. Now, *gently*," he stressed as he pressed his fingers painfully into the sides of my neck, "sink your fangs into the vein until you feel the pop. Then you will suck the blood and count to five. Then you will retract the fangs and close the wound. Understood?" I nodded nervously. "And if you stay longer than five seconds, I do not care that you are like a grandson to me, I will rip your head from your body."

"Eri..." Sera warned.

"I want to set all expectations, mia bella. Now let's do this before the fighting out there makes its way in here."

I nodded and stopped my right leg from shaking. Don't screw this up. Don't screw this up. Eris will kill you, don't screw this up. With a deep breath, I concentrated on the vein in front of me and bit. It took a second before I felt the pop of the vein, and instantly blood came rushing into my mouth. One, one-thousand. Two, one-thousand. Sera's blood was soothing the burning in my throat. Three, one-thousand. The warm feeling was spreading all over my body, bringing energy and relief. Four, one-thousand. The taste, the feeling, it was hypnotic, addictive. Five, one-thousand.

Eris' fingers dug painfully into the sides of my neck, causing me to pull out of Sera's wrist. "Close the wound," he said without letting up on his grip. Quickly I licked the two small holes on Sera's wrist and watched as they closed, squeezing out two tiny droplets of blood. Eris took his wife's wrist, licked the trailing blood away, and kissed the wound.

Sera patted my cheek, and I could see how tired she suddenly looked. "Rest, young one," she said and stepped into Eris' waiting arms.

"Thank you, Sera," I said softly, suddenly flooded with guilt.

Eris helped Sera around the bed. "Do as she says, Wills. We will all need to be at our full strength for what lies ahead."

As the door closed behind them, I put my legs up on the bed and laid back on the pillows, wondering how exactly I would fall asleep. The world had turned upside down, and we had somehow all been forced on the underside trying to claw our way back.

Vampire sleep was completely different than human sleep. Whereas when I was human, I would drift off to sleep and ease back awake. Vampire sleep was more like opening and closing a door. You were asleep and then you weren't. There was no sense of feeling rested, but you had energy where there wasn't before. I opened my eyes and flinched at how different my sight was. Things were so clear that I could see the details of the individual dust motes floating about. Colors had dimensions I'd never seen. Even the bedspread felt different under my fingertips, and I could hear various conversations happening in different parts of the house. Apparently, my transition to being a vampire was complete. Reflexively I took in a breath and caught scent of something else in the room. I jerked up and found Jax sitting quietly in the chair in the corner.

He raised his eyebrows and held his hands up. "Just me."

"Sorry," I replied. "So...that's how you smell? Like I can smell you now?"

"I guess it's a compliment that you couldn't smell me before, but yes, you'll find everyone has a more noticeable smell. Nice nap?"

I rubbed my eyes and swung my legs over the edge of the mattress. "I guess. I feel better, but everything is really different."

"I'd say so. Can't say you ever sucked on my grandmother before today."

An awkward silence fell between us before I could stutter an answer. "She...she made...me."

He laughed lightly, but then a sadness settled back in him. "This is weird, man."

"I know. It was this or death." He nodded his head, but there was still a sense of uncomfortableness. "Hey, did you catch what my dad said about what Cam did to his own kids? What did he mean by that, do you know?"

Jax shook his head. "I'm assuming it has to do with me and Livy being true hybrids, and that everyone else knows something we don't."

I waited a few beats before asking, "Have you heard anything from Liv?"

"No," he replied and his right leg started to bounce nervously.

"Do we have a plan yet? What are we..."

"Jared's been able to make contact with Connor. They've killed all the Warriors that Ada and Devy sired. They're starting to pull out those they don't trust, and interrogating them. They just took Julian into custody."

My stomach sank. "Shit."

"Grandfather, Aunt Kyla, and Uncle Alex just got here."

"Really? How long was I out?"

"Couple of hours. Grandfather is beside himself."

"I'm sure. Are my parents out there?"

"Your mom is passed out and your dad is outside."

"Wanna go into the living room, then?"

He shrugged and rose from the chair. "Sure."

His tone was so odd, depressed maybe. Even standing in front of me there was sadness pulsating from his body.

"You ok?"

"I don't know," he replied weakly. "I just feel...off."

"Do you..." I began and then had to swallow the lump in my throat, "could it be Olivia? Could you be feeling what she is, like before?"

He considered it, looking around the room and purposely not making eye contact. "Maybe. Let's get some air, ok?"

I nodded and followed him out of the room. The living room opened up only a few feet away, and by the front windows with Cam and Devy stood Victor. In a word, he was seething. His brows were firmly creased and set over his eyes while his lips were curled in a deadly snarl. He looked up as I stepped over near the couch, although his face didn't change.

"Well, at least one good thing has come out of this," he said and jutted his chin at me.

Alex gave me a sympathetic nod from the couch, but Kyla pulled herself away from the discussion she was having with Awbie in the kitchen and hugged me tightly. Her orange hair floated around me and tickled my nose. As she pulled away, it was amazing how much more detail I could see in her face, hair, everything.

"You'll get used to it," she winked.

"Was I staring?"

She patted my cheek. "But you were cute doing it, so you're forgiven."

Completely embarrassed, I smiled and looked down at the floor. From the corner of my eye, I could see that Jax had pressed himself up against the wall behind us. I looked over at him and could see that he wasn't completely with us. His eyes were darting from side to side while his head and face flinched a couple of times. There was definitely some kind of twin action going on.

"Connor says they definitely took him toward your quarters," Jared said, looking up from the laptop he was hunched over.

"Who?"

Cam looked up and shot me a fearful look. "Julian."

"So then Connor was right," I began, "looks like they're hauled up in that area of the manor. Olivia could be in there."

"It's possible," Victor replied.

"Then what's the plan?" No one answered. "If we think Olivia is being held in your quarters, then let's go in and get her."

"With what army, William?" Cam said tersely.

"We can't just sit here..."

"I know you love her, but do not think for a minute that you want to save her more than her mother or I do. It is taking every ounce of energy I have not to jump out of this window and rescue my daughter. But what would that get us? How would that help the other Warriors who are being hunted inside the walls of the manor? It is not just about Olivia, as hard as that might be to say. There are others that need saving, and we simply do not have near enough numbers to do anything but get ourselves killed."

"But they're keeping her hidden for a reason, we have to…"

"We have to get our numbers up and pray that they are keeping her as leverage, and therefore leaving her unharmed."

"Then let Jax and I go," I yelled in frustration. Devy straightened his shoulders and gave me a warning look, but I didn't let up. "With just the two of us, we can sneak in, get her, and get out."

"How naïve of you to think it would take so little to accomplish that."

"But we have to try!"

Suddenly Jax groaned behind me and I turned around to see him keeled over. I touched his shoulder, but he jerked up violently and slapped my hand away.

"LET GO OF ME!" he shouted and I noticed his eyes weren't focused.

I grabbed him by the shoulders and shook him. "Jax! Are you feeling Olivia?! What's happening…"

"NO!" he yelled and a sharp pain suddenly struck my head. I was no longer myself, but I could see I was being forcibly held down while Miller climbed up toward me, a horrible grin on his face. It was a nightmare being pushed into my head that I couldn't get away from. As he placed his body on top of mine two words reverberated in my head so loud it made my teeth chatter – HELP ME!

The connection broke and I fell to my knees. The other vampires in the room were clutching their heads, they had all seen what I had. Jax was lying in the fetal position on the floor. From the kitchen there was an agonizing, guttural scream. It was Awbie. Her legs had given out and Kyla was struggling to hold her up. Everyone in the room was dazed, confused, and horrified.

I looked to the front of the house where the three leaders of our coven stood. "Can we go and get her now?" I shouted.

Cam lunged toward the door, but Devy wrapped him up by the shoulders, although he was struggling to hold on. It took both Victor and Alex pushing back from the front that even remotely stopped him, but eventually they all ended up in a dogpile on the floor. Mom came running down the hall, Sera just behind her, both with bewildered looks on their faces.

"Wha-what happened?" Mom asked as she ran across the room to where Awbie now laid on the floor sobbing.

Jax pressed himself up and looked around, finally finding me. His face was green, and then he started to heave. Quickly I picked him up off the floor, and ran him toward the sliding glass door. Just as we approached the door, my dad opened it with a very confused look on his face. I pushed him aside and ran Jax out to the edge of the patio.

"Is he ok?" Dad asked as he came up next to me.

At that exact moment, Jax vomited onto the grass.

"Does he look ok?" I snapped.

"Is there anything…"

"No, Dad. You don't want to be a part of this, so just go sit down and relax while the rest of us have our lives torn apart."

He flinched, and backed away slowly. Guilt instantly settled in, but I couldn't feed into it since Jax started to shake. Not knowing what else to do, I held him tightly against my chest. He cried and grabbed at my shirt, twisting it and turning it in his hand.

His breathing became staggered and he began to rock back and forth. "Did…did you see it."

I swallowed my emotions down as I answered, "I did."

"I could…feel it. I'm not sure how that's even possible. Wills, I felt him lick my face and…and…I felt it, all of it."

It took all my strength not to breakdown. I squeezed him tighter, maybe more for my sake than his. They were hurting Liv, and we were here doing nothing. We had all failed her.

Slowly Jax began to calm down, and eventually he pulled away from me. "I'm gonna check on Mom and Ada," he said and wiped his mouth.

"Yeah, man," I replied and helped him up to a standing position.

He was still shaken, but pushed my hand away when I tried to help him toward the sliding glass door.

Once he was inside, I realized I was alone with my dad, the man who only hours earlier would have preferred that I had died than be Turned. He was stretched out in one of the long patio chairs, but it was hard to look at him, so I turned away. I took in a deep breath, noticing the smells of dirt and pine, and other scents I couldn't decipher yet. When I closed my eyes to take in another breath, Miller's devilish face flashed before me and I jerked my eyes back open.

"Son?"

I looked back over my shoulder. "I just need some air, and then I'll go in so that my mere presence doesn't offend you."

He didn't respond so I took in one last deep breath. As I turned to leave, he stood from his chair and put his hands up. "It's not that I'm offended…"

"Really? I think you were very clear. You'd rather be burying me than talking to me right now."

Tears welled in his eyes, and his bottom lip quivered as he replied, "I'd rather be talking to my human son, my boy with the blue-green eyes and pink cheeks. And now I…I never wanted this for you. Seriously, Will, look at what's already happened today, and there's obviously something else that's happened that I don't know about."

"Yeah, well it just involves your niece and goddaughter," I said and his face fell. "Miller is attacking her right now, literally right now, and Jax felt it, saw it, and it just got pushed to all of us so we got to see it too. Hence why he's out here throwing up, and Awbie's crying on the kitchen floor."

Dad covered his mouth with his hand, placing his other hand on his hip and turning away. "This is the life you wanted?"

"What else should I be, Dad? I tried being a doctor and it nearly killed me. I tried my whole life to be what you wanted me to be, and it sent me to the looney bin. Is that the son you'd rather have? All drugged up and walking around like a zombie, but at least he's not a vampire. Is that it?

"You would always talk about how your dad *didn't* want you to be a medical doctor, and how much grief he would give you. And then you'd look at me and tell me I could be whatever I wanted to be. Do you remember that?" He looked down at the ground. "Well, I figured out what I am supposed to be, Dad. I guess you should have been more specific in what you really meant. You always said you never wanted to be like your dad, but you're just like him. You were only happy when I was going to be what you wanted me to be."

I stepped toward the sliding glass door and he countered me, placing his hand on my chest. "You're right. I am just like my dad. It makes me sick to think I've become just like him, but…they didn't have to Turn you."

"Yes, they did."

"There had to have been other options, Will. Cameron has always resorted to the most drastic options."

"Dad…" I sighed, frustrated at his unwillingness to listen. "Fine, we'll do it in terms you'll understand."

"I don't know what you mean."

"Lacerations to the face, neck, arms, chest, abdomen, and legs," I began, and I could see his medical mind start to click. "Broken nose, periorbital hematomas, multiple rib fractures, dislocated left knee, probably something broken in the leg but I was in too much pain to really pinpoint it. Considering the hits to my abdomen and back, there was probably some organ damage, kidney and liver maybe. Then there was the stab wound to the abdomen through to the back, and I was left to bleed out on the floor. I had to have lost several pints of blood. Shock started to set in when Cam and Devy finally asked permission to Turn me. Devy could feel that I was dying, so I took the opportunity to live, Dad. I didn't want to leave you all like that.

"So, is that enough? Is that close enough to death for it to be ok to be Turned? When I was lying there on the floor bleeding out, my last thought was of you and Mom. I wanted you both to know that I loved you. Now think about how when I clawed myself back to life, you and Mom are there screaming that you wished I was dead. What am I supposed to do with that?"

"We're not perfect, Wills," he said and sighed loudly. "And you're right, with all those injuries and blood loss you wouldn't have survived. But...I just keep thinking that if you hadn't been with them, none of that would have happened to you in the first place."

"True," I replied. "I probably would have killed myself by now, and I don't mean that lightly. The Warriors saved my life by showing me my calling."

"And now you're no longer human, Will. That's going to take some getting used to."

"But you've been around vampires for over twenty years now."

"They are not my son!" he snapped, and then brought his voice down. "If you're ever a father, you'll understand."

The thought of Liv popped in my head, and suddenly none of this was important. "We're not going to solve this tonight."

"You're right."

"But I'm still your son, and right now I need my dad," I said, putting my hand up to my eyes to hide the red tears I knew were coming. "They're doing god knows what to Liv, and I'm stuck here..."

Dad pulled me into his shoulder, patting my back to try and comfort me. He didn't say anything, although what could he say? Anything said would either be insensitive or hollow. His embrace might not have been exactly as it would have been when I was human, but I was taking what I could get.

After a minute, I backed away and turned around to wipe away any red tears that might have escaped. A light breeze wisped past and with it came a strong scent that made the hairs on the back of my neck stand on end. It was a mix of animal and aftershave, if that made any sense whatsoever, but it was the animal part that made my defenses go up immediately. I looked to my right where fifty feet away three tall, heavy creatures stepped out from the edge of the woods. As more stepped out from the wood line in front of me, I realized what they were and guided my father behind me.

"Get inside," I said softly as I pushed him toward the sliding glass door, keeping my guard up at the dozen or more werewolves now coming out of the woods and onto the yard.

Once Dad was inside the house, I jumped inside and slid the glass door shut. "Guys, we have a prob…" I began but then turned around to find Tosh and Beckett Dawes standing by the front door. "Oh thank god," I sighed, making both of them smile.

Beckett Dawes was considered a grandson of Victor's because his father was a Warrior at one time, but he had been scratched by a werewolf and therefore became one himself. End of story, he became the pack leader of a wolfpack, married Tosh, and they had two boys. Normally I'd see Tosh a couple times a week when she'd bring the boys to class, that was until they started showing signs of becoming wolves themselves. It had been a while since I'd seen Beckett. He was average height, but broad and muscular in the shoulders with powerful legs. His bow was strapped across his chest, which made me wonder if his bow was more dangerous than him as a wolf.

"I hope that's your pack outside," I said and gestured behind me with my thumb, "or else we've got a problem."

Beckett laughed. "Yes, that's my pack. Sorry to scare you, it's just easier for them to stay in wolf form rather than spend the energy on phasing back and forth," he said and then looked over at Victor and Devy. "We have twenty-two wolves. That's the entire pack minus the four we left behind to watch over the ranch."

Twenty-two, that sounded like a good number, although I literally had no idea. While Beckett continued talking, Tosh stepped away from him and came to stand in front of me. She took in a soft gasp of air, and then realized she was staring.

"So it's true?" she asked, peeking from underneath her lashes.

"Good news travels fast," I replied sarcastically. "You just got here, did you walk in and they were like, 'hey, thanks for coming, Will is a vampire now."

"Something like that," she replied with a sigh.

"Where are the boys tonight?"

"They are having a night with Grandma and Aunt Nikki," she replied with a nervous sigh. "Hopefully it's just for one night."

"Are you fighting with us too?"

"Victor told us both to never stop training, that someday we'd need it," she said, unzipping the small duffle bag in her hand and pulling out the handle of a whip. "I never thought I'd ever use these things again. I just can't believe what's happened." She looked up at me with tears forming in her eyes. "It's like my childhood home is burning."

"The world is definitely upside down."

"Guys," Jared cut in to everyone's conversation and looked up from his laptop. "Julian's dead. Connor just confirmed. They've..." he paused and shook his head. "Everyone they've killed, they've put their head on a spike in the midnight garden. It's a message for anyone..."

"We know what the message is," Cam interrupted.

The room went silent. I thought about Roberts moments before he died, how brave he was up to the last minute. And young David, scared but proud until the end. Then Julian, whose blood was in me, had helped save me. All of them were brave and loyal, and were now on display in a disgusting medieval way. There was nothing Miller and his men wouldn't do. They had no honor, they had no respect. They were pure evil.

"We need to go now," I said, breaking the unbearable silence.

"Will, we still only have a quarter of the bodies we need," Devy replied. "Our other reinforcements won't be here for another couple of hours, and even they are not enough."

"Things are not going to get any better, our odds aren't going to get any better, and they will continue these...these...atrocities!"

"Child," Victor said in a low, scarily powerful voice, "as a Warrior you need to learn patience."

"But..."

"We have to wait or else we will be completely destroyed. Who can we save if we're all killed? Who will be left to fight the evil then? You are hours old, child. Although your enthusiasm is commendable, you must let us do what we do best, and find something to busy yourself with."

I nodded sheepishly and looked down at the floor. A moment later, someone placed their hand on my shoulder. When I finally looked up, I found Eris giving me a sympathetic smile before pulling me down the hallway.

"Jackson? Come help us," Eris called down the hall, and a moment later the three of us were standing in the middle of the main bedroom at the other end of the house.

"What are we doing?" Jax asked, still seeming a little unnerved from what had happened earlier.

"Well," Eris began in his usual light tone, "while we wait for the powers-at-be to finally take some action, why don't the two of you go through the armory."

"The…armory?" I asked.

"Yes, of course," he said and pointed to floor. "Under the carpet you'll find the compartment I added to house my collection. Sera complained I had too many weapons at the island house, so I started keeping them here."

Jax and I looked at each questioningly. Something about this seemed odd, but with nothing else to do, Jax and I rolled up the carpet and placed it in the corner. In the floor was a large rectangular door carved into the floor with a bronze latch.

We looked over at Eris to do the honors, but he gestured to the floor. "Well come now, get to work."

Jax and I looked at each other again, something wasn't right. Eris loved nothing more than to show his collection of weapons, especially his swords, yet now he seemed insistent on having us handle his prized possessions. Reluctantly, Jax and I lifted the door in the floor.

"And she said they would never be used, well look at us now," he said as we began carefully pulling the swords and other weapons from the compartment, and placing them on the bed.

"Where's Vlad?" Jax asked.

"He's pulling in some of our old friends to help," Eris replied. "But like the Assassin said, we are still a few hours away from getting everyone here. It's a shame, really."

"What is?" Jax asked as he took a broadsword from my hands that had to have been nearly four feet long.

Eris shrugged. "I was just thinking," he began in a whisper, "Olivia is in a secluded area of the manor. It's a shame they couldn't send someone in just to get her. If we are all to die in the face of battle, wouldn't it make sense to rescue at least one member of the familia? If only they could spare…two people to rescue Olivia, individuals who really knew the ins and outs of the manor, maybe even knowledge of…a secret tunnel or two." He shook his head and sighed. "But what do I know, I am merely an instrument of death, not a hero that rescues people."

At this point both Jax and I had frozen. We both knew what Eris was doing, he'd done it our whole lives. Besides being an instrument of death, he was a master manipulator.

"Well," Eris shrugged with a big sigh, "I guess I will leave you to it. But, perhaps leave the Masamune katana swords, they are originals after all."

With a flourish, Eris left the bedroom and closed the door behind him. Jax and I were still frozen and looked at each other blankly.

"Which ones are the Masamunes?"

I shrugged and jumped out. "Let's just assume any samurai sword is a priceless Masamune. But honestly, do you think he just brought us in here to pull weapons out of the floor?"

He shook his head. "No, I think my grandfather is trying to manipulate us to rescue Livy."

"So…" I said, and let the word hang in the air for several seconds, "we're going to…do that?"

"Fuck yeah," he replied, and I sighed with relief. "If Eri brought us in here away from everyone else, he's laying the groundwork. If we leave, he'll give us some cover."

"How are we doing this," I whispered.

"Well, Eri is right that we should use the tunnels. There's one that goes right up to a hidden door in my parents' quarters. But how do we get in?"

"We went out through a hidden grate today," I replied. "It's on the same side of the manor as the suite. If I can get us to the grate, can you navigate to the room?"

"It's worth a try," he said, and became pale. "Anything to get her out of there. Of course, that's as long as they don't have that entrance covered by a shield, or found that tunnel, or the hidden door."

"We have to try."

"You realize everyone here is going to be furious at us." I nodded. "They may not make you a Warrior because of it."

"I don't care. We have to save Olivia."

"Well, let's hope they don't see us as we run."

"Run?"

He smirked. "Are you planning on going out the front door?"

"Oh, yeah, I guess not," I replied and opened the window in front of me. "Do you think this is what Eris expected us to do?"

He laughed. "I expect if we haven't left in the next few seconds, he's going to come through that door and throw us out the window himself."

I nodded and gestured to the open window. Jax easily climbed through and I followed, landing on the ground softly. As we stepped away from the house, we both noticed that the curtains of the front window were thankfully closed and we bolted toward the woods.

We could be running to our death, but neither of us cared. We could both be stripped of our Warriorship, but neither of us cared. Liv was all that mattered, and she was worth losing everything.

Chapter Thirty-two

Olivia

My parents' room had always been a place of comfort. A place that wasn't consumed by battle and strategy meetings, but instead family movie nights wrapped in blankets, special breakfasts with Grandfather, and playing dress-up with Mom and Auntie Kyla. It was the closest I could ever get to feeling what others described as home.

But now, as my insides throbbed, it was all tainted. My childhood memories were torn apart by the horrendous act that was inflicted upon me. A new guard was on duty, and Niall was curled up in his corner. He'd been a coward and let his own father do the most heinous and disgusting things to me. I wanted that shield down so that I could inflict enough pain on him to drive him into insanity and beg me for mercy as much as I had screamed for it myself.

"You could have stopped him," I muttered and Niall looked up at me.

"Bullocks," he replied. "If you think…"

"I think you're a coward," I interrupted. "A fucking coward who sat in the corner and watched as his father raped his fiancée. No matter how much you hate me, I didn't deserve this. You spineless, fucking coward."

Niall stood up from the floor and came to stand right up to the edge of the shield. "All you had to do was tell him what he wanted."

"I can't tell him what I don't know."

"For fuck's sake, Olivia, he's not going to stop! Just end this."

I pushed myself up from the bed, grunting at the pain as my body screamed at me to stay still. "If you want to end this, then just kill me. I don't know any other way to say it in order to get it through your thick skull. I don't know anything! All I do know is that you are the biggest *coward* that ever lived. What man lets his father..." I had to stop from saying the words. "Fucking coward."

Niall was quiet for several moments, his anger simmering just below the surface. With a breath, he raised his eyebrows and held his head high. "Well, I warned you, and you chose not to listen. And if you are too bloody stupid to tell him what he wants to know, then best of luck to you, Olivia. Whether you know anything or not, my father will not stop, and he will not let you go. Just like my mother, I hope you like being a whore, because that's all he's ever going to allow you to be."

With a condescending smile, he turned and walked out of the room. Once Niall closed the door, it was only me and the lone guard holding his shield around me. He was slighter than the others, but just as stupid looking. His blonde hair was slicked back with so much gel it looked like a shiny hair helmet. He gave me a sickening grin and then licked his lips.

Tears started streaming down my cheeks again. I was so alone. No one was coming for me, there was no one left. Painfully I laid back down on the bed on my side, being sure to keep an eye on creepy Mr. Hair Helmet. My hand slipped into the pocket of my robe and pulled out Will's cross necklace. The chain was tangled over my finger while the cross swung from side to side, catching the light every now and then. Emotions were starting to bubble over and I had to squeeze my mouth closed tightly with my other hand to keep them in. I refused to grieve in front of Mr. Helmet Head.

"I 'eard 'e cried like a baby, that one," Mr. Helmet Head said with a nasty smile. "When they kill 'im, yeah, like a wee lit-ul baby."

He was baiting me, so I looked away and bit into the corners of my mouth to keep quiet.

"Now your dad and pedo uncle, I 'eard they showed their necks before we cut off their 'eads," he continued, and the metallic taste of blood filled my mouth. "Ooh, but your mum," he said and gave a disgusting whistle, "it's a shame she got away. The things I'd do to 'er. Oh yes, I would..."

Suddenly he stopped speaking and my eyes flew up. His mouth was hanging open as his eyes squinted in pain. Invisible strings lifted him off the floor and two blurry figures bolted out of a door hidden in the wall. The shield popped like a bubble, and Helmet Head fell to the ground.

My brain was slow to really understand what was happening until one of the figures shook me by the shoulders. It took me a moment to even recognize Jack looking back at me.

Livy, can you... was all he said in my head before I bolted up from the bed and hugged him tightly, pressing my mouth into the meat of his shoulder to muffle my louds cries that were borderline screams. Jack's arms were squeezing me so tight that I was stunned and humbled by his fear. Too soon he let go of me and pulled my face up to meet him.

"We don't have much time," he said aloud and I looked over his shoulder to see Mr. Helmet Head lying lifeless on the floor, while the other figure that had come in through the secret door still had his back to me.

"Who is that," I asked softly, jutting my chin over Jack's shoulder.

He pressed his lips firmly together and reluctantly opened himself up. The other figure straightened up and exhaled loudly before turning around.

Will. Somehow, Will was standing only a few feet away. But...how. I leapt from the bed and just as I placed one foot on the carpet, Will looked me in the eye and I slid clumsily to the ground. His eyes. His eyes were black and dead, not the deep blue I'd known all my life.

"No, no, no," I cried loudly as Will knelt down in front of me. The closer his black eyes came, the louder I sobbed. He wrapped his arms around me and pressed his cold cheek against mine, making me shiver and flinch.

He pulled away from me and cupped my cheek with his cold hand. "Liv, I know," he began, thin red tears forming at his bottom lids. "Believe me, I know, but we don't have much time. We have to get you out of here before our forces storm the manor. Ok? Liv, we have to move."

Will went to stand up, but I squeezed his wrist and he froze. "Our forces?"

He nodded. "Your dad and Devy have been working..."

"They're alive!"

"Yeah, what did..."

My head fell into my hands as I cried loudly. "They told me they were dead. You, Ada, Devy, all of you were dead and Mom..." I jerked my head up and looked over at Jack. "Is Mom ok?"

"Yeah," he replied softly and sympathetically, "she and I got out together with Uncle Jared."

The walls were crashing down around me. For hours I'd thought my love and my family were dead. Once again, I began to cry loudly in my hands. Both Will and Jack leaned against me, wrapping their arms around me protectively, maybe in some way trying to put me back together enough to leave.

"Livy, we need to get out of here," Jack said again.

I nodded and wiped my face, but then looked down at myself and pulled at the collar of my robe. "I can't stay in this."

Will looked up at Jack who jutted his chin toward the back wall. "You'll have to wear something of Mom's, but make it quick."

Gently, Will lifted me from the floor and I melted into his side as we walked to the opposite side of the room to my mother's walk-in closet. Once inside, Will settled me up against the center island while he began to rummage through the various drawers. Eventually he came to me with a pair of grey capri sweatpants and a maroon sweatshirt that had "Southern Girl" written in cursive across the chest. It was my mother's favorite, oldest, and softest sweatshirt she owned. I tried not to cry at the fact that he knew exactly what I needed.

Will placed the clothes on the island just next to me, and I froze. I was scared to take my robe off. When I didn't move, his hands went for the tie of my robe.

"Don't..." I snapped, taking a step away and then freezing with my hands in front of me. I looked up at him and started crying again. "I'm sorry."

Slowly Will took a step back. "No need to be sorry."

I shook my head. "No, Will, you don't understand. I...Miller, he..."

"I know, Liv," he interrupted.

"What do you mean...you know?"

Will held my gaze, but struggled to find words. "Jax...he felt...somehow your connection got through and he pushed an image to us."

"Us?" I said, and bile started to rise in my throat.

Will took a breath and rested his hand on mine, only his black eyes were staring back at me, and it was unnerving. "There are so many things that we need to talk about, Liv, but we simply do not have enough time right now. So, I'm going to turn around, and you need to change into those clothes so we can get out of here."

I nodded nervously and he turned his back to me. With hands shaking, I untied my robe and reached for the sweatpants first. Once I had pulled

HEART OF BETRAYAL ~ 339

them on, I shrugged into the sweatshirt and said, "There should be some sneakers in the corner. Mom and I wear the same size."

Will nodded and moved to the furthest corner of the closet while I dug into the drawer nearest to me for a pair of socks. When I turned around, Will had a pair of bright turquoise and grey sneakers in his hands. I leaned over and groaned as I slipped on the socks and sneakers.

"Are you in pain?"

"I don't know why it's taking so long to heal," I replied while bending over slightly and braced myself with a hand on the wall.

"A vampire hurting you versus a human…"

"Five," I snapped. "There were five of them, five Vamps against me. I did everything I could to fight them."

His dark eyes bore into mine as he squeezed my shoulder. "*No one* is blaming you or judging you, Olivia. If you're in too much pain, I'll carry you, or Jax can if you don't want me to…to touch you. Whatever you're comfortable with, we'll do it, but we have to leave now. Please? Please let me get you out of here."

It was hard to look at him. He held out his hand and I nervously allowed him to guide me out of the closet. When we stepped into the bedroom, Jax was pacing back and forth between the couches, and he abruptly stopped when he saw us.

"We've gotta go," he said, looking at his watch. "We've wasted way too much time. Ada and Devy will be here soon."

Jax took a step forward, but with a horrible sound, there was suddenly a sword's blade sticking out of his abdomen. I screamed as he was lifted a foot off the ground by an invisible force. It was my dream, but instead of Will, it was my twin being skewered by a sword. Will rushed forward, and just as he approached Jax, the area between them shimmered and revealed Miller with several of his men including Mason holding the sword that was impaling my brother.

Miller laughed and nudged Mason who then pulled the sword away, causing Jax to fall into a heap on the floor. Will pulled him away from the edge of the shield and pressed his hands into Jax's wound.

"You Warriors never learn. There are always more of us hiding somewhere," Miller said and then looked over at Will. "Didn't I kill you?"

"You tried."

Miller harumphed and shook his head. "Well, I won't make that mistake again. Before this is over, I will carry your head like a trophy, you can be assured of that."

Jax groaned and I crawled over to him, taking his hand in mine and squeezing it tightly. Blood was seeping out between Will's fingers from the wound, and it took everything not to start crying again.

"I do want to thank you," Miller began, "we were beginning to wonder if your family was going to wreak vengeance or hide. It is nice to know that our preparations aren't in vain. We have some lovely surprises for your family when they decide to attack us. So thank you, for all your help.

"Mason, ensure there are two guards shielding them at all times. Only I can give the order to take the shield down. There can be no more mistakes."

"Yes, sir," Mason replied and wiped his bloody sword on the side of the couch before leading all but two guards out of the room.

"Holy shit, this really hurts," Jax grunted as he tried to move.

"It sure does," Will replied. "That's the same sword he used on me."

"Wh-what?" I cried.

"We have to kill that fucker."

"Jax, stop talking. Liv, grab a pillowcase so we can apply pressure."

I nodded and crawled to the bed, grabbing one of the pillows and ripping the pillowcase off. Will lifted Jax's shirt and pressed the pillowcase firmly into the wound causing Jax to groan.

"How long does it usually take you to heal from something like this?" Will asked as the blood began soaking through the cloth.

"Dunno," Jax replied, drunk with pain. "Never been impaled before."

Will squinted his eyes at the joke and lifted the pillowcase slightly to peek at the wound again. "Liv, keep applying pressure," he instructed and I replaced his hands with mine.

"Wh-why? What are you…"

Before I could finish, Will reared his head back, extended his fangs, and scraped them down his forearm. Thick, dark blood bubbled up from the two parallel tracks. Will pulled my hands and the pillowcase away from Jax's abdomen, and allowed his blood to ooze down into the wound. When he pulled his arm away, I placed the bloody pillowcase back onto Jax's wound and applied pressure.

"Wills to the rescue," Jax muttered while Will licked his wounds closed. Jax reached up and squeezed my arm. "Livy?"

"Yes, Jack-Jack," I replied, fighting back tears. "What is it?"

"We are in so much trouble."

Chapter Thirty-three

Olivia

With the help of Will's blood, Jack finally began to heal. Recovering from the shock of what had happened to his body took a little longer. It struck me how lucky my brother was to have never been injured prior to today. In all the missions he had helped on, he'd never even had a broken bone, let alone a stab wound through and through. A bit of his usual cockiness seemed to have faded slightly, but who knew how long that would last.

It had been almost two hours since we had been caught and Miller informed us about the "surprises" that awaited our family. The atmosphere was tense and awkward between the three of us for several reasons. One, our family would be pissed at Jack and Will for coming here on their own. Two, they had given up any element of surprise my family had at attacking the manor. Three, we all knew what had happened to me.

I was sitting on the floor with my back pressed up against the side of the bed, hugging my knees tightly into my chest. The pain and cramping had finally begun to subside, and the bruising on my wrists and ankles had disappeared. Will was sitting near the nightstand, stealing looks and glancing away when I would catch him. Jack, on the other hand, was a pacer. He paced, and paced, back and forth, and back and forth, it was enough to drive you nuts. Jack's pacing was getting closer and closer to the large blood stain on the carpet. How didn't he see it? Closer, and closer...

"Jack, could you not step there?"

He stopped and looked down. "Oh shit. Sorry, I wasn't paying attention. What happened there?"

My head fell back against the side of the mattress as I closed my eyes and replied, "That's where they killed Julian." It was very quiet so I opened my eyes and found both of them staring at me. "What?"

"They killed him in front of you?" Jack asked with concern.

I closed my eyes again and sighed. "Yep. And even as the sword was coming down, he was only concerned about me. So yeah…that happened."

"I'm sorry, Liv," Will said softly.

Images of Julian's final moments flashed in my head. I think I was most astonished by how calm and brave he had been until the final moment. He was such a complex man that few ever gave him the time of day. Of course, in his job he had to stay so rigid and firm, but for whatever reason he showed me a softer and caring side.

"I don't think I've ever told you this," I said as I lifted my head and looked at Jack. "When Aidan kidnapped you, when you were at the camp…"

"Yes, lovely memories to be bringing up right now," he interrupted, but I continued.

"Aidan and Goran put you on that electrical machine…"

"Again, memories I'd rather you not bring up at the moment."

"Once everything had calmed down, we were in here and all these people were coming in and out. Julian…" I paused and smiled at the memory of Julian standing awkwardly near the doorway, "he…he brought me a doll."

"A doll? Julian?"

I smiled and nodded. "Yeah, it was this old-fashioned Victorian doll, but…I loved that doll. No one else did that, you know?"

"I remember that doll," Jack said. "I used to think it would kill me in my sleep." I laughed. "I never knew where it came from."

"He would send me hand written letters when I was at University, and they wouldn't say much about anything, but they were so…I don't know, we could just be honest about what was going on in our lives and I knew that he would never tell Ada or Mom. It was nice."

"Who did it?" Will asked.

"Mason," I replied.

Will shook his head. "He seems to have had a big day."

My heart sank at the thought that Mason had something to do with Will being Turned. But I wasn't ready to hear about it. "Well, I got a couple of good shots in before…" Nope, I still couldn't say it.

Jack knelt down in front of me, placing his hands on my knees. "I'm sorry, Livy."

Tears leaked from my eyes because I was so shocked at how loving and compassionate his simple words were to me. We had been so contentious for so long I wasn't used to having even the slightest kind word from him.

Did you really see…what…what happened?

He looked away for a moment and then pressed his head into my knees, his tears soaking through the fabric of my sweatpants. But before we could even begin to broach the subject, the manor's alarm began to wail. Jax whipped his head up, and looked between me and Will.

They're here, he pushed to me and I nodded.

A second later Will nodded, and my stomach flipped at the realization that Jax could now talk to Will like he did with other vampires.

Jack looked back at me. "Are you ok to move?"

I nodded.

"Oi!" the guard closest to us shouted over the wailing alarm. "Separate yurselves, or we'll do it fur ya."

Jax put his hands up and scooted a few feet away from me. Suddenly the door burst open with a very unlikely Warrior running inside the room.

"Tori?" Will muttered under his breath.

"What are you guys doing?" she said to the two guards and ignoring us. "They're here! Miller needs everyone on the front lines." The two guards looked at each other and then back at Tori, but they didn't budge. "Are you deaf?"

"Sod off," the guard replied. "The Master says we stay 'ere until 'e pulls us off. So sod off." Tori squared her shoulders and gave a condescending smile as she walked across the room. "Oi! You can't…"

"Like hell I can," Tori replied and pulled the curtains away from the French doors that had a view all the way out to the gardens. The three of us quickly stood from the floor, and even from this distance we could see both werewolves and vampires coming out from the tree line. A line of Miller's men formed a tall shield in front of them. "Do you see what's coming at us? There's a whole other team coming at us from the front too. Do you want to tell Miller you couldn't help because you were keeping a shield around these stupid kids?"

The two guards swapped worried looks and then stepped closer to the double doors, watching the line of wolves and vampires slamming against the shield. But what the guards didn't notice was that Tori had now positioned herself right behind them, and with two quick pulls of a trigger, she shot them both through the heart. The shield disappeared before they fell to the floor.

Jack leapt over to Tori and gave her a high-five. "You had me fooled for a moment."

"Thank you, Tori," Will said behind me, making me flinch and turn around to find him with his hands up defensively. "Sorry."

"No, I'm sorry," I replied nervously.

"It's ok, Liv. We're going to be ok now."

Tori snickered. "Not so fast, hot shots. We still have to get through that line. Do you even know how much trouble you two are in?" she said and pointed to Will and Jack.

"I have a vague idea," Jack replied and Tori rolled her eyes.

"Your father is pissed, but we need your help to get them through that shield. Can you...do your thing?" she said and pointed to Jack's head.

Jack exhaled and nodded. "Yeah, but that's a lot of Vamps to push." He looked over at me and extended his hand. "But you can help me."

I shook my head. "I...I can't do...I can't do anything."

"Yes you can," he said calmly and gently took my hand. "We've done it before. We can do it, Livy."

"Last time it was against each other."

"Then this time we'll do it together."

My teeth bit into my lips as I nodded and allowed him to pull me closer to the French doors. He looked me in the eyes as he took my other hand and squeezed it tightly.

We can do this, he said in my head.

Tears streamed down my cheeks as I closed my eyes. With our palms squeezed tightly together, and both our minds open to each other, I could see all the white lights surrounding us, but two especially close to us.

"Will, Tori," Jack began, "hold onto something, we won't be able to filter the two of you out of this."

I opened my eyes just in time to see Will and Tori run to my mother's closet and shut the door. I looked at Jack in confusion. "They'll still get hit."

"Yeah, but they won't fly as far," he laughed, and then became very sober. "We're in this together, Livy. I've got you." I nodded and squeezed his hands as he pulled them up between us. "Can you see the lights?"

"Yes, I see them."

"Ok, push everything you have in three, two, one," he said and with a deep exhale both of us pushed everything we had, releasing a massive wave of energy. The burst was so powerful that both of us fell backwards onto the floor. As I rolled to my side, I watched as Jack pushed himself up clumsily from the floor and stumbled to the doors. "It worked!" he shouted, and helped me to my feet.

Once I was steady, he ran to the opposite side of the room and opened the closet door. While he checked on Will and Tori, I looked out onto the gardens and watched as our people broke through the line of Miller's men and began tearing them apart. The war had begun. I'd escaped from this world so I wouldn't have to see this, and now I was smack dab in the middle of it.

"Liv!" Wills shouted and I turned around. He waved me over to the secret door in the wall. "Liv, come on, we have to go!"

I nodded and ran to him, taking his hand and ducking into the stairwell with Jack and Tori right behind us. "Where are we going?"

"Hopefully the way we came," he replied. "There's a hidden grate…"

But before Will could finish, an explosion rocked the area below us. Will draped himself protectively around me as debris flew up the stairwell. As the dust settled, Will stood up and gently pulled me up beside him.

"Everyone ok?"

"Yeah," Jack replied as he and Tori brushed themselves off. "I'm guessing that was the surprise Miller was talking about."

Will headed down the few remaining steps and jetted to the left around the corner. A second later he re-appeared so quickly that the dust swirled around him like a dozen little tornadoes.

"The whole corridor is caved in. We can try and dig our way out."

Jack shook his head. "Let's go the other way, there's a tunnel near the prison cells that'll take us up through the vaults."

The rest of us nodded, allowing Jack and Tori to lead the way this time. Even through the solid stone surrounding us, you could somehow still hear the sounds of battle happening above us. The tunnel was dark and growing increasingly damp as we got closer to the prison cells. I squeezed Will's hand tighter, and he pulled me into his side in response. In my head

I was trying to map out where we were in the manor, but it was nearly impossible with the darkness and strange sounds echoing around us. But I had faith in Jack. He and Will played in these tunnels all the time when we were young. Besides Grandfather, Ada, and Devy, I would bet that few knew these tunnels as well as they did.

We took a sharp right and came to a four-way intersection. Jack and Tori were about twenty feet in front of us, and as they crossed the intersection, a soft beeping began to sound. Jack turned around quickly and thrust his hands out in front of him. Will screamed in pain as he was thrust backwards, dragging me with him as another explosion erupted in the center of the intersection.

I hit the stone floor first and a loud crack came from my shoulder. Will fell next to me, but then repositioned himself to cover me as stone and wood and other debris flew over us. My ears were ringing, and it was difficult to breathe because of all the dust and Will's weight on top of me. Eventually he shook his head and looked at me.

"Liv, you ok?" he coughed and wiped the dust off his face.

"Can't…breathe."

Quickly he rolled off and then hovered over me. "Sorry. Are you ok?"

I took in a few breaths before replying, "My shoulder."

He nodded and gently sat me up, although I could already tell my shoulder was not right as it hung at an odd angle. Carefully Will placed his arm around my waist and pulled me back up against the wall.

"Will! Olivia!" Tori called in the distance. I looked to my right to find a good amount of the surrounding walls and floor from above had caved into a tall pile of stone in the center of the intersection.

"We're here. Olivia has a dislocated shoulder," Will replied while he gently began to exam my arm. "Where's Jax?"

"Head injury," she replied.

"How can you tell?" Will laughed and I narrowed my eyes at him. He flinched slightly and then looked down at me. "Your brother is fine. He's telling me to go fuck myself."

I sighed with relief and let my head fall back against the wall. "Did he push you right before…"

"Yeah. They must have triggered something when they ran ahead of us. I heard the beeping, but then felt his push," he said as he pulled me forward and began feeling along my shoulder and arm. "If he hadn't, we would have been in the middle of that explosion."

Pop!

I screamed in pain after my shoulder was popped back in place. "You could have given me some warning."

Will brushed my hair away and kissed me gently on the forehead. "And then you would have tensed and your shoulder would not have gone into place." He pulled my chin up. "Feel better?"

I nodded as I rolled my shoulder back. "I know you didn't like being a doctor, but you sure are good at it."

He laughed lightly, but then something crossed his face causing him to close his eyes tightly and rest his forehead against mine. His breath was strained as it wafted against my face. I placed my hands on either side of his face and we held each other in that moment, silent and painful, and knowing there was not enough time to say all the things we wanted to say to each other.

"Guys?" Tori called from the other side of the cave in.

"We're here," Will replied, reluctantly sitting up straight.

"Jack?" I called and then looked to Will. "Why isn't he talking to me?"

"Because my head hurts," Jack yelled back.

"But you talked to Will."

"Yeah, that's why my head hurts."

"Tori, is he bleeding?" Will asked.

"Yes, but it's slowing down. We can't..." Tori began but was interrupted by another explosion somewhere on the other side of the manor, but close enough that the walls shook around us causing more dust to fall. "We can't stay in these tunnels!"

Will stood from the floor and exhaled loudly before looking up. The hole in the floor above us cast a shimmery light down on the mountain of rubble that separated us from Tori and Jack. He looked down at me and asked, "Think you can climb that?"

I rubbed my shoulder which only complained slightly. "I earned the name Monkey for a reason."

He smiled and helped me to stand, watching me for a moment before yelling back over to Tori, "We'll have to go up. Jax, are you..."

"Yeah," Jack groaned from the other side. "I'm fine, let's go."

Will held out his hand. "Ladies first."

I nodded nervously, took his hand, and reached up to the first block of stone that looked semi-sturdy. Slowly I pulled myself up the mound of rubble toward the large opening above. Halfway up, my right foot slipped on some loose stone and shot out from under me. My left arm was unable to hold me from the weakness in my shoulder and I slid down several feet before Will caught me and held me in place.

His eyes were wide with fear as I dug my fingers back in. "Guess that shoulder is a little weaker than we thought."

I forced a smile and together we climbed up the rest of the way. Tori and Jack were already at the top waiting for us. Jack's headwound was definitely worse than I imagined. There was a large gash from the right side of his forehead to his jaw, and blood had seeped all the way down to his chest. Will tried to look at it, but Jack slapped his hand away.

From the top of the stone mountain there was at least a five-foot gap to the edge of the hole above. It would be an easy jump for everyone else, but I worried if my shoulder would have the strength needed to pull up and out. Then there was the worry about who might be waiting for us when we climbed out.

"I'll go first and make sure the coast is clear," Tori said firmly. "Then I'll give the signal for Jax to go."

"Then I'll give Liv a boost," Will continued. "Jax, you help pull her up if her shoulder gives way."

I hated being the weak one. "I can do it."

"Of course you can," he replied. "It's just a precaution in case your shoulder gives out."

After a nod from all of us, Tori bent her knees and flew out of the center of the opening. A moment later she gave the all-clear for Jack.

He looked back at me. "Just jump and I'll catch you."

"Ok, see you up there," I replied.

A moment later he jumped up and grabbed onto the edge of the opening, swung his legs forward and then on the back swing launched himself up and out.

Will leaned down and laced his fingers together for a foothold.

"I'm not a weakling, you know."

Will looked up from his hands. "No one is saying that. Your shoulder is weak, that's all. I'm going to give you a little boost, and trust your brother will catch you. We've all got you, Liv."

I sighed and Will laced his fingers together again. Just as I placed my foot into his hands, he threw me up in the air and I held my right arm up. In an instant, my brother's hand surrounded my forearm and pulled me out of the opening. Quickly he pulled me into the small alcove where Tori was looking out around us. A second later she gave a whistle and Will jumped out of the opening like a gazelle. The sight made me shutter.

Once the four of us were nestled in the alcove, I realized we were across from the dining hall, and the noises around us were finally settling in. Vampires were tearing each other apart on either side of us. It was chaos. No wonder no one noticed us coming up out of the ground. But it was the screaming from above that caught our attention.

"The donors," I said as I pulled on Tori's arm. "We have to help them!"

"I was ordered to get you all out of here," she replied and I shook my head.

"They are more helpless than we are. I'm not going until they're safe."

Tori looked at Jack and then down at Will for any kind of opposition, but she didn't get it. "Fine," she sighed. "But you explain this to your father."

"We will," Jack affirmed and the four of us ran out from the safety of our alcove.

It was only seconds later that we realized why there was so much screaming. The spiral staircase, the spine of the manor, was falling apart. Large chunks of stone were crashing down to the floor below while cracks spread like veins up the edges of the staircase. Dozens of donors were frozen in fear, screaming for help as the staircase pulled away from the landings and then began to pitch.

Jack and Will sprang into action and pushed to hold the base in place. Other donors were gathered at the edges of landings, desperately trying to pull those stuck on the stairs back to safety. Tori pulled me out of the way just as another large chunk of the staircase fell from above. Someone screamed and I looked up quickly to find a male donor hanging from one of the ledges.

"Tori, come on," I shouted and climbed up on the banister without waiting for an answer. I had climbed these stairs more times than I could count. With pieces of stone crumbling at every foothold and finger grab, it just meant I had to climb faster than I ever had even with my shoulder groaning at me. When I reached the fourth level, I leaned down and pulled the donor up with all my strength onto the main part of the staircase.

"Thank you," he cried and I pulled him to his feet.

"You all are going to give me a heart attack," Tori shouted behind me.

"Take him," I said, and handed the donor over to her. "Get everyone to the back stairs and lead them outside through the side door. It goes almost directly into the woods. They'll have a chance."

She shook her head as we traveled up the rest of the stairs to the fourth landing. "I have my orders…"

"Then you have new orders now, Tori," I shouted. "They need you more than we do. Now go!" Tori pressed her lips together in a fine line, but I wasn't budging. "I'll go down to the other levels and direct them out. Please, Tori."

She sighed and pushed the poor donor onto the fourth-floor landing. "And you all will follow?"

"We'll find our way out and I promise this will not come back on you."

Tori nodded and led the donor down the corridor. Quickly I climbed back down the staircase, which was now beginning to sway. One by one I helped the other donors back onto the closest landing and instructed them to run down the back stairs. Third floor, second floor, and by the time I reached the first floor, the famous spiral staircase was in shambles.

"Livy, come on!" Jack yelled up at me as the staircase began pitching forward. Jack let go first as I jumped down, and then pulled Will away. The three of us bolted as the spiral staircase, fell away and crashed into the main dining hall. The impact forced all of us down on the floor.

Even with the ringing in my ears, I heard someone yell, "The wolves can cut through the shields!"

Only a few feet away, several wolves were clawing at Miller's men, and their deadly sharp nails were cutting clean through the shields. The men hiding behind those shields didn't know what to do. They seemed to possess little skill. As the wolves sliced away the shield, a Warrior would swoop in and take care of the rest. Blood and bodies were falling all around us.

Suddenly Jack pulled me up from the floor and jutted his head toward the main entrance. Freedom. I reached back to Will who was only a few feet behind us.

"Run, Livy, run!" he shouted as he pointed toward the front door, and my stomach dropped at the familiarity.

"Will, no…"

Another explosion burst out in front of us only inches from the front doors. Jack and I were blown several feet to the left, both of us bouncing hard on the stone floor. My head was pounding and my ears were ringing. Slowly I stretched my eyes open and everything seemed to be in slow motion. Dust and stone fell and floated around us. My heart was beating in my throat, which seemed to be the only sound I could hear. Finally, my eyes focused and I found Uncle Alex hovering over me. His mouth was moving, but my ears and my brain hadn't caught up enough to decipher what he was saying.

I looked to my left and Jack was rolling onto his side. I looked to my right and saw lifeless bodies lying on the floor. Slowly I looked back up at my uncle whose mouth was moving extremely fast although his words were inaudible.

"Will," I whispered, and then coughed violently from the dust in my throat.

Uncle Alex looked behind him and then back at me, his words still not registering. Painfully I rose from the floor and pushed Uncle Alex's hands away. In front of me was an enormous hole where the front of the manor used to be, and an even bigger mound of stone piled up on the floor where the explosion had emanated from. My brain still wasn't working, but my body immediately reacted and began digging at the pile of rubble.

"Olivia!"

The voice of my uncle finally broke through my fog, but I didn't stop digging. "Will is down here!" I shouted.

Uncle Alex pulled my hands away and held them tightly. "We will find him."

"I'm not leaving without him."

Uncle Alex sighed, shook his head, and then turned toward the mountain of rubble.

"Jax!" he called, and my brother stumbled over. Uncle Alex knelt down and dug his hands firmly into the mound. With a loud grunt, I watched as my uncle lifted a mountain of stone off the ground. He was a real-life Atlas holding the world on his shoulders. Jack ducked into the opening, which was only about a foot tall, and began pulling other rocks away and calling Will's name. Quickly I crawled across the floor and helped clear the area. A moment later, Will's fist broke through the stone. It took both Jack and I to dig around and pull Will up through the opening. Once he was clear, Uncle Alex dropped the mountain back down on the floor, shaking the ground around us.

Will laid between me and Jack, his face paler with dirt and dust. His arm was draped across me while he nuzzled his face in between my neck and shoulder. I was exhausted, traumatized, and wanted to take a moment to breathe, but it seemed that everyone else had different ideas.

"Come on," Uncle Alex began and lifted Will off of me. "Everyone into the courtyard."

"Tori," I said, but then coughed up more dust. Uncle Alex squinted his eyes at me. "Tori…and the donors. We…sent them out the side door. We need to…"

Uncle Alex put his hands up to stop me and then snapped his fingers. "Connor! Grab someone and help Tori with the donors. They're…"

"I'll go," Jack said as he stood from the floor and brushed himself off, but then looked down at me. "Unless you want me to…"

"Go," I interrupted and he disappeared. I turned to Will and helped him brush the rocks and dust out of his hair. "Are you ok?"

He nodded with wide eyes. "A little shocked I'm alive right now." He paused and then looked down at himself. "As alive as a vampire can be, I guess."

He looked at me guiltily and I couldn't hold his gaze.

"Come on, kids, we need to get out of here," Uncle Alex shouted and waved us forward.

Will extended me his hand and pulled me up off the floor. We supported each other down the corridor toward the courtyard. Once we had made our way outside, I gasped. Warrior after Warrior was on his or her knees, hands up by their ears while Ada, Devy, and Grandfather walked slowly back and forth in front of them.

I looked up at Will confused. "The traitors," he whispered in my ear.

"But there are so many," I replied in awe. "And these are the survivors."

We stayed pressed up against the wall where it seemed the safest. From here it was easy to see they were separating the naughty Warriors from Miller's men. It was then that I saw Niall being walked out, and I dug my fingernails into Will's arm. But what about Miller? Where were Mason and Duncan? Were they dead? Could they all be thankfully be dead?

"Despite your treachery," Ada yelled at the Warriors on their knees, "we will give you a choice." As he looked down the line of those he had known for centuries, he caught sight of me huddled with Will at the opposite end. He froze for a moment and then looked down at the ground, his eyes tightly closed. After a moment he shook away his emotions and continued, "You will have a choice – defend yourself at trial, or be executed this very moment."

"Ohmygod," I moaned, feeling the strength of my knees begin to falter. I pushed against Will and stepped across him. "No, I can't, I won't stand and watch…"

Then I froze and Will walked right into me causing us both to crash to the ground.

"Liv?" he asked, pulling at my arm, but then followed my gaze to the line of Miller's men being walked out into the center of the courtyard.

Without answering him, I bolted up from the ground and launched myself at the two men who had held me down by my wrists.

"NO! They don't get a choice," I shouted as my fists and feet came down upon their shields. "They…don't…not them!"

My knees finally gave out and I fell into the ground weeping violently into the grass. Suddenly I was pulled up by my shoulders, and Ada's red-stained face was looking down at me.

"Them!" he growled and pointed at the two men. "Were they there?"

My head fell into his chest and I nodded as I soaked his shirt with my sobs.

"Take your shields down or we will," Ada shouted. I began to shake, and Ada pulled me tightly into him. "Beckett, I need a wolf! Eris!"

I opened my eyes slightly, only seeing through the thin slit of space under Ada's arm. The two men had backed themselves up against the courtyard's wall, their hands shaking as they continued to hold up their shields. One of Beckett's wolves lumbered over to them and showed his claws, but they still held their ground. The wolf swiped his deadly claws across their shield, slicing through it like tissue paper, and Eri jumped into the thin space with his broadsword. I buried my head into Ada's chest at that point. I wanted them dead, but I didn't want to see it happen.

"Baby girl?" my mother said softly next to me.

Instantly I lifted my head and found Mom kneeling in the grass. Her clothes were torn in several places, blood splattered across her chest and covering her hands. Sometimes I forgot that my mom was just as much of a Warrior as everyone else, and she was just as deadly as Eri. She dropped her daggers in the grass and with Ada's help I fell into her waiting arms. The area around us was still in chaos, but in that moment, I was in the safety of my parents' arms, and I could finally breathe.

Eventually I lifted my head from my mother's chest and began to look around. Bodies and decapitated heads were strewn about. Eri stood protectively in front of us, his sword still dripping with blood. When he caught my eye, he spoke to me in Italian saying that his sword would cut through the world to find each of my attackers.

"Thank you, Eri," I said, interrupting his tirade. It was too much to take in at the moment. Looking over at Ada, I asked, "What are you going to do to Niall?"

"We will figure that out, but I promise we will hold him accountable for what he has done."

"Where is Miller?"

He shook his head. "We have not seen him. It is rumored he Projected away once we breached the perimeter."

"But…what about Duncan and…Mason?"

Ada shook his head again. "No one has seen them."

"So, they're still out there!" I shouted and began to hyperventilate.

Mom pressed her hands on either side of my face and brought my eyes in line with hers. "We will find them, Olivia. We will turn this world upside down to find them, but you are safe now."

I shook my head and began to cry again. My skin was crawling and I was panicked that Miller would just appear at any moment. "No, no, I can't be here. I don't want to stay here. I need to…"

"I'll take her," Will said and knelt down in front of us.

"Where will you go?" Ada asked firmly.

"I'll take her back to Ollie's," he whispered and looked back at me. "Want to go back to Daddy O's? Mémé is there, she'll be waiting for you."

I looked up at Mom and then over to Ada, seeking permission in some way, and receiving it instantly. Will extended his arms, lifted me up from the ground, and carried me down the length of the courtyard with the sounds of torture and death occurring behind us.

"Going through the manor is too dangerous," he said in my ear. "I'll have to jump the wall."

I nodded and snaked my arms tightly around his neck. He was Will, I knew he was, but he felt different, he sounded different, he even smelled different. He bent down and jumped the ten-foot wall with ease, and I tried not to cry into his chest. He was Will. He was Will. I loved Will…but more so, I loved human Will.

Once we had landed on the other side of the wall, the gravel crunched under Will's feet as he ran to one of the Warrior's black SUVs. He opened the passenger door and I sank into the thick leather seat. Will was in the driver's seat only a second later and quickly started the engine. As I pulled my seatbelt across my chest, I looked out through the windshield and saw what was left of the manor. Smoke and dust still rose from the skeletal remains of the main entrance. In some areas you could see straight inside through the massive holes and cave-ins. But it appeared our battle hadn't gone unnoticed.

"Are those sirens?" I asked and clicked my seatbelt into place.

"Yes, I think they're coming up the hill."

"You should go the back way."

He nodded and steered the SUV toward the hidden drive located at the other side of the manor. "The manor will never be the same,"

"In more ways than one."

"Everything is going to be ok now, Liv."

I shook my head and took one last look at my home. "Nothing will ever be ok again."

Chapter Thirty-four

Will

The ride from the manor to Ollie's place was eerily silent. Olivia was curled up in a ball and shutting out the world. I didn't dare speak let alone try to touch her. There was a protective fortress around her, and there was nothing I could do or say to make her feel any better. For most of our lives together, that had been my role in her life. Now I was helpless, and I could see she was about as disgusted with me being a vampire as my parents were.

Seraphina was already waiting at the door when we pulled into the driveway. Olivia didn't even wait for me to put the SUV in park before she opened the door and ran into her grandmother's arms. Once they disappeared inside, I took my time getting out of the truck – double checking that the gearshift was in park, no debris on the seats, and the lights were off – just about anything to delay having to go into the house. Finally, I pulled myself out of the truck and checked the tires, the headlights, and then began to pick the bugs out of the grill.

"Are you coming in or not?"

I turned around and found my mother standing in the doorway with her arms crossed in front of her chest. "Depends if I'm welcome."

Her eyes were red and swollen, and she looked exhausted. "You and Jax sneaking out was really stupid, and it scared everyone half to death, which is really saying something since most of the people that were here were already technically dead."

"I had to try and save her," I replied.

She paused as tears welled up in her eyes. "I'm not sure I can get used to this, Will. It's...it's a lot."

I took a deep breath in and stuffed my hands in my pockets. "Today I've been falsely accused of treason, tortured, killed, brought back to life, saw the woman I love being assaulted, been told by my father that he would rather I was dead than a vampire, held captive, been hit by two bombs, and buried in five feet of stone by a third. But by all means, I understand that this might all be a lot for *you* to handle."

She took a breath before replying, "Damn, and all this time I thought for sure you were more like your father. If that wasn't the Snider side of the family coming out, I don't know what was."

"I'm sorry, Mom..."

She put her hand up to stop me. "No, I'm sorry. Your dad and I are...our grief is only because we love you so much. You're my little man, Will, and now you're...this, and with everything that happened to Olivia, I just...I don't want to be a part of this anymore. It's too much. Our family, all our families have sacrificed too much. How is any of this worth it?"

"We can make sure none of this happens to anyone else."

She gave me a cynical smile. "Spoken like a true Warrior."

Without another word, she turned and stepped back inside. Needing a little space between us, I waited a few seconds before stepping inside the house myself. Mom disappeared down the hallway toward the bedrooms, passing by Sera as she came out of the bathroom.

"Where's Liv?"

Sera smiled and gestured toward the couch. "She iz in with your fazer," she replied.

"Her wounds have healed, I'm not sure what else..."

"Zhere are some ozer zhings to discuss, some...womanly zhings."

Feeling as though the floor was falling out from under me, I sat down on the couch and Sera took a seat at the other end. "She's on birth control...she told me that the other day. That means she can't be...you know. Right? He couldn't have..."

Sera patted my hand gently. "Zhere will be much for her overcome. She needs our love, not our worry."

I nodded at the same time my dad came out of the bathroom. As he closed the door behind him, I could hear Olivia click the lock on the door.

Even here at Ollie's, what I would consider a sacred place, she was still terrified.

"How is she?"

Dad opened his mouth, and then closed it with a big exhale and a shake of his head. "Her injuries have healed, physically she's ok. In regards to the other…issues, I told her about the options available to her. There's not much else I can do for her. She's suffered significant trauma, and she'll need counseling. I wish I could do more for her right now…"

"As do we all," Sera interrupted.

Dad nodded helplessly and pointed to the hallway. "I'm going to check on your mother. Yet another woman I can't help today. Maybe later we can…talk?"

"Sure," I replied and sank further into the couch.

Dad disappeared down the hall and Sera headed into the kitchen. "If I know ma petite singe, she will be hungry."

"That's a good bet," I replied and found comfort in the noises of her puttering around the kitchen.

About that time, the shower in the bathroom went on and stayed on for twenty agonizing minutes. In that amount of time, Sera had made guacamole, chicken tenders, and chocolate chip cookies. I guess she intended to cover all angles of her granddaughter's potential hunger needs.

Frustrated, and unable to handle all the overwhelming smells coming from the kitchen, I retreated into the front bedroom. It was the same bedroom I'd hidden in after being Turned, and had fed on Sera, something I wasn't sure I would ever get over. As I sat down on the mattress, I heard the shower finally shut off, but it was at least another fifteen minutes before Olivia opened the bathroom door. She gasped once she stepped inside the bedroom, and I instantly felt guilty.

"Sorry," I said and sat up. "I just needed to rest my eyes for a few minutes."

Liv nodded and closed the door. "Sleep sounds good."

"Sera made food for you if you want it."

She shook her head. "I'm not hungry." I tried to hide my reaction to the three words I'd never heard come out of her mouth, but she read my face instantly. "Guess I've never said that before."

"No, I don't think you have." She forced a thin smile and I stood from the bed. "Why don't you try and get some rest." She nodded and stepped toward the bed. "I'll give you some privacy."

"Can you stay with me?"

"Liv, I'll stay with you forever and a day," I replied and sat back down on the bed.

I pulled back the blankets on her side of the bed, but she froze, so I froze too. After a nervous moment, she climbed inside, pulled the bedspread up to her chin, and turned onto her side toward me.

"What's supposed to happen now?" she asked with a sniffle which caused a wet curl to fall in her face.

Cautiously I moved my hand and took the curl between my fingers before tucking it behind her ear. The diamond earrings I'd given her sparkled up at me. It was the first time she hadn't flinched when I touched her. Already I knew it was going to be a long, painful road for her. I only hoped she would allow me to help her and love her along the way.

"First thing, I think you need to get some sleep," I began, leaning back over to my side of the bed to give her back her space. "And then we'll just take it from there, see what you feel like doing."

"I'm afraid of what I'll see if I close my eyes."

"What do you mean?"

She wiped her eyes with the edge of the bedspread and replied, "The last two times I fell asleep around you, I had dreams."

"What kind of dreams?"

She looked up at me with teary eyes and swallowed hard before continuing. "Like the dreams I used to have when I was little, when I would see...things, future things."

"You saw what was going happen today?"

She shook her head in frustration. "No, not really, I just...I knew something was going to happen to you, but it was so hazy and I couldn't...I didn't want to believe it."

My head fell back against the wall. "You told me you had a bad feeling about the mission. What did you see?"

She sniffled, causing me to look back down at her. "I saw Miller and...you got stabbed in the back with a sword, but that ended up happening to Jack...or is that what happened to you too?" My eyes widened and I blinked several times in surprise.

"The stomach, not the back," I replied and her eyes filled with tears again. "But it's not something you need to worry about now."

"I could have stopped it," she cried. "That's what I keep thinking, I could have stopped all of this. I was just too scared of it. It's been so long I didn't know how to deal with it. I could have stopped it."

I shook my head. "I don't think you could have, Liv, and you can't think that way. Your dreams were always a warning, but there was nothing you could ever really do about them."

"Then what's the point?"

I sighed and placed my hand gently around her shoulder. "Ask your mother, I guess. Her dreams were the same way, weren't they?"

She nodded and rolled into my side. "I don't want to fall asleep."

"I'll be right here," I replied, my eyelids suddenly feeling heavy.

"What if I have another dream?" she asked, her voice sounding sleepy.

"Then tell me about it. Tell me all about it, Liv, and we'll figure it all out. It's what we do. It's what we've always done."

"We have a lot to figure out, Wills."

I squeezed her shoulder gently, pulling her further into my side without feeling any kind of resistance. "We have all the time in the world now, Liv."

When she didn't answer, I glanced down to see that her eyes were closed, her face soft and relaxed. She was so beautiful and peaceful, and it tore me apart that the peacefulness would be short lived. She was right that there were so many things we'd need to figure out, but being a vampire now, I truly did have all the time in the world. Despite it all, I had finally become what I had always wanted to be. How many people could say that?

William James Ryan. Sire number seventy-nine of the Warrior coven. Coven leaders Cameron Burke and Devin the Warrior Assassin. Sires of the mighty Victor. Sire of the ancient Alastor. I was part of their legacy. I, William James Ryan, Warrior.

Epilogue

Jackson

To put it plainly, the manor was now a shithole. The front of the building was gone. The spiral staircase, probably the most iconic structure of the entire place, was lying in pieces in what used to be the dining hall. Holes the size of Texas were blown in the tunnels causing concern about the structural integrity of the building. Everyone's biggest question, was the manor salvageable? And in turn, would the Warriors ever recover?

My life thus far had been a waste. I was always waiting for something big to happen, some sign that would show me my purpose. After nearly six hours of sifting through rock, I had decided this was that sign. It was time to leave. I would step through the enormous holes in the walls, and try my hand at a life that was own, and not governed by my family's heritage and expectations.

Mom didn't take the news very well. She cried for nearly ten minutes, and hugged me with an iron grip for nine of them.

"But where will you stay?" she sobbed as she wiped her face of tears.

"I don't know yet. I'm just going to drive, and when I find a town I like, I'll set up there."

"But you don't know anyone," she cried and Ada covered his mouth to hide his laughter.

"That's kind of the point, Mom. You let Livy go half across the world for almost five years. I'm just talking about one year in one or two states over. It's what someone my age is supposed to do."

She hugged me again. "I know, but now?"

I patted her arm and then pulled her away from me. "If I stay now, I'll never go. I need to do this, Mom."

She wiped her face again, and kissed my cheek with her usual three kisses in quick succession. She cupped the same cheek with her hand as she said, "Just remember you can always come home."

"Well, it's not much of a home anymore."

She nodded sadly. "But still, we're here…if you don't like it out there."

"Bri, love," Ada interrupted, placing his hands on her shoulders and pulling her away from me, "let him go. It's his turn."

She nodded and wiped her face...again.

With a hard swallow of emotions, Mom shifted her shoulders back and forced a smile. "Call us when you stop, ok? Whether it's for the night, or whatever. I need to know you're ok."

"I will," I replied and she reluctantly walked back to the manor.

Ada watched her for a moment, as he always seemed to do, and then gave me an apologetic smile. "She has had a hard day."

"I think we all have."

"Yes, but when it comes to her babies, her emotions are tenfold," he said and then gave me his serious fatherly look. "Are you sure about this?"

I nodded. "Yes. I have money saved, and I can tap into the Trust if I have to. I hate leaving you like this, but I have to, Ada. I need to try and do something for myself."

"I understand, son," he replied, and I felt the acceptance I needed. "We have been spoiled to have had you with us this long."

"I know it's a bad time..."

"Jacky," he interrupted, "no one should have to stay here right now. Go and do good things, find yourself, son."

"Thanks, Ada," I replied and accepted his hug gratefully.

"And since you are leaving," he said as he pulled away from me and dug into his pocket, "you should have something nice to ride in."

Ada pulled his hand from his pocket and held up the remote control to his vintage Aston Martin. He had always had a love for cars, but especially his Aston Martin.

"Really?"

"Only as a loner, of course."

I laughed and took the remote from him as though it was a bar of gold. "Thank you, Ada."

He hugged me one more time, kissing my temple and saying, "I hope you find yourself, Jacky. I really do."

When he pulled away, I could see the red tears lining his eyes, and his attempt at holding them back. He gave me a quick nod and retreated back to the pile of stone that used to be our home.

I sighed nervously, but then felt a jolt of energy from the car remote in my hand. Before Ada could change his mind, I ran to the Aston Martin, threw my bags into the back, and sank down into the leather seat which melted around my body. With the slightest touch, the masterpiece of machinery roared to life, and I took one last look at the manor. For the first time in my life, I was nervous, and that made all of this even more exciting. Cautiously I pulled away and traveled through the black gate that was more greyish brown with all the dirt and rock dust that had been flying around. I waited until I was completely around the corner before pressing on the gas. The powerful engine almost made me cum in my pants as I sped smoothly around the tight curves coming down from the hills.

Are you still coming? Livy's voice suddenly echoed in my head.

My stomach flipped. It wasn't that I had forgotten, I was hoping she had changed her mind.

You're sure about this? I asked back.

Everyone's asleep, you have to come and get me now.

I'll be there in twenty minutes.

Make it faster, please. I won't be able to face him if he wakes up.

With a sigh, I tightened my grip on the steering wheel, and pressed the gas even further. Most of this was my fault. Once I had made my decision to leave, Livy was the first person I told, mainly because I could tell her without having to say the words out loud. It was like a practice run before having to tell my parents and watch my mother have a meltdown. Livy's immediate response was asking me to take her with me.

I don't know why I agreed to it. Maybe it was guilt, maybe it was some sick form of understanding what she'd just been through. I could easily understand why she didn't want to stay here. And although I worried how my parents would take her leaving too, even more worrisome was how Will would take it. But in true Morgan fashion, which sometimes dominated over the Burke genes, I decided I wouldn't worry about that today. So, after I packed a few of my things, I snuck into Livy's bedroom, stuffed some of her clothes into my bag, and purposely didn't tell Mom or Ada that she was leaving too. She could face the music herself.

The normal twenty-minute trip was cut down to fourteen, and I only ran five red lights. Ollie's house was so secluded that there were very few streetlights, making the winding roads pitch black, but the Aston Martin just glided along seamlessly.

I'm thirty seconds away, I said to her. *Be ready, I won't pull into the driveway.*

Ok, I'll come out to the road. Thanks, Jack-Jack.

I was about to answer her when I slammed on the brakes at the sight of something in the road. Forcefully I pulled the steering wheel to the left and the car finally stopped sideways in the road. Once the smoke from the tires cleared, I realized that Eris was standing next to the car. He bent over and waved at me through the window.

I rolled down the window. "Uh...hey, Eri, sorry about that. I thought you were an animal or something."

He tilted his head curiously. "Really? Well, I have been called worse."

I forced an awkward laugh. "Do you uh...always stand...in the road?"

"After today, I am on high alert to anyone who would come near our familia. I heard you coming from a mile away, little one, what are you doing up here?" Eris quickly looked to his right, just as Olivia began crossing the driveway. "Staging a breakout?"

"Something like that," I replied.

"Do your parents know?"

"About me, yes. About her, not yet."

He nodded as Olivia tentatively approached the car. She looked at me panicked through the windshield.

"It's ok, Livy," I replied aloud and waved her forward.

Eri looked between us and said, "Do you have money? As your nonno, I worry about these things."

Livy smiled, which was good to see. "I think we're ok. Well, Jack-Jack is better off than I am. I'll have to dip into the Trust."

"Nonsense," Eri replied. "Whatever your parents refuse to provide, I will send you. It's what we nonnos do."

"Thanks, Eri," Livy said and kissed him gently on the cheek. "Just please, don't tell Mom or Ada yet."

"And what about Will?"

Livy looked sheepishly down at the ground and replied, "I left him a note."

Eri sighed with a curt nod and whispered something into Livy's ear before kissing her on the cheek. "Buona fortuna, my little ones."

And just as quickly as he had appeared, he vanished into the house and Livy jumped into the passenger seat.

"We need to go, *now*," she said and slammed the door shut.

"Let's get one thing straight," I began, and pulled a U-turn. "This is my journey, my life change. You are here on my coattails and will not bark orders at me. I will drive the car, I will decide where we stop, where we eat, and where we eventually live. Got that?"

She nodded and curled up in the seat. "I just need to get out of here."

Once we were headed back down toward the city I asked, "So...you left a note?"

"Yeah," she replied as she tucked her hair behind her ears and looked out the window.

"Your earrings are gone." She didn't answer. "Livy?"

"I don't know what you're talking about!" she snapped.

I rolled my eyes, mainly at myself since I'd voluntarily put myself into this situation. "The diamond earrings that Will stupidly gave you on your eighteenth birthday that you threw away, but somehow have been wearing the whole time you've been here, and are now no longer in your ears."

It took her nearly thirty seconds to answer. "I gave them back...with the note."

"He is going to kill us, both of us. Mostly you, but both of us at some point. Damn, Livy."

She started to cry and it was tough not to feel bad. A few days ago I would have told her to go fuck herself, but now...well, now I had to help her. Gently I placed my hand on top of hers, and she flipped her hand over and squeezed mine. Eventually she turned over, pulling my arm into her chest and laying across the console. Never had my sister been so vulnerable, or needed me so much.

"Once we settle, we'll find a counselor or something. Ok?"

She nodded against my arm.

"And you need to call Mom and Ada."

She nodded again. "Will is never going to forgive us, is he?"

"Probably not."

STAY TUNED FOR BOOK SIX IN THE

Blood-Borne Series

VISIT **WWW.CR-QUINN.COM** FOR THE MOST UP TO DATE
INFORMATION ON THE BLOOD-BORNE SERIES AND
OTHER PROJECTS FROM C.R. QUINN

Acknowledgments

I don't think anyone would ever "thank" 2020 for anything, but without the forced quarantine, lack of social gatherings and distractions of family-time, this book would never have been finished. Hopefully this novel has allowed you to escape as it did for me.

About the Author

C.R. Quinn is a budding author whose prior accomplishments include a bachelor's degree in Biology, surviving the corporate world for over twenty years, and a singer/dancer/actor/director in community theatre. She lives in Connecticut with her husband, and is lucky to be the stepmother to two wonderful children, and now a grandmother to three darling grandchildren. C.R. Quinn comes from a family of storytellers whose stories will be showing up in books and plays of their own.